CHERYL HOLT

The Way of the Heart

ZEBRA BOOKS
KENSINGTON PUBLISHING CORP.
http://www.kensingtonbooks.com

ZEBRA BOOKS are published by

Kensington Publishing Corp.
850 Third Avenue
New York, NY 10022

All Kensington titles, imprints, and distributed lines are available
at special quantity discounts for bulk purchases for sales promo-
tion, premiums, fund-raising, educational, or institutional use.

Special book excerpts or customized printings can also be
created to fit specific needs. For details, write or phone the
office of the Kensington Special Sales Manager: Attn. Special
Sales Department. Kensington Publishing Corp., 850 Third
Avenue, New York, NY 10022. Phone: 1-800-221-2647.

Zebra and the Z logo Reg. U.S. Pat. & TM Off.

ISBN 0-8217-7871-4

First Printing: December 1999
10 9 8 7 6 5 4 3

Printed in the United States of America

Chapter One

Portsmouth
February, 1812

Jane Fitzsimmons stopped to glance in the mirror, wondering when Gregory, her cousin and brother-in-law, would step through the door. She wanted to look absolutely perfect when he did. A single strand had worked loose from her carefully braided hair, and she expertly pinned it back into place.

As usual, she was harried from the morning of busy commerce, but the major accomplishment of the previous day made all the hard work enjoyable. Finally, she'd found a land-owner willing to part with some of his hardwood forest at a reasonable price. The long months of her planning had been worthwhile.

Of course, her father and Gregory had actually negotiated the arrangement, and being men, they would receive the credit for the contract. Heaven forbid that a woman should know anything about business or have a head for numbers. As always, her part in the entire affair had been carefully hidden in order not to offend the sensibilities of the seller.

But it was Jane who first realized the need for a new source of timber, Jane who located the small forest, Jane who saw the hidden value, the easy access. The price offered, shipping arrangements and the other thousands of details that would bring the beautiful logs to the Fitzsimmonses' Shipworks had been her doing. Father and Gregory had simply followed her instructions and put the finishing touches on the deal.

Taking a moment to enjoy the view, Jane glanced out across the busy shipyard where dozens of men scurried about their tasks. She took note of the ships in various stages of completion. Two were nearly finished and already in the water, a half-dozen others were up on huge scaffolds as they slowly took shape.

It was a grand time to be in business, and with the hazardous state of the world, there could be no business better than shipbuilding. Everyone needed ships, it seemed. Bigger ones. Better ones. And they all turned to Fitzsimmons when they wanted the best. Two centuries of building the best for England had given them a name around the globe that meant quality and durability.

Jane glanced down at the papers in her hand, looking at the figures on which she'd been working. War was spreading on the continent, and war meant people needed to buy things. Not just ships. Her plan was to start a new branch of the family business, using Fitzsimmons's ships to import and export around the globe as England grew desperate for more supplies.

The possibilities for increased wealth were staggering. She looked at her papers again. Very likely, it was a sin for one family to be able to earn so much when there were so many who had so little, but they had the knowledge and the tools. And they had worked hard for so long, no one could say they hadn't earned every penny.

The knob on the door turned, and Jane's father, Charles Fitzsimmons, stepped into her office. Jane's heart fluttered slightly. With mealtime upon them, no one was supposed to be in the rooms, which was the very reason she was waiting for Gregory. They would have their first chance to be alone in weeks.

At age fifty-six, Charles Fitzsimmons was healthy and robust but short and stocky, still carrying a full head of white hair, complemented by a bushy mustache and heavy eyebrows. His skin was red and ruddy from years at sea, trying out their ships and perfecting the working parts to make their products better and better.

"Hello, daughter." He smiled as his energy filled the room. "I thought everyone had gone."

Jane casually slid the papers she was holding under her desk blotter. Although she'd outlined the plan to Gregory, and he'd been heartily enthusiastic, she hadn't broached the subject of her ideas for expanding the business with her father and wasn't quite ready to speak of it. "Hello, Father." She walked around the desk and stood next to him. "I was too excited to eat. After yesterday's news, I can't seem to take my eyes away from the 'Works."

"Aye." He nodded in agreement. "It all came together, didn't it?"

She blushed as she realized she was waiting for a compliment which would never come. It wasn't Charles's style to toss them about. " 'Twas marvelous."

He moved to the window. "It's a beautiful sight, isn't it, girl?"

"Yes." Jane sighed, as she moved next to him. "Yes, it is."

For a time, they were content to watch in silence, lost in their thoughts. They'd passed many hours like this in Jane's nineteen years. From the time she was a small girl, she'd been enchanted by her father's offices, hanging around, making herself a pest. As a widower, he'd done his best to turn her into a gently reared female, but nothing had worked. Unlike her older sister, Gertrude, who thrived on all things domestic, Jane had fought every attempt to turn her onto a more docile path until he'd simply given up on his attempts to keep her at home.

Her life, like his own, revolved around the family business.

"Everything always looks so grand from up here."

"I never get my fill. The ships look so beautiful."

"Yes, they do." He turned to look at her, immediately struck again by how much she looked like her mother. He had not particularly loved the woman, as he'd never give in to such a silly emotion over a female, but she'd been a good wife in the few years she'd been joined to his side. Jane took after her in looks. She was a petite thing. Although he wouldn't be so bold as to touch her now that she was a grown woman, he imagined that both his hands would fit neatly around her small waist with room to spare. The heavy braids in which her hair was bound hid its rich, chestnut color. Her lips, ruby red, always looked delightfully pouting; her brows raised in questioning surprise.

Good Lord, but she was a pretty thing. And smart as a whip, too. Too bad all the looks and talent had been squandered on a daughter. He shook his head, not able to see much for her in the future. She simply couldn't continue in her role at the Shipworks. Change was coming and long overdue.

Jane's bright, emerald green eyes widened. "What is it, Father? Is there something you wish to say?"

"No, child. I was simply thinking how much you looked like your mother."

"I'm honored. I always thought she was very pretty." It pleased her immensely when he spoke of the woman she barely remembered.

"She was, girl. She was quite exceptional." His memories of the woman were distant. She'd been a gentle woman, always even tempered and sensible. If not exactly warm to her bedroom duties, compliant enough. She'd been understanding over his love of the shipyard and the long hours he put in, and had steadfastly shouldered her responsibilities toward his other daughter, Gert, a child by his first wife. Gert had never been an easy person for anyone to like, but Jane's mother had managed to do her best.

Charles sighed. All these years of toil. All his attempts to father an heir to carry on the family name. He'd been married to his first wife for ten years, sired one daughter and lost the woman to childbirth. He'd been married to the second for eight and finally sired another daughter. After all the years, all the attempts, all he had to show for it were two girls. One who was not particularly bright and who was particularly unpleasant. The other, a beautiful, delightful, intelligent young woman who could have been all things if she'd been born a male, but, because she hadn't, simply could not continue her steps toward taking his place.

He was no fool. He was older, tired, and knew it was only a matter of time before arrangements had to be made. A transition of power arranged. Jane would be so hurt.

Oh, well, she's just a woman, he thought to himself. Once she was married and had a few children clinging to her skirts, she'd forgive him for what he was about to do to her.

He turned to leave, then paused. "Oh, I'd forgotten the reason I stopped in. I left my reading glasses here."

Jane had found them earlier. She reached in a drawer and pulled them out, quickly handing them over.

As soon as the door clicked behind him, she returned to the mirror, hating the fact that she was dressed in one of her usual gray day dresses. She always dressed in the most modest of clothing. Charles insisted she needn't waste money on anything else. Her hair was severely pulled behind her head, her neckline high, her sleeves long. More than a few times, she'd wished Gregory could see her in flowing skirts and delicate curls.

A light knock sounded on the door and her breath caught. Gregory! She pinched her cheeks, hoping to add a small bit of color, then said quietly, "Come in."

Gregory Fitzsimmons quickly and quietly stepped into the room, and her heart fluttered as he closed the door. He was so terribly handsome with his fine blond hair the color of wheat, his smiling blue eyes. And he was dashing in his sapphire waistcoat which exactly matched the shade of his eyes.

"Jane, my darling." He stepped forward, reaching for both her hands. Holding her at arm's length, his eyes took their fill, carefully cataloging the curved hips, the slim waist, the small breasts. He pulled her into his arms and inhaled deeply of the scent of lavender he always associated with her.

"Gregory, how I've missed you."

"And I, you, little one."

Jane's stomach was tickled by those silly butterflies that always seemed to arise whenever he touched her. "I didn't think you were coming."

"I arrived as quickly as I could." He didn't offer, and knew Jane would not ask, where he'd been, which was a good thing. They rarely discussed his marriage to Gert, and Gregory would never have admitted that he'd just come from their marital bed. After being out of town for several weeks, he'd had to get back to the business of making a babe with his wife. He desperately needed an heir to present to Charles, but his wretched wife was proving to be every bit as infertile as her mother had been. "Kiss me, Jane."

She raised her lips, and the familiar tingle started in her fingers and toes. As his lips chastely met hers, she instantly felt the heavy swelling in her breasts and the odd stirring in the woman's place between her legs. Her body was waiting for so much more, needing so much more to happen. Each blissful encounter left her feeling increasingly unsatisfied. Desperately, she wished that, instead of an uninitiated, timid virgin, she was an experienced woman of the world who knew the ways to lead Gregory to greater heights of passion.

"Oh, Jane," he whispered, "I want you so much. I'll die if I don't have you soon." He'd wanted her so badly, and for so long, that the pain was nearly unbearable. "Tell me you've made up your mind and my wait is ended."

Jane had had enough conversation with her friend, Elizabeth Carew, to understand what it was Gregory wanted from her, but from the woman's frigid descriptions of coupling, she wondered if she should give in to Gregory's desires and let him take her maidenhead. Somehow, she doubted the ultimate act would extinguish the fire burning in her veins. But he wanted it to happen so much.

"I love you, Gregory."

"I love you, too, darling," he responded with what sounded like sorely tried patience.

Jane frowned and buried her face in his chest. She hated to continually disappoint him, but couldn't make up her mind to give herself to him. Putting off the decision yet again, she raised her face and found his lips. Her attention was so wrapped up in him that she did not hear the opening of her office door. Did not see her father standing there, watching. Was not aware of anything but Gregory until she heard her father clear his throat.

Guiltily, the pair of lovers jumped apart. In the ensuing silence, Charles Fitzsimmons stared them down. Once they were completely cowed, he said quietly, "I came back to remind Jane that we would be having a late supper tonight. I have business which will detain me. I see it's a good thing I returned when I did."

"Sir, if you'll permit me ..." Gregory made an attempt to mollify him.

"No. I will not. If you will excuse us, I wish to speak with Jane alone."

"It's all my fault, sir. I take full responsibility."

"As well you should, young man. Jane has barely left her girlhood behind. You are a man full grown. Now leave us."

Jane looked at the floor, listening to the click of the door. In the silence, she finally raised her eyes to meet her father's unrelenting stare. "I'm sorry, Father," she whispered quietly. "I am so ashamed."

"I should hope so, because I can't remember being so disappointed in someone in all my born days."

His words slashed liked a knife, and she looked back at the floor. "I'm sorry," she offered again, feebly.

"How long has this been going on?"

Jane thought about lying, but figured he would learn the truth from Gregory. "For the past year, sir."

"Are you still a maid?"

God, that he would have to ask such a thing. "Yes, sir."

"I am most upset. Look at me, daughter." Jane raised her eyes. "You will go home at once. To your room and stay there. Am I clear?"

"Yes, sir."

"You will join the family for supper, and then you and I will speak of this again in the library after our evening meal is concluded."

"I will be there."

Charles left her standing there, alone in the quiet.

Charles took a last bite of his evening meal and leaned back in his chair, surveying the dining room from the head of the family table. His eldest daughter, Gert, sat on his right next to her husband. Jane sat on his left. As always, he took a moment to ponder how two different mothers could produce such incredibly different children.

Gert was a thoroughly unpleasant person, unhappy with her lot in life. Even as a child, her sour disposition had colored all their lives. Her frigid disposition was so distasteful that he could hardly fault Gregory for turning to Jane for affection.

Looking at his other daughter, he admitted that only a fool would fail to be attracted to Jane. She was pretty in a fresh, young way that wasn't fading as she aged. Her beauty seemed to grow with each passing year as her body adapted to its womanly shape. At fourteen years, she'd been like an ungainly colt trying to steady its balance. At nineteen, she was gracious and lovely.

Her nature was kind and pleasant. She found joy in her work and was one of those lucky people who embraced life with open arms, ready to do battle and to succeed with all challenges placed in her path.

Oh, if she had only been born a boy!

Charles shook his head. The familiar lament had traveled through his head thousands of times. There simply was no reason to rehash the unfairness of it. She was a daughter, and he could do nothing about it except to avert the coming disaster.

The others had finished their meal. It had been a long, silent, tedious affair. He cleared his throat and looked at Gert, then Jane. "If you will excuse us, ladies, Gregory and I will have our port."

"Certainly, Father," Gert said obediently and rose. Jane followed her from the room, not casting her eyes at either man. As she reached the door, Charles said to her back, "Jane, I need to speak with you when I've finished with Gregory. Please wait in the library."

"Yes, sir," she murmured as she stepped into the hall.

Charles cut off Gregory before he could make any more lame excuses. "I have made arrangements for Jane. She will be leaving us shortly. I will have your word on one thing."

"Anything, sir. You have but to ask."

"You must promise me that you will not be alone with her between now and the day she leaves. I'll have no last-minute lovers' trysts. Am I clear on this?"

"Certainly, sir."

"She swears she is still a maid. Is that correct?"

"Yes, sir." Gregory had the sense to color slightly at having his father-in-law ask such an intimate question.

"Her innocence has great value for me in what I'm about to do, and I'll have it jeopardized because of your behavior. You've caused enough trouble. I'll have no more." Gregory looked so forlorn, he decided to have pity on the young man. Over the years, he'd had his doubts about Gregory, but his son-in-law was growing more useful all the time. Especially now that he'd come up with the idea for expanding into the import-export markets. It was a grand scheme, and frankly, Charles was quite surprised that Gregory had thought of such an outrageous, wonderful idea. Maybe there was hope for him yet.

He leaned back, his worry lines slackening, and smiled. "So how are your attempts at starting your family? Any news to report?"

"Nothing, sir. I'm trying my best."

"Try harder. I want that grandson."

With that, Charles rose and left Gregory to drink his port alone. 'Twas time to end Jane's suspense.

She stood when her father entered. Although he'd never been a violent man, she feared now what he might do. If he beat her, she could hardly complain that it wasn't deserved. She couldn't imagine what other punishment he could possibly have in mind for her.

"Sit, daughter." He moved to his chair behind the big desk and motioned to her to sit across from him. Unlocking the top drawer, he pulled out the papers his solicitor had delivered earlier in the evening. Jane was pale and quiet, awaiting his verdict, her hands folded in her lap. Surely, she'd never imagined this.

"I could spend a great deal of time talking about how upset I am by the state of things, how disappointed I am by your behavior, and how ashamed I am to see how you've acted. But, since I'm sure you already know all those things, I leave my words to your imagination. I'm sure you know what I would say were I to lecture you about your conduct."

"You're right, Father. I already know everything you would say to me." She hoped she was looking contrite enough to suit him. Although she hated being caught, she hated more the thought that it would now be so much more difficult to arrange meetings with Gregory. She loved him so much. "Once again, I do want to say how sorry I am."

"Save the regrets, daughter. Let me continue." He opened the folder. "I have decided that it is time for you to marry."

Jane let out a shocked gasp. "Father, you can't be serious."

"I've never been more serious. If you are interested enough in men to cavort with Gregory in your office, you are certainly ready for marriage and what it brings."

Jane had had three previous offers of marriage from local gentlemen close to her own age and two from older men who were acquaintances of her father. He had consulted her feelings each time and had graciously turned away all offers. She had no wish to marry. Especially when a husband would take her away from her home. Which meant away from Gregory. "But the other times . . . the other times, you let me make the decision."

"That was because I felt it was right at the time. You were too young. I've changed my mind now. You're nineteen, and it's time you wed."

"But I've no suitor at the moment. I'm not anywhere near a marriageable state." Suddenly her heart caught in her throat. Had he chosen someone for her without her knowledge or consent? She pressed a nervous hand between her breasts, wishing she could still the furious pounding of her heart. She could barely force the words out. "Unless, of course, you have someone in mind for me . . ."

Across the desk, he saw her eyes go wide with understanding: he'd chosen. He read all the emotions there. Betrayal, fright, anger. This was for the best, he kept reminding himself. Looking down at the papers, he spread them out in front of her, trying to keep the meeting as businesslike as possible. He couldn't abide a woman's hysterics, and although he'd never seen Jane stoop to using them, there was a first time for everything.

His voice was calm and even. "Because of our family's wealth, you have a fine dowry. You are also beautiful, graceful and generous. All combined, you are an excellent catch. Any man would be lucky to have you, and I have found five who need to be lucky right away. You may have your pick."

Jane laughed in astonishment, looking at the papers in front of her. They appeared to be personal histories of some sort. "I am to select from these papers you've set in front of me?" *Unbelievable!*

"No. You will leave for London on Friday. All five gentlemen are there now awaiting your arrival. You will meet with each one and make your own selection."

Her eyes met his in challenge. "And if I refuse?"

"I will make the selection for you."

Jane felt a chill move up her spine. How could he do this to her? "May I ask where you found these *fine* gentlemen?"

"My solicitor contacted a solicitor in London who prepared a list for me."

"I see. And why would these *fine* gentlemen be so interested in marrying me?"

He paused, as though trying to find a delicate way to tell her the truth, but she realized the reason immediately. " 'Tis the money, isn't it? They all need money."

"Yes."

He said it without a trace of shame. He was prepared to auction her off to the neediest man! With as much sarcasm as she could muster, she asked, "Are you so certain you can get any of them to settle for a pitiful merchant's daughter like myself? Look here." She pointed at one paper, then another. "This one's a baron. This one's an earl. Are you so certain they're ready to sully their blue blood by mixing it with some of mine?"

"You'd be surprised what a few pounds will accomplish," he said coldly. Pulling all the papers together, he put them in the folder, then handed it to her. She refused to reach for it.

"Just how soon am I supposed to woo one of these fine lads into asking for my hand?"

"Two weeks. You have two weeks to make a selection. And two weeks after that to marry."

"And if I don't?"

"I already told you, I will make the selection for you. You are nineteen. You have no say in the matter. I am offering you a choice out of courtesy."

Tears finally started to race to her eyes. He really meant it. He was actually doing this to her. Refusing to let the tears fall, she swallowed hard before she spoke again. "What about my position at the Shipworks? You're letting me go as your daughter. Am I being let go there as well?"

Charles cleared his throat, not anguished in the least by the lie he was about to tell. "If your husband agrees, you may resume your duties in six months' time." It was a complete fabrication. He had no intention of ever letting her back into the family business. "I want you to take that long to establish yourself in your new family situation."

"Six months? Six months?" Jane stood suddenly and raced around the desk, falling at his feet, her face resting on his knees. "Father, please, I'm begging you. Don't do this to me. The shipyard is my life. It's ours. I've helped you. I have so many dreams to make it better. I have the best idea right now . . ."

He cut her off. "Jane, stop this." He knew exactly what he was taking from her, how much she loved their family business, but it couldn't be helped. Taking her hand, he stood and brought her to her feet. "I will have my way in this. You cannot dissuade me. If you do not do as I say, I will put you out. You will have no home here. You will have no place in the 'Works. Now go to your room and begin preparing for your journey to London. I know after you've thought on this for a time that you will see it's for your own good."

Chapter Two

Phillip Wessington, Earl of Rosewood, rolled onto his back and shielded his eyes from the glint of sunlight. His manservant, John Graves, seemed to garner a particular enjoyment from forcing another day on his master and always pulled back the curtains with gusto. This day, he seemed unusually gleeful about the event. Phillip groaned and pulled the bedcovers over his head.

"None of that, milord. Time to rise and face the day."

"Go away," he muttered.

"I can't, sir. This is the third time I've tried to awaken you. I can wait no longer. Your afternoon appointment will arrive at any moment."

Phillip pulled the covers down to his chest, squinting viciously at the bright light. "What appointment?"

"Your solicitor, Master Thumberton."

Phillip groaned. The man never brought any good news. If he was coming by, it could only mean more trouble. "Why didn't you tell me?"

"I did, sir. Twice yesterday." Graves glanced across the bed to the well-rounded, blond woman snuggled next to the Earl. Oblivious to the suddenly lighted chamber, she snored lightly. "I guess your thoughts were otherwise occupied."

Graves had never made any attempt to hide his dislike of Lady Margaret Downs. Margaret was well aware of his feelings and loved nothing more than to provoke the man at every turn. Phillip was not in the mood for either of them to go at it. Especially if Thumberton could arrive at any moment.

Sitting up on the edge of the bed, he moved too swiftly, swinging his legs to the side, and the pain behind his eyes nearly took off the top of his head. God's teeth, but he shouldn't have drunk so much the previous night. He flopped back, his head hitting hard against Margaret's stomach.

She woke with an unladylike, "Oooph."

"Don't you dare move a muscle."

She struggled to the side, and his head hit the mattress, wrenching another groan from him.

Even just awakened, she was very pretty. Her blond hair fell in glorious disarray, her blue eyes twinkled, her lips curved with just a hint of pout. Loving the opportunity to taunt Graves, she glanced his way to be sure he was close enough to notice, then let the bedcovers fall to her waist. Her magnificent breasts were in full view, the large nipples erect, the tips pink, the surrounding skin the color of cream.

She stretched her hands over her head and purred like a cat. "Have pity on his lordship, Graves. You know he was up all night." She placed particular emphasis on the word *up*. Seeing Graves's look of distaste, she giggled. "Why did you wake us so early?"

"It's almost three, ma'am. If I thought it was any of

your business, I would tell you that his lordship has an important appointment in a few minutes. But, since it isn't any of your business, I won't mention it."

Margaret turned a pout on Phillip. "Darling, I don't understand why I must put up with such insolence from a servant." She hated Graves and the power he had over Phillip, and she constantly attempted to get Phillip to let him go. "I'm a guest. He shouldn't be able to speak to me so."

Phillip closed his eyes and rubbed his temples. Graves was the only one who would continue to work without his salary being paid, and the only one who could tolerate Phillip's bad habits enough to stay. The true facts were none of Margaret's business, however. Let her think what she wished.

"Margaret," Phillip hissed. Her voice usually sounded as sweet as spun honey, but this morning it grated like cart wheels on the street. "Have mercy on me. I can't referee in my condition." Slowly, he sat up, waiting for the room to quit spinning. "I'll need a bath," he told Graves.

"Already done, sir. It's next door in your bedchamber." When the Earl hesitated, he asked, "Do you require assistance, milord?"

"No. Just give me a minute." Phillip stood and moved cautiously toward the door, his legs acting as though he'd never walked on them before.

"And the . . . *lady*?" Graves's emphasis on the word "lady" indicated that there wasn't anything about her that made him think she was one.

"Feed her. Bathe her." Phillip glanced over his shoulder at his paramour. The last thing he needed was for Thumberton to see her. "Stay up here."

"For how long?" she whined.

"Until I ask you to join me."

"Oh, you're dreadful . . ."

She unloaded a string of complaints about his character, but he had already stepped into the adjoining room and Graves closed the door to cut off her litany.

"Silence. Thank God," Phillip muttered as he slipped into the tub of steaming water.

Margaret had been a reigning princess of the Season eight years earlier when her father presented her at the age of seventeen. She'd had her choice of marriage offers and had judiciously selected an older gentleman with a handsome income who conveniently died three years later, leaving her a beautiful, young widow with a steady income, a fine home and a ranking place in society.

She and Phillip had been lovers for the past year, but he couldn't call her his mistress, for that would have indicated that he supported her in some fashion. Usually a suitable bed partner, lately she'd grown tiresome with her tantrums and demands. For some insane reason, she'd even hinted that they should marry.

At age thirty and without an heir, he needed to wed again, but his first marriage, over a decade earlier, had been so disastrous that he couldn't imagine ever going through the process a second time. The few occasions he'd tried to envision such a thing, Margaret's face certainly never came into focus as the mother of his child. Since he could only become the father of a legitimate heir through marriage, and since he'd sworn off the wedded state, the chances of his ever producing an heir were slim to none.

Oh well, he thought to himself, *if something doesn't happen soon, there won't be anything for anyone to inherit anyway.*

Graves yanked his depressing thoughts back to the

present moment as he doused the Earl with a bucketful of water. "Should I shave you, milord?"

"No time. I want to get this unpleasantness over with as quickly as possible." He stepped to the mirror. With nearly two days of growth covering his face, he looked horrible, but he couldn't seem to work himself up to caring. "Let Thumberton see the real me. What do you think, Graves? Will I scare him off?"

"Perhaps, milord."

With Graves assistance, he dressed hurriedly and headed downstairs to the library.

Dudley Thumberton, a short, older gentleman with a cumbersome belly and huge sideburns, sat patiently in a chair. There was no use getting worked up about Phillip's tardiness. He'd show when he was prepared to and not a moment before. There had been so many meetings since Phillip's father had died eighteen months earlier, and the respected solicitor had grown used to the man's bad habits. He didn't approve of them, but he was used to them.

"Good afternoon, sir," Phillip said briskly in his best Earl-like tone. He stepped across the room, shook the solicitor's hand without quite looking him in the eye, then scooted behind the desk, welcoming the little bit of protection it offered from the man's stern presence.

Thumberton gave him a thorough once-over from head to toe. "For pity's sake, Phillip, couldn't you even be bothered to shave?"

Thumberton had been his father's solicitor and his grandfather's before that. He'd watched Phillip grow from a child to a wild adult, living a life full of spirits and debauchery. He wasn't about to coddle the man.

"I was running late. I assumed you'd rather have the meeting begin on time than wait while I continued to complete my morning bath."

Thumberton glanced rudely at his timepiece and raised an eyebrow, silently reminding Phillip that time was quickly marching toward evening. Outside in the hall, Margaret's gay laughter tinkled as she walked past the room. "Really, must you continue to consort with that strumpet? Have you any idea how it looks to others?"

Phillip winced, hoping she wouldn't have the audacity to poke her nose into the room, then breathed a sigh of relief as her voice drifted farther down the hall. He resisted the effort to squirm in his chair. Whenever he was in Thumberton's presence he could barely shake the feeling that he was still a young child. He wished he could dismiss the man, but hiring another solicitor would require that he pay some amount of retainer. Thumberton continued to work for free out of loyalty to his father and grandfather.

Phillip sat back in his chair, acting as though the solicitor's words meant nothing, even though he was seething inside. "What brings you by, Thumberton? More dreadful news, I suppose."

"Actually, yes, there is more bad news. But also a proposition I think you'll find worth entertaining."

"Let's have the bad news first."

"They are going to try to seize Rosewood."

The ancestral estate? The enormity of it quickly shattered his composure. "What? But . . . but . . . I thought you told me it was encumbered. That the old man couldn't gamble it away."

Thumberton shrugged. "I've done my best, lad. I've told you numerous times: the debt is so grand, we simply can't expect creditors to walk away from it. There's too much at stake. They're ready to try anything to grab a piece of it."

Phillip's rage began to spark, causing his throbbing

head to pound even harder. "Why didn't you tell me before it came to this? Didn't you think I might be interested?"

"Phillip"—Thumberton took a deep breath, calming himself; fighting was a waste of time—"we've been negotiating for months. I've sent you letter after letter. If you'd read any of them, you'd have been apprised of the seriousness of the situation."

"I didn't get any letters," he insisted bitterly.

Thumberton stood, moved around the desk to Phillip's side, opened a drawer. Over a dozen sealed missives were carelessly tossed inside. Casting upon him a silent stare, the solicitor noted that Phillip had the decency to redden. He moved back to his seat. He had always hoped for so much more in the boy, had always liked him immensely, but what chance had he ever had to grow to be a good man?

In his most gentle tone, he said, "You must take charge of this situation."

Every discussion they'd had since he'd assumed the title led back to this. Phillip simply had no interest in tackling the problem. The situation was so desperate, the debt so immense, that he had no idea where to begin. Throughout his life, everyone had taken care of him. That's what he wanted Thumberton to do now.

"Fix it, sir. Isn't that what you're supposed to be so good at?"

With an exasperated sigh, Thumberton rubbed his eyes, then held out his hands in supplication. "We have had this discussion so many times, and I grow mighty weary of it. You must do something."

"What? What would you have me do? Mint some coins?"

"Don't jest, Phillip. It's much too serious for that. I simply meant that you must at least begin making an attempt to change the outcome. Go to Rosewood. Make sure the crops will be planted. Make sure the tenants are paying their share. Show your creditors that you're making progress toward payment. Give them some hope of change, instead of . . . of . . . spending your nights as your father did. You can't continue to live as if there is no end to the money and no beginning to your responsibility.''

Phillip raised a dismissive hand. "Go farming? Is that what you're telling me? I should return to Rosewood and grow crops?"

"You own some of the finest lands in all of England, Phillip. For centuries, they have been the bedrock of your family's fortune. You must get the business back on track, or I'm sorry to say disaster is upon us."

"Disaster is already upon us."

"Yes, yes it is," the solicitor agreed, "but I have an incredible proposition for you. It will stop the foreclosure actions against Rosewood and the other properties. It will pay off your creditors. By the end of the month, you will have enough left over to begin rebuilding the family business so that the land is once again producing necessary income."

"Have I inherited a fairy godmother?"

"In a way. I've had contact with a wealthy merchant in Portsmouth who wishes to find a suitable husband for his daughter."

Phillip went still. "A husband? You wish to marry me off?" He started to chuckle; then the laughter grew and grew until he was wiping away tears of mirth. "Oh, sir, this has made my day." He continued to laugh, until he looked once again at the old man's eyes. Not a trace of warmth or friendship lingered there.

" 'Tis a fine family. The Fitzsimmonses. They build ships. I'm sure you've heard of them."

Of course he had. Only an illiterate would not know who they were. "And what? Such a well-respected family, with so much money, they can't find a match for their girl? What is she? Ugly? Fat? Deformed? Demented? Tell me."

"I do not know why they wish to wed her. But the father wants to, and he wants it done quickly. Before the month is out."

"How much is her old man offering to rid himself of her?"

Thumberton pulled out some papers and laid them on the desk for Phillip's inspection. Phillip whistled. "He must really, really want to send her on her way."

"Someone will snatch her up in a heartbeat with this kind of dowry."

"And how did I become the lucky man? Did you offer me up for auction on the block?"

"You're not the chosen one, yet. She's meeting with five gentlemen and will be allowed to select from the lot of you. I have no doubt, with your womanizing skills, you could easily win her hand."

"Lucky me." Phillip's brow wrinkled momentarily as, for some reason, he experienced a moment of annoyance that he was expected to compete with four others. For many years, he'd been one of England's most eligible bachelors, and leaving his poverty aside, he still was. He leaned back in his chair and rubbed his eyes. To what a state his world had fallen.

"Before the month is out, your problems could be solved. Your creditors would be satisfied. You'd be wed and could set about starting your nursery. You'd have a lovely wife." Thumberton liked this part. He truthfully felt that marriage to a good woman would cure many of Phillip's faults.

"So she's lovely, is she?"

"Her father insists that she is."

"I'll just bet he does." Phillip pointed to the folder. "I assume there's no blue blood running in the veins anywhere."

"No, sir. They are merchants. But, as I said, from an old and distinguished family."

"And what about your insistence all this time that I make another proper marriage for myself? That I continue the line and all that malarkey? Have you changed your mind?"

"No, but matters are simply too grievous now to worry about the lofty state of your wife's position. You need to consider the lofty state of her purse."

Phillip stared at the man who, in many ways, had tried to be a father to him over the years. As a first and only son, he'd had all the respect and honors due him throughout his life, but he'd had very little guidance. Tutors threw up their hands and left. Servants ran crying from the halls. His widowed father enjoyed the circuit of parties and night life. Thumberton had been one of the few adults to look kindly on him. He'd tried and usually failed in attempts to give direction, but Phillip couldn't follow him this time.

"No. I don't think so. I have a plan to stave things off."

"What could you possibly have planned?"

"I've been offered a betrothal contract for Emily, and I'm seriously considering it. The gentleman would pay me ten thousand pounds for her hand. Certainly that amount of money would keep the barbarians at the gate for the time being. We'd have some breathing room."

Thumberton, for one of the few times in his life, was speechless. Emily. Darling Emily, with her beautiful ebony curls and smiling blue eyes. That the Earl would even consider doing such a thing to his daughter was beyond all the solicitor's imaginings. After many decades of serving the most wealthy and influential families in the country, he'd begun to think nothing could shock him. With a desperate attempt at maintaining control lest he leap across the desk and grab the despicable whelp by the throat, Thumberton asked quietly, "And when would the happy vows be exchanged?"

"This autumn. On her twelfth birthday."

"And who, may I be so bold as to ask, would be the lucky bridegroom?"

"Frederick Morris. He's always had a fondness for the girl."

Thumberton swallowed his outrage. Morris was four years older than Phillip. There had always been rumors circulating about the man, that he had an unnatural interest in young girls. The solicitor suddenly felt sick at his stomach. "He is a pervert and—"

"He is a neighbor and friend I have known all my life," Phillip broke in.

Thumberton shouted over him. "He is a pervert. How could you imagine such a dastardly thing? She is a child. Your only child. At the rate you're going, perhaps the only one you'll ever have!" The outrageousness of Phillip's comments caused tears of anger to well in his eyes, and he wasn't embarrassed to have the Earl see them.

"We have been through this before," Phillip roared back, refusing to be swayed by the emotion pouring from the old man. "No one will ever convince me that she is my daughter."

"You're right. We have been through this many times. And I've told you time and again: she is your daughter, conceived and born during the marriage. In the eyes of God and the law, she is your child. Her welfare is your concern. She is your responsibility . . ." Finally, words failed him. 'Twas simply wasted breath. He wanted nothing more than to remove himself from the Earl's presence.

"We finally agree on one thing: Emily is my responsibility, and I will do with her as I see fit. She can bring me a great deal of money to help alleviate my problems, and I intend to use her to accomplish my goals." Phillip said the words forcefully, but it was the first time he'd spoken aloud of the possible betrothal. The words left an unpleasant taste, but he refused to let Thumberton know. After all, Phillip was the employer in the room, Thumberton the employee.

"Fine, your lordship."

Phillip knew he'd pushed too far when the old man resorted to addressing him in such a fashion. He tried to lighten the conversation. "So, thank you for attempting to ease my problems with the idea of marriage, but I simply cannot accept. Please send my regrets to the Fitzsimmons woman. Make it sound as though I'm heartily sorry I won't be able to meet her. You know all the right things to say." He picked up the papers Thumberton had scattered on the desk and held them out to the man, and a chill rippled up his spine as Thumberton refused to reach for them.

The solicitor eyed him silently for a moment or two, then stood. "I'm sorry, sir, but you will have to find someone else to notify her. Or perhaps you will have to do it yourself."

"I'm ordering you to do it, Thumberton."

"I'm very sorry, sir, but I am no longer taking orders from you. As of this moment, I consider my long association with your family to be terminated."

"Good God, man, you're quitting?"

"I'll send your files with a messenger first thing in the morning, so you will have them to present to your next representative."

Phillip was shocked and a little frightened. "I'll not accept them. You were the solicitor for my grandfather and father before me. I am pleased with you."

"But I am no longer pleased with you. I have an income that is more than adequate, and I do not need the meager amounts I could ever hope to receive from you." Thumberton turned to go, frustrated and so upset over Phillip's plans for little Emily that he thought he might actually fall to his knees and find himself begging on the girl's behalf.

"I do not give you permission to leave."

"It matters not to me."

Thumberton took a step toward the door, but Phillip was quicker, heading him off before he could get away. He meant to shout more orders at the old man, forcing him to obey by the very weight of his position, but one look at the cold outrage in the man's eyes stopped him short. He said quietly, "Wait, sir. Please don't leave in such an angry state."

"Phillip—" Thumberton swallowed, then started again. "Wessington, your father was a gambler and a womanizer. He had many faults, but for all of them, he was a kind, gentle and generous man. In all the years of our acquaintance, I never knew him to intentionally hurt another soul." Tears surged to his eyes again, and he wiped them away with the back of his hand. "I always had such great hopes for you. No matter what you did, how you acted, what trouble you caused, I told myself that deep down, there was a good man waiting to come out. I have waited for thirty years, and it has not happened.

"That you would even consider doing such a horrendous thing to Emily—" His voice broke, and he pushed Phillip aside and stepped past him. "I wash my hands of you. I simply *wash* my hands of you." Walking briskly toward the door, he brushed his palms across the fabric of his jacket as though Phillip was something despicable that had stuck to him.

Phillip stepped back into the library and seated himself behind the desk. He was shaking. Surely, Thumberton couldn't mean to abandon him at such a desperate time. Especially over something so silly as a marriage contract for Emily. Girls were married off by their families all the time. It was the way of things. Thumberton's attitude was so misplaced.

Even though Emily was three days away, safely sheltered out of his sight at Rosewood, she continued to plague him. Her mother, Anne, had been a whore. A beautiful one, certainly, with an outwardly sweet and gentle disposition. Phillip had met her and fallen in love when he was seventeen. Anne, who was three years older, had been a calculating woman who'd carefully played her cards to get exactly what she wanted. He had married for love, only to find out later that she had married for title and position.

Looking back, he was quite sure she hadn't even been a virgin on their wedding night. In his youthful inexperience, he hadn't noticed. When the babe was conceived, he'd already caught her in bed with his best friend, Richard Farrow. How many others had there been? He'd suffered through three long years of marriage until she'd had the grace to die of influenza, and he no longer had to suffer her cruel manipulations and infidelities.

He had been left to raise the child.

Shaking his head in disgust, he walked to the sideboard and rummaged through the contents, searching for something stronger than wine. The few bottles were empty, and he rang for Graves. The man appeared, taking much longer than necessary, but Phillip could hardly chastise him. He was the only one who agreed to stay after all this time.

"Where is Lady Margaret?"

"She grew tired of waiting, sir, and asked me to tell you that she would meet you at the scheduled time tonight."

Phillip was greatly relieved. Margaret insisted on long, involved, sexual relations every day upon waking. The last thing he needed at the moment was the headache of satisfying her. "Good. I've decided to go to my club for a time. Could you have the carriage brought 'round?"

Graves cleared his throat and looked around the library, trying to carefully choose his next words. "Actually, sir, there's a slight problem with the carriage . . ."

"What?"

"Some men came with papers while you were talking to the solicitor. They took the carriage as payment for something or other."

Phillip shook his head and sighed. What a state! "Thank you, Graves. I'll ring if I need anything else."

Graves took his cue and left quietly. Phillip flopped back in his chair. Glancing at the clock on the wall, he realized he'd barely been awake for an hour. He leaned forward on his elbows, resting his head in his hands. If he'd been a weeping sort of man, this would have been the time for it. All the years of his life, he'd followed his father's example on how to live the privileged life of a wealthy aristocrat. He'd drunk and gambled and debauched women with reckless disregard and without a thought to the family's finances.

What no one had ever bothered to tell him was that his father, for most of his life, had never tended the estates, had never managed the money. As the years passed, his gambling addiction had grown until, by the time he died, there was hardly anything left.

Moving his hands from his eyes, he saw the papers

Thumberton had left behind. A wife. A huge dowry. He pondered the possible consequences from all angles. Marriages in his social group were arranged all the time. If the liaison were carried out, he wouldn't be the first man to marry someone he barely knew. However, he would be the first he knew in his position to marry so far below his station.

"What the hell!" he muttered to himself. It wouldn't hurt to meet the woman. Give her a good look. She would certainly solve all his problems, and if they eventually married, it wasn't as if he had to care about her.

He rang for Graves again, who many minutes later appeared. "Graves, send a bottle of French brandy to Thumberton."

"Certainly, sir."

"With a note from me: Humblest apologies or some such nonsense. Tell him I've decided to consider his advice, and I'll hold off on my decision about Emily." Graves raised an eyebrow. If he'd heard of the plan through the servants' grapevine, he didn't let on. "And tell him I'd be delighted to meet with Miss Fitzsimmons."

Chapter Three

Jane stood on the cliffs, looking out over the sea. The cold winter wind whipped at her cloak. How she loved this place! At three hours from her father's home and only slightly out of the way for the trip to London, she couldn't bear the thought of traveling past without stopping.

Behind her stood her small cottage, the only thing in the entire world that was hers and hers alone, inherited from her long-deceased mother, along with a small stipend for a widow, who lived in and cared for the place. Everything else, even the clothes on Jane's back, belonged to her father, purchased with his money. Although he'd paid her a small allowance for her work at the family business, it had been more pin money than anything else. Available for purchase of hair ribbons and the like.

She'd never minded in the past, but now, faced with his treachery, she wished she'd long ago demanded a salary. She'd have socked it away, bit by bit, until today, when she needed to flee; she'd have been able to run to France or Italy. Perhaps somewhere even more exotic, like Jamaica or the Colonies. Anywhere that would shelter her from her father's demands.

Picking up a rock and hurling it over the ledge, she shook her head. It was too late for wailing over her fate. She was to marry a stranger and that was that. If her father's decision hadn't been so ludicrous, she'd have laughed at the irony of it.

For years, she'd said her prayers every night, thanking the good Lord for giving her Charles as her father. She knew early on that she had been born to do things with her life besides cooking, sewing and birthing children, and she'd felt grateful that her father had seen how she was different from other women. At least that was what she'd always believed.

Now, she'd learned the truth. He had humored her, tolerated her, let her amuse herself at the family business, but the first time it became inconvenient for him to have her around, he'd decided to dump her onto some other man's hands. She'd never had an inkling that he'd do such a dastardly thing.

When she'd looked into the future, she'd always seen herself working side by side with him, helping him build the business until one day, after he passed on, she would sit at the head of the table, directing its affairs. Marriage was always the farthest thing from her mind.

Looking over her shoulder, she could see her best and only friend, Elizabeth, waving from the door of the cottage. Short and plump, with springy, blond curls and rosy, dimpled cheeks, she looked like a painted doll. Pregnancy had added color to her cheeks and a gleam to her eye. Only four months into her time, she'd jumped at the chance to accompany Jane to London, hoping to have the opportunity to shop for the babe.

Closer to the cottage, she grasped Elizabeth's freezing fingers and pulled her through the door, both of them having to push it shut against the fierce wind.

Initially, Elizabeth had resisted Jane's decision to stop at the cottage. She had wanted to press on to London, wanting Jane to have every possible moment to consider her life-altering choice. Her own husband, Edward, a distant cousin betrothed to her at birth, was far from the most passionate or demonstrative man, but he was steady, kind and dependable. Jane could do much worse.

"You were outside for nearly two hours. Whatever were you pondering all that time?"

"You know exactly what I was thinking about."

"Have you had time to examine the papers on the various gentlemen?"

"Not really. I thought perhaps we could look through them together after we've eaten."

"Oh, that would be great fun." Elizabeth led her to the small, cozy kitchen, where she ladled hot soup as she looked over her shoulder. "I wonder if any of them are dashingly handsome?"

"Really, Liz," Jane rolled her eyes. "It matters not to me."

"But a handsome husband can cause a wife to overlook many of his faults."

"I care not for his looks. I'm just marrying because my father has commanded that I do so if I wish to return to my work. I don't intend to have much to do with my husband. I don't care what he looks like, what he does, or where he goes as long as he leaves me be."

"Your husband might have something to say about that." Elizabeth chuckled as she joined Jane at the table.

"Besides," Jane continued, "no one could be as handsome or as dashing as Gregory."

Elizabeth bit into a slice of crusty bread and watched Jane through her lashes. Because of her close relationship with Jane, she'd known early on of her friend's infatuation with Gregory, which began shortly after he had wed Gert. Jane had just turned thirteen, a young woman with romantic notions filling her head. Gregory had played on her emotions, showing her attention, listening to her ideas and encouraging her in her endeavors, all the while moving their relationship from one step to the next in what Elizabeth felt was a slow, but carefully planned, seduction.

Although Jane was nineteen now and nearing twenty-years of age, she was an innocent in many ways. Elizabeth blamed Gregory for every bit of this sorry mess and couldn't for a moment understand why Jane was the one having to pay for what had happened.

"I know you think you love Gregory," she began.

"I don't *think* I love him, Liz. I know I do. And he loves me. That's why I can see how this is the very best thing that could have happened."

"Yes, I agree. 'Tis best for you to forget about him and start your own life with your own husband. Nothing good could have come from walking the path down which Gregory was leading you." Although Jane's father had chosen a harsh method with which to remedy the situation, Elizabeth was secretly glad that he'd decided to remove her from Gregory's clutches. The man was a scoundrel and a cad. Even now, when she'd been banished from her home because of the rogue, Jane couldn't see clearly that he had had any complicity in what had happened. She was loyal to a fault, but in this instance, her loyalty was so misplaced.

"No, you silly goose. That's not what I meant." Jane

broke off a chunk of bread and dipped it in her soup. Gregory's pressure to join physically was becoming unbearable, and Jane wanted so much to please him by doing the right thing, but she couldn't decide what the *right* thing was. Thinking she might have found a solution to her problem, she decided to test her idea on Liz, hoping it would sound better once she spoke of it aloud. "All along, Gregory has wanted us to become lovers in the marital sense of the word. I was thinking that I could relinquish my virginity to my husband, and then, when I return home, Gregory and I could be together just as he always wanted."

Elizabeth had just swallowed a mouthful of broth and struggled to keep from choking. Looking around to see if Mrs. Higgins might have rushed to the room at the scandalous declaration, she looked at Jane in shock and whispered, "You would commit adultery?"

"No," she answered hesitantly, wanting to deny the truth in Liz's question. "My marriage won't be a real union. I'm simply going through with the ceremony in order to please my father and win my way home. I will have no feelings for this man I marry one way or the other."

"Oh, my dear Jane . . ." Elizabeth sighed. Finished with their meal, they retired to the parlor to sit by the fire. Jane shuffled through the packet given to her by her father.

"Let's begin with this one," Jane suggested, completely oblivious to her friend's distress. "Phillip Wessington, Earl of Rosewood . . ."

"Jane." Jane stopped talking as Elizabeth reached for her hand. "As your friend, I feel I must say something to you about this plan of yours."

"What plan?"

"What plan?" she hissed. "Your determination to cuckold your husband. To commit adultery."

"How could you possibly consider it adultery?" Jane waved a hand, trying to appear confident by dismissing Elizabeth's concerns.

"Have you gone mad?"

"Why do you ask? Because I refuse to peacefully give in to my father's disgusting scheme? Gregory is the only man I will ever love. You know how horrid Gertrude is to live with; she abuses him terribly. He's so misunderstood, and he needs me desperately. I can't simply abandon him."

"But Jane, my friend, when you marry, you will have to go to bed with your husband."

"Only on my wedding night. To consummate the thing."

"You don't know that. You're to live with him for six months before returning home." *If he will ever let you return . . .* Elizabeth thought it highly unlikely, but she wasn't about to address that sticky problem at that moment. "He will very likely expect you in his bed every night upon retiring. On occasion, in the mornings when he wakes." She leaned close and whispered, her eyes wide, "Perhaps even in the middle of the day! It will change you in ways you can't imagine. It is so private . . . so personal. I know your heart, and I can't imagine it is something you could do with one man and then with another."

"But you said yourself that it is dry duty at best."

Elizabeth blushed slightly. Edward took his marital duties very seriously but, not being a very emotional type, he wasn't very good at it. An extremely devout man, committed to the Bible's instructions on procreation, he did his duty nightly, but felt that nudity was a great sin. They'd never viewed each other unclothed. "With most couples, it is. But since I left my maidenhood behind, I've heard women talking. Some say there are men who are very good at it. Who give great pleasure in the act and expect to receive great pleasure in return. What if your husband is one of these?''

Jane shook a handful of papers in Elizabeth's face. "Do you really think that one of these men, whose only means of finding a wife is by being paid to accept her, could actually be very good at his marital duties? Really, Liz, think about it.''

Wrinkling her pretty brow, Elizabeth conceded, "I suppose you're right.''

"I'm sure that none of them are any happier about marrying than I am. We will consummate our marriage, and that will be that.''

"You do make it sound simple, but I think you're forgetting one very important thing.''

"What's that?''

Elizabeth rubbed a hand over her slightly raised abdomen. "What if you lie with Gregory and the two of you make a babe? How would you explain it to a husband with whom you have no marital relations? And some of these men''—Elizabeth pointed to the top sheet—"like for instance, this Earl of Rosewood, they will need an heir. How could you risk it? To cuckold such a husband might cost you your life!''

"Hmmm,'' Jane mused, tapping a finger against her lip and not wanting to show her friend how the thought had confounded her. Why couldn't there be an easy solution to alleviate the situation in which she found herself? "I had not considered a babe. Father would never let me come back to work if I was increasing.'' She flopped back against the sofa and wailed, "What am I going to do?''

Elizabeth patted her friend's hand, feeling terrible to

have forced the first crack in Jane's calm facade. She had enough to worry about without any added stress. "It will all work out, Jane. You'll see." She forced a bright smile. "Now, let's read more about the Earl."

Phillip sat at the small dinner table which had been set in Margaret's bedchamber. Everything was done up in red, black and gold. The remodeling had been completed recently, and Margaret thought it was the height of fashion. Phillip thought it looked like Monique's boudoir. Monique was his favorite whore at Madame LeBlanc's.

Margaret entered the room with a flourish. The bodice of her gown was cut so low that, as she leaned forward, Phillip wasn't sure how she kept her nipples from popping over the edge. As it was, he could see where the pale, creamy white skin of her breasts met the pink areolas.

He kissed her lips, then the valley between her breasts. She smelled like roses.

As she seated herself across the table, Phillip watched as she signaled to her servant that they were ready to begin the intimate meal. So lovely, so perfectly matched to himself, she was one of the few women he'd ever met who thoroughly enjoyed the same life of debauchery he did. She drank, gambled, engaged in casual sexual liaisons. She could be as crude, crass and foul mouthed as any man, so very few things ever surprised or upset her. 'Twas a pity that he couldn't marry her.

Instead, he was reduced to seeking the attentions of a commoner. A merchant's daughter, one who was no doubt hobbled by dim wits or an ugly face. Even worse would be to find out that she was a shy, retiring little mouse of a woman. While other men in his class loved to woo and cuddle with females who appeared to have air between their ears, he hated women who couldn't speak up for themselves, and he absolutely abhorred long, silent evenings sitting next to some silly chit who had nothing interesting say. Surely, Jane Fitzsimmons would be all horrible things rolled into one.

They'd nearly finished the first course before Margaret realized she didn't have his undivided attention. "Phillip, what is the matter with you this evening? I hate it when you ignore me."

"I'm sorry," he murmured halfheartedly. "What was your question?"

"I ran into Morris last night. I was simply wondering if you had come to a decision about the betrothal contract for Emily." Although Margaret would never admit it in a thousand years, she was the one who had actually encouraged Morris to press his suit for the girl.

Of course, Margaret would receive numerous benefits out of the deal. Although she'd only spoken to the girl a handful of times, it was obvious that the child hated her. Margaret had no intention of putting up with the girl's rude behavior, once she and Phillip were wed. The child was also quite pretty and, in a few short years, would grow to be a ravishing beauty. Margaret would rather die than have to chaperon her around London while all the available young men swooned over her. Plus, when Margaret considered the staggering expense required to present a young woman, she shuddered. If any money was to be spent on jewels and gowns, it would be spent on herself. She wanted the child out of their lives.

All innocence, she looked deep into Phillip's eyes. "Have you decided whether the child should marry?"

"I don't know. I was planning on it, but then I talked

with Thumberton yesterday, and he seemed to think that—"

"Pah!" Margaret waved a dismissive hand. "That old snake. I don't know why you keep some of those people on retainer."

Because he works for free—out of loyalty to my father. Phillip wanted to shout, but he held his tongue. He shrugged instead. "He gives me good advice."

"I'm sure he does, darling." Margaret could sense she'd touched a nerve. For all Phillip's failings, he was terribly loyal to those working for him. He refused to shed any of the dead weight who gave her so much trouble when she stayed at his various houses. Well, they'd all be dismissed after the wedding. She'd show Phillip how to hire help who could hold their tongues and keep their opinions to themselves. "But you are the girl's father, and no one could possibly have a better idea of what's best for her," she said.

"Nevertheless, I've decided to wait a few weeks while I ponder the situation further. There's plenty of time." Phillip reached for his wine and took a long swig, indicating that the topic was closed for discussion. Thumberton's words had left a bad taste in his mouth. For, while he truly had no feelings for the girl one way or another, he would not want to intentionally hurt her.

"I say, dear"—Margaret interrupted his thoughts again—"talking with you this evening is turning into a major chore." She threw down her napkin. "Are you going to attend the poetry reading with me on Wednesday afternoon?"

"No. I've an important engagement that's just come up." Initially, Phillip had thought about keeping his meeting with Jane Fitzsimmons a secret, but these things had a way of leaking out.

"What?"

"I'm meeting with a young lady."

"Phillip, I've told you before, if you decide to engage in intimate relations with someone other than myself, I suggest you keep it a secret from me. You know I've a terrible temper, and I seem to have developed a jealous streak where you're concerned. I really don't think I could be responsible for my actions."

Phillip chuckled. "It's nothing like that. Actually, I'm meeting with a woman from Portsmouth. Her father has invited marriage offers, and I'm thinking of making one."

Margaret eyed him carefully, wondering what her response should be to this man who had been her steady lover for the past year. He wasn't joking, that was certain. But how could he even consider such a thing? The bastard!

Letting him see her turmoil over the pronouncement would never do. She decided to face the statement with her usual, detached reserve. "Marriage? Why, Phillip, how cute!" Her laughter twinkled. "That is such an absolutely adorable idea. Wherever did you come up with it?"

"Thumberton arranged the meeting for me."

"Oh, isn't that special." She swirled her wine in her goblet, considering the coming days. "And who is she? A babe ready for presentation? A widow? Anyone I know particularly well?"

"I doubt if you know her. She's a merchant's daughter. Her father is willing to part with quite a bit of cash to procure the union."

This bit of information soothed Margaret's emotions considerably. If Phillip was considering a marriage, the money must be substantial, but if the father was ready to part with such a sum, the woman had to be some sort of ball and chain around the man's neck. What could possibly be wrong with her?

The possibilities, of course, were endless. Margaret would find out what flaws the woman possessed, and she would see to it that Phillip saw them, too. No way could he develop an interest in the woman. Margaret simply wouldn't allow it.

Chapter Four

Jane knew that what she was doing was a very bad idea, but she couldn't help herself. The official meetings with her five gentlemen didn't begin for another day, and she dreaded having to make her selection from the stilted, dry introductions she would endure at the small apartment her father had rented for her stay in London. The conversations would be polite, boring; the gentlemen callers practicing such reserved behavior that it would be impossible to learn anything at all about them from their mere presence.

She needed to do something that would tell her more. So, although it was the height of impropriety and rudeness, she'd decided to meet them first on their own turf.

Starting with the Earl of Rosewood, Phillip Wessington.

Raising a hand, she knocked briskly on the door, her heart pounding at the outrageousness of her actions.

There was a chance the Earl wouldn't be at home, or that he would be so affronted by her audacity at calling on him unchaperoned that he'd want nothing more to do with her, but she'd had to come.

For too many years of her life, she'd done as she pleased, run her own schedule, made her own decisions. It was difficult to change after nineteen years. She wanted to meet the Earl, and if he was upset by her appearing on his doorstep, so be it. His very reaction at seeing her make such a bold move would tell her very much about his character, much more than she would be able to learn when *he* called on *her* the next day.

She took a deep breath and knocked again. The Earl's residence was an imposing place in Mayfair. Only the Quality lived in the neighborhood as evidenced by the few fancy carriages passing by. There were none of the street hawkers and peddlers that she'd traveled past only a few blocks away.

One last time, she knocked and was rewarded by the sound of footsteps coming toward the door. A kind-looking man, short and trim in his mid-thirties with graying hair and a clean-shaven face answered. As she reached for the card she had buried in her reticule, the man took in her functional gray day dress and the trim, tidy hair, braided and wrapped around the back of her head. Under his scrutiny, she felt horribly underdressed.

Wishing she'd taken more time with her appearance, and wondering if the man would close the door on her before she said her piece, she held out her hand. "Hello, my name is—"

"John Graves, here, my dear. I must say we'd about given up on you."

"What?" Jane asked, confused.

He hustled her through the doorway and across the

foyer. She found herself traveling quickly down unfamiliar hallways as Graves talked. She had to hurry to keep up. "The Earl's friends are already here. Cook's frantic. And, of course, I refuse to serve them. Even I have my limits." He paused for a moment, hurrying her past and through a door. "Here we go, then."

They'd entered the kitchens. A plump, older woman bent over a long table, arranging small finger foods on a tray. "Cook," Graves said, "the girl is finally here." He looked over his shoulder at Jane. "What's your name, dear?"

"Jane, but I think there's been some mistake. I . . ."

The cook looked up from her work, eyeing Jane so thoroughly from head to toe that she felt naked. "Oh, Lud, you're a pretty one. Graves, did you forget to tell the agency?"

"No, Cook. I told them."

Jane couldn't help asking, "Told them what?"

Cook responded, "Not to send any pretty ones. We just end up losing them afore they're trained and then having to start again with another. It's such a bother."

"Why do you lose them?" she asked in a voice that sounded nothing like her own.

Cook rolled her eyes, turning her attention back to her work. Graves stepped up and efficiently tied an apron around Jane's middle. "There's no time to change, but your dress should do for now. The Earl will hardly notice, and if Lady Margaret says anything"—Cook harrumphed at this—"simply beg her pardon, then come back downstairs. After you finish with these few trays, we'll have some minutes alone. I'll be able to show you to your room."

With that, he was already moving out of the kitchen and along the hall. Jane realized they thought her a new, just-arrived servant of some sort and wanted to correct the misimpression before things went any further, but Graves's back was disappearing so quickly, she was afraid she'd lose him in the corridors.

She meant to set the tray aside, but Cook looked at her so sternly that she didn't dare leave without it. Oh, well, she'd hand it to Graves with apologies as soon as she caught up with him. She turned to leave.

Cook's gruff voice stopped her. "The Earl's got a roamin' eye for the pretty ones. Don't let it settle on you."

She paused as understanding dawned. "Surely, you don't mean . . ."

The older woman gave her a knowing look. "Just be careful you don't find yourself alone with him, if you get my meanin'."

"Cook, do you mean to say that he tumbles the servant girls?"

"Only if they're willin'."

"Oh, my heavens . . ." Jane was blushing. "But why would so many of them—"

"He's handsome as the Devil's own, that one is. And a smooth talker where the ladies are concerned." Cook motioned her to follow Graves. "Keep a square head on your shoulders. You'll do all right."

Jane hustled out, tray in hand, her head whirling with Cook's admonitions about her prospective husband. A rake and scoundrel who wasn't above having his way with the servants. What had she gotten herself into? Graves was waiting patiently at the top of the stairs. "Graves, I think I should—"

"You look ill at ease, Jane. Did Cook say something unseemly about the Earl?"

"Just that he . . . well . . . he likes the ladies. She said I should be careful."

"The old bat." Graves chuckled. "Don't listen to her. He'd never do anything you didn't want to be done."

"High praise, indeed," Jane responded with a raised brow.

Graves laughed. He was a quick study where people were concerned, and he'd liked the looks of Jane from the moment he'd opened the door. The girl definitely carried herself well. Just the thing they needed in the dreary house. He leaned closer. "I don't mean to tell tales, but you might as well know the truth of it if you're looking for steady work. These days, you need to worry more about whether your wages will be regular than whether or not the Earl might take a fancy to you."

He was busy leading her up the stairs. "But . . . but . . ."

Outside a closed door, he paused and whispered, "You know the trick. Just remain invisible. Smile at the Earl. Stay out of Lady Margaret's way." Jane opened her mouth to try one more time to correct the misunderstanding, but Graves prevented it by opening the door to the parlor. He gently nudged her inside.

She stared around the room. If she'd half been expecting all to turn in her direction and point fingers, unmasking her silly charade, she'd been sadly mistaken. Dressed as a servant, carrying a tray, her appearance in the door went unnoticed.

A quick mental count showed four men and two women, all in various stages of casual dress. Jackets were discarded, cravats missing, sleeves rolled back. One woman, a voluptuous blonde, was particularly beautiful. Her gown was cut low, and the fabric across the bodice so sheer that Jane could make out the soft rounding of the woman's breasts and the large protruding nipples. She was sitting on the lap of one of the men, her head tipped back in laughter.

Jane was embarrassed to see so many strangers in such

a state of dishabille. They were drinking spirits, touching each other. In her closely sheltered life, she'd never imagined that people would socialize in such a scandalous state, and she briefly wondered if the two females might be some type of loose women, offering themselves to the men. What had she gotten herself into?

Her eyes scanned the room as she looked to see which one was the Earl and found him in a second. She took a quick breath. Cook had certainly been right. He did look like the Devil's own, with a full head of black hair held back by a leather thong. A few dark strands hovered over his forehead. His brows were wedged across intelligent but hard, eyes—eyes that looked as if they'd seen too much. They were black, too, like his hair or perhaps it was just a trick of the light. He'd missed his shave for the day, and the dark stubble on his cheeks only accented the high cheekbones and aristocratic nose.

His shoulders were impossibly broad, his shirt undone halfway down his chest, and the dark chest hair poking through was stark against the white fabric. His chest narrowed to a thin waist and hips. Even though he was sitting, his legs looked impossibly long. With one ankle laid casually across his knee, he looked like a pirate or highwayman, a man who appeared to be thoroughly relaxed but who might spring into action at any moment.

He sat by himself at the end of the room, intentionally distanced from the others, in an oversized chair. His sleeves were pushed back, and his forearms were covered with the same dark hair that swirled across his chest. His fingers were long and elegant. Twirling the contents of his goblet, he listened with apparent half-interest to the blond beauty sitting across the room on another man's lap.

Through the clink of silver and glassware and the

lively chatter, Jane thought it a good time to make her escape. She crossed the room to set the tray where Graves had instructed her. The route took her directly past the Earl's chair. As she stepped by, he gently reached out a hand and laid it on her wrist, stopping her while he selected a handful of orange slices. Up close, he was even more handsome than he'd appeared from across the room. She could feel the warmth of his skin through the fabric of her dress.

Phillip looked up into the eyes of the female servant he'd never noticed before. There were so few left these days, and the new ones Graves hired came and went quickly, having no long-standing loyalties to the family and not wishing to remain if wages were slow in coming.

She was a pretty thing, with smooth, creamy skin, chestnut hair and emerald green eyes. A tad on the thin side for his taste, and her hair a bit too severe in that tight braiding. He'd definitely love to see it free and flowing down her back. If she stayed, perhaps he would, maybe in her nightclothes some evening, sneaking down the hall to the kitchens. He could just imagine her stretched out beneath him on his bed, the long auburn locks decadently arrayed across his pillows. He rubbed a thumb in a slow circle across the inside of her wrist and felt her tremble. Yes, there were definite possibilities with the chit.

He smiled up at her and whispered, "You're doing fine. Don't be nervous."

With that all-consuming gaze focused on her, she was like a deer trapped in the carriage lamp. Unable to move or speak, she looked her fill, wondering what it would be like to have a man like the Earl shower the full force of his attentions on her. But, then, he winked at her, and the spell was broken. The man was impossible. She'd only been in the house ten minutes, and he was already making advances.

It was the perfect time to flee, and she took a step toward the door just as she realized the blonde was talking about the Earl and his meeting with Miss Jane Fitzsimmons the next day. Knowing she was being incredibly naughty, she stepped back along the wall, hovering near the drapes. What a chance!

The blonde leaned forward, her gown barely constraining her large, round breasts. "So, Wessington, dear, share your secret with everyone. It will make the evening so much more entertaining."

The Earl sipped his wine and appeared bored with the idea. "Really, Margaret, I'm sure there are many more important things we could discuss."

"Hardly." Margaret waved him off as if he hadn't spoken. She had everyone's attention. "Wessington is thinking about marrying!"

There was a long, silent pause as his friends digested the news.

Finally, one of the men laughed. "The old ball and chain, eh? Who's the lucky gel? Don't tell me you managed to snag Farthington's daughter."

Another said, "Can't imagine her old man would let his darling marry this rake."

They all laughed.

Another said, "Can't imagine this rake would settle for a silly, little virgin like Farthington."

Everyone laughed again; then Margaret continued. "Oh, it's even more delicious than imagining Wessington sawing away between the thighs of some wide-eyed blueblood." She paused with dramatic effect. "He's decided to settle for a merchant's daughter." There was a particularly vicious gleam in her eye, and Jane decided then and there that she despised the woman. Needing to do something with her hands before she threw something, she picked up the tray and started offering it to each individual.

"A merchant's daughter? Really, Wessington, I heard the rumors about your finances, but how low are you willing to stoop? There really should be a limit imposed. We can't be diluting the blood by marrying just any old one."

The other woman, dressed as shockingly as Lady Margaret, leaned over to better see the Earl. "Have you gotten a look at her, Wessie?"

Margaret answered. "Oh, he doesn't need to see her. He doesn't care about how she looks. It's only the size of her purse that matters."

"Yes, well," one of the men put in, "even in these necessary unions, it's nice to stumble on a pretty face."

"Or a nice arse," another added.

"Or an ample set of duckies," yet another chimed in. "Always nice to suckle a juicy pair."

Jane flushed with embarrassment. Margaret, in a silent bit of communication with the Earl that Jane couldn't begin to understand, waved a dismissive hand. "I've done some checking on the girl, myself. She's plain and thin. Homely as a post they say, with mousy brown hair and a mousy personality to match." Her eyes gleamed wickedly as she looked at the Earl, then glanced at the others. "I hear her father's trying to marry her off at the first offer. None around her home will have her."

The other woman said, "Well, if she's got plenty of money, and there's no one near her home who'll have her, you certainly should do some checking."

"And," Margaret added, hitting at the Earl's most vulnerable spot, "I'd certainly be requesting a midwife to check her. Wouldn't want to find a bun in the oven, now would you, Wessington?''

Jane paused in front of Margaret, waiting for the Earl to say something in her defense, one kind thing that would soften the harsh words of his friends.

The Earl looked over at Margaret and said blandly, ''Her money's the same color as everyone else's or so I hear.''

If Jane had been standing next to the Earl, she'd have dropped the tray on him. As it was, she was standing in front of Margaret. She tipped the thing just right, making sure every bit of the pastries slid down the woman's bodice and onto her lap.

Margaret screeched and jumped to her feet. ''Of all the clumsy, idiotic . . .'' she sputtered. ''You blithering fool!'' Her eyes blazing, she reached out and took a swing. Jane saw it coming and jumped back before the slap could land on her cheek.

''Margaret, stop!'' the Earl shouted in his most authoritarian tone, his command bringing a halt to all movement in the room. He stepped to Jane and took her hand in his own. ''Are you all right, my dear?'' he asked softly.

Not wanting him to see the tears of rage burning in her eyes, Jane curtsied low in his direction. ''I most humbly beg your pardon, milord.'' Before he or anyone else could say or do anything, she jerked her hand back and scurried away, Margaret's bitter words ringing in her ears all the way down the stairs.

''Really, Wessington, the caliber of the servants you hire is absolutely beyond imagining. I expect that horrid girl to be beaten, then discharged. Just look what she did to my gown . . .''

Graves was lurking in the shadows, peeking curiously toward the noises coming from the parlor. Jane untied the apron and held it out. " 'Twas nice to meet you, Mr. Graves. Thank you for giving me a chance, but I just don't think I'm cut out for this line of work."

She was out the door and running down the street before anyone thought to stop her.

Chapter Five

The next afternoon, Jane sat on the stiff couch, waiting for the arrival of her first caller, Phillip Wessington. She'd risen early, taken hours with her bath and toilette, so long in fact, that Elizabeth began to think that perhaps she really was taking the matter of marriage to heart by trying to look her very best. Elizabeth was partly right. Jane was trying to look better than she ever had, but not for any reason her friend could have ever imagined.

To think that the cad had the nerve to plan to wed an innocent victim, a woman like herself, who would then be exposed to his life of intemperance and debauchery. She shuddered, just thinking about what might have been her fate if she'd politely met the Earl in her apartment, taken a look at his handsome face and compelling physique, and decided to marry him based on the one tightly controlled and chaperoned encounter.

The previous afternoon's fiasco had given her a renewed purpose for her meeting with the Earl, which was scheduled to begin at any moment. Remembering his attitude set her temper flaring all over again. She'd spent all night trying to calm herself enough to be able to face him again. As morning dawned so did her idea on how to get even.

A hand knocked loudly on the door downstairs. The woman hired temporarily to cook and look after them opened the door, and voices could be heard.

Elizabeth leaned over and squeezed her hand. "Jane, this is so exciting, isn't it? And I've never seen you look lovelier."

The servant announced the two men, Wessington and his solicitor, Thumberton, who had arranged the entire sordid episode. Elizabeth bade the woman show them up, and Jane took a last quick glance in the mirror, making sure nothing was out of place. She hid a wry smile. Liz was right: She'd never looked better.

Her chestnut hair was artfully scooped onto the top of her head, cascading down in soft ringlets which curled delicately around her face. Her dress, although not as fancy as anything the Earl would be used to, was conservative but stylish. Showing just a hint of bosom, the high waist emphasized her slender figure. The green color brought out her lovely emerald eyes and set off, in startling contrast, the red highlights in her hair.

Thumberton was the first to enter. He was a pleasant older man, and, from the gentle look in his eyes, Jane knew she wouldn't be able to be unkind to him. He was only doing his duty. She flashed him a welcoming smile as he bowed over her hand.

Phillip entered the small salon a step behind Thumberton. Graves had spent hours primping and preening his master until Phillip felt as though he were a cock being prepared for the fight. *Or a lamb for the slaughter*, he thought ruefully.

The thought of marrying again was distasteful. He'd wooed Anne and married her at such a young, foolish age. So much in love and so ready to live happily ever after, only to have his romantic yearnings crushed by her repeated infidelities. And this from a woman he'd known and loved! What terrible things could happen being wed to a woman he didn't even know? To be bound and shackled to a stranger was unthinkable.

Forcing off the morbid thoughts that had plagued him since he'd agreed to the stupid meeting, he stepped into the room. Nobody was forcing him to marry, he reminded himself. Nowhere was it set in stone that he was bound to this woman or that he owed her anything. He was taking a look, that was all.

Nothing prepared him for the female sitting on the sofa, making introductions for herself and her friend. She was lovely, with flowing chestnut hair that curled gracefully around her heart-shaped face and striking emerald eyes that sparkled like a green summer lawn. Her nose turned up slightly at the end, her cheeks were rosy and dimpled. Her trim figure was perfectly flattered by the cut of her gown. The creamy, white skin of her bared bosom hinted at small, but perfect, treasures hidden beneath. Phillip actually felt his body stir as a vision of himself, buried between her shapely thighs, flew unbidden through his mind.

There had to be something wrong with her. Her looks were flawless, so perhaps she had a voice like a screech owl or the personality of a shrew. Listening to her chat with Thumberton put an end to both thoughts. Her voice was soothing and gentle, her manner soft-spoken and delightful.

Through his reverie, he realized he was being introduced. He stepped forward as Jane Fitzsimmons extended her hand. " 'Tis a pleasure to meet you, Lord Wessington."

"The pleasure, lovely lady, is all mine." He bowed low and kissed the back of her hand. Her skin was smooth and soft, and she smelled of lilacs. Her fingers were slim and elegant, the nails perfectly manicured, and he imagined the feel of them wrapped around his hardened shaft as he taught her how to pleasure him. Where the notion came from he couldn't say, but it sprang freely into his mind.

The afternoon was turning out to be much more interesting than he could ever have imagined.

Jane watched the Earl as he leaned over her hand. Gregory was the only man she'd ever been close to, and he'd always smelled of an overpowering cologne that she hadn't particularly cared for. The Earl had a clean, manly scent all his own. A fresh soap smell, mixed with tobacco, leather and other things she couldn't describe. His head of beautiful, dark hair hovered before her eyes. If she hadn't already known what a despicable cad he was, she'd have welcomed the temptation she was feeling to run her fingers through it.

Fine thoughts for a woman who had only been away from her beloved for a matter of days!

Wessington touched her hand, his moist breath brushing her skin, his warm lips lingering much longer than was appropriate under the circumstances. Jane knew he was flirting with her. He wanted her money badly enough to do anything for it—even if it meant trifling with someone he detested. Well, he could have his fun and so would she.

As he released her hand and rose, she gave him her most winning smile, and a question furrowed his brow. "What is it, milord?"

Phillip was surprised that she so quickly read his expression without knowing anything about him. "I don't mean to be forward, but when you smile like that, Miss Fitzsimmons, it seems as though I must know you from somewhere. Have we met previously, and, I am embarrassed to ask, have I forgotten the occasion?"

Jane's heart fluttered for a moment. He couldn't possibly have paid enough attention the previous afternoon to connect her with the serving girl in his drawing room. "No, sir, I'm sure not." She smiled again as Wessington and Thumberton settled themselves across from the two ladies. "I must say I would certainly have remembered even a chance encounter with you."

The Earl wasn't ready to let it rest. "Have you spent much time in London?"

"Hardly any, sir. I've been to the city only four times previously in my entire life. The last time was almost three years past."

"Perhaps, in Northampton, then, where many of my family's properties are located."

"No, I've never had the pleasure of visiting there. Perhaps I simply have one of those common faces that blends easily with others."

"Hardly." He flashed her the smile that had never failed to melt a female heart. "There is nothing about your lovely face that one could consider *common.*"

They chatted as strangers do, all the while, everyone keenly aware of the true reason for the Earl's visit. Thumberton steered the conversation after the initial introductions, relieved to see that Phillip was behaving himself and showing the manners that had been so carefully drilled into him at an early age but which he so seldom chose to use. He actually seemed to be quite taken with Miss Fitzsimmons, and Thumberton heaved a great sigh of relief. She was lovely, well educated.

She'd be good for Phillip and an excellent mother for Emily.

Thumberton was thrilled.

Elizabeth quietly watched Phillip Wessington as much as she dared without being caught staring. He was tall, dark and handsome as well as charming and funny, and he conversed with ease on a number of topics. There was an air about him of self-possession and self-assured-ness that made it seem as if he filled up too much of the room simply by being in it. He obviously knew how to woo a woman, for his gaze, when he trained it on Jane, was thoroughly encompassing, and he listened and watched her as if nothing or no one else existed in the world. To think that this man had materialized in the flesh from Jane's list and could very likely end up as her husband!

Elizabeth was thrilled.

Phillip was a master at playing a woman. His earliest memories were of women falling all over themselves to please him. He'd had a lifetime of it. He knew how to draw them in, to make them open themselves up in a way they did to no one else. When talking to him, they felt important, comfortable, cherished and valued. He was better at playing this game than any man he knew. And he was playing it now with Jane Fitzsimmons, giving her the full force of his attention, and liking every bit of what he saw.

While her looks were nothing that he'd expected, neither was her manner. If she'd had any reservations about marrying so far above her station, it didn't show. While most women were thoroughly overcome by his position and personality, she didn't seem to be the least bit intimidated. The woman was no shrinking violet, hiding behind her fan while flashing coquettish looks in his direction.

Even more amazing was the fact that she had actually been *working* at the family business for several years, and if she was to be believed, had quite a responsible position at her father's side. She'd thrown out the admission proudly, as if daring him to chastise her or be offended at the prospect of his future wife having such a scandalous background.

Secretly delighted, he had no problem with educated, strong women, preferring them to the blithering, gossiping ninnies raised by members of the *ton*. But he was a quick study, and he also saw a great possibility looming with Jane as his wife.

Phillip hated accounting, numbers and oversight, but Jane appeared to thrive on such things. She was hardly the type to want to sit around embroidering all day and would want something valuable to do. He would be more than happy to let her busy herself with the situation at Rosewood; then he could stay in London with friends, gambling and carousing just as he'd done for all of his adult life.

Of course, they'd have to spend time together occasionally to breed an heir, and from looking at her and watching her, he could see that bedding her would definitely be the least of his problems. Those green eyes, those ruby lips, the pert breasts. Just imagining what it would be like to twirl those two lovely nipples between his fingers made his fingertips start to itch.

Phillip was thrilled.

Jane was watching Wessington very carefully. She found it easy to read his expressions and, with each passing minute, could see how the idea of marrying her was seeming less offensive. While she wasn't sure what she'd said, she could tell the exact moment when he'd come to the decision that a union with her might be just the thing he needed. Without even realizing what was happening, Wessington was being reeled in to his doom.

Jane was thrilled.

The two hours they'd allotted for the meeting was quickly drawing to a close. Thumberton was the first to notice after glancing at his timepiece. "I see our time is almost up. I must say, Miss Fitzsimmons, that it has been a delight to meet you." He'd already talked with Phillip in advance about what his response should be if he was interested in pursuing the matter by meeting again, and the boy didn't disappoint.

"Yes," Phillip added, "I must say I've enjoyed this time very much. If you have no other plans for this evening, I'd like to ask you to join me for supper." He smiled at Elizabeth. "With Mrs. Carew and Mr. Thumberton joining us, of course. I realize it's quite bold of me to issue such an invitation on such short notice, but Thumberton has instructed me that you're under some time constraint in making your decisions."

It was all Jane could do to keep from cheering at how well things were going. "Yes, I do have a very short time to make decisions. I'm eager to get on with them."

Phillip took this as a positive sign. "I'd like to speak further with you about your thoughts and plans." He paused for effect. "And about mine." He smiled at Elizabeth again. "And I have a box at the theater. After dining, perhaps you ladies would care to join me for an evening of entertainment."

"Oh, that would be positively lovely," Elizabeth gushed. "The theater, Jane. Just imagine! Wouldn't it be fun?"

"I don't know, Elizabeth." Jane paused, watching the smile in her friend's eyes turn to a question. "Actually, Lord Wessington, I've had a bit of time to think, and I don't think we'd suit." Wessington sat ramrod straight in his chair, obviously surprised that a lowborn chit would have the audacity to refuse him, but it was Thumberton who seemed most openly surprised, as if she'd dashed dozens of unnamed hopes and dreams.

"If you'll beg my pardon, Miss Fitzsimmons," Thumberton said slowly, feeling the irritation rolling off Phillip in waves and wanting to quell it before he unleashed his harsh tongue on the young lady, "these things should often be decided after a little more reflection. Perhaps you might spend some time tonight with Mrs. Carew, and we can talk again tomorrow."

"Actually, I don't think it would do any good to think on it any longer." Jane rose and casually walked to the sideboard, poured herself a fortifying glass of wine as she glanced over her shoulder. "I'm sure you'd agree, milord, that you couldn't possibly settle for a merchant's daughter." She leaned forward slightly, as if baiting him, and carefully repeated the harsh words one of his male friends had uttered in his parlor the previous day. "After all, how low are you willing to stoop? There should be a limit imposed. You aristocratic types shouldn't be allowed to marry just any old one."

Phillip's cheeks were flaming red. He knew there were those who felt exactly as she'd implied. At a different time in his life, he was probably one of them. Now, with his feelings toward marriage significantly cooled by his first experience, he no longer cared who married whom. "Really, Miss Fitzsimmons, if that was what I believed, I would never have come here today."

Jane was incensed that he didn't seem to recognize that she'd thrown the words of his friend in his face. The encounter in his parlor had obviously been so insignificant that he didn't even remember it. Her anger started to rise along with her voice.

"I realize how disappointed you must be that I'm not

interested in you as a husband, especially when you are so smitten with the size of my *purse.*"

"Jane," Elizabeth hissed, completely mortified by her friend's comment. "Where are your manners?"

"I left them at home. This is my choice, my life we're talking about." She turned her furious gaze back to Wessington, altering her voice to do a good imitation of the male friends who had teased him. "Even in these necessary unions, it's nice to stumble on a pretty face"— she laid a hand on her cheek—"or a nice arse"—she brushed a palm along her hip—"or an ample set of duckies. Always nice to suckle a juicy pair." She ran a hand seductively across her bosom.

"Jane!" Elizabeth shrieked.

Phillip watched in stunned amazement as the gentle, pleasant woman he'd enjoyed for two hours turned into a whirling termagant. He couldn't imagine what he had done to cause the change. The words she was using seemed familiar, but he couldn't place them.

Realizing that Mrs. Carew and Thumberton were both looking to him for answers, he said calmly, "Miss Fitzsimmons, it seems I've displeased you in some way, and I'm not sure what it is I've done. Let me say that I never intended any slight. I came here with an open mind and an eager heart, wondering if an arranged marriage could be a possibility, but—"

"Really, Lord Wessington? Would you truly and seriously consider marriage to me when all your friends are spreading the word that I have a *bun* in the oven?" Jane raised the wine goblet she had in her hand and hurled it at the fireplace where it shattered most effectively. "Now, get out of here before I dump a tray of pastries on you as I did to that doxy you were entertaining in your parlor."

"You!" Phillip roared, coming to his feet.

"Jane, oh Jane, what have you done?" Elizabeth asked in wide-eyed wonder.

Jane kept her furious gaze locked on Wessington's, but answered her friend. "I only made the lucky decision to find out what this scoundrel is really and truly like, and I'm happy to say that I've saved myself from a life of heartbreak and humiliation."

Phillip crossed the room in three angry steps, standing nearly nose-to-nose with Jane, his entire body quivering with rage. "You break into my home—"

Jane placed her hands on her hips and shouted, "I didn't break in. I was invited."

"—unannounced and unwelcomed, and you have the audacity to be upset about what you saw and heard?"

Thumberton stepped closer, laid a hand on Phillip's arm, but the Earl shook it off. "Excuse us, Thumberton," he said in a quiet voice filled with fury.

"Phillip, I don't think—"

Phillip whirled on his advisor. "That was not a request. It was an order. Go! And take Mrs. Carew with you. I will only be a moment."

Jane welcomed the chance to be alone with the blackguard. She had more than a few things she wanted to get off her chest. "Yes, please, Master Thumberton, do give us a moment of privacy."

Elizabeth, blushing red, found her voice, "Jane, I don't believe it would be at all appropriate for you to remain in here alone with the Earl."

Jane peeked around from behind his broad torso. "You needn't worry about his temper, Liz. He didn't bring along any of his whores, so there's no one to strike me. And as for my virtue, I have it on good authority that he only tumbles those servants who are willing."

"God's teeth!" Phillip roared again, whirling back to face her.

"Sir, you will not blaspheme in my presence!"

"I will damn well speak in any manner I choose."
Only inches separated them, and Phillip was secretly
amazed and impressed that the chit had the fortitude
to stand her ground. Her rage burned as hotly as his
own, and she stood toe-to-toe, ready to give as good as
she got. "Thumberton, take Mrs. Carew and leave this
moment." Phillip used his most authoritative voice,
knowing that neither of them would dare argue, and
he stood still while he heard the shuffling of feet. The
door clicked shut behind them. He took a step forward,
but the woman didn't move a muscle or bat an eye.

Between clenched teeth, he said, "I give you credit
for having the most audacity of any woman I have ever
met."

"And I give you credit for being the lowest, most
despicable man I have ever met!"

"Hah!" he shouted. "You are the one who imposed
herself on my party. On myself and my friends." He
wanted to shake her. "Do you have any idea with whom
you're dealing?"

"Do you, sir? I am not one of the half-brained nitwits
from your social circle. I am not one of the whores you
cavort with in the middle of the afternoon."

"You will not disparage the women who choose to
visit me in my home."

"Oh, you're right of course," she answered in her
most condescending tone, "I can leave that to your
servants. They know best what your female friends are
like. So tell me, did you and your Lady Margaret have
a good laugh after she was allowed to nearly assault me?
I'm sure 'twas an added measure of entertainment for
all of you."

"We did not laugh about it. I was quite upset. Contrary

to what you wish to believe, Miss Fitzsimmons, the servants in my houses are well treated."

She wasn't swallowing it. "Especially all those girls who came as maids but left as women."

"Where did you hear these outrageous things?"

"Do you deny it, milord? That you love nothing better than seducing a sweet young thing?" She turned away and fiddled with the items on the sideboard. "Get out of my sight. I can't bear to look at you."

There she was, doing it again! As if she were the noblewoman, and he some lowborn lad. "You will not dismiss me," he shouted again. He reached for her arm and whirled her back to face him. "I will have my say."

"Then say it and go."

Phillip pulled himself up so he towered over her. She didn't even blink. No fear. No embarrassment. No respect or deference. Just a complete lack of regard for all he represented. "I came to you in good faith, wondering if perhaps a beneficial union between us was possible. I can see that I was completely misled by my solicitor."

"Pray tell me, sir, in what manner were you misled?" The very picture of innocence, she fluttered her eyelids.

The sweet, mocking smile was too much. It was time to strike back. "He told me he'd found a sweet, virtuous young woman, from a good family, who was considering marriage. Obviously, nothing could be further from the truth. I find you rude and unpleasant. In possession of an uncontrollable temper. A woman whose lack of common sense lets her wander into impossible situations." No reaction. Best to hit where her pride ran truest. "A woman who comes from such a disreputable family that her own father allowed her to involve herself in the family's commerce. I could *never* take such a one as you to wife."

"Yes, it's so horrible that I have a head for figures and trade," she said sarcastically, "but at least *my* family's business was alive and thriving when I left Portsmouth. What say you of yours?"

Phillip knew he had to leave the room immediately or he just might strike her. The nerve! The gall! For this stranger, this commoner, this *woman* to question his life was beyond imagining. "I'll take my leave now, Miss Fitzsimmons. You have insulted me, my title, my family. I wouldn't marry you if you were the last woman on earth."

He turned to go, and she shouted at his back, "And I wouldn't have you if you were the last man!"

A glass smashed against the door, but he kept walking as though he hadn't noticed. Thumberton and Mrs. Carew were huddled together at the bottom of the stairs, obviously trying to make out the words of the loud argument. Thumberton was holding Phillip's hat and cane, and Phillip reached for them and headed for the door. "Come, sir, escort me out of this madhouse."

Chapter Six

Jane stood at the window, looking out at the cold, gray day and listening as her fifth and final suitor retreated down the stairs. Outside, one hearty soul braved the weather and passed by on the street below.

"Are they gone?" Jane whispered as Elizabeth returned from seeing him and the solicitor off.

"Yes, thank goodness." Sensing her friend's mood matched the gloomy day, she joined her by the window. "What are you thinking?"

"That I could probably go down and pluck that man off the street and he'd be better than any of these imbeciles Thumberton has sent to me." She started to giggle, Elizabeth joined her; then the giggles turned to laughs. As they both recalled the meetings of the past two days, the laughter grew until they were both nearly doubled over. Jane moved from the window and flopped back on the couch. "Ahhh, I can't believe this. I haven't met such an offensive person in a very, very long time."

"I imagine poor Master Wiley was a nice enough sort, but his mother! Could you possibly imagine living with that woman day in and day out?"

Wishing she could jump out the window and disappear, Jane shook her head. What a disaster the past two days had turned out to be!

Each of the men she'd met had been horribly distasteful. Poor Jerome Wiley, the man who'd just left, was just one of the peas in a terrible pod. With the exception of Phillip Wessington, not one of them had any looks to speak of, no charm, personality or charisma. He possessed all. Wessington was the only one who could carry on an interesting conversation. He had been the only one to ask about her life in Portsmouth. She'd been so inconsequential to the others that not a single one had asked her anything about herself.

Elizabeth's gentle voice broke into her painful reverie. "Whatever are you going to do, Jane?"

"I don't know. I can't imagine that Father had any idea of the type of men Thumberton would provide for me to meet. Can you imagine what he'd say if I brought one of these men to Portsmouth?"

"Well, I do think he'd be quite pleased with the Earl of Rosewood."

"Don't dwell on it, Liz." Jane sighed. "Thinking of him just makes all of this so much worse. We've got to figure out what to do." The folder with the information about the gentlemen was laying on a side table. Jane picked it up and absentmindedly leafed through the pages again. "I really like Master Thumberton; he seems like an astute man. I can't imagine why he would have felt any of these men would be appropriate. Not just for me, but for any woman. Can you imagine any poor female shackling herself to one of those clods?"

"No, I can't."

"Perhaps if I talked with him. Maybe he could reason with Father. He could explain the problems with the choices. Get me an extension of Father's deadline while we search for someone more appropriate."

Elizabeth smiled sadly. "Dear, I whispered as much to him yesterday after your gay blade departed. He said the instructions from your father were very clear. That absolutely, under no circumstances, would you be granted more time."

"Oh, Liz, what am I to do?"

"Well, I do have one thought."

"What is that?"

"I know you have quite a few angry feelings for the Earl, but put them aside for a moment."

"Why should I?"

"Well, if you forget about the things you witnessed at his house, he is quite a spectacular gentleman. Handsome, educated, most likely well built in the appropriate places."

"Liz, for heaven's sake." Jane blushed slightly, looking embarrassed, but she'd never reveal that the flush was due to a strange heat that seemed to creep over her whenever she thought about the Earl. Her imagination was ripe, and she'd already passed many unpleasant moments wondering what was hidden under his clothes. For some reason, it was impossible to put the man entirely out of her mind as she wished to do.

Elizabeth saw the red cheeks and waved a hand. "No, no, don't be getting embarrassed on me now. This is too important. Hear me out. He's probably well schooled in the acts which take place in the marital bed. He offers a title, estates, respect. Imagine being married to a member of Parliament!"

"Right." Jane snorted. "As if the lazy oaf could tear

himself away from his women or gambling long enough to attend any sessions.''

"You agreed to hear me out. Do you want my thoughts on this or no?"

"All right, all right. Tell me."

"Anyway, when you hold Phillip Wessington up against these others, it's almost as though Master Thumberton was stacking the deck against you."

"What do you mean? You think he actually selected some unsuitable candidates to make Wessington look better?"

"Think about it." Elizabeth was pacing back and forth as the thoughts circled in her head. "Of course, that has to be it. Don't you see? He did everything he could to make the Earl appear to be the only logical choice."

"I suppose you're right. But he's a very well known and respected solicitor. Why would he play such a game?"

"Imagine if you'd never stopped by Wessington's townhouse. You knew nothing at all about him except what you learned in this very room. Would there have been any question about whom you would select?"

"No, none," Jane had to admit.

"That's the answer then. I'm sure of it." Elizabeth sat next to Jane. "For whatever reason, Master Thumberton wanted you to select Wessington, and he did everything he could to make sure you would."

"He just didn't know I was likely to skew the deal by taking matters into my own hands."

"Yes, and as you said, I like him a great deal. I trust his judgment. There must be some reason he fancies the Earl."

"I can see that now. That sly old fox."

Elizabeth took her friend's hand and squeezed it tightly. "Jane, I know it would be a bitter tonic for you to swallow, but I think you need to talk to Master Thumberton first thing in the morning. Ask him about the Earl. Find out why Thumberton feels such loyalty to him and has such a need to help him out in this way. Perhaps there's still a chance for you.''

"You think the Earl might still be interested in me? Oh, Liz, that's foolishness. I've lost my chance, I'm afraid.''

"You don't know that you have. He's as desperate as you are, or he wouldn't have let Thumberton drag him here in the first place.'' Elizabeth squeezed her hand tighter and leaned closer. "Jane, I have loved you like a sister since we were young girls. I couldn't bear to have you married to one of those idiots Thumberton brought by for you to meet. I know the Earl has his faults in your eyes, but perhaps he has some redeeming qualities also. You need to find out, and see if Master Thumberton can fix things for you. If our friendship has ever meant anything to you, please say you'll do this for me.''

Jane knew, as usual, Liz was right. It was just so difficult to think of asking Thumberton to cajole Wessington into meeting with her again, but the distasteful task had to be completed. Elizabeth knew it and Jane did, too. She turned to look at her friend. "All right, Liz. I'll go talk to him in the morning.''

Graves entered the room as Phillip stood in front of the mirror, yanking and pulling on the cravat he could not seem to tie into any semblance of order. He and the Earl had a very different relationship than most gentlemen had with their menservants. Because of Phillip's financial state and his inability to hire quality people or keep large numbers on staff, Graves filled many roles: valet, secretary, doorman, footman. Simply relieved to have a job after the misadventures at his last position, he was more than happy to do most of what the Earl required.

"Allow me, sir." Graves reached for the cravat.

"Graves, thank heavens. I thought I'd surely choke myself to death before I finished with the bloody thing."

With a few swift moves, Graves had it neatly tied. "There you are, sir, and you're looking quite dashing tonight, if I may say so."

"What do you want, you pirate?" Phillip eyed him suspiciously. "If it's a raise, the answer's no."

Graves chuckled. "It's a sad day when a man can't make an innocent comment about appearances without having his motives questioned."

"I've yet to hear you make an *innocent* comment about anything. Out with it. What do you want?"

"Actually, I was just wondering if you'd had time to cool off after yesterday's unfortunate"—Graves paused as he searched for the word that would adequately describe the Earl's meeting with Jane Fitzsimmons without setting off his temper again—"ah, yesterday's unfortunate incident."

"So it's an *incident* now, is it? Last night, 'twas a *disaster*. This morning, 'twas a *debacle*. Why the whitewash all of a sudden?"

"Well, since you've calmed considerably, I thought perhaps we should discuss what you must do next."

Phillip enjoyed his private moments with Graves very much. From the first, there'd been ample evidence that he held strong opinions about things and people and was going to share them whether or not anyone wanted to listen. The man was loyal, smart and possessed a great deal of common sense. Because Phillip felt that many times he possessed none of his own, he was usually more than glad to listen to Graves's ramblings. The man could nearly always pierce to the heart of the matter with little trouble.

"And what must I do next?"

"Well, we've been discussing the possibilities . . ."

"We? God's teeth, not advice from the servants again. I know you people gossip, but didn't anyone ever explain to you that you're not supposed to let on that you do?"

"Well, sir, who understands you better than Cook and some of the others who've served you since you were a boy? They know what's best, whether you want to admit it or not."

"You could at least humor me and pretend it was your own idea, rather than letting me know that I'm the subject of unremitting discussion and debate." He shook his head in amusement. "So what say all of you?"

"You must talk to Master Thumberton and have him approach Miss Fitzsimmons with your apologies so you can set up another meeting."

Since he'd never passed a more unpleasant afternoon or suffered through such a river of insults and foul besmirchment of his character, the very last thing Phillip ever intended to do was speak again with Jane Fitzsimmons, but he was curious about the whisperings of the staff. "And the purpose of this meeting would be for what?"

"Well, to begin again the discussions about the possibility of your marriage to the young woman. Cook and I were quite taken with her."

Phillip raised an eyebrow. "Since you were the ones who let her in without checking her papers, I wouldn't throw that in my face just now if I were you."

"She was delightful. Smart, pretty. Well spoken."

"Let's not forget rich."

"No, let's not. You could, of course, do much better. But you most certainly could do much worse."

Graves's eyes shifted to the bed where Margaret's red silk negligee was still draped over the end. Refusing to argue over the woman, Phillip ignored the insinuation. "So all of you would have me wedded to Miss Fitzsimmons. After yesterday's fiasco, how are you advising I proceed?"

"Well, flowers to begin with, in copious amounts. And, of course, some bauble or other. Something simple but elegant. You're the lady's man. I'm sure you can think of something appropriate."

"And the purpose of these gifts would be . . . ?"

"To show how sorry you are for the unfortunate misunderstanding."

Phillip moved toward the door, and Graves followed him out into the hall and down the stairs. "There's the problem with your plan."

"What's that, milord?"

"I'm not the least bit sorry. Jane Fitzsimmons is a madwoman. I was already married to one, and I'll not wed another. The only good thing about yesterday is that I found out what she was truly like before taking any steps down the road toward matrimony."

They reached the foyer where Graves had the Earl's hat, gloves and walking stick waiting. He assisted Phillip with the gloves. "So there's not a chance, then?"

The man looked so forlorn that Phillip almost felt sorry to have dashed his hopes. "I'm sorry, Graves. But there's not a chance in hell." He opened the door and stepped out. The night was a miserable one, extremely cold and a freezing drizzle had begun falling.

"Your cloak," Graves offered before Phillip could ask for it.

Phillip smiled. Finding Graves was perhaps the only good thing that had happened to him in the past few years. "I'll probably be very late. Don't wait up for me."

"If you're sure, sir."

"I am. Enjoy your evening, Graves."

"You, too, milord."

The hackney Graves had arranged was waiting by the front gate. Phillip handed the driver the last few coins in his pocket, climbed in without assistance and relaxed back against the seat. In a few hours, he was due to meet up with Margaret. Even though she'd spent the previous night in his bed, their relationship was strained after the incident in his parlor. And, of course, Margaret had been only too delighted to find out that the serving girl and Jane Fitzsimmons were one and the same.

He wasn't in the mood for Margaret or any of her friends, but since they'd accepted the invitation several weeks earlier, there didn't seem to be a way to avoid the party without causing talk. More talk—about himself and his financial problems or about his relationship with Margaret and where it was headed—was the last thing he needed right now.

To fortify himself, he'd spend a few hours at his club. Gambling and drinking had a way of shoring up his beleaguered spirits.

Inside the club, he left his cloak and other trappings and walked through the crowded rooms toward the gaming tables in the back. All along the way, acquaintances stopped him for a drink or a chat. Though feeling like an incredible leech, he couldn't help feeling glad that he'd been offered several drinks which meant he wouldn't have to add them to his already excessive account.

Several different games of chance were available for the evening. Phillip selected dice and moved to the empty seat to which a friend waved him. He crossed the room and was welcomed with vigor by the revelers who had obviously been at it for hours before he'd arrived.

Phillip waved to one of the housemen to request the voucher he needed to sign for the night of credit which would allow him to play. It was something he'd done almost nightly for over a decade. The man didn't approach right away, and Phillip became annoyed by the delay. Just as he was ready to seek out the man himself, another appeared at his elbow.

"Begging your pardon, Lord Wessington, but Master Stevens desires a word with you."

Stevens owned the establishment as had his father and grandfather before him. He was an interesting sort of fellow, polite to the members of the *ton,* but Phillip always received the impression that he didn't care for any of them very much. That gave them something in common, since Phillip didn't care much for the members of the *ton* either.

He'd been invited back to Stevens's private rooms many times in his life, so he didn't think anything of the invitation. He simply followed where he was led.

"Wessington." Stevens nodded in acknowledgment of the Earl's entrance, then looked at his servant. "Close the door, would you? I don't wish to be interrupted." The man left silently.

"So what have you for me today?"

"Nothing, actually." Stevens, a man near Phillip's own age, was a handsome sort. Blond and blue-eyed, but with a rugged look about him that the ladies seemed to adore. "I needed to speak with you before you began playing. Something important's come up."

Phillip was instantly on alert. The only topics they'd ever discussed in this room had to do with what new types of enjoyment they could create to ease their own boredom and that of their friends. "What?" was all he could think to say.

"Unlike some other clubs, I have a limit on how far my customers can go into debt. I'll not be responsible for having a man's family tossed out on the streets."

"I know that about you. I've always admired you for it. But what has it to do with me?"

"You've finally managed to exceed your limit."

Phillip's outrage was matched only by his embarrassment. Years of breeding and training kept him from sputtering. "Your point?" he asked in his most aristocratic tone.

"I'm sorry, Wessington. I've known you for a very long time, but I simply can't carry your losses any longer."

"You're saying I'm cut off?"

"Actually, I'm saying you're no longer welcome. Not for spirits or meals or play. I don't want you back. Not even as someone's guest."

Phillip glared at him. The man didn't even have the sense to appear ashamed at his treatment of a peer of the realm. Poverty had a way of making everyone equals. He rose. "You miserable whelp, my grandfather was a charter member of this club. My father one of its premier members."

"I know, Wessington. And both of them always paid their bills. In full and on time, I might add."

"I'll see you ruined for this." Phillip immediately knew it was the wrong thing to say. Without money, he had lost much of his power, and Stevens ran one of the most exclusive, most popular clubs in the city. Everyone wanted to be a member.

"No, you won't, because that would mean you'd have to tell people why you were asked to leave. I promise this meeting will be our secret. If anyone asks why you haven't been 'round, I'll spare you any embarrassment and simply say I hadn't noticed." Stevens rose so they were facing each other. "I know you don't believe me, but I'm really doing this for your own good. Come back when you can pay. Once you're back on your feet, you'll be welcome. Not before. I'll not let you in."

"You bloody bastard!" Phillip forced the words between clenched teeth, but he turned to go without further comment.

The doorman was waiting with his things. Without any excess expression of temper, he shrugged into his cloak. He didn't want anyone to have a hint of the unpleasant moment he'd just endured. The word would spread soon enough.

He stepped out into the night, wishing there was someone leaving at the same time so he could grab a ride, pretending that the lift was accepted simply because it was convenient. No one came out behind him, and he refused to linger on the steps like some kind of beggar.

Up and down the busy street, hackneys raced to and fro as people hurried to their evening's entertainments. But Phillip Wessington, the eighth Earl of Rosewood, the sixth Earl of Ravenwood, the fifth Baron of Abbeysford, did not have a coin in his pocket to hire one of them. Alone, embarrassed, angry and disgusted, he pulled his hat low to shield his face and began the long, dreary walk toward home.

Chapter Seven

Phillip could not have said what twist of fate brought him to the front of the small townhouse occupied by Miss Fitzsimmons. After leaving his club, he'd begun heading home, but his mind was in such a jumble that instead of turning where he should have, he'd just kept going. If anyone had asked, he'd have said he was just wandering, taking a casual stroll in the misty evening, but apparently, he'd had a direction in mind all along.

So far, he'd managed to keep the extent of his financial dilemma a well-kept secret, but now, with his banishment from his own club, there'd be no stopping the flood of speculation and rumor. He trusted Stevens. The man was as good as his word and wouldn't tell anyone, but his employees would gossip with his servants and then his servants would gossip with others. On and on it would go until every member of the *ton* would be aware that he'd been cast out. Knowing the fickle attitudes of the people who comprised Polite Society, it could very possibly start a string of expulsions, ending only God knew where.

A picture of Jane Fitzsimmons's face flashed before his eyes. He thought of how she'd looked the previous day, standing in her rented drawing room, matching him word for word, shout for shout, insult for insult; fists on hips, an angry blush on her cheeks, her breasts heaving as she raged at him. He and his friends had hurt her, and somewhere in his jaded heart, he felt embarrassed and sorry that she'd seen him at his worst and been treated so horribly in his presence.

As his hand hesitated while reaching for the latch on the gate, the front door opened. Phillip walked on casually, to disappear in the shadows, then turn to watch the scene play out behind him. Miss Fitzsimmons stood silhouetted in the doorway by the lamp she was holding, saying good-byes to Mrs. Carew and two other companions who appeared to be going out for the evening. She watched until their coach pulled away, then closed the door.

Phillip stood for a long time, wondering what to do. Miss Fitzsimmons appeared to be home alone, perhaps without even a maid for company, so there'd never be a better time to speak frankly with her. A light appeared in an upstairs room, most likely the drawing room where they'd met the previous day.

Without thinking further, he once again approached the gate, opened it quietly and walked to the door. He didn't know if she'd answer so late in the evening, and if she did and saw him standing there, she'd very likely refuse to let him in. In the darkness, he reached for the knob and turned it. The door opened. She hadn't bothered to lock it after her friends departed.

"Silly country girl," he whispered as he stepped into the darkened foyer. If nothing else came of this night, at least he'd take the opportunity to explain to Miss Fitzsimmons some of the dangers of living in the city.

Letting his eyes adjust to the shadows, he stood for a few minutes. As he suspected, there were no noises coming from the back of the house. There were either no servants in the rented abode or they'd already retired for the evening. He could see a speck of light under the door to the drawing room. Shedding his wet hat and gloves, he laid them on a small table, then started up the stairs. The fires had been banked for the evening, and the place was freezing.

At the top of the stairs, he waited outside the drawing room, listening for sounds. Not hearing any, he quietly opened the door a crack and peeked in. A single lamp burned, and a cozy fire in the small hearth warmed the room. Miss Fitzsimmons was standing at one of the windows, obviously deep in thought, peering out into the rainy night.

In the time he'd been outside pondering his next move, she'd changed from her evening dress and was wrapped in her nightclothes. A thin robe, with the tie cinched tightly at the middle, accented her slim waist and the gentle flair of her hips. Her shoes were gone, replaced by a pair of heavy, wool socks. Her beautiful chestnut hair fell loose and long down her back and just brushed the tops of her hips. In the firelight, it gave off red and gold highlights. He could just make out her profile, the furrowed brow, the way her teeth worried her bottom lip. She looked so lovely, so forlorn and vulnerable, that he had to restrain himself from rushing across the room to take her in his arms.

Not wanting to frighten her, he stepped fully into the room so that she'd see him when she turned around. "If I had a coin in my pocket," he said softly, "I'd say: a penny for your thoughts"—he held his hands in a gesture of peace, palms out—"but since I haven't a coin, I guess I can't say it."

"Lord Wessington."

"Hello, Miss Fitzsimmons."

"Hello." Jane supposed she should have been shocked to see him standing there, but she wasn't. He had so fully occupied her mind for the past few hours, it was almost as if she'd conjured him up.

In the shadows cast by the fire, he looked dark and dangerous. His hair, wet from the rain, had been slicked back with his hand, and a few wayward locks dangled in disarray over his forehead. Although he was clean shaven, the angles of his face seemed sharper and more defined. The rain had soaked through whatever outer garments he'd been wearing, and the cloth of his shirt was molded tightly across his shoulders and the upper part of his chest. His tall, broad form filled up too much of the small room.

His tie was gone, a few buttons were undone and the shirt's sleeves rolled back, much as they had been the afternoon she'd stopped by his home for that disastrous visit; she was given the same view of the dark hair that swirled across his chest and forearms. Jane couldn't believe how her fingertips tingled, wondering what it would be like to touch some of it with her hands. *Would it feel silky soft? Harsh and springy?* She shook off the thoughts. He was too handsome for his own good, really, but the arrogant rogue certainly knew it.

"May I join you?" Phillip asked, gesturing toward the fire. "It's dreadfully cold out in the hall. I'm letting out all your warm air."

Realizing that he was studying her as intensely as she was studying him, she reached for the lapels of her robe and pulled the front tightly over her chest, hoping to cover every inch of her nightgown. "You shouldn't be here, sir. I'm not dressed. This is highly improper."

He smiled and took a step farther into the room, closing the door. "There's no one to know, and I won't tell if you won't."

"Mrs. Carew could come down at any moment."

"I was standing out on the street. I saw her leave."

"Oh . . ." She was unused to letting a man see her in such a state of undress. Her own father had never seen her without her shoes on, and here she was in front of this stranger wearing hardly anything at all. "Still, even though she's not here, I can't let you stay. It's terribly inappropriate."

"I'm soaked to the bone. Would you cast me back out onto the wet streets without a chance to warm myself?"

"No, I don't suppose I would. I haven't a servant about, but I could fix you some hot tea. Would you care for some?"

"No. Just let me stand by the fire for a few minutes."

"If you like." He walked to the hearth, holding his palms out to absorb the heat of the flames, and he was perfectly silhouetted by the firelight. He was a beautiful male specimen. Much different from her beloved blond-haired, blue-eyed Gregory, but beautiful nonetheless. "Whatever are you doing walking about on such a night? Didn't your mother ever tell you you'd catch your death out in weather like this?"

He looked over his shoulder. "Actually she never had the chance. She died when I was a babe. And your mother? Is that what she would say to me?"

"Perhaps. If she were still with us, but she died when I was a young girl."

For a long, silent moment, they stared at each other. As it was their first communication of private information, this small exchange hovered in the air, taking on significant meaning in the dark and quiet house. Jane broke the moment first, walking to the sideboard and rifling through the contents.

"I don't drink spirits myself"—she poured some amber liquid into a glass—"but I believe this is a French brandy. It should take the edge off." She held it out, and he reached to accept it, their fingers brushing as the container passed from one hand to the other. Phillip's hands were cold, and Jane's were warm, and each had the strange sensation of wanting to wrap theirs around the other's, he to absorb some of her warmth, she to share some of hers.

He downed the contents of the glass in a quick swallow, then held it out while she poured him another. This one he sipped. "Thank you. It does help very much."

Because he was staring down at her so intensely, Jane walked over to the window and rested her hip against the sill. Wessington followed, leaning against the wall with one hand and sipping from the glass held with the other while he stared out at the quiet street. "You were lost in thought when I stepped into the room. What were you thinking about?"

Jane hesitated momentarily, wondering if she should lie, but quickly realized it was time to speak frankly. "I was thinking about you."

"And what were you thinking about me?"

"I was trying to decide what I would say to you if I could convince Master Thumberton to arrange another appointment between us."

"What had you decided would be appropriate?"

Jane worked one of her toes back and forth across the floor. "Oh, I suppose something about how sorry I was for the things I'd said to you. About your family and your home and your friends."

"Are you sorry?"

She shrugged, and a corner of her mouth lifted in a smile. "Not really, but I probably would have made the apology anyway."

Phillip chuckled. "You have an interesting style, Miss Fitzsimmons. And what else were you going to say, if Thumberton could have arranged this meeting?"

"I was preparing to do a bit of groveling."

"I can't imagine that you're very good at it."

"I'm horrible, but I was going to start practicing."

"Pride's a bitter tonic to swallow, isn't it?"

"Yes. I hate it."

He chuckled again, and the sound did something to her insides that she didn't like very much.

"And you, milord, if you could have found me at home alone in my drawing room, what were you thinking you'd say to me?"

"Oh, I suppose something about how sorry I was about the things you witnessed in my home and about how you were treated there."

"Are you sorry?"

"Actually, yes, I am. I'm very sorry." Phillip turned from the window to face her, his dark eyes sincere and intense in the dim shadows. "I hope you'll accept my sincerest apologies."

"I do, sir. Thank you. And I hope you'll accept mine. For coming there uninvited and for behaving as I did later on. I'm sorry."

"Accepted." He took a final sip of the searing liquid and set the glass on the sill. Leaning a shoulder against the wall, he folded his arms across his chest. "You never did tell me why you stopped by."

"It just seemed like a good idea. I have to make such a life-altering decision in such a short amount of time, and I didn't trust myself to do it simply through the short meetings Master Thumberton had scheduled for me here. I decided to do a little investigating on my own. It seemed a wise choice at the time, but . . ."

"Not later."

"Well, let's just say I didn't stop by anyone else's house."

"And how did your other interviews go?" Phillip was fairly certain they hadn't gone well.

"Quite badly, actually. That's why I have another meeting scheduled with Master Thumberton tomorrow morning. My friend, Elizabeth, convinced me that he is a decent sort of man, and if he is so taken with you, you must have some redeeming qualities. I was planning to ask him what they are." She didn't like the way he hovered so closely by her side, watching and studying her, his eyes so intense they seemed to be able to read her very thoughts. She turned her gaze to the fire. "What do you suppose he'd say?"

"Oh, probably some hogwash about how I'm a man with a decent heart and high moral standards, but because of the life I've led and the things that have happened to me, my stronger attributes are well hidden."

"Would he be right? Are you a man with a decent heart and high moral standards?"

Phillip paused for a moment, wondering if he should lie, but eventually deciding that it was time only for the truth. "No, I don't think so."

Jane was startled by the admission. She lifted her gaze to his once more and saw the twinkle of mischief in it. "Do you have any redeeming qualities?"

As Phillip pondered the question, he ran a hand through his damp hair, then sat next to her on the windowsill. "Not a one, I'm afraid." The admission might have been funny if it hadn't been too true.

"You're being too hard on yourself. There must be something."

"No, I think you had it right in the beginning. I'm a bit of a scoundrel and a cad. I drink and gamble and carouse. I've never worked a day in my life. I have no hobbies or interests. I'm simply the first and only son of a titled family. Not much was ever expected of me except that I would be just that: the first and only son. I'm frightfully good at enjoying all my position entails. I try to make the most of it."

"So you're a little bit spoiled, are you?"

"Perhaps more than a little bit."

His smile now was genuine, and Jane couldn't believe the things he was admitting. She'd never talked so candidly with a man in her life. "And you insist on having everything your own way?"

"All the time."

"And the entire focus of your day is to enjoy yourself?" Jane didn't need to look at him to know he was nodding in agreement. They both continued to stare at the fire, but he chuckled. That twinkle in his eye was back.

"Of course, if I had a little more money, I'd enjoy myself a great deal more. It's the dickens trying to make do without. I don't have the slightest idea how to go about it."

"Why are you walking in the rain?"

"Because my last carriage was confiscated by creditors, and when I left my club a while ago, I hadn't any pocket coin to hire a cab for the ride home."

Several emotions warred inside her, the strongest seeming to be pity for him and his fallen state. What must it be like to be such a proud, well-known gentleman and to have everything being taken away a bit at a time? His world was tipping off its axis as quickly as her own.

"I have some money in my reticule. Remind me to give it to you before you leave."

"I'm too embarrassed to accept your coins."

"I don't mind giving them to you. Really. I can't bear the thought of you walking alone out in all this rain."

Phillip sighed. "I'm pitiful, am I not?"

"No, I don't think so. And I'm sorry for your troubles."

He shook his head. "Don't be. I bring most of them on myself." He slipped his hand into hers, lacing their fingers together.

At the sudden, intimate touch, Jane looked up into his eyes. It occurred to her that he was much too close. With their hands entwined, she couldn't help but face, once again, the inappropriateness of the situation. Except it didn't feel inappropriate. It felt perfectly normal to be sitting with him, holding hands in the firelight, while they exchanged confidences. "I think we've a bit in common. I seem to have brought most of my own problems on, also."

"How's that?"

"Being here in London, trying to find a husband."

"And you feel marriage is a problem for you?"

"Well, I hadn't planned on it, you see."

"Not now? Or not ever?"

"Not now, certainly. Perhaps not ever. I don't know."

Phillip shifted slightly, taking in her profile. She wanted to look sideways, but they were already too close and any movement on her part would bring them even closer.

Out of the blue, he asked, "May I call you Jane?"

Jane's stomach tickled at the way her name rolled off his tongue. So slow and sensual as though she'd never heard a man speak it before. She knew that propriety dictated the use of her first name was too familiar and she should say no, but she couldn't. "I . . . I guess that would be all right."

"Jane, you're very pretty and have such a pleasing manner. Surely, you had many suitors at home seeking your hand. Why have you not been married before now?"

"Well, my father was very kind about letting me make my own decision about the thing, and I turned away a few gentlemen."

"Why?"

"Because I enjoyed my work at the Shipworks too much, and I was afraid a husband would insist I curtail my duties." And, she didn't add, the young men who had come courting all seemed too tame. None of them had set her heart fluttering or sent chills down her spine. If she had decided to marry, she had always told herself that she had to do better than so many of her acquaintances had done. Elizabeth was typical, with her stodgy, boring husband. Jane shuddered at the thought of such a dull, depressing existence. She'd go mad living such a life. Better to stay single.

"So tell me, if your father was so understanding all this time, why is he suddenly in such a blasted hurry to marry you off?"

"Oh, that . . ." Jane wasn't sure how much to tell him without revealing her family's private business. On the one hand, her love of Gregory was not something he needed to know about. On the other, if he might consider marriage, she did owe him some kind of explanation for her dire circumstances. She settled on middle ground. A little of the truth, but not all. "Well, there was a gentleman, you see, to whom I'd taken a fancy, and my father didn't feel he was appropriate for me."

"Ah, yes, I do see very well, indeed." Phillip wondered who the fellow was. A sailor? Perhaps one of the ship-

wrights working at the Shipworks? "And are you so
willing to blindly go along with his wishes?"

"Well, he is my father, and he's ordered it, so I have
no choice, but I'm also doing it for personal reasons."
Jane wondered what he'd say, but she had to know.
"He's forbidden me to return to my position at the
business until I've been married at least six months.
Only then may I come back to work."

"It means so much to you, this job?"

"Yes. I couldn't possibly marry someone who didn't
understand that it means everything to me."

A smile lifted the corners of Phillip's mouth. If they
ended up married, he'd never let her return to Portsmouth. If she was so bound and determined to work at
something meaningful, he had plenty of tasks to keep
her occupied at the Wessington properties. In time,
she'd forget all about her own family's business.

"Yes, I can see how it would be important to you.
'Twould be a travesty for you to be kept from something
you enjoy so much." The lie came easily enough, and
he didn't feel a touch of guilt for voicing it. Everything
was working out much better than he'd hoped or
planned.

Chapter Eight

Jane stared down at their joined hands. His thumb had begun tracing circles across her palm. It was strange that such a simple movement in such an innocuous spot could send butterflies cascading through her stomach. The gesture was making it hard to concentrate. She realized that he was speaking again, but with her attention completely focused on the subtle movement of his thumb, she hadn't noticed. "What did you say, milord?"

"I said: 'Perhaps we have more in common than we thought.' Perhaps we should talk about the need we both have to marry." He only needed to find out one more thing about her. His responsibility to the title required him to provide an heir, so he'd have to bed her occasionally. While he didn't need a sexual whirlwind in his bed—he had plenty of those—he wanted someone who was at least willing to learn and participate in the experience. He started his experiment by playing with her hand.

She tried to pull it away, but he wouldn't let go. "I don't think you should be doing that."

"Why?"

The force of his gaze required that she meet his. Up so close, she noticed, for the first time, that his lashes were long and dark. Beautiful. "Because it's not proper, and we hardly know each other." She tugged again, but he raised the hand to his mouth. Her eyes widened in surprise as he stretched her fingers back and pressed a tender, gentle kiss to the middle of her palm. His lips were warm and soft.

This time, she tugged harder and rose, moving away and across the room to stand before the fire. From one small kiss, not even on the mouth but on the hand, her emotions were in turmoil. She was in far over her head and not certain how to swim to safety.

Phillip knew she wanted to break the tension between them, but he couldn't allow her to do so. He had to know how far he could push her and how she would respond, so he followed and stood behind her. Resting his hands lightly on her shoulders, he nuzzled his face in her exquisite long tresses, inhaling the scent of lilacs hovering around her.

"Why are you doing this to me?" she asked with a shaky voice.

"Because I want to touch you. I know you're an innocent, but surely you know we would have to touch each other in intimate ways if we were wed."

"Yes, I know."

"I want to know how it feels to touch you. I want to know if you enjoy it."

His whisper tickled the hair resting along her ear, and when he placed a kiss there, he stepped closer, letting his body, chest to thighs, touch hers along her back and buttocks. He felt her stiffen, hesitate, then relax, the slight easing bringing her into closer contact.

He pulled the sweep of her hair to one side, baring her neck and a bit of shoulder, then settled his lips on the creamy expanse of skin. As his mouth nipped and sucked, he lowered his hands along her arms to wrap around her stomach, so he could ease his loins against her backside. He was hard as a rock, and either she was too inexperienced to know what she was feeling or she didn't care.

"Marry me, Jane."

"Oh, Lord Wessington," she groaned, "I don't know." The moist lips, the biting teeth, were wreaking havoc with her senses. The arms encircling her, the broad shoulders and tight chest pressed so closely, and his lower body against her bottom!

Lord Wessington was aroused by her and not afraid to let her know. The very idea that she could excite such a man inspired a new burst of flutters across her abdomen and down to that secret place between her legs. Wrapped in his arms, she felt beautiful and desirable. Wanting to increase the feeling, she tipped her head to the side, baring more skin for him to torment. She raised a hand, resting her palm against his cheek and gave a tug, urging him closer.

He chuckled, but responded eagerly, increasing the pressure. "Marry me," he whispered again.

Jane closed her eyes at the lovely agony he was inflicting with his mouth. The feelings he stirred were so naughty, so shocking, but so wonderful that she wouldn't have stopped him for anything in the world. Her breathless voice, usually so full and sure, sounded as though it belonged to someone else. "What can you give me through marriage that I don't already have?"

"I will give you my name."

"I have one that's respected around the kingdom and across the seas."

"I will share my title."

"I've no need of one."

"My homes."

"I already own one that is perfectly fine."

"Then what is left but my passion?"

He turned her, and she came willingly. His lips moved across her eyelids, brushing gently over each one before moving across her brow, down her cheek, along her chin. They left a trail of fire as they moved, and she waited eagerly for his to join with hers, but she was left to groan softly as he moved past, only to create new sensations by nuzzling under her chin, along her neck.

She placed her own kisses in return. Learning the feel of his cheek, his forehead. More daring, she raised her fingers and ran them through his thick, dark hair. It was soft and full, still damp from the rain, and she loved the way it sifted through her fingers as she worked her way to his shoulders. They were broad and strong, and she could feel his muscles shifting and changing as he wrapped his arms around her. She was completely surrounded by him, by his arms and legs, his thighs, one hand running up and down her spine, the other resting on the small of her back, urging her closer to the fire.

At the corner of her mouth, he nipped in invitation. Lifting her mass of hair, he cradled her head in his palm. His voice low and seductive, he whispered, "I'm going to kiss you, Jane."

"Yes, please," she murmured against his lips.

It was all the invitation he needed. He tasted and cherished her sweetness and warmth as his desire surged to aching heights. To his surprise, he was enjoying this moment more than he'd thought possible. She was fresh, and pretty, so different from the jaded women who filled his nights that he'd almost forgotten what kissing could be like.

Women like Margaret, with their sexual skill and prowess, could provide interesting diversion with their experience, but their innocence was long gone, their sense of wonder long forgotten, their actions all seeming to have a hidden motive. Jane's surprise was genuine, her enjoyment honest, her delight intoxicating.

Her lips were full and beautiful. As he moved over them, a small sound of pleasure escaped from the back of her throat, and she trembled slightly in his arms. He was certain that there was a hidden passion buried in her, waiting to be let loose; and much to his surprise, he wanted to be the one to free it.

She hesitated at first, not certain of what he wanted as he guided his tongue along her teeth, teasing them until she felt its tip touch her own. Immediately, she understood the pleasure he was offering and accepted him inside, her tongue dueling with his. His own groan of pleasure escaped as she stood on her toes and wrapped her hands behind his neck to pull him deeper into the embrace.

He welcomed her closer, her robe now open, the sheer fabric of her nightdress barely offering any resistance at all to his senses. Plump, round breasts, the tiny peaks hard with arousal, were pressed against his chest. Her heart thundered beneath them. Those long, shapely legs were captured in his own, the muscles of her thighs flexing and changing as she shifted against him. The mound of her femininity was wedged tightly against his aroused male part. The taste, the scent, the feel of her were so overwhelming, he couldn't bear the thought of stopping.

Over the past year, Gregory had provided her with

numerous opportunities for fond embraces, but none of them had prepared Jane in the slightest for Lord Wessington. His tongue was inside her mouth, moving back and forth in a rhythm with his hips that Jane instinctively sensed must be the rhythm of mating. He was completely at ease with his arousal and unashamed to have her feel the hard length of him pressed against her stomach, and there seemed to be so much of him there!

The pressure of his hips at the V of her thighs was incredible and created a heated fire through her breasts, down her stomach, causing a painful ache between her legs. As his mouth and hips played their dastardly games, his hands never stopped for a moment, roving across her body, seeming to touch every inch. They stopped on her buttocks, kneading the soft flesh as he pulled her ever closer, leaving nothing to the imagination.

When she'd agreed to let him kiss her, she'd envisioned something along the lines of Gregory's chaste embraces—embraces which would be sweetly enjoyed and easily ended. With Wessington, the sensations were simply too intense, and she wasn't at all sure how to stop what they'd started.

There was not enough air in the room for breathing. Wrenching her lips away from his, her breathing labored, her voice unsteady, she begged, "Lord Wessington, please. A moment please . . ."

Phillip pulled back, aware of nothing in the room except Jane. Her lips were swollen and wet from his kisses, her eyes wide with wonder. "Marry me." It was an order this time. His mouth descended to kiss and nibble at the pulse pounding against her throat.

"Lord Wessington," she sighed, twisting her head in a slight effort to pull away. The motion simply provided him greater access.

"Say my name."

"Wessington," she sighed again.

"No, my given name: Phillip. I want to hear it on your lips."

"I can't. I can't . . ." she shook her head in protest, and he couldn't wait for more as he once again covered her mouth with his own.

The kiss went on and on as he tasted, sampled, seduced. Before she knew it, somehow she was on her back on the sofa with Wessington stretched out at her side. His hard thigh rested across her womanhood, his knee pressing in a slight rhythm which her hips seemed bound and determined to match. The lace holding the front of her nightgown together began to give way as his fingers deftly worked it loose. It wasn't until she felt the hot, rough callus of his palm resting in the valley between her breasts that her body began to fully shout an alarm.

She reached for his wrist, trying to stop him, but not managing before he was able to close his fingers around a nipple. The pleasure and the pain of it was exquisite—searing wet heat between her legs—and she tried to twist away. Holding his hand still, pulling her lips from his, she panted, "Please, milord. Please, we must stop."

"No. Not now. Let me . . ."

"Please," she begged.

"I don't want to stop, love. I need you."

To hear such a man as the Earl whispering that he needed her was nearly her undoing, and even as she protested, her traitorous body was offering full acceptance of his ministrations. Her back arched, offering her breasts up for closer attention.

Phillip was so caught up in the moment that he wasn't thinking clearly. He wanted to drink his fill, to bury himself, to never leave her side. His lips moved down the creamy white of her throat to the warm valley between her breasts, where he planted long, moist kisses against her silky skin.

"You're frightening me."

"Don't be afraid," he whispered. "I would never hurt you."

One part of her wanted him to keep doing exactly what he was about. The throbbing in her breasts, with his lips only inches away, was unbearable. For some strange reason, she wanted to beg him to nuzzle under the fabric of her gown, to place his lips on her nipples. Some secret feminine part of her seemed to know that, by doing so, he could ease the painful agony he was causing, but her mind continued to shout that she must stop.

She twisted again, trying to move so his lips were no longer touching her in such an intimate fashion. "Please, Wessington . . ."

It took several moments for the reality of what Jane was saying and doing to sink in. All Phillip knew was that he was hot and hard with desire; he wanted to have this woman, to bury himself deep within her right here on the sofa. The need to absorb some of her freshness, some of her spontaneity, some of her innocence was simply too overwhelming. Something wonderful, something extraordinary seemed to be beckoning. If he could only hold her close enough, he might find out what it was. But, as she continued her efforts to squirm away, better sense eventually prevailed.

While he wanted to burst between her thighs and ease the terrible ache between his own, he knew he couldn't. She was looking up at him, her eyes a mixture of awe, fear and surprise. More slowly than he should have, he pulled his hand from beneath her gown, making sure he fully caressed each breast one last time. Immediately, she clutched the front together.

God, she was lovely, with her swollen, rosy lips, her aroused breasts heaving against the thin fabric, her hair tousled and fanned out beneath him. "You're very beautiful, Jane."

"Whatever must you think of me!" she admitted with a quiver in her voice. "I'm sorry."

"I'm not." Still lying pressed against her from forehead to toes, he ran a gentle hand up and down her spine.

"Is it always like this when you . . . when you . . . ?" Not knowing how to address such an intimate topic, she couldn't find the words to finish her question, so he finished it for her.

"No. It's rarely like this. This was special. Which makes me think we will suit just fine."

His decision made, he slid off the couch to the floor, kneeling beside her and helping her sit up. Keeping her hands wrapped in his, he said, "I cannot promise you undying love and devotion, simply because we've not known each other long enough for such powerful feelings to grow between us, but I can promise to always honor and respect you. I will be a good husband to you, and I hope, in time, that friendship, trust and respect will grace our relationship." Phillip didn't think any of these things were possible to achieve through the wedded state, but necessity caused the lies to roll easily off his tongue. "Jane, will you do me the great honor of accepting my hand in marriage?"

It was simply impossible to remain unmoved by the sight of this handsome man kneeling in front of her, proposing marriage. What woman on the whole of the Earth could have resisted? "Yes, I suppose I will."

"Good." He gently kissed her forehead. "We'll meet

with Thumberton in the morning to sign the papers. The wedding will be done before the end of the month. Will that be acceptable?''

Jane's mind was in a whirl. She could hardly think, hardly plan. "Yes," she finally responded, "yes, I guess that will be acceptable.''

He stood and helped her to her feet. "I'd best get going before your friend returns.''

Jane flinched. In the passion of the last few minutes, she'd completely forgotten Elizabeth. Thank heavens, she'd not returned early. Now that sanity had reasserted itself, Jane could once again act like the gently reared woman she was. "Would you like a few coins, Lord Wessington? For the ride home?''

"Perhaps." He smiled as she found her purse and handed over the contents. "Although, I must admit I feel as if a great weight has been lifted off my shoulders. I might prefer to walk in the crisp night air.''

Jane escorted him down the stairs to the front door. It was cold in the lower rooms, away from the fire and the heat of Phillip's body. In the foyer, she helped him into his cloak and gloves, wondering at the intimacy between them, and enjoying it much more than she probably should. As he donned his hat, she could feel his eyes on her, but she simply stared at his chest, wondering why her heart felt so heavy at a moment which should have been bringing her great joy.

Phillip couldn't help noticing her forlorn countenance, the sad, almost haunted look in her eyes. Once again, he felt that unusual tug at his heartstrings. Where Jane was concerned, he couldn't seem to shed his need to offer comfort. He rested a finger under her chin and lifted her gaze to his. "You don't look very happy for a woman who's just agreed to wed.''

"I'm happy enough, I expect.''

She looked thoroughly miserable, which made Phillip want to laugh aloud. Women all over England would give anything to be in her shoes. For over a decade, hordes of mothers had thrown their unwed daughters at him, hoping to marry their girls into the title of countess. Every woman he met, from Margaret on, dreamed of the possibility of this moment. Now, he'd finally asked a female to marry, and she looked as though she'd rather visit the barber to have a tooth pulled. "Then why the sad face?"

"I always thought I would marry for love."

"Jane . . ." He was completely enchanted by her ability to honestly state her emotions. He squeezed her hand. "Love is a fleeting emotion which fades in time. Trust me on this. For a marriage to last, a person needs to rely on other, stronger, more dependable traits."

"Aren't you the least upset that you must enter into an arrangement like this?"

Phillip shrugged. "In my social circle, marriages are always arranged. They're never made for love."

"It seems so wrong."

"But it's the way of things." She was shivering slightly, and he pulled her into his arms, running his hands up and down her back. "Get back to your fire."

"I will."

"Until tomorrow, then." He brushed a light kiss across her lips. "And, for heaven's sake, turn the key when I leave. You never know who might wander in off these London streets."

"You are right about that." She smiled then, closing and locking the door behind him. Her tread and her heart were heavy as she climbed the dark stairway back to the drawing room. It seemed strangely empty without the Earl's presence filling it up. She flopped in anguish onto the couch where only moments before Wessington had cradled her breast in the heat of passion.

"What have I done?" she asked the silent room. She'd cast her lot, she'd picked her man. What was ever to become of her?

Chapter Nine

Margaret tapped her foot in time with the music as her eyes carefully scanned the crowd, looking for Phillip. With his height and broad physique, it was hard to miss him. He was simply one of those men who turned female heads wherever he went, and with his reputation as a scoundrel, every woman wondered in her heart what it would be like to enter the room on his arm. Even the young girls couldn't help glancing at him out of the corners of their eyes when they felt their mothers weren't looking.

Phillip, for his part, was so used to female adoration that he barely seemed to notice all the commotion he caused.

"Eat your hearts out, you silly twits, for he is mine," she muttered as she glanced at the door again. As usual, he was late, which irritated her. Their current host had added amusements upstairs. Although she was one of

the few females who would be allowed, she needed
Phillip's escort.

Frederick Morris was making his way toward her. A
small man, with light brown hair and cold blue eyes,
his cheeks were so smooth that Margaret wondered
sometimes if his beard had ever begun to grow.

Although he was a few years older than Phillip, he
appeared much younger. From behind, with his petite
size, small hands and delicate features, he looked like
a teenage boy until you stepped closer and saw the age
lines around his eyes.

The whispers about Morris abounded, but he was
welcomed by all members of the *ton*. The rumors about
his sexual perversions were just that: rumors. If they
were true, Margaret didn't care, and for the most part,
neither did anyone else.

'Twas the lot of females to service men's wishes and
desires. Margaret's own father had done so by marrying
her off to a lecherous, but wealthy old man whose very
touch had made Margaret's skin crawl. Once upon a
time as a young girl, she'd believed in love and happily-
ever-after, but her father had quickly disabused her of
those notions on the day he'd announced whom he'd
chosen as her husband. Life's realities were reaffirmed
on her wedding night. There was no such thing as love.
Each man—or woman—had to look out for himself,
because no one else was going to.

The trick was to figure out a man's weakness, then
learn how to use it to gain whatever you wanted or
needed. Which was exactly what she'd done. Morris was
fascinated by young girls, and he'd set his sights on
Emily Wessington. He was so besotted that he was willing
to pay a fortune to have her. Phillip needed money.
Margaret wanted Emily gone and Phillip happy. Therefore, a union between Morris and Emily was perfect.

Everybody would get what they wanted, except Emily, of course. But she was a child, and a female, so who cared what she wanted or thought about the entire affair?

"Lady Margaret," Morris greeted her as he bowed over her hand. "How nice to see you. You're looking lovely this evening."

Margaret knew she was one of the most beautiful women in the room, but still she managed to accept the compliment graciously. "Thank you, sir. It's kind of you to notice."

They chatted politely for a few minutes, until Morris gave up any pretense at social banter. "Will Wessington be here tonight?"

"He was supposed to be here already. He's late."

"I haven't heard from you in weeks. What's his thinking?"

"He's still considering your offer."

"What does that mean?"

"It means he's still considering it."

"Last time we spoke, you said you had him convinced."

"*Nearly* convinced, Morris. Not completely." Margaret regretted the necessity of doing business with such a disgusting little weasel, but sometimes, a person simply wasn't allowed to choose her partners. "Give me more time."

"How much more? I first approached him with the idea six months ago." Morris's voice rose slightly in agitation. He'd been wanting to get his hands on Emily for years.

"He's having trouble reaching a decision."

"Well, I'm tired of waiting. I want an answer."

"He's got the betrothal contract sitting on his desk. I've seen the papers. I think he just needs an extra push in the right direction. Perhaps if you raised the amount of the offer.''

"It's already at ten thousand.''

"How about twelve-five? Could you swing it?''

"Yes, but that's it. If he refuses, I can't go another pound.''

"Good, I think that will bring him 'round. His financial problems may be a bit steeper than we know. A little extra cash should be just the thing to aid in the decision-making process.''

"I hope you're right. I'm so tired of this uncertainty.''

"Patience, my dear Morris. All good things come to those who wait. Now . . .'' Just then, Phillip entered the room, his presence announced by the doorman. He seemed in a heady mood, flush with color and excitement. Margaret loved to see him in such a state. He would be an animal when they were alone together later. "Look, there's Wessington. I'll speak with him, and I'll send a note 'round tomorrow.''

Morris drifted away into the crowd, and Margaret stood her ground, watching Phillip make his way to her. It took many minutes, as he stopped to chat with numerous acquaintances.

"You're late.'' She wasn't going to mention his tardiness, but the words popped out of their own accord.

"Yes, I am. I had some last-minute business to tend to. It couldn't be helped.''

It was as close to an apology as she'd ever get from him, so she didn't push it. "I'm dreadfully bored. I've been waiting to go upstairs.''

"You should have gone without me.''

Margaret bit back her retort. As much as she felt they were having a serious relationship—or as serious a one as two people such as themselves ever had—he always refused to act as though it meant anything at all. "Let's go now, shall we?"

"Certainly."

They casually strolled through the rooms to the back of the house where a servant stood guard. With a quick nod, he stepped aside and let them pass.

Only a select number were granted entrance to the seedier side of the celebration. Most people would have been scandalized to know such things occurred just over the heads of those attending a most proper ball filled with marriageable young ladies. The goings-on were so foreign to the minds of most, especially women of delicate countenance, that even rumors of such things failed to reach their ears.

A few dozen people, mostly men but also some of the more jaded women, filled the darkened rooms. Beds were available for those who wished to engage in fornication. A Chinese opiate was dispensed for those who enjoyed the lethargy and dreams it evoked. In the middle of the main room was a small stage complete with a large bed. On it, a prostitute was busy with a well-known gentleman. Others could take turns with her later—alone or in groups.

Margaret loved watching sexual displays after sampling opium, so she headed for the corner. Of late, she seemed to reach for the pipe sooner and more often, but she didn't care. The sensations it created were too delightful to pass up.

Wessington stopped her before she reached it.

"What?" she asked, wondering why he cared what she was doing.

"I want to speak to you. Privately." *While you're still in a condition to listen,* he thought but didn't voice his opinion.

"That's a good idea. I've something to tell you as

well." She turned and walked back to the hall. Wessington led her past the row of doors until they found an empty room at the end. He bolted the door, then lay back on the bed, loosening his cravat and shirt.

"You go first," he commanded once he was comfortable.

"I spoke with Frederick Morris before you arrived."

"What did he want?"

"He simply mentioned that he hadn't heard from you about the contract."

"That's because I haven't made up my mind."

"That's what I told him. He asked me to pass on his interest, and to let you know that he's willing to increase the price."

"To what?"

"Twelve thousand, five hundred."

"He's that eager, is he?"

"Well, Emily is very lovely."

Phillip just shrugged. He'd never paid enough attention to the girl to notice. Still . . . he couldn't decide. Morris would just have to wait until he could. At least now, the pressure was off to reach a hasty decision.

"I'm not going to decide now."

"I understand." She moved to the bed, lay next to him and rested a hand on his chest. "Good heavens, Wessington, you're soaking wet."

"I've been walking."

"You're joking."

"Not at all. It's lovely outside. Plus, I needed to clear my head. I had some good news for a change. It's going to be 'round town by tomorrow, so I wanted to be the one to tell you."

His attempt at dramatic effect was almost humorous. "Well, then, get on with it. What news?"

"I've decided to marry."

He stated the fact with no hesitation, as though they were discussing the weather instead of Margaret's future. The words were so far removed from what she'd expected that, at first, she felt as though he'd whispered in some exotic Arabic language she didn't understand. She sat up and looked him in the eye. "What did you say?"

"I'm marrying. I've proposed, and she's accepted."

"You can't be serious."

"I am. We're to be married in two weeks. We sign the papers tomorrow morning."

Margaret swallowed hard. While she'd just spent hours impatiently waiting for him to arrive at the blasted party, he'd been off proposing marriage to someone else! She wanted to kill him. She wanted to weep. She wanted to laugh at the absurdity of it all. "But what about us?"

"What about us?"

"I always thought that we would—"

"That we would marry? I swear, Margaret, sometimes your thinking truly astounds me."

Margaret flushed a bright red. She'd never let the bastard know how much his remark had cut. "We suit very well."

"For an affair, yes, but I've always told you we would never wed." He noticed her agitated state. "Please, don't go hysterical on me."

"As if you'd be worth hysterics." She stepped off the bed and moved toward the fire, taking the few seconds to rearrange her features and regain her composure. "So, who's the lucky girl?"

"The heiress I told you about."

She whipped around in surprise, laughing rudely. "You can't be serious. You can't mean the one who was playing servant girl in your home?"

"The very same."

"That plain little mouse? You'll eat her alive."

"I seriously doubt it. And while we're on the subject of my new bride, I'd appreciate it if you'd keep your opinions about her to yourself. I've no desire to hear them."

"Fine, but I can't believe you're seriously considering this."

"I'm not *considering* it. I've made up my mind."

"But whatever are you thinking? She'll expect a husband. A *real* husband."

"I'll be a *real* husband. We're having a ceremony."

"No, you idiot. She'll expect you to play house. To chaperon her, and escort her, and make it home for supper and be there for breakfast. To spend your holidays 'round the fire with your loving family. She'll expect you to be a father to her children." Margaret rubbed her eyes and laughed again, more wickedly this time. "I can just see it: the great ladies' man, Phillip Wessington, bouncing a brat on each knee while a third tugs at his coat."

"It's not going to be like that."

"Isn't it? How can you be so certain?" She walked to the table in the corner and helped herself to a large swig of brandy. "And what about love? She'll expect love from you. Fidelity and loyalty. You've no idea how to give any of those things."

"I've no intention of giving them."

"It will begin on your wedding night when you make love to her the first time. She's just a girl, Phillip. A young, impressionable commoner who thinks that going to bed with her husband means something important. You'll touch her and caress her with the simple intent of opening her to ease your way, and she'll think she's in the beginnings of the greatest love affair of all time."

"You're reading too much into this."

"Am I? When was the last time you bedded a virgin?" Margaret knew she had his attention. "She loved you after, didn't she?"

"They all did."

"Of course, they did. That's how virgins are. They don't understand reality."

"So what are you saying? That I should marry, but never consummate the bloody thing because my wife might misunderstand my intentions?"

"No, that's not what I'm saying. I'm just trying to help you understand how ludicrous this idea is. If you need an infusion of funds, you have only to ask me for them. I'll give them without a thought and save *you* all this trouble and this *girl* all the coming heartache."

"You're too generous and too kind," Phillip said with more sarcasm than was necessary. The only time Margaret was generous or kind was when she wanted something in return. As for her offer of money, the inheritance from her late husband was pocket coin compared to what Phillip required to square his debts.

She wanted to try to talk him out of his decision, but she knew from his tone that further argument was futile. If she'd learned one thing about him after all this time, it was that he was a hardheaded, stubborn man who made up his mind and forged ahead without regard for the consequences. It was time to move on to more pressing matters. "So, Wessington, if you go through with this idiotic idea of yours, what of us?"

"What do you mean?"

"What's to become of us now that you're entering the state of holy matrimony?"

"Nothing's to become of us."

She gasped, unable to believe it. "We'll never see each other again?"

"Of course we will. We'll see each other all the time." He held out a hand, urging her back to the bed, all the while thinking of the coming changes and of how Jane Fitzsimmons's money had rescued his way of life. Things were working out perfectly. "I may be getting married, but that changes nothing."

Chapter Ten

Jane had thought this day, the day after accepting a marriage proposal from a titled, handsome, powerful man, would be so much different. More romantic or more exotic.

Instead, she sat alone and stared out the window of her new bedroom, and her gaze followed the slope of the gardens as they dipped toward the River Thames. There were a few splotches of color down below, but for the most part, everything was gray and dreary. On a bright summer day, the view was probably spectacular, but for now, all she could see were fog and mist.

She had arrived at the Earl's home just outside London in the past hour, after receiving instructions from Thumberton advising her that the Earl wished her to retire to the new locale. His note said Wessington had a small, private estate just minutes outside the city, and Jane was expecting a nice-sized family home similar to the one she'd grown up in. As the new carriage swept her up the long, winding drive, she realized that nothing had prepared her for the incredible bit of architecture waiting at the end.

It seemed a palace to Jane, slightly rounded, with the outer wings curving as though it had two arms waiting to embrace new arrivals. There were three stories and twenty-five sets of windows across the front. Never having been inside such a place, she couldn't imagine how many rooms there must be.

The center court was full of wagons driven by teamsters who were unloading goods and furniture. The place was buzzing like a beehive from all the activity, and Wessington seemed to be already refurbishing the house.

The staff had received her politely, then shuffled her off to her rooms. Feeling left out and unneeded, she huddled quietly, trying to stay out of everyone's way, and wondering if anyone would remember she was there so they could offer her supper.

Upon waking early in the day, she'd advised Elizabeth about her acceptance of the Earl's proposal and told her that she could return home. Elizabeth had protested halfheartedly, but seemed relieved when Jane insisted she go. She left as soon as her bags were packed. Already, Jane was wishing she hadn't sent her away.

"You've made your bed . . ." She sighed for the hundredth time and turned away from the window as a knock sounded at the door. She opened it to find Graves standing there.

"Well, well, if it isn't my favorite serving girl," he began with a friendly smile.

"Ah . . . You do remember! How terrible!"

"How could I forget the woman who possessed the courage to provoke Lady Margaret into a screaming fit?"

"Don't remind me," Jane said, pulling him into the room. "And if you ever tell anyone about it, I'll have you drawn and quartered."

"I believe you." They stared at each other for a moment, then burst into laughter. Graves gave her a mocking bow. "If I may be so bold, may I say: Well done on snagging the Earl."

"Don't pat me on the back too heartily. I think the color of my money had a great deal more to do with it than the way I batted my eyelashes."

"Don't sell yourself short, Lady Jane. I don't think all the money in the world would have moved him if it wasn't something he truly wanted to do."

"Really? Hmmm . . . I'll have to consider that. And, please, call me Jane. Drop the 'Lady' part. It sounds so silly. Everytime someone uses it, I find myself looking 'round, trying to see if there's another person standing behind me."

"Jane, it is, then. And call me John."

"Hello, John. It's so nice to see a friendly face. What are you doing here?"

"I'm here to *facilitate,*" he said the word in an exaggerated way that made her laugh, "the coming festivities."

"I'm so glad. I wasn't sure what was to happen next."

"I'll be here to guide you through it. And Master Thumberton will arrive shortly with papers and instructions. I thought you might like to freshen up a bit and perhaps have a bite to eat before he arrives."

"I was wondering if I'd ever be fed. I had visions of everyone forgetting I was here, and I'd be found years from now, nothing but a starved skeleton."

"This place is intimidating, isn't it?"

"For the likes of me, it certainly is."

"Wait until you get to Rosewood and the other country estates."

"I was afraid you'd say something like that."

"Well, first thing first. I've taken the liberty of finding you an abigail. The Earl said you hadn't brought one from home."

"I've never had one. I'd be too embarrassed to start now."

"The Earl will insist, I'm afraid."

"But, I wouldn't know how to act."

"Well, your maid will. Her name is Meg, and she's a great friend of mine. She's worked and lived around the Quality for a good many years, so she'll be a terrific help at answering all your questions and getting you moving in the right direction. She's had a good bit of education, too, so I think the two of you will get on famously."

"When do I meet her?"

"Now, if that's all right."

"Certainly."

Graves opened the door and motioned into the hall. Meg entered, a plump, pretty thing who looked Irish with her reddish hair and blue eyes. She smiled through her curtsy, and dimples graced her cheeks. From the way Graves was looking at her, Jane wondered if there was more between the two of them than he'd led her to believe.

Meg rose. "I'm very pleased to meet you, Lady Jane."

"Not so formal, Meg. Just 'Jane' will do nicely."

"All right." She smiled good-naturedly. "Now then, let's get you prettied up for your meeting with the solicitor, and you can show all those old bats downstairs just who it is they're dealing with."

Without waiting for comment or protest from Jane, she shoved John out the door, and an hour later Jane descended the long, sweeping staircase for her meeting with Dudley Thumberton. Meg had efficiently redone her hair and reworked her dress by adding a scarf and tugging at the bodice to expose some cleavage. Since Jane's father had always felt that money was wasted on excessive clothing, and that what a person wore should be extremely discreet, Jane felt pretty but scandalously clad.

Thumberton waited in the library. As she entered, he was seated behind the desk, looking through papers in a file. "Hello, Master Thumberton."

"Ah . . . Miss Fitzsimmons." He smiled broadly.

"Please call me Jane," she requested as she crossed the room.

"Then you must simply call me Thumberton. Everyone does." He came around the desk and bowed over her hand. "I say, you're looking lovely. Becoming engaged has had a marvelous effect on you."

"I doubt if that's the cause, sir. Everything's happened so fast I can hardly fathom that I've a marriage in the near future."

"Hardly time to catch your breath, eh?"

"Not a second."

"That's Wessington for you. When he makes up his mind about something, there's no stopping him." He held out a chair. "Sit, my dear. Sit while we talk."

"He does move quickly, doesn't he? I can't believe all the activity 'round here. Is he further extending himself financially in preparation for the wedding?"

"Well . . . ah . . . you see . . . ah . . ."

Jane was amused to see how her question flustered the solicitor. He was probably not used to women asking questions about finances or women asking questions about their husbands' actions. She reached across the desk and patted his hand. "It's quite all right, Thumberton. I expect I know a great deal more about finances than the Earl ever will, so you might as well get used to my asking.''

"Yes, I suppose you're right.'' He took out a handkerchief and mopped at his brow. "That's probably for the best actually. He's never taken much interest in the financial side of things.''

"I'd say that's the root of all his problems.''

"I agree wholeheartedly.'' He looked around the room, as though the Earl might be lurking behind the drapes listening to his admissions.

Jane laughed gently as she recognized the panicked look on his face. "Don't be so worried, sir. Perhaps we could forge our own working relationship and use it as a way to keep the Earl on the right track.''

"How so?''

"We could have frank discussions about finances, and we can both work from different angles to make sure that we stay in the black.''

Thumberton breathed a sigh of relief. Jane was turning out to be everything he'd hoped for. He reminded himself to say another small prayer of thanks when he retired for the evening. "I would have to say that your idea is an exceptionally good one. Since you will be charged with managing the household accounts anyway, you might as well see the entire picture. You'll be better able to judge when and what to spend.''

"My thoughts exactly.'' She leaned forward again, and they shook hands to seal their bargain. "So tell me, is the Earl going into further debt to prepare for the wedding? Because if I'm the cause of all this spending, he certainly doesn't need to be doing it.''

"He has a heavy responsibility to the properties. They've been seriously neglected for decades. I imagine he'll be spending quite a bit getting things squared away. Once you've been married for a while, you'll begin to understand his duty to the land and all the people who depend on him.''

"I have some idea of it now, and I know I'll learn more, so, yes, I understand that he has a duty to the estates. But that's not my question. How is he paying for all of this?''

Thumberton almost seemed embarrassed when he answered. "Actually, the money has already changed hands.''

"But I haven't signed the papers yet.''

"Your signature was not required. Your father sent me a signed contract months ago.''

"Months ago?''

"Yes. All I needed was the Earl's signature.''

"Let me see the contract.''

He hesitated, then said, "I guess that would be all right.''

Jane took her time looking through the pages, scanning the words and terms. She'd understood that her father had done this because of Gregory, but now, to learn that he'd had this plan in the works for months! It was hard to grasp the depth of this latest betrayal.

Thumberton studied her intently. "I'm sorry. I thought you realized about the money.''

"I just thought I'd be signing. Along with the Earl. That he'd be here today. Will I be seeing him?''

"No. You'll probably not see him until the day of the wedding. Now that the money is in his accounts, he's dreadfully busy.''

"Really? Too busy to see his fiancée before the ceremony? After all, I've only spoken to the man twice in my life.''

Thumberton, more than anyone, wanted Jane to have as limited a view of Phillip as possible before the joining. Although the contracts were signed, and she couldn't back out, there was always a chance she might try to refuse to go through with the ceremony. No sense letting her get too close a look. "Don't take this personally, Jane."

"Why shouldn't I? This is my life we're talking about. When is the wedding to be? Or don't I need to know?" Her tone was angry and accusatory, but she felt she had every right to be upset. It was *her* wedding, too, not just his. Perhaps he could have consulted her about a few of the insignificant details, like which day it would be held.

"Please don't be perturbed," Thumberton said to quiet her. "Because the ceremony needed to be held so quickly, Phillip felt it was best if he took the matter in hand. It's been scheduled for two weeks from today."

"Has he selected my dress?"

"No. He's left that to your discretion."

"How kind."

"However, he has arranged for the woman who will create it for you. She's to visit you tomorrow and will begin working on your bridal gown and your trousseau. Currently, she's the most sought-after seamstress in London. Phillip wishes you to be most fashionably accommodated."

"Nothing but the best will do for his new bride, I suppose."

"Exactly."

"I believe I understand the situation." Jane shook her head. "Is there anything else I should know before I blindly follow all of you down this path?"

"There is one other matter. I regret that I must be the one to discuss it with you, but I'm afraid the matter can't be avoided." He cleared his throat, turned bright red, cleared his throat again, shuffled through some papers. "Ah . . . the Earl insists that you be tested . . ."

He was too embarrassed to finish the sentence. During their meeting the previous night, when Phillip had dragged him out of bed and begun giving him pages of tasks that needed immediate attention, he'd insisted that Jane agree to it. Thumberton had tried to get him to see reason, but Phillip's past still hung too heavily around his neck.

Jane waited on the edge of her seat during the long pause. It appeared Thumberton was never going to finish his sentence. "Tested for what?"

He stared at the desk, unable to look her in the eye. "Because of the haste surrounding your marriage, he asks that you"—Thumberton's voice fell to a near whisper—"submit to a test by a midwife to ascertain that you are still a maid and that you are not already with child."

"What?!" Outraged, Jane jumped to her feet.

"Please don't ask me to repeat it. I don't think I could."

"I've never been so insulted in all my life. The nerve of that wretched man." She started pacing around the room, working her hands over one another. "I won't do it, I tell you. I've had to quietly watch while my father completely ruined my life, and I was forced to accept his stupid plan that I marry a stranger. I've done everything that was required of me, but I will not sit here now and have my character besmirched in such a fashion. Not by the Earl of Rosewood or anyone else! Do I make myself clear?"

"Yes, but sit, dear. Please."

Jane paused for a moment, looking at the anguished features of the older man. He was only the messenger, and she truly felt sorry for him. She walked back to the chair.

"I know how upsetting it is to hear such a request

from your future husband," he said, "but I must tell you that Phillip feels he has a valid reason to ask. Lest you think horribly of both of us, I should like to tell you why he is asking, but I think he would be extremely upset if he knew we had discussed it. So, I only ask that you promise not to mention this conversation to him."

"All right, you've my word. I'll say nothing about it."

"Phillip was previously married."

Jane inhaled sharply. For some reason, the information hurt.

"He was very young, just seventeen, but he met and fell in love with a woman who was three years older. His father and I tried to talk him out of it, but he wouldn't listen."

"Whatever became of her?"

"She died of illness a few years later."

"What has this to do with me?"

"Let us just say that she was not the most faithful wife, and because of her actions during the marriage, he's developed a severe distrust of everyone that's never abated."

"How do you know all this to be true?"

"Phillip found evidence with his own eyes, and when his wife turned up with child later on, he swore the baby was not his own flesh and blood."

"And the child?"

"Will be your daughter."

Jane gasped again. How many more things was she to endure in one day? "Her name?"

"Emily. She's eleven years just now."

Thumberton pulled a small locket from his pocket and opened it. There was a tiny miniature of the young girl inside. It was too small to get a good idea of what she looked like, except that she had dark hair and blue eyes. "Where is she?"

"She lives at Rosewood the year 'round."

"Will she come for the wedding?"

"No. Phillip would never think to invite her."

"Why ever not?"

Thumberton prevaricated, wondering if he should really spill the truth, but the matter of Emily was too important. She needed a protector, and he hoped more than anything in the world that it would turn out to be Jane Fitzsimmons. "I will be frank, Jane, although I hope this information is not too shocking for your ears."

"It's all right, sir. Just tell me."

"Phillip could never be convinced the girl was his own flesh and blood. Since she was conceived and born during the marriage, he is legally obligated to claim paternity and see to her needs, but he's never felt an obligation to do anything more."

"Who cares for her?"

"The people at the estate do their best. But governesses come and go. She has no tutor just now. I fear for her future, I truly do."

"But surely the Earl would never let anything terrible befall her."

Without responding directly, he leaned forward and said, "I know I have no right to ask, but I am desperate to know that the girl has someone looking out for her interests. She is such a charming, pretty thing. I know you'll come to care for her. Will you watch over her?"

"First, sir, tell me one thing," Jane responded, thoroughly moved by his emotion. "I was very surprised by the choices of men offered to me as possible candidates for marriage. Did you arrange it so I would select the Earl?"

"You've found me out, I'm afraid. After your father first contacted me, I had some research done on your background, and the moment I received the report, I decided that Phillip would be the ideal choice. I did it all for Emily, and I'll not say I'm sorry for it. Would you see to her for me?''

"Yes, I will. You have my word." She stood, indicating the meeting was over. "But, as to the Earl and his request that I submit to his *test,* you may tell him for me that he will rest in Hades before I'll ever do it. He can learn what he wants to know on our wedding night and not a moment before."

Chapter Eleven

Jane waited in the marital bed. The numerous pillows were arranged behind her back, the bed covers draped lightly over her feet. The skimpy white nightgown—or negligee as Meg had called it—hardly covered anything. The tiny straps left her shoulders and arms bare, the lace bodice hovered precariously across her bosom. It was gathered down the front by a pink ribbon, and Meg had loosened the ties, allowing tantalizing hints of skin and cleavage. The fabric was so sheer that nothing was left to the imagination.

She'd wanted to cover herself more completely, but Meg wouldn't hear of it, insisting that Wessington was a man of the world, greatly experienced in loving and that Jane must learn from the start how to win and keep his affections and interest. Her heart was pounding, her body tingling with the anticipation of what would happen once he stepped through the door from his adjoining bedchamber.

Meg had helped with her bath and her hair. From the preparations and advice, it was clear that her unmarried abigail had more than a passing knowledge of what went on between men and women. As Meg brushed and powdered, lotioned and perfumed, she kept up a continual recitation of what Wessington might ask, what he might expect.

Jane had only heard about half of what Meg was saying—things about her hands and her mouth. Now, as she waited alone in the silence for her husband to appear, she realized how much Meg had simply been trying to ease the tension. There was much more to this than she'd ever imagined.

"It will all be worth it," she whispered to herself. "Everything I've done will be worth it." Marriage was the ticket she would use to eventually return home.

The knob on the door turned, and her heart started to pound as Wessington stepped through the opening. Bathed and dressed in his nightclothes, he was so tall. So handsome. And he was her husband. 'Twas nearly unbelievable that such a man had joined himself to her.

His robe of dark green velvet was loosely cinched at the waist. The cloth hugged his form too tightly for there to be anything underneath. It appeared that her husband liked to carry out his lovemaking without any clothes on, which meant she would know more about him after her first night of marriage than Elizabeth knew of hers after two years. The thought was exciting and terrifying at the same time.

The lapels of the robe had pulled apart slightly, and on his chest she could see the swirls of dark hair which tapered in a line down toward his abdomen. Luckily, the edges were crossed over one another at his waist so her eyes could not follow that line as far as they seemed to want to go. The outline of his sex pushed against the fabric. In the dark shadows, it was hard to tell, but it looked as though he was already aroused.

He stepped into the room, closing the door behind him. As he moved, she caught sight of nearly all of his bare leg. It was long and slender, with muscled thigh and calf. The same dark hair that covered his chest also covered his leg. His feet were bare, and she was fairly certain it was the first time she'd ever seen a man's feet. They fascinated her, but embarrassed to have him catch her staring, she lowered her eyes to the bedcovers.

Phillip stared across at his wife. Sitting in his own room, readying himself, had been agony. Just thinking about her and what was coming had made him hard as a poker. But now, after seeing her!

She was lovely.

Beautiful chestnut hair hung loose in long waves down her back, the ends resting around her hips against the bedding. A rosy red flushed her cheeks, her creamy white skin glowed in the candlelight. Her bare throat gave way to slender shoulders, those to the gentle swell of her plump breasts. Through the delicate lace of her gown, he could see pink nipples, hard and fully pressed against the fabric. A tiny waist flared to slim hips which disappeared under the covers.

Her eyes were glowing green, and he remembered thinking them more beautiful than a green lawn on a fine summer day. She stared at the bedding, embarrassed to look at him, her fingers working nervously back and forth across the smooth blankets. She appeared to be trembling slightly, and he wasn't sure if it was caused by the coolness of the room or the excitement of the moment. Perhaps 'twas a little bit of both.

He wanted to groan. He wanted to shake her. He wanted to bury himself, hard and deep and fast, with little regard to how much it hurt. He wanted to love her slowly and gently, showing her how wonderful and erotic it could be. He wanted to take her again and again through the night. Hard and rough. Soft and slow.

If he lived ten lifetimes, he couldn't imagine meeting any other man who could find such a delectable woman through an arranged marriage. She looked to be perfection itself. Any man in his right mind would be cherishing the moment. Phillip was dreading it, so perhaps he was not in his right mind. He'd always wondered.

"Hello, Jane," he said softly. With the only noise in the quiet room being the occasional cracking of the log in the fire, his voice sounded too loud. She appeared to jump slightly, or flinch, on hearing it.

"Hello, Lord Wessington." Jane couldn't seem to look up at him. Her heart was pounding too hard, her nerves were too rattled. In the past few weeks, she'd kept moving forward by reminding herself that she was simply going through with this for Gregory and her father. Now that the moment of coupling with her husband had arrived, she was beginning to suspect that she'd made a mistake somewhere in her assessment of the situation. The problem with that being she couldn't back out now.

Wessington was her husband, which gave him the right to do anything to her, and she had to agree to participate. While mentally she had convinced herself that she wanted to go through with it because she was eager to learn what would happen under the covers, her body seemed to have finally realized the full extent of what she'd be required to do.

Meg insisted that Wessington was a man of great sexual experience—how Meg knew that to be so, she'd never said, and Jane hadn't dared to ask—who would guide her gently and skillfully through the change from maid to wife. Jane wanted to participate eagerly and willingly. She wanted to experience every wonderful moment, wanted to enjoy, rather than endure, the loss of her virginity. She wanted to cherish, instead of dread, the moment he breached her maidenhead. She wanted to welcome him with open arms, rather than sit there trembling in fright.

She wanted all those things and more from the night ahead, and she could have them, if only she could get her body to cooperate. The air in the room suddenly seemed to have vanished, and she couldn't breathe. With great effort, she had to force her lungs to work. In, out. In, out. In, out, she told herself, trying to help them regain their own tempo, but her coaching didn't seem to do much good.

Phillip watched her carefully. Over the last two weeks, he'd let these next moments play out in his head hundreds of times. What he should say. What he should do. How he should do it. The words of comfort and praise he should use. Although he let the details change in various ways, there was always one constant ending. She'd be gently taken; he'd be greatly satisfied.

In none of his mental scenarios had he dared prepare himself for the reality of what was about to happen. He, Phillip Wessington, the great lover and user of women, who had bedded every type, color, style, age and size of female, did not plan to make love to his wife.

He'd had his share of younger, less experienced women. Some virgins, some barely so. Any number of girls had thought they were in love with him simply because they'd mated a time or two. Girls didn't understand the way men perceived sexual contact. Therefore, the act could take on hideous importance for some of them, and they were likely to blow the meaning of it all out of proportion. Young women believed in love and commitment and happy endings.

Phillip believed in none of those things, and he didn't want to kindle those feelings in his new wife. He simply wanted to consummate their union and go about his business without any of the messiness that marital "love" could cause. Jane had none of the jaded experience of the women in his social set, and she would never understand how little meaning the sexual act really had.

If he made love to his wife as he should, if he was kind and gentle, supportive and tender, she would read so much into it. He could see it in her eyes and the tense trembling visible across her shoulders and arms as she waited for him to approach the bed.

He wanted to blame it on Margaret, to be able to tell himself that he was simply doing this to avoid any further fighting with her. But that wasn't the case. The sad fact was that, for once, Margaret had had a point. Jane would fall in love with him. The closeness and connection she would feel would grow into something so much bigger than it was. She would want him to be a real husband, a real father for her children. Phillip had no idea how to be either of those things and no desire to learn.

Or so he told himself. If there was a tiny voice in the back of his mind telling him that he was really just scared about Jane and the feelings he might develop for her if he let his guard down, he completely disregarded it. She was beautiful, seemed kind and genuine; all traits he told himself he'd never find in a woman. If he let himself get too close to her, to her pure heart and gentle nature, there was a very good chance that the ice surrounding his heart would begin to melt away, drop by drop. He was terrified to find out what was hiding underneath. Better to never know what would be left.

Not wanting to scare her, he walked to the edge of the bed and eased down. Her fingers were still nervously working along the top coverlet, and he folded his large hands around her small ones to stop the nervous motion. Her skin was like ice, and at the gentle touch, she raised her eyes to his. He wanted to groan aloud at seeing how lovingly she stared up at him.

"I'm sorry," she said just above a whisper. "I seem to be rather frightened all of a sudden."

"Don't be afraid. It won't take very long."

"Really?" That seemed a strange admission. Meg had insisted it would go on all night and maybe into the next day. "How long would you guess?"

"Just a matter of minutes, and the pain goes away quickly."

Jane nodded, curious. Either Meg or the Earl was terribly mistaken about the coming event. "Shall I take off my gown?"

Wanting to be helpful, and not sure of how to go about it, she reached for one of the tiny straps, but Phillip stopped her. "No, that's all right." His hand moved over hers and brought the strap up onto her shoulder once more. Again he nearly groaned, as he touched her smooth, bare flesh. Her pulse pounded in her throat, and it took every bit of his willpower to keep from leaning close and pressing his lips to the throbbing spot. He dropped his hand back to his lap, and closed his eyes for a few moments, trying to quell the rising tide of his desire.

When he opened them, Jane was staring intently.

"Is something the matter?"

"No, Jane."

"Why are you staring at me? Is it the nightgown?"

He didn't say anything, speechless that she could possibly imagine that it was anything but exquisite.

In distress, she tried to rise. "Oh, I knew it was all wrong. I'm sorry, sir. I let Meg convince me that I should wear such a thing, but I realize it's quite a bit shocking for . . ."

Phillip rested his arm across her waist, easing her back against the pillows before she could remove herself from the bed. "The nightgown is fine, Jane. It's very beautiful. *You* are very beautiful."

Jane blushed from her toes to her forehead. Never had she imagined that a man's words could create such a stir on the inside and the outside. "How do we proceed, then? I hate not knowing what to do."

"Well, I know what to do, so don't trouble yourself."

"All right."

"Just lie back against the pillows."

As he instructed, she lay back on the feather and down. Her hair fanned out behind her head, encasing pale skin and white lace in a wrap of deep auburn. Her lips appeared a more rosy red, her eyes a more brilliant green. The lace of the gown tightly covered her bosom, completely outlining the gentle slope of her breasts. Their hard points jutted proudly, on display, and he could make out their pinkness through the tiny holes in the stitching of the lace.

His eyes continued to travel down, to her waist and beyond. At the juncture of her thighs, he could see the dark hair covering her mound. It was a deep red, slightly darker than the hair on her head, discreetly sheltering her secret place. He wanted desperately to lower his head and inhale the essence of her through the fabric. Instead, he rose slightly and pulled the covers back the rest of the way, exposing her long legs, which turned out to be a grave mistake, since looking at them stirred visions of how they would feel wrapped around his waist while he pounded himself between her thighs.

Look at her feet! he ordered.

God's teeth, even they were sexy. Slender, with delicate bones and graceful arches. She, or perhaps Meg, had painted the nails a light shade of pink, the color of her nipples. The dab of color against the white of the bedding was incredibly erotic. He wanted to start with her toes, sucking them one by one into his mouth and working his way up from there. But he didn't.

Allowing himself one bit of pleasure, he raised his hand to her face, traced across the planes and bumps, learning the features. Certain he felt a light kiss against his hand—he didn't want her kissing him!—he moved on. Down her throat, taking longer than he should have to feel that alluring bit of throbbing pulse. To her breasts, tracing them over and over, circling his palm around them, learning their size and weight, pressing against the centers and feeling the nipples press back, until the moment she became too brave and covered his hand with her own—she couldn't be allowed to enjoy this!—increasing the tension.

To her waist, the ridge of her navel, till he rested his hand against her mound. He rubbed a few slow circles with the heel of his hand, and, damn, if her hips didn't respond slightly with their own demand.

The woman was a natural. With proper guidance, she'd be a hot, passionate bedmate. Resisting her was torture.

As though burned by the realization, he pulled his hand away.

Jane, though afraid of the actual joining to come, was thoroughly excited by her husband. His gaze seemed a tangible force, creating heat and fire wherever it landed, as though he were actually touching her. She felt hot and cold all over.

As his hand passed over her face, she caught that

male smell, one that was distinctly his, and inhaled deeply. Some ancient, animalistic part of her seemed to know that smell, to have been seeking it out all of her life, and as he passed on, she wanted to hold his palm to her face so she could continue to enjoy and capture his essence, but she didn't, settling instead for placing a light kiss against his palm.

He seemed to notice, nearly jerking his hand back, then moving instead down her neck to her breasts. They were nearly screaming for his attentions, aching and full. As he touched and manipulated their shapes, chafing his callused palm across the hardened tips, she bit her bottom lip, refusing to give voice to the sound of agony wanting to escape from somewhere deep inside her.

The discomfort was so great that she finally grabbed for his wrist, trying to force him to apply greater pressure. He did, but only for a moment, squeezing her pained nipple between thumb and finger. Then ... nothing! 'Twas so unfair.

As his fingers lightly brushed down her stomach, she resisted the urge to grab for him again, to bring his hands back to where her body so desperately wanted them. Back to the gentle rub and massage across her nipples. Just as she thought nothing could feel better, he touched her again, between her legs, smoothly circling his hand, creating new sparks of sensation between her thighs, then across her stomach, up her arms and down her legs.

She'd thought the ache was in her breasts, but no, it was here. Hotter and more potent. Not knowing what else to do, how to ease the agony he was creating, she flexed her hips against his hand, her body seeming to know that an increase of pressure would make her feel better.

As with her breasts, the moment she flexed against him, he pulled away. It almost seemed as though he didn't care to touch her. Was she doing something wrong? Perhaps she was supposed to sit immobile. Oh, the embarrassment of not knowing what was appropriate was nearly unbearable.

Phillip raised his eyes back to hers. They were so distressed. Unable to resist giving her a moment of comfort, he rested his lips against her abdomen, pressing a light kiss against her stomach; then, rubbing his cheek against the soft lace, he allowed himself one small moment of pleasure while he learned the scent of her. As he burrowed his cheek, she rested a hand on the back of his head, and sifted her fingers through his hair, in an intimate, affectionate gesture. As though she'd done it to him thousands of times in her life. As though they loved and cherished one another. As though it was the most natural thing in the world.

Enough! With greater speed than he'd intended, he jumped away from her and sat up. She bent a knee as he moved away. The gown had a slit up the side which allowed her naked leg to reveal itself all the way to the upper part of her thigh. The silky expanse of skin was covered by a gentle down of her dark hair. He could barely refrain from running his hand up the inside of her leg to her knee, up to her thigh and higher, until . . .

"What is it, sir? What have I done?"

"Nothing, Jane. Nothing. Everything's fine."

"No, it isn't. I can tell by the look in your eye. I told you I don't know what to do, but I'm eager to learn. If you'll just show me, I'm sure I'll get it right."

Phillip remembered the night in her rented parlor two weeks earlier when she'd seemed able to so quickly and easily assess his moods. She was doing it again, as though she'd always known him. At times, she seemed to know him more than he knew himself. Deep inside, he keenly felt the lonely weight of all the years when he'd never been close to anyone. When no one had cared for or about him and he'd cared for and about no one in return.

Once again, he sensed that there was something important here. Something vital and fresh which he could grab hold of if he dared.

What would it be like to let his guard down? To let this woman close enough to enjoy a friendship with her? To trust her and care about her?

No. No. He was too far gone to even think such a thing. Best to get back to the messy business at hand and get it over with as quickly as possible. His eyes quickly scanned the room, and he saw what he was looking for on her dressing table. He leaned forward and placed a gentle kiss on her forehead. "Turn over, Jane. And lie on your stomach."

"What?"

"Lie on your stomach." She hesitated for a moment, trying to decide if she should. He gave her an encouraging nod and helped her ease herself into the welcoming mattress. Once she appeared comfortable, he grabbed the pot he'd spotted.

He moved off the bed and quickly got back on. Raising up on her elbows, she glanced at him over her shoulder. Her long hair was in such disarray that she couldn't see him, but she could feel him kneeling behind her. "What ever are you doing?"

He reached for her rope of hair and pushed it to the side, only to wish he hadn't. Her eyes, more startlingly green than he'd seen them so far, were staring at him curiously. "I've grabbed a pot of cream. It will ease the way for me and, I hope, lessen the pain for you."

She seemed to accept the explanation, or at least was

too shy to ask more questions. He loosened the ties of his robe, then scooped cream out of the pot with three fingers. Slowly, wanting to prolong the moment for some reason, he stroked the white stuff up and down the length of his shaft. He was hard when he'd entered the room, and from touching and smelling her, his condition had increased until now he was in a painful way. The cream felt delectably carnal, forbidden, and for a moment, he seemed fourteen again and wondered if he'd embarrass himself before he could become impaled between her legs.

Deciding not to test fate, he reached for her and rested his hands against the backs of her thighs. She flinched. "Shhh . . . it's all right. I'm just going to raise the hem of your gown." In a slow movement, he lifted the thing up her legs, past her hips and waist, over her head, leaving her buttocks bare and exposed. They were two perfect globes, creamy and smooth like the rest of her. Above, two beautiful dimples tempted his lips, but he refrained. The cleft between beckoned, but he kept his hands to himself.

Barely breathing, she lay perfectly still. Every sound seemed magnified. Every one of his movements overly made. This didn't seem right, but he kept insisting that he knew what he was doing. Movement again and touch. A knee between her thighs. Then another. Curly, rough hair, abrasive against her skin. Hands, gently easing her legs apart.

He leaned closer and whispered, "I'm going to touch you. In your private part. I want to put some cream on you, too."

No response came to her, so she lay rigid and tense as his fingers drifted across the cleft of her bottom. Without any hesitation, he touched her where no other person had ever touched her. The cream was cold, her body hot, and as his finger slipped inside, she tried to clench her legs together. The movement seemed to pull his finger more deeply inside. She was certain she wrenched a groan of frustration from him, but she didn't care. The touch was so unwelcome, so impersonal, that she was beyond caring if she was doing things correctly or not.

He worked one finger back and forth several times; then another joined the first. She tried to turn again, but his other hand steadied her back and wouldn't let her up.

"What are you doing?"

"I'm preparing you a little. So it won't hurt quite so much." Phillip closed his eyes in agony. From their small amount of touching, she was wet and ready for him, her moist lips fairly crying into his hand. Then she clenched tightly, squeezing against his fingers. Sweet, sweet agony. There were no other words to describe it. He removed his hand, making a slow, leisurely circle across the bud of her womanhood. It was exposed. Hard. Waiting for his ministrations and attentions. He could almost feel it against the tip of his tongue.

Sweet Jesu, what am I doing?

Reaching under her stomach, he gripped her around the waist, raising her slightly to insert a pillow under her. Her backside was now raised up, a delectable offering for whatever he wanted to do.

Jane was holding her breath again. He'd touched something, some small place, that previously she'd not known existed. It sent fire and ice shooting through her veins. The pain was so exquisite she nearly cried out. All too quickly he moved his hand away.

Again! she wanted to beg. *Please, husband, again,* but she didn't. She lay immobile while he reached under her and slipped the pillow under her stomach. Hands on both buttocks now. Then to the backs of her thighs. Slipping to the insides. Pressing her open. His body weight shifting across and over.

As he eased himself down onto one elbow, his robe still on and flowing over them like a velvet blanket, she began to realize what he intended. His hand was between her thighs, the blunt, hard positioning of his sex up against hers. He eased his hips to increase the pressure.

"No, Wessington. No, please. Not like this." She started to squirm; then, when she realized he wasn't stopping, she gazed over her shoulder. "I want to see you."

For a brief moment he considered doing what she requested. Rolling her over. Making love to her as he'd always imagined it. Kissing her lips. Suckling at her breasts. Tasting and tonguing the moist petals of her womanhood. But he couldn't. One kiss, one stroke of the hand, and he'd be lost. "It will be quicker this way. And it will hurt less. Trust me."

It seemed as though agonizing minutes passed while she stared at him with those probing emerald eyes. God, how he hated them! They looked straight to the center of his black heart.

"If you insist," she finally said, turning her head back to face the pillows. Phillip began again the moment she turned her head 'round. The pressure between her legs increased further. She tensed as his fingers tightened against her thighs.

"Relax, Jane."

"I can't. I'm sorry." It was impossible with the pressure between her legs. What did the blasted man expect?

"Don't be sorry." He pushed his hips closer, then stopped, knowing he'd reached her barrier. "Take a deep breath." He waited, feeling her lungs fill with air.

"Let it out slowly." She did so, and seizing on the bit of relaxation brought about by her exhale, he impaled himself to the hilt. To her credit, she didn't cry out, though he thought she was going to.

Phillip couldn't believe how aroused he was. She was tight and slick. The cream he'd used, coupled with her virgin's blood and her body's juices had created a hot, slippery paradise, his for the taking. As she tried to turn to look at him, her body naturally clenched tightly around him. Suddenly, the heat in his groin began to rage out of control, and he could no longer hold back.

His hips began to move back and forth. While he could have spilled himself with a few deep thrusts, he found her so exquisite that he couldn't bear to end it so quickly. He began slowly, then increased the tempo, pumping faster, letting the tension build until his universe darkened, the sun burned brighter than the brightest star. His entire body tensed, and he completely spilled himself against her womb.

Jane lay very still as he thrust deeper and deeper.

All at once, his entire body slackened, and she felt his full weight on top of her, pressing her into the bed. At first, she wondered if he'd died, but gradually, she could feel the steady beat of his heart thundering against her ribs. Perhaps he was asleep or unconscious. She could barely breathe and wondered briefly if she might suffocate before help arrived. Worst of all was that his male part was still buried deeply between her legs.

Just when she was thinking that perhaps she should try to call for Meg, he surprised her by nuzzling a kiss against her ear. With whatever small amount of leverage she had, she elbowed him in the ribs. "Get off me, you bloody bastard. Now."

Phillip rolled onto his side, but as he was reaching for her, she scurried away to the far side of the bed. As far away as she could get without stepping onto the floor. As she'd wanted to do for what seemed an eternity, she curled her legs to her chest, wrapped her arms around them. Rocking herself gently, she let silent tears start to fall.

The silence was oppressive. Why didn't he just leave? He shifted on the bed, and she flinched, wondering if he intended to reach for her again. She'd kill him if he touched her just now. She'd murder him, right here in their marital bed. If she had to hang for it in the morning, she'd go to her executioner with a peaceful heart. She felt ravaged, torn, beaten, more unloved than she'd ever been in her long, lonely life.

He laid his hand on her back, and she straightened. "Don't you dare *touch* me."

"Jane . . ." He stared across the bed, at her body huddled in upon itself like a newborn babe's. Her shoulders were shaking slightly as she shed silent tears. His decision to couple with no emotional involvement between them had been a good one, but if that was true, why did he feel so wretched? In all his years of loving women, he'd never treated one so callously as this. "It was better to do it this way."

"Better for whom?" she asked, then laughed bitterly. "I was so sure that you would know how to do it. That you would know how to show me the way of it. I am the world's biggest fool."

The prick at his loving skills injured his pride. "I know how to make love to a woman, Jane. It's just better for us not to be too involved with each other."

"Oh, yes, *Lord* Wessington." Her voice was heavily laced with sarcasm. "Heaven forbid that you show any kindness to me. I'm just your *wife*. No wonder they make sure we remain virgins until this night. Who would ever go through with marriage if they knew this horrible experience was awaiting them?" The tears that had been falling silently were becoming a dreadful flood, and she could no longer hold them back. She refused to let him know she was crying. "Leave me be."

"Jane, I think we should discuss things."

"I've no wish to speak to you at the moment. If you have any decency, you'll leave now."

"Jane . . ." He reached for her again, wishing there was some way to explain why he'd done what he'd done, but the words were like ashes in his mouth. His mind kept saying that he'd done the proper thing, but his heart kept shouting something else again. He felt despicable. "I want to . . ." What?

"Just go. Cease this torment."

He hesitated, then stepped off the bed. "Shall I ring for Meg?"

"God, no. I don't want anyone to see me like this."

Phillip cinched his robe across the waist, covering the slash of blood across his thighs. He moved to the door of his chamber. She looked so lost, so forlorn. So injured and hurt. By his hand. By his actions. He wanted to say the right thing or do the right thing, but he wasn't sure what it could be now.

"Good night." She didn't respond, and he stepped through the door and closed it softly.

Jane waited, tense and anxious, until she heard the click of the door as it closed behind her husband. She waited a few minutes more, just to be sure that he wasn't returning. Then she fell to the floor, fumbled in the dim light for the chamber pot and found it just in time. She retched over and over again until there was nothing left. Too weak to stand or even to crawl back to the bed, she managed to drag a blanket to the floor, where she leaned against the wall in the dark shadow of the corner. Huddled there, alone and frightened, she fell asleep.

Chapter Twelve

Meg lay on her stomach, burrowed down in the soft bed, when she heard the click of the knob at her door, but she was too tired from her night of frolicking to open an eye just yet. Besides, she'd know the soft step of that foot anywhere. Only a moment later, warm lips brushed against her ear. A hand reached beneath the covers and fondled her breast.

"Rise and shine, lazy bones," Graves whispered.

"Now?" She groaned. "What's the time?"

"Five. Just past. The Earl's been to his room and gone."

"He's probably still cuddled with his wife."

"Maybe, but I didn't want to poke my nose in." Graves had seen the Earl in all sorts of situations with numerous ladies and, in the past few months, had woken him nearly every day with Margaret by his side. "I doubt the Earl would mind if I saw them in bed together, but I don't think Jane would care for it."

"Yes, I suppose you're right." Graves moved back as she shrugged off the covers. "I'd better go check. If he's gone, she'll be wanting a bath. And perhaps someone to talk to." Meg wiggled her eyebrows at the thought of learning a few more juicy tidbits about the Earl's love-making abilities.

Dressing quickly, she sneaked down the hallways. The entire household was still sleeping, and she didn't want to wake anyone. Jane was so lovely, and the Earl such a randy devil, that Meg couldn't imagine he'd have left her alone already, unless, of course, she was so drained from her first night of ecstasy that she was sound asleep.

Silent as a mouse, she opened the door to Jane's bedchamber. The fire was out so it was very cool, the candles burned down so it was dark. She lifted her own candle toward the bed, surprised to see that it was empty, the bedcoverings barely mussed. Making a quick circle to make certain they weren't going at it on one of the chairs or on the floor, she walked around the room and lit the lamp. At the backside of the bed, she stopped dead in her tracks.

Jane was on the floor, braced into the corner, her hair a disheveled mass, and she was barely covered by the blanket thrown over her legs.

"Jane . . ." Meg squatted, then knelt, taking her hand. Her skin was cold and clammy.

"What?" Jane jumped slightly, opened her eyes, squinting into the candlelight. "Oh, Meg, thank the Lord it's only you."

"Whatever happened?" Of all the things she'd imagined, this was definitely not even close to being one of them. "Let's get you up, dear. Can you stand?"

Jane seemed to think about it for a moment. "Yes, I guess I can. I'm a little stiff."

"How long have you been down here?"

"Most of the night, I expect. I guess I fell asleep."

Meg extended a hand, helping her to her feet.

"Sit, Jane. Here." Meg moved her toward the bed.

Jane pulled away. "No, not on the bed. I don't want to sit there. I don't want to sit there ever again."

"All right. This chair, then." She moved it close to the fire, then held Jane's arm as she walked her to it. Jane limped a little and winced with each step. How hard had the bastard ripped into her? Meg shook her head in distress. This was so at odds with everything Graves had ever told her about the way the Earl treated his lady friends.

"I'm going to go find someone to light the fire, and I'll ring for a bath."

"Please, Meg"—Jane reached for her arm—"I don't want anybody to see me like this. You know how they'll talk."

Meg knew all too well, but she needed help and couldn't leave Jane in such distress. "How about Graves? He'll be extremely discreet. I swear it."

Jane thought for a long moment, then agreed. "But only him."

"I'll be right back."

Meg returned momentarily and stoked the fire. While it kindled and Jane warmed herself, Meg stripped the bed.

Graves entered by himself. Whoever had helped him carry things up the stairs had been dismissed at the door. Meg helped him bring the hip bath into the room and fill it with hot water. When it was ready, he walked to Jane's chair and smiled down at her, care and concern clear in his eyes.

"I've really done it now, haven't I?" she asked through a flood of tears. "Binding myself to him this way . . ."

Graves flashed a pained look to Meg, then reached

down and took Jane's hand and squeezed it. "I don't understand him, Jane. I truly, truly don't."

Jane looked from Graves to Meg, caring so much for these two wonderful new friends she'd found swimming in this sea of enemies and sharks. "It was the most horrible thing that ever happened to me. Quite a statement about a girl's wedding night, wouldn't you say?"

Meg fell to her knees in front of the chair. She and Jane embraced each other, while Graves held her hand, stroked her hair and whispered comforting words. They stayed with her until she cried herself out. Once the tirade ended, Jane seemed embarrassed. With a shaky voice, she said, "I guess I'll have that bath now."

"You'll feel so much better once you're cleaned up." Meg helped her to her feet as Graves headed for the door. She stopped him with a look. "Where will you be?"

"I've things to attend to."

Meg could tell by the firm set of his jaw that the *things* he referred to had to do with finding the Earl and giving him a piece of his mind or perhaps more. If Graves found himself in trouble again, there'd be no help. "Don't you dare go downstairs."

The stern tone of Meg's voice brought Jane's head 'round. "What is it? What's wrong?"

"He's got his mind set to go after the Earl. Who knows what kind of trouble he'll get himself in."

Jane was touched. She couldn't remember a time in her life when someone had volunteered to stand up for her.

It was touching.

It was frightening.

"Graves, I'm ordering you to go back to your room."

"I've things to attend to, Jane."

"No. I don't want to see your face about before nine or so."

Graves looked ready to burst. "What your *husband*"—the word rolled bitterly off his tongue—"needs, and I'd say has probably needed for a good share of his life, is to have his arse kicked." He bowed slightly. "Beg pardon, ladies, for my language."

"Yes, you're probably right. But not now, not over this. And definitely not by you." Jane stepped to him and held out her hand until he took it in his own. "I need you here to help and guide me. You can't give him a reason to send you away."

Meg moved closer. "She's right, John Graves. You know she is."

"Promise me you'll do nothing." Jane squeezed his hand. "Say you'll return to your room once you leave here."

He bit back all the words he wanted to say and stood silently, fuming at the two women.

"Promise me."

"All right, you've my word. I won't do anything. I won't say anything."

"Thank you." As Meg nearly collapsed with relief, Jane turned to her. "I want you to go with him to make sure he stays out of trouble."

"But I should help you bathe."

"Actually, I'd rather be alone. I'll clean up, and then take a bit of the fresh morning air. I need to clear my senses and decide how to face the days to come."

"If you're certain . . ."

Meg looked so torn between her duties to her lady and to her lover that Jane's heart ached. What would it be like to love someone so much? "Go." She smiled. "Don't worry about me. I'll ring as soon as I need you again. Enjoy the last few hours of the night together."

While she wanted to have a long luxurious bath, she didn't want the Earl walking in while she was naked and thinking he could exercise his marital rights. If he wanted her again today, she'd kill him. She truly would.

After soaking as long as she dared, she dressed herself in a comfortable day dress, leaving behind her corset and other trappings. Feeling refreshed, she wanted to get out of the house to the fields beyond, perhaps to walk along the river and watch the sunrise while she planned her next move.

Quietly, she tiptoed down the stairs. No one was about yet, and probably no one would be for several hours. She made it across the foyer without encountering guest or servant. Heading for the back of the house, she stepped into one of the huge sitting rooms, intending to slip out a back door onto the terrace and down to one of the pathways leading through the gardens.

Whispers stopped her only a few feet into the room. A man and a woman were having a romantic assignation on one of the couches. The back of the couch faced her so she couldn't see who it was, which was just as well. What kind of people were these friends of her husband's that they would couple on one of the divans where anybody might walk in? The woman sighed, the man groaned and Jane blushed bright red as she turned to go, hoping to back into the hall undetected.

But the woman's voice stopped her cold.

"Yes, right there. Oooh . . . you know how I like that." Lady Margaret.

The man chuckled. "You are such a glutton for pleasure." Her husband.

In all her life, Jane had never imagined she had tendencies toward murder. While killing was rare, it happened, and whenever she'd heard of it, she'd been unable to fathom the rage required to take the life of another.

Now, upon hearing her husband whispering love words to another woman a few short hours after their wedding, she knew. Quiet but determined, she retreated to the hall.

Because of the hours she'd spent alone at the Shipworks, her father had instructed her in the use of firearms. She'd always kept a pistol nearby, although she'd never had occasion to use it. There was a collection of pistols in the library, neatly arranged on display in various cases. Wessington owned several varieties of the Dragoon pistols so favored by British cavalry soldiers. She chose the one with the longest barrel; it looked intimidating. Then she headed back to the sitting room.

Although she walked quietly, as she approached the couch and stepped around the end, she realized she could have made any amount of sound and neither of the lovers would have noticed. They were too caught up in what they were doing. She tucked the pistol into the folds of her skirt, hiding it from view.

Lady Margaret was stretched on her back, Wessington on top of her. He was shirtless. She was dressed in some sort of exotic red underclothing trimmed in black, which, when fully in place, would have barely covered her torso. Unfortunately, the top had been lowered and her breasts were on full display. Jane had to admit that they were quite something. Full and round, the nipples large and nearly a dark purple color. And hard. Very, very hard. Her husband's hands were making sure of it as he stroked one between his thumb and index finger.

Margaret arched her back, offering them up. "Quit teasing, Phillip. You know what I want."

The world seemed to move in slow motion as Jane watched her husband's mouth begin to descend to the woman's breast. Her rage exploded. "Yes, Wessington, by all means, you know what she wants. Quit teasing her."

The lovers both paused, as if their minds could not fathom where the third voice was coming from. At the same time, they looked to the side and saw Jane standing there. Phillip jumped to his knees. Margaret shrieked and tugged at her bodice, trying to find enough of the scanty cloth to cover her swollen mounds.

"Jane . . ." Phillip squeaked. So shocked was he by her sudden appearance, he could barely say her name.

"Yes, Lord Wessington, it's Jane. Your new, beloved lady wife. So nice of you to remember my name." She was so angry her entire body was shaking. "I see you *do* know how to make love to a woman. I was doubtful last night."

"Whatever are you doing down here?"

"I might ask you the same question, but I can see the answer with my own eyes."

Phillip rose off the couch to his feet. "Jane . . . I can explain . . ."

"I doubt that you can."

By now, Margaret had adjusted her bodice and had slipped into a robe which covered her from shoulder to foot but was skimpy enough to see through. Sitting up and covered, she was back to her cocky self. "Jane, you're making too much of this." She looked bored by the whole affair. Her lips hinted at a slight smile, showing just how amusing she felt the situation was. "Everyone knows that Phillip and I are good friends."

In an authoritative tone that surprised all of them, Jane responded, "You do not have my permission to call me by my given name. Ever!" She glared at her husband who looked as though he'd just swallowed a toad. "What does she mean by *good* friends?"

Margaret chuckled. "Don't be such a silly goose, Countess. What do you think I mean?"

Phillip managed to find his voice again, some of his aristocratic demeanor returning. "Shut up, Margaret, and leave us. I wish to talk to my wife alone."

"No," Jane countermanded, causing Phillip to raise an eyebrow and Margaret to chuckle again. Tears surged to her eyes, which surprised her. She thought she'd cried them all out earlier with Meg and Graves, but she refused to let them fall in front of these two despicable people. Faced now with the fact of her own naïveté—it had never occurred to her that her husband might currently have a *leman* or that it was Margaret—she was nearly too ashamed to ask, but she had to. "Is she your mistress?"

Phillip sighed, then answered quietly, "Yes, Jane, she is."

The audacity, the impropriety, the lack of respect were beyond understanding. "You brought this *woman*, this whore, into my home and invited her to stay as a guest during our wedding celebration? How could you do such a thing to me?"

Margaret's light voice tinkled. "Actually, Countess, it's the Earl's home. I'd say he can invite whomever he wants."

"Shut up, Margaret," both Jane and Phillip shouted at the same time.

Jane pulled the pistol from behind her skirt, causing the lovers to gasp. "I've got one shot, and for the life of me, I can't decide who deserves it more."

"Really, Countess," Margaret offered, waving a hand in dismissal, "if you're going to shoot someone every time your husband takes a lover, you'd better stock up on plenty of ball and powder."

The remark was the last straw. Jane turned and fired

point-blank at her husband. He had the good sense, coupled with the agility, to duck just in the nick of time, and the explosion whizzed past where he'd been standing only moments before. If he hadn't moved, she'd have blasted his heart out.

For long seconds, no one moved. The trio was so stunned by the fact that Jane had actually fired the pistol. A woman, a wife, simply was not allowed to attempt murder against her husband, especially when that husband was a peer of the realm. Smoke hung heavy in the air, sifting silently to the floor.

Phillip was the first to act, jumping to his feet and reaching for the weapon. "Give me that thing," he ordered.

Jane threw it at him, then jumped next to the fireplace and grabbed a poker which she held so threateningly he stopped in midstep.

Sounds came from out in the hall. Several servants now huddled in the doorway, as well as a few guests who'd jumped out of bed at the sound of the shot. In their various stages of half-dress, they would have appeared comical if the scene hadn't been so shocking. What the Earl and Margaret had been doing was so apparent that people were standing openmouthed. Jane could already hear the scandalous gossip which would be sweeping London before the day was out.

With others in the room, she wasn't fearful of what her husband might do or say. She took command, looking to him first. "I will speak privately to you—later." Without giving him a chance to respond, she turned to Margaret and waved the poker. "As for *you*, you will leave my home within the next fifteen minutes, and if I ever have the misfortune to see you near my husband again, I'll kill you where you stand."

Margaret, refusing to be put down in front of any

members of Society, scoffed. "I'll not leave unless the Earl asks me to."

Just then, Graves entered the room, barefoot and wearing trousers, but tucking his nightshirt in at the waist. "What the bloody hell . . . !" He stared at the three of them, at the two lovers barely dressed, at the pistol on the floor; he smelled and saw the gun smoke hovering in the air. "Oh, no . . ." He turned to Jane.

"Graves, Lady Margaret is just leaving." She turned to him in a magnificent fury, and everyone standing in the hall jumped out of her way. "Come with me."

"And you told *me* to behave myself," Graves muttered as he, then Meg, then several other servants followed Jane to Margaret's rooms.

Jane methodically pulled out valises and trunks. "Pack it. Pack it all. I want all of her things sitting in the front drive in fifteen minutes. Meg, see to it." She looked to Graves. "Have a coach brought 'round to take her back to London immediately. If you have to, place her—bodily—inside. Tell me when she's gone. I'll expect to hear from you in twenty minutes."

"Yes, Countess." Graves left, and Jane followed him out, turning down the hall and walking back to her own room, oblivious to the smiles and silent applause of her staff. Jane was now their heroine.

Chapter Thirteen

Jane sat at the window, looking out. Carriages had been pulling out for hours as various wedding guests decided the festivities had come to a quick halt. Curiously, as the afternoon drew to a close, there were also many carriages and horses coming into the drive, the drivers or riders stopping for a moment, then leaving again. She couldn't figure out what that was about and didn't want to. There were too many other things on her mind.

It had taken most of an hour to get Margaret down the road. After her departure, Jane had sat alone, wondering what to do, what was going to happen. Shooting at one's husband was a very serious affair. There would undoubtedly be consequences.

No matter what, she could not stay in London, living on the fringe of Wessington's social life, ashamed to go out because people might see her and recognize her as the jealous shrew who fired at her husband simply because he was making love to his mistress. The members of the *ton* were so immune to taking partners outside of marriage that they were sure to wonder what all the fuss was about.

Yesterday, Jane would have wondered herself. After all, in her naïve state, she'd been thinking she could do the same thing to the Earl, but now that she'd recognized the intimacy of the marital act, such behavior on her part would be unthinkable. With a grimace of distaste, she thought of the times Gregory had tried to coax her to bed him without regard to how it might affect Gertrude. How little Jane had understood what he was truly asking her to do! To think that she'd almost acquiesced.

Elizabeth had tried to explain it to her and had failed, but she couldn't fault her friend. How could one adequately explain what a man did to his wife under the bedcovers? It hurt to imagine her new husband engaging in such a private moment with another woman, but it hurt more to realize that he hadn't really wanted to do it with her. His lack of regard for her as a partner— in fact, his seeming distaste for her—was a cruel blow. He obviously knew how to perform the marital act in a passionate manner, but he hadn't cared about Jane enough to show any interest in an affectionate coupling. The knowledge hurt.

A knock sounded, and Graves entered as she continued to stare at the latest horseman making his way to the front door. For not the first time that day, she wondered why such a good person as John Graves would serve a cad like her husband.

"Whatever made you come to work for Lord Wessington?" she asked.

"Actually, he rescued me, after a fashion."

"Really? How?"

"Oh, I had a bit of trouble with my last employer."

Jane shifted slightly so she could see him. He was standing across the room, his hands full of envelopes. "What happened?"

"My last employer turned his attentions on his children's governess. She was a sweet thing. Young and alone. He got her in the family way and then kicked her out. She had nowhere to turn."

"What did you do?"

"Let's just say I tried to make him see the error of his ways."

"You struck him?"

"Actually, 'beat him bloody' would probably be more adequate. I was jailed in Newgate. Lord Wessington somehow heard about what had happened. He bribed some people and brought me to his home."

"Did the two of you know each other previously?"

"No. That's what makes me shake my head about him sometimes. He can do the most wonderful thing, and then it's almost as if he has to do something dastardly to prove that he didn't mean to do anything good in the first place."

"And the girl? Whatever happened to her?"

Graves paused, wondering momentarily if he should share the secret. He made up his mind quickly because he trusted Jane and knew it would be safe with her. " 'Twas Meg."

"Meg?" Jane could barely conceal her shock.

Graves misread what she was thinking. "None of it was her fault. I hope you won't think badly of her."

"You know me better than that. I'm just surprised is all. And the babe? I didn't realize she had any children."

"She doesn't. The babe was stillborn."

"How does she come to be working for Wessington?"

"Lord Wessington let me bring her here. He let her stay with me while she was increasing and through her childbearing time. He gave her a job after that."

"I can't believe that he would show such kindness to another."

"I know. Not when you see how he acts at other times. It's almost as though he's two people. Deep down, he knows how to do the right thing. It's just hard to get him to do it. But that's why I haven't given up on him. If I thought there was no hope, I'd have left months ago."

Jane sighed. Maybe Graves hadn't given up on Phillip Wessington, but she had. In her eyes, there was nothing worth saving. "So, has he sent for the constables?"

"No. He shut himself in the sitting room after this morning's . . . ah . . . adventure . . . and he hasn't come out."

"Do you think he will send for them?"

Graves merely shrugged. "I'd like to think not."

For the first time, Jane's eyes strayed to the envelopes in his hands. It was a large stack, with several dozen items. "What have you there?"

"You're not going to believe this."

"What?"

"They're invitations. For you. They've been arriving all day. Ever since the first group of guests left early this morning."

"Invitations? Whatever for?"

"Teas, poetry readings, musicales. Several are for more formal events, for which the Earl has already received invitations, but it seems London's finest hostesses want to be certain that he brings you along."

Jane was wide-eyed. "But why would they want to meet me?"

Graves shrugged again. "Have you spent much time around the Quality?"

Jane shook her head.

"They're a fickle lot. Too much time on their hands. Too much money. So few things to care about. Easily bored because of it."

"I'm just a dash of excitement in their otherwise dull existences?"

"That's about the size of it, I'd say. I don't think Lady Margaret is especially liked, either. Everyone probably just wants to get a good look at the woman who gave her her comeuppance."

Jane took the stack and rifled through a few of the offerings near the top. "I'd rather poke my eyes out with a sharp stick than spend one of my afternoons doing any of these things."

"My feelings exactly." Graves chuckled. "So what would you like to do?"

"I have a plan."

"Am I going to like it?"

"I doubt it." Jane stood and headed for her large wardrobe. Since only a handful of items for her trousseau had been finished, it contained few things. "I'm leaving, and I'm going to need your help to get going."

"What if your husband will not allow you to go?"

"Then, I'll go anyway. I don't see how he can stop me."

Phillip sat in the large chair in the corner. The door had only been knocked upon once in all the hours he'd been secluded inside, when one of the servants had worked up the courage to ask if he wanted dinner. His curt no had sent the woman scurrying away. Everyone else had had the good sense to leave him alone. On the opposite side of the room, the spot where the pistol shot had hit the wallpaper, was a dreadful hole with a sooty black rim around it.

Better the wall than his heart, he supposed, although he wasn't sure.

No matter how much he tried to convince himself that there were no similarities between the current situation and the one he'd encountered with his first wife, Anne, he had to admit that they were exactly the same. The only difference being that he had actually shot his wife's lover, crippling him for life. Even now, as he closed his eyes, he could picture the two of them, could feel the rage and the pistol in his hand, could see the look on Richard's face as he accepted his fate that he would be shot and killed by his lifelong best friend.

If only he could reverse his life somehow, go back in time, to that fateful day. How different, he'd always wondered, would his life be now, if his best friend and wife had not betrayed him so despicably? Would he be a better man? A kinder man? A more trusting man? Would a change in the past make any difference at all, or would he simply be what he'd grown to be since that day: a distrustful, lonely fellow, who cared about nothing and no one?

Jane's angry words seemed still to reverberate in the room. *You brought this* woman, *this whore, into my home and invited her to stay as a guest during our wedding celebration? How could you do such a thing to me?* He was truly ashamed of what she'd witnessed and how he'd behaved. Over the past years, he'd done so many horrible things that he was surprised he could feel shame about anything, but he did.

When he'd invited Margaret to attend the wedding, it had seemed only natural. The marriage seemed so inconsequential, the vows so meaningless. As far as Phillip was concerned, it was simply the celebration of the end of his poverty. He wanted all of his friends and acquaintances to be there. Margaret was one of them and had been for a long time.

As for their assignation, he hadn't planned on it in the least, but after leaving Jane's room, he'd spent hours in the quiet darkness of his own, fixated on his memories of her lovely breasts, her beautiful face. His shaft had been rock hard, the soft sacs below aching with unreleased agony. To escape his self-imposed prison, he'd gone downstairs. Margaret had arrived only moments later, almost as if she'd been waiting for just such an encounter. He'd put nothing past her. By the time she'd offered herself up, he'd have accepted a tumble with a street whore to ease some of his suffering, so he wasn't about to refuse her.

But then his wife had walked into the room, and nothing would ever be the same again.

Well, he had to go speak with her. Certainly, enough hours had passed for a calm and rational discussion about their future. He rose and went into the hall, almost expecting a gaggle of servants to be hovering outside. No one was around, and he made his way undisturbed to the door of his wife's chamber. Upon opening it, he found her alone and, much to his surprise, packing her bags.

"Oh, John, I'm going to need a . . ."

She turned, obviously thinking he was Graves. In midstride and midsentence, she stopped when she saw him. To his surprise again, she gave a low curtsy. Hovering there until Phillip wondered if she'd ever rise, he scowled. "For pity's sake, Jane, get up."

Jane hated showing any sign of meekness, but she could be in grave danger if he was still angry. She wanted to leave, and she didn't want to find out what would happen if he refused to let her go. "What is it you wish, milord?"

He looked about at her trunks. "What are you doing?"

"I believe it's obvious, Lord Wessington."

"God's teeth, Jane, will you call me Phillip?"

Jane refused to accept his invitation as a courtesy. "I'm packing to leave."

"I am your husband. When were you going to tell me? Or was it going to be a surprise?"

"I was just about to come downstairs."

"How kind of you to think of me."

She couldn't help but notice the biting tone in his voice. Wessington was a man used to giving orders and having them obeyed without question. Graves had warned her it would be difficult to convince him to accept her plan. Walking to the writing table, she lifted the stack of invitations, handing them over.

"What are these?"

"Invitations for me. They've been arriving all day. It seems that I am suddenly the talk of the town, and I've no wish to be. I am not one of the women to whom you are accustomed. I am highly embarrassed"—she paused, red color flushing her cheeks—"and deeply ashamed. I do not wish to show my face 'round any of these people. I simply could not bear to have them tittering and gossiping behind my back. You know that's what will happen if I remain."

Phillip thought about arguing, but he knew all too

well that she was right. "Where are you planning to go? I thought your father had refused you permission to return home for another six months."

"I was thinking I would go to Rosewood."

"I've no desire to leave London just now."

"Actually, sir"—she looked down at the floor—"I hadn't planned on you accompanying me."

"Well, good. I've no desire to."

"I could meet our daughter, and—"

Phillip cut her off. "I have no daughter."

"Oh, how silly of me." She'd wanted to have a polite discussion without further incurring his wrath, but at his dismissal of parentage, she was unable to keep the sarcasm out of her voice. "I'd forgotten. Emily is simply another one of those people you don't care about. That seems to be the pitiful story of your life, doesn't it?" Needing something to do with her hands, and somewhere to look besides at her husband, she walked to the bed and began folding one of her dresses. "So tell me, sir, is there anything that matters to you? Anything at all?"

"Not really." He shrugged off a world full of possible friendships. "I warned you before we wed, Jane, that I've no redeeming qualities. If you thought I was joking, I'm sorry. I was very serious."

Jane looked at him over her shoulder. Although he was trying to remain aloof and unemotional, all she could see was a lonely, solitary man. "It must be terrible to be so alone. I'm sorry for you. I hope you will find something in your life that makes you happy." In a small part of her heart, she almost wished she'd be there to help him. Almost. She closed the lid to the last trunk and turned to face him.

"If I allow you to go"—Phillip tried to act as if he were still pondering whether to let her, but he could see that she'd go no matter what; one part of him was hurt that she'd leave him so soon, another glad that she was going so he could go about his life undeterred—"what are you planning to do there?"

"A great many things. I've devised a plan for my father's business, to expand it into imports and exports. I need to finalize the details, and that should occupy a great deal of my time."

Phillip wondered if it was the bartering chip she would use with her father to gain his permission to return home. "This is a plan you've thought up yourself?"

"Don't look so surprised, milord." Jane snorted. "Believe it or not, I actually possess a great deal of intelligence."

"I didn't mean to offend you."

"Well, you did. This is something I've been working on for the past two years. I'll enjoy the quiet time to finish it. And Graves and Thumberton tell me there's a great deal of work to be done at Rosewood. Many things need attention. I could begin to see to them."

For the longest time, a precious moment hung in the air between them. It hovered, tempting one or the other to grab hold. A chance at peace. A chance for a truce. A chance for much more. Neither quite knew how to wrap their fingers around it.

Phillip said, "I'm sorry about this morning."

"Sorry for what? Doing it or getting caught?" Phillip looked as though she'd just struck him, so she turned away, tidying up the last of her things. "If you want to be sorry for something, perhaps it should be for the previous night. For ruining something I'd been wondering about and waiting for all my life."

"I thought I was doing the right thing."

"It doesn't matter. At least I know it's not an experience I shall ever want to repeat." With her back to him, she couldn't be sure, but she thought he took a step toward her. The idea of his touching her now, after everything he'd done, was too revolting. She straightened her back and heard him stop. Speaking toward the wall, she said, "I don't have any money for the mail coach, but if you could lend me a few pounds to pay the fare, I'll repay you as soon as I'm able."

"The mail coach? No, you'll take my carriage."

"I've no wish to impose."

"You're my wife. It's not an imposition. You'll take it."

"I'd like Meg to accompany me, so I have a friend when I arrive."

"Yes."

"And John Graves. There will be much to accomplish around the estate. I'll need a trustworthy assistant."

"No, I can't spare him."

Graves had said the Earl wouldn't let him go. How could she take Meg away from John? Oh, well, they'd have to work it out. "And if you could replenish one of the Rosewood accounts, so I'll have a bit to rehire staff and purchase necessities . . ."

"Certainly."

"I'll try to be frugal."

"Jane, it's all right. I trust you with the household accounts."

"Well, then . . ."

"Well . . ."

Jane couldn't believe the tears that had welled to her eyes. Leaving was what she wanted, wasn't it? She never wanted to see her husband again. Never wanted to look at him or hear him speak or converse with him. Then why did she feel so forlorn? Perhaps it was just the stress of all that had happened in the past two months. The weight of it seemed to be crashing down finally. Struggling for composure, she swallowed hard against the lump in her throat, pressed a thumb and finger to the bridge of her nose, urging the tears back from wherever they'd sprung.

She turned to face her husband one last time. "I hope things work out for you, sir. Truly, I do."

"I'll stop by Rosewood this summer. During my visiting."

"All right. Please let us know when you're coming, so we'll be expecting you."

"I will." Phillip couldn't believe the overwhelming urge he suddenly felt to get down on his knees and beg her not to go. If she left there would be no chance for any sort of reconciliation. He'd never have her for a friend or a lover. They'd never share confidences, tell stories, laugh and play together.

But he didn't want that, did he? Hell, no. He didn't want a wife. He didn't want Jane. He had her money, every penny of it, so tightly wrapped in his fist that she didn't even possess the few pounds it would take to pay her fare to the country. That was all he needed. Her money. His whole, rich life, filled with beautiful women, with drinking and gambling and debauchery, beckoned to him like a bright beacon. He couldn't wait to relish the days and months ahead.

If all those things were true, why did he feel so wretched?

"If you need anything, contact me."

"I won't ever need anything from you." *And if I did, I wouldn't ask,* she added silently.

"All right, then." Phillip was embarrassed that she thought him such a poor excuse for a man she'd never turn to him for help. Too late. This was the relationship he'd wished for; now he had it.

"Good-bye, sir."

"Call me Phillip."

Jane shook her head and walked out of the room.

Chapter Fourteen

Emily Wessington, dressed in a split skirt that looked very much like trousers, bounded out the front door of her family home. Mrs. Smythe, the head housekeeper who had lived and worked at Rosewood all of her life, saw her go just as she slipped past the bottom of the stairs. Knowing that the older woman would try to force her back inside in the midst of one of the first nice spring days, Emily increased her speed. The idea of spending the afternoon cooped up in the schoolroom was unthinkable.

Mrs. Smythe despaired over Emily's lack of supervision, but even though she worried about Emily constantly, there were only so many hours in the day. Trying to ensure that the household ran, that there was coal to heat a few rooms in the winter and food on the table for those who'd chosen to remain about the place took up all of her time.

Emily danced outside into the sunshine, smiling

broadly as she realized how easily the housekeeper had given up the chase. Removing the boy's cap she'd carefully hidden in her pocket, she tugged it onto her head and started shoving her hair under the brim. The previous autumn, she'd seen a troupe of performers at the fair and had been fascinated by the possibility of doing tricks with animals, but it was so hard to do any good moves with her curls always falling in the way.

Just as she finished with the last strand, Richard came around the corner. With one real and one peg leg, he limped carefully as he headed her way with her horse. In her small world, he was one of the few adults who seemed to have aged over the slow passing of the years. He looked older, with sad lines around his eyes and his dark hair gone nearly white, but he was still handsome.

Her horse was one of the few left on the estate, though once upon a time her grandfather had boasted of owning one of the finest stables in all of England.

"Well, well, missy, aren't you a sight today. How did you get past Mrs. Smythe in that outfit?"

"I ran out before she could say anything."

He laughed, glad the housekeeper hadn't had the opportunity to cause her any distress. Emily had had too much of it in her life, and he'd vowed from the day of her birth, when Phillip had taken one look at her and promptly left for London, to be the best friend she could have. A best friend in a world where no one wanted her.

She was so pretty, standing there with her unruly ebony curls tucked under her hat. By hiding her hair, she'd only accented her perfect, heart-shaped face. Her blue eyes, as blue as the summer sky, stared out at him over rosy cheeks and ruby lips. What a man-killer she would grow to be in a few years. And, with her kind-hearted nature and pleasant manner, the gentlemen would be falling over themselves to win her hand.

How Phillip could go through life without recognizing the gem he'd sired was a complete mystery to Richard. The idiot's stupid pride kept him from admitting that she was his daughter. Only a blind man would fail to see their resemblance. In every way, she was the spitting image of Phillip Wessington. The only hint that she'd had a mother was in her astonishing blue eyes.

"So what will it be today, Mistress Emily? Running leaps? Daring handstands?"

"You know I can't do any of those things."

"Oh . . . all right." He smiled. "How about standing on his bare back?"

She managed to mount the horse by herself, but Richard steadied her while she rose to her feet. He dropped out the lead line, and the horse, seeming to know the value of his cargo, took tiny, slow steps in a measured circle. Both man and girl were so engrossed in their practice session that neither of them noticed the carriage coming up the drive. Emily concluded her ride by dismounting with a somersault which landed her on shaky feet next to Richard.

A woman's laughter and clapping of hands brought them up short. They did not have many visitors anymore. A neighbor might stop. Morris came occasionally, wanting to check on Emily for her father, or so he said. But rarely anyone else.

Emily stepped forward. The carriage looked new and bore her family's crest on the side, which immediately caused her heart to pound. Had her father decided to arrive unannounced?

His visits were a double-edged sword which left her happy and desolate—happy because she loved him so; desolate, because with each visit, she hoped in her tender heart that he would show her some attention, some kindness. But he never did.

She didn't know why he didn't care for her. If someone would only tell her the reason, she'd fix herself. Everyone said he liked her just fine, but she knew it was a lie. Her father hated her, and she had no idea of the cause. More than once, she'd wondered if he was disappointed she'd been born a girl.

The carriage door opened, and a woman stepped out onto the ground without waiting for any help from the footman. She had reddish brown hair, pulled back and braided about her head, and was wearing a simple gray dress with white collar and cuffs. Emily's first reaction was one of dread. Had her father finally gotten around to sending a new governess?

"What a wonderful trick," the woman gushed enthusiastically. "I've never seen anything like it."

"May I help you?" Emily asked.

"I hope so. I'm here to meet Emily Wessington and the head housekeeper, Mrs. Smythe."

"I'm Emily Wessington." She raised her chin as though to dare the woman to say something about her manner of dress. She was almost disappointed when the stranger didn't seem to notice what she was wearing.

"Well, now that you say your name, I can see that you are. The resemblance to your father is uncanny."

"Are you my new governess?"

"Goodness, no."

"Who are you then?"

"Jane Wessington."

Emily wrinkled her brow. "I don't have any relatives by that name."

"Oh, dear, I'm wondering if the Earl's message never made it." Jane had expected some sort of welcome—

if not one with open arms, at least some acknowledgment by the staff and Emily. Whatever to do now?

Seeking assistance from wherever she could find it, Jane turned her attention to the crippled, white-haired man who'd been helping Emily with her horse. When they'd first pulled up the drive, Jane had thought him elderly. Now, up close, she could see that he was probably the same age as her husband. His white hair, and the sad lines on his brow and cheeks, made him look older. "And who might you be, sir?"

Emily knew that she should never tell her father, or anyone else who might know him, that Richard was still at the estate. Richard's presence was just one of the many secrets they all kept from him. No one would ever tell her why her father hated Richard, too, but he could never know that Richard was on the property. If he did, he would send him away. Emily couldn't bear the thought of losing her friend or of hurting him in any way.

She stepped in front of him, blocking him from Jane's view. "He's no one. I mean he's someone, but not anyone you'd be interested in. He was just . . . ah . . . looking at my horse. Thinking of buying it since it's one of the last ones left. But he was just leaving." Emily flashed Richard a pleading look, hoping he wouldn't argue.

Jane couldn't figure out what was wrong. For some reason, Emily was lying, and lying badly, about the white-haired man. She obviously didn't want Jane to know who he was. Well, there were bigger hills to climb at the moment. "Perhaps we'll meet later."

"Yes, perhaps we will," the man responded guardedly, his gray eyes taking in every detail of Jane, from head to toe. "Are you Emily's new tutor?"

"No, I'm . . . Oh, it's difficult to explain, and I'm

famished from my trip. If I could find a bite to eat and a spot of tea, I'm sure I'll find it easier to explain everything."

"Explain it now."

The man insisted, not in a forceful or rude manner. In some way, he'd made the words seem like a polite request. Jane wasn't certain, but it seemed as though he might not let her into the house unless he knew her business. "Actually, I'm *Lady* Jane Wessington. I'm married to the Earl."

The silence was almost deafening, as if even the birds and spring crickets had been stunned by her declaration. From the look of the two people facing her, the announcement had been a complete mistake.

Emotions rushed across Emily's face. Confusion, anger, caution. Surprise. "I don't believe it."

"It's true, Emily. I'm sorry to blurt it out like that."

"But Father never said anything."

"He was supposed to have sent a message."

The man interjected. "Please don't mind us. We're just surprised. We never received any word."

"I understand. Really, I do. It all happened so quickly, I can hardly believe it myself sometimes."

"But if you married Father, that would make you my . . . my . . ." Emily looked as though the word were too distasteful to be spoken aloud.

"I'm afraid so. I'm your new stepmother. Believe me when I say it seems as strange to me as it does to you."

Emily ran a hand through the air vertically, indicating Jane's unassuming hair and dress. "But you're so plain!"

"Emily!" The man's rebuke was sharp. "Mind your manners! Apologize this instant."

"No, no, it's all right." Jane, wanting only to ease the girl's distress, took no offense. "I do look a sight, don't I? 'Twas easier traveling in such a fashion, but I would greatly love to clean up and rest a bit. Then I'll answer all your questions."

"Of course, Lady Wessington," the man said. "Let's get you inside. Mrs. Smythe will be beside herself." He looked at Emily who stood by, pale and barely breathing. "Why don't you run ahead, Emily? Tell Mrs. Smythe that we've a guest." He looked back at Jane and offered his arm. "Oh, pardon me, I mean a new addition to the household."

Emily didn't move, but continued to stare at Jane. Although Jane couldn't quite read her emotion, there was nothing kindly in it. Perhaps it was hatred; perhaps it was envy. She wasn't sure. "Go in now, Emily," she said softly. "I'll be along in a moment, and we'll talk as long as you wish."

"I don't want to talk to you. Ever!" The girl spun around and raced for the door, quickly disappearing inside.

Jane glanced at her companion and sighed. "Well, I'd say I handled that perfectly, wouldn't you?"

"Please forgive her. I don't know if anyone's mentioned it to you, but Emily's relationship with her father is a difficult one. I'm sure she's just wondering where she'll fit in now that he's married."

"Funny, but I've been wondering the same thing about myself. I'd say she and I have a lot in common."

Jane spent the first few days learning her way about the house, memorizing the names and faces of the small staff who had remained on the property, discovering some of the workings of the large household. The only thing she didn't learn more about was Emily, who kept a discreet distance, never joined her for tea or meals and never seemed to be present when Jane was in the room. Jane left her alone, knowing she'd come around when she was ready.

By the beginning of the second week, her life was becoming routine. Meg and Graves had arrived. Graves had resigned from Wessington's service when the Earl refused to let him come to Rosewood. They were working with Mrs. Smythe to get the household back in order. With the two of them taking over so many tasks, Jane had finally found the time to begin examining the estate books. To her surprise, they were up to date, carefully kept and appeared to be extremely accurate.

After spending most of the day perusing the numbers, she came to the unmistakable conclusion that the estate was like a ferocious, starved sea creature, intent on devouring everything in its path. Great amounts of money were expended, but very little seemed to be generated in return. No wonder the Earl had found himself in financial trouble.

Jane knew how much money he'd been given as her dowry. While it was a large amount, it was clear that in a few years they'd find themselves right back in the financial doldrums if something wasn't done and done quickly to change the course of things. Jane wasn't sure what action to take, and she doubted if the Earl knew. But someone had to know.

Mrs. Smythe happened to be walking down the hall at the moment and poked her head in the library door, inquiring after Jane's comfort.

Jane commented, "I've been reading over the estate books, and they're very well put together. Tell me, who has been charged with the responsibility these past years?"

"Master Richard, Lady Jane," Mrs. Smythe answered without thinking.

Ah, the mysterious Richard Farrow. "Is he about at the moment?"

"I believe he's down at the stables with Emily."

"Would you send word that I need to see him immediately?"

Mrs. Smythe worried over her bottom lip, wondering if she should say something, all the while knowing she couldn't refuse to carry out her lady's order. "I'll see to it, milady," she finally said.

"Don't look so disturbed, ma'am. I only wish to speak with him."

Richard appeared some time later and stood silently in the doorway, watching Jane pore over a long string of numbers. She finally noticed him and looked up as he straightened. "Pardon me for staring, milady. I didn't know you'd be taking an interest in any of the properties."

"From these numbers, I'd say it's high time someone did."

He shrugged. "We've tried to maintain as best we could."

"I wasn't judging. Please sit." She indicated the chair across from her, but felt quite certain that Master Farrow was much more used to sitting behind the desk than in front of it. "The books are very well kept. And I can see that you've expended a great deal of effort on a losing cause. It has been *your* effort, hasn't it?"

He remained politely silent.

"So tell me, sir: what is the grand secret? You work here, but you don't. You live here, but you don't. You manage the financial affairs, but you don't."

Her statements finally brought a smile to his lips. "I will tell you the truth, milady, but I ask only this: if you decide to tell your husband, please promise you'll not mention Emily's knowing about me."

"Knowing what about you?"

"That I'm here."

"Why shouldn't you be here?"

"Because Phillip would be most upset." He squirmed slightly in his chair. "He and I grew up here together. We had a parting of the ways many years ago."

"You're no longer friends?"

"To put it bluntly, Lady Jane, your husband hates me. If he found me here, he'd run me off at pistol-point."

"But you keep staying, helping with the land, with the animals, with Emily."

He shrugged again. "My family has served here at Rosewood for centuries. It is my home, the only place I've ever lived. I love it here, and Phillip has hated it for many years now. If I hadn't seen to things all this time, who would have?"

"And my husband? Who does he think is running things?"

"I really don't think he worries on it overly much. He only stops by once a year for a few days, usually in the summer while he's traveling to someplace else. Whenever something important happens, I send word to Master Thumberton, who passes it on to the Earl for decision. He's never asked where the information comes from; I believe he thinks Thumberton has a man here who's in charge."

Jane rubbed her eyes. "Unbelievable."

"I'm sorry, milady. I didn't mean to distress you."

"You haven't. I'm just shaking my head because my husband is so witless when it comes to running these huge estates. How can he expect things to continue in such a fashion?"

"I don't know his thinking, but I do know that many changes are needed."

"Yes, I agree. I hope you're ready to get to work. I've need of a good teacher so I can get my hands 'round the root of the problems."

"So, you'll not tell your husband I'm here?"

"Master Farrow"—Jane raised an eyebrow—"I've come to the early opinion that what my husband doesn't know, won't hurt him."

Richard smiled in secret accord. "Lady Jane, it shall be my pleasure to have you as a student. Let me begin by saying that we are sitting on some of the finest farmland in all of England . . ."

Chapter Fifteen

Phillip struggled into his coat. The new tailor had created some excellent items, but this one's sleeves were a bit tight. Looking over his shoulder, he hoped to see his new manservant stepping through the door, ready to offer assistance. Of course, he did not. The fellow was impossible. He was never around when needed, and always seemed to be underfoot when he wasn't.

Cursing John Graves, he yanked at his cravat, which ruined the knot so he had to tie it all over again, causing the curses to flow even more freely. The man had only worked for him for three years. How could one become so attached to a bloody servant in such a short time? The ungrateful wretch. Just as things were looking up, he'd run off. Phillip had tried to find him, had even suffered the indignity of having a Bow Street runner make inquiries, but the man seemed to have vanished.

In the time they'd spent together, Phillip had never asked about his family, background or life, so he had no idea where Graves had come from or to where he might return. All Phillip knew was that the man was gone and apparently gone for good.

"I hope you're starving in the streets, you bloody ingrate!" Phillip muttered as he headed down the stairs. At the bottom, with still no sign of his manservant or anyone else, he stood silently fuming. Where was everyone?

He needed his wife. He needed Jane in London to see to all this nonsense, to hire these people and to manage them. That was what wives did! What was the sense of marrying if one's wife refused to carry out her obligations? She hadn't even stayed long enough to receive the trunks of new gowns for which she'd been fitted. The accursed things filled several closets in the house, a silent and damning reminder of everything that was wrong with his life.

Cursing himself for a fool for letting her leave, and cursing her much more fluently than he'd done with Graves, he walked to the small cloakroom in the hall and found his own bloody cloak and hat. Just as he started for the door, his manservant appeared.

"May I be of assistance, milord?" the man asked in a bored voice.

"Go take a nap or something." Phillip waved him off irritably and walked outside. His carriage was not waiting as it was supposed to be. After several minutes, he heard the sound of horses' hooves and wheels turning. The driver, another name and face to learn, rushed the horses up the path.

There had been a constant influx of new people as he'd tried to return his house to some of its earlier grandeur, and he'd run into problems every step of the way. Excellent servants were quickly swept up and kept by their employers. Phillip had been forced to rummage through the remaining dregs. Now his house was filled with people he didn't know, people who didn't care about him and people he didn't care about.

Things would have been so much different if Jane had remained. He wasn't sure how he knew, he just did. For the thousandth time, he cursed her again. How could a woman he barely knew, who'd been nothing but trouble from the moment he'd met her, continue to plague his mind every moment of the day and night? Well, the Season was quickly coming to a close, and people would begin returning to their country estates in the next two weeks. He had half a mind to postpone his visiting and head straight to Rosewood. He'd put his foot down and order her back to London, although he wasn't certain what he'd do with her if she returned.

The past night as he'd sat in his cold, silent, dreary bedchamber, pondering the miserable state of his life, he'd realized that he'd grown to be such a despicable cad that even his own wife wouldn't live with him. Once upon a time, the knowledge wouldn't have mattered. For some reason, it mattered now, more than he wanted it to. Something about those marriage vows, repeated before God and the assembled company, had had more of an effect on him than he'd imagined possible.

He approached the carriage. "I'm attending the Miltons' ball. Do you know the place?"

"Certainly, sir," the driver said with a tip of his hat.

The carriage took off with a jolt, and Phillip relaxed against the smooth leather seat, but, as the driver twisted and turned through London's streets, Phillip knew the imbecile had no idea where they were going. It took three times as long as it should have to reach their destination.

There were numerous balls going on that night, each one fancier and more excessive than the last, as all tried to wring as many seconds of enjoyment as possible out of their remaining time in London. Phillip had selected to begin the evening at the Miltons' for the simple reason that it was the least likely spot to run into Margaret.

Ever since the fateful morning after, he'd avoided Margaret like the plague. Whenever he thought about contacting her, he remembered how Jane had looked, standing there shocked and hurt and humiliated. He couldn't bear many repeats of that mental image, so he'd sent Margaret a note, telling her they'd have to lie low for a time until the gossip and scandal abated, although he fully intended never to see her again.

The only downside he could see was that splitting with her had wreaked havoc on his sex life. As a man used to finding release wherever and whenever he chose, the situation left him surly and in a constant state of discomfort. It had gotten so bad that he was seriously considering keeping a prostitute at one of the finer brothels.

For now, he was unattached, which meant he was seen with various women, but with his self-imposed restriction of not escorting the same one more than three times in a row. Tonight it was the Russian countess.

Entering the ballroom, he huddled along a side wall, scanning the crowd, looking for but not seeing her. As he continued his visual search, his eyes widened as they settled on a chestnut-haired woman across the room. From the side, she was the spitting image of Jane, but just as he wondered if she'd slipped back into the city without notifying him, the woman turned and he could see from her pinched expression and dour look that there was a close resemblance, but she was not Jane. She was too plump, too plain, and too miserable with herself and her surroundings.

She was dressed in simple clothing, outdated and terribly modest for the occasion. The white-haired older gentleman on her right wore a jacket that looked like something a seafaring man of high rank might wear. The balding younger man on her left was the only one of the three dressed appropriately for the affair. Watching the woman as she stood, morosely out of place between the two men, he had the worst sense of foreboding.

He made his way to the side of Lady Carrington, an old friend and lover before her latest marriage. She made it a point to know everyone's business, but she also knew how to keep a secret for her close friends. He slipped next to her. "See that odd-looking trio over there?"

"Certainly. How could one miss them?"

"Who are they?"

"You truly don't know?" Phillip shook his head as her laughter rippled quietly around the two of them. From a passing waiter's tray, she picked up a glass of champagne. "Take this," she said, handing it to him. "You're going to need it, and more than a few people are watching, so try not to show any reaction."

"To what?"

"To what I'm going to say." She raised a brow. "They're your in-laws."

It took every ounce of his self-possession to keep from spewing the mouthful of champagne he'd just sipped.

His face carefully blank, he swallowed, then took another long drink. "You're joking."

"Not at all, dear heart. It's Charles Fitzsimmons, with his older daughter and his son-in-law. They're richer than God, or so I hear." She paused, waiting to hear how Phillip would respond.

"So I hear," he said neutrally. "What are they doing here?"

"The old gaffer's in town to announce some new venture for the family business. Meeting with bankers and other people in the industry."

"About what?"

"I guess his brilliant son-in-law came up with the idea to branch out into exports/imports, using the family ships or something. It's very big news. Very big, if you're interested in that sort of thing."

Phillip frowned. "But . . . 'twas Jane's idea."

"What was?"

"Nothing." He had no desire to get into a discussion of his wife's business acumen. Clutching his glass, he surreptitiously eyed his in-laws, knowing he had to go introduce himself. The people in attendance who knew his relationship to the Fitzsimmonses had to be circling like sharks, waiting to watch the meeting. With great reluctance, he started across the room.

Proper etiquette required that he ask the hostess, or someone else who knew the Fitzsimmonses, to make an introduction. Since he could think of no way to tell Lady Milton that he'd never met his in-laws without creating a huge wave of gossip, he walked purposively and stepped in front of Charles, acting as though they had always known each other. He gave a polite bow.

"Sir, please excuse my forward behavior, but I couldn't wait to make your acquaintance. I am Phillip Wessington."

"Wessington?"

Charles Fitzsimmons eyed him for several seconds, looking perplexed, as though the name was familiar but he couldn't quite place it. God's teeth, the man had recently handed over his daughter, plus tens of thousands of pounds, and he couldn't recall the name of the man to whom he'd given it all! He added acerbically, "Jane's *husband.*"

"Oh, Wessington. Yes." The man extended a hand, giving Phillip's a hearty shake, but oddly, his eyes were nervously scanning the surrounding crowd.

Phillip said, "It's good to meet you, sir."

"And you, my boy. And you." He cleared his throat. "Is . . . ah . . . is Jane with you?"

"No. She's retired to one of my country estates."

"Yes . . . well . . . pity we'll miss her," Fitzsimmons said, though he didn't look saddened by the fact at all. He looked greatly relieved. "May I introduce Jane's sister, Gertrude?"

"Madam." Phillip bowed over her hand, and Gertrude curtsied politely enough, but the look she gave him was one of complete distaste.

Charles continued. "And your brother-in-law, Gregory Fitzsimmons."

Gregory had paled, as though he'd just received a great shock. "You're Jane's husband?"

"That's what the minister said at the end of the ceremony," Phillip responded sarcastically.

"I meant no offense, sir. I'm just surprised. We had heard she'd married an Earl, but . . . ." Gregory couldn't find the words to express his shock at the handsome, virile nobleman standing in front of him. He'd pictured Jane's husband as some frumpy, balding, obese fellow. Not this man! He cleared his throat and adjusted his cravat which suddenly felt much too tight. "Jane is very much like a beautiful jewel. I hope you realize what a gem you have in your possession."

"I assure you, I do," Phillip said, as Gertrude glared at Gregory with incredible malice. Phillip looked from father to daughter to son-in-law and felt a stab of compassion for Jane. How had she managed to remain so vibrant and unsullied after spending her life around these people?

Although he didn't mean it in the least, he felt obligated to say, "I'd like to invite you to dine with me while you're in London."

"I'm sorry, Wessington," Charles said, "but we're leaving for Portsmouth tomorrow."

"What a pity we'll not get to know one another better." Phillip sighed with relief. A dreadful evening avoided!

"I should like to speak with you, though. Privately. Do you know this house? Is there some place where we could talk?"

"Yes," Phillip answered, motioning down a hallway. "The library is this way."

When they would have followed, a look from Charles kept Gregory and Gertrude rooted in their places. Phillip silently led the way and ushered the man into a room, then poured each of them a glass of brandy.

"I don't usually indulge in spirits," Charles mentioned as he accepted the glass. "Dulls the mind, you know? But I believe I will just this once."

The more words the man spoke, the happier Phillip was that he wasn't going to have to socialize with him. He never trusted a fellow who didn't drink. For the first time, he noticed that the older gentleman seemed uncomfortable. He was sweating profusely, his cheeks red and overheated. "Are you feeling all right, sir?"

"I've felt a bit under the weather all day." Fitzsimmons tugged at his collar. "Probably the excitement of seeing Gregory's plan put into action. And the stress of being away from home. Never did like to travel."

"I understand."

"So, how is Jane?"

"Fine," Phillip lied. No way would he tell his father-in-law that he hadn't talked to her in three months.

"The wedding went off without a hitch?"

"Yes."

"And the money? The transfer was satisfactory?"

"Certainly."

Charles took out a kerchief and began mopping his brow, feeling more discomfort by the moment. "I've a bit of a confession to make."

"What is it, sir?"

"When I required Jane to wed, I did it to force her out of the family business."

"Why was that necessary?"

"Well, she was so capable, you see, and so interested. I'd let her dally at it for years, and I have to admit, I'd come to rely on her. But my years at the helm are coming to a close, and I simply couldn't have her continue. I expect she'd have wanted to take charge."

Phillip couldn't help but marvel at how protective he felt of Jane at hearing of her being manipulated by this pompous ass. He knew the answer, but asked anyway just to irritate the older man, "Why couldn't she?"

"Because she's a female, of course." Charles looked at him as though he were the thickest man alive.

"Of course," Phillip responded dryly.

"I've no sons, so I've been grooming Gregory for years to take over when I retire. I occasionally had my doubts about his capabilities, but with his new plans for expansion, I see that I was right all along."

"And you're certain Gregory's the man, are you?"

"His plan is brilliant. Simply brilliant."

"Well, good for you. I'm sure Jane will be glad to hear of it."

"Her thoughts on the matter are neither here nor there." Charles shrugged. "What I want is a commitment from you."

"In what regard?"

"When I commanded Jane to find herself a husband, I promised her that, if she carried out my wishes, she could return home after spending six months adjusting to her new life. Perhaps she's mentioned it?"

"Yes, a time or two."

"I figured six months would be plenty of time for her to find herself with child, and her maternal duties would then overwhelm her. Working on that situation, are you?"

Phillip felt himself blushing. The audacity of the man! "Is there a point here, sir?"

"Of course, there's a point. You'll not let her return, will you?"

"No. I've no intention of allowing her to return." He'd do everything in his power to see that she was never put upon by these dreadful people again.

"Good. Good. I'll not let her back. I'm sorry to strap you with the problem, but she's very headstrong and used to getting her own way. My fault, I suppose. I always indulged her." He took a long sip of the brandy, then coughed ferociously.

Fitzsimmons's pallor seemed to have increased with each passing moment. Phillip was actually becoming alarmed. "Are you certain you're all right?"

"Perhaps if I just sit down for a bit." He moved as though to step to the chair, then stopped. With a puzzled look, he gasped for breath then collapsed to the floor.

"For pity's sake, Fitzsimmons! What are you about?" Phillip rushed to the hall to call for help.

Chapter Sixteen

Jane leaned back against the chair and raised her hands over her head in a long stretch. It felt good to be working so hard, to be doing things that were so necessary.

Although she'd never imagined it at the time of her marriage, she was needed at Rosewood. The people who lived and worked at the estate, along with those in the surrounding villages who depended on the solvency of the properties for their welfare and incomes, welcomed her attention and management. And, much to her surprise, she found that she needed them; their support, interest and respect were touching and overwhelming.

With Richard's careful guidance and shrewd suggestions, everything was falling into place. Within five years, they'd be far into the black, and within ten, the estate would, once again, be one of the most productive in England.

There was a strange, unexpected satisfaction in

accomplishing so much. People from the village were returning to work. In a very short time, she'd begun providing gainful employment for so many, helping them feed their families, and people were grateful, thankful for the efforts she'd made on their behalf.

Curiously, she'd never felt such gratification while working for her father. Because she was a female, the men actually building the ships were kept far away from her. Her contact had been mostly with the accountants and the clerks working in the offices. All of them had been polite, helpful, but none of them had ever looked to her with thanks in their eyes for putting bread on their table.

And her father . . . Over the years, she'd thought he appreciated her help, that he welcomed her assistance and cherished her for her abilities, but now, upon looking back, there hadn't been much pride in his attitude toward her.

The Fitzsimmons Shipworks was her life. It was her future. Her birthright, but for the first time ever, she felt no joy in the thought of returning to it. With a twinge of regret, she noticed on the calendar that her possible departure for Portsmouth could come in as soon as two months. Then what? What if she went home? To Father, with his harsh, demanding ways. To Gertrude, with her cruel, hurtful words. To Gregory, who would once again begin pressuring her to do something she now knew was wrong and impossible.

Better to stay at Rosewood, except that she wasn't sure she belonged here either. If Emily's attitude was any indication, she never would. The girl simply was not warming to her in any sense. While Jane's original plan had been to leave her alone while she came to terms with her father's marriage, she was now having second thoughts.

With everything else running so smoothly, it was time to take the matter in hand. However, if she couldn't even get the girl to sit down for a chat, how could she ever dress her appropriately or calm her manners?

Closing the account book in front of her, she looked up just as Meg stepped into the room. Meg had truly blossomed in the warm, country sunshine. Her skin was tan and healthy looking, her red hair radiant from the time spent outdoors. Jane smiled. "Ah, just the person I was looking for."

She carried a large basket of fresh-cut flowers which she began arranging. "I picked these myself. What do you think?"

"They're lovely. All my favorites."

"What did you wish to see me about?" Meg asked casually as she worked at the bouquet.

"Well, Graves once mentioned to me that you'd worked previously as a governess."

Meg's fingers stilled, her eyes stared at the desktop. She finally sighed, " 'Tis true, Jane."

"Did you enjoy it?"

"Well, yes, I did enjoy it." She swallowed hard. "What is it you wish to know?"

"I was wondering if you'd be interested in becoming Emily's governess. She's desperately in need of some guidance and attention. I can't think of anyone who would be better suited."

"Oh, Jane." Meg flushed bright red. "I'm very flattered that you think so highly of me."

"Of course, I do. Why wouldn't I?"

"Well, I'm afraid I wouldn't be the least bit appropriate to guide a young girl to womanhood."

"Nonsense. I can think of no one better."

"But there's something I need to tell you . . ."

Jane leaned forward and wrapped her hand around

Meg's. Squeezing tightly, she said quietly, "There's nothing you need to tell me. I've learned everything about you that I need to know, and I don't need to learn one iota more."

Meg raised her eyes to Jane's. "You've known all this time?"

"Graves told me quite awhile ago."

"That rat!"

"He felt he was protecting you. Don't be angry."

"But doesn't it matter? What happened to me?"

"Not a whit."

"I feel so unworthy because of it. You're certain?"

"More certain than I've been of anything in a long time. Emily has been entrusted to my care, and I can't think of anyone I'd rather have helping me watch over her."

"Thank you, Jane." Meg's eyes brimmed with unshed tears. "Thank you so much."

"Does that mean you accept?"

"Yes, I do, but I'd say we've got our hands full."

"I'd say you're right."

They talked at length about what to do with the girl, how to calm her down and round the rough edges without quashing her energy and natural appeal. It would be a daunting task.

After Meg left, Jane was turning her attention to another project just as the butler poked his nose through the door, looking for Emily.

"Master Morris has come to visit her," he announced.

"Who is Master Morris, might I inquire?"

The butler cleared his throat and looked away. "He is a neighbor, milady. And a good friend of your husband's. He stops by regularly to converse with Lady Emily to ensure that her needs are being accommodated in her father's absence."

"Please show him into the day room. Offer refreshments."

"Already done, milady."

"Thank you, sir. Inform him that I will be down shortly to meet with him."

The butler bowed his way out of the room, and Jane closed the book on top of the stack. As she stepped around the desk, she caught sight of a pair of small, dust-covered boots sticking out from under the drapes. Emily, the scamp! How long had she been hiding and listening? She must have heard the entire conversation with Meg.

Jane walked to the door and closed it, pretending to have left, then stood quietly. Not more than a minute passed before the fabric rustled and the girl slipped out, silent as a mouse. She walked to the desk and began rifling through Jane's papers.

"Eavesdropping is dreadfully impolite."

At the sound of Jane's voice, she jumped sky-high. "Lady Jane, I didn't know you were still here."

"Obviously." Jane crossed her arms over her chest and tapped a toe against the flooring. "Well, what have you got to say for yourself?"

Emily fidgeted, pulling at the sides of her dress, a dreadful brown thing that she'd outgrown. The sleeves were too short, the hem too high. Looking everywhere but in Jane's direction, she said, "I was lost?"

"Try again."

"I was looking for something?"

"Again." Jane made a whirling motion with her hand, urging the girl to hurriedly run through her string of lies.

After three more inane attempts, Emily threw up her hands. "I give up. I was snooping. There! Are you happy now?"

"Actually, yes I am. Very happy. When we speak to one another, I'd like to think that we could always tell each other the truth."

"Why?"

"So I'll know what you're thinking and feeling."

"Why ever would you care about that?"

"Because you are my daughter, like it or not. And that means something to me."

Out of the blue, she asked, "Why did you marry my father?"

Jane thought about prevaricating, but it wouldn't be a good beginning for the two of them. "My own father decided it was time I wed. He commanded that I find a husband. To speed matters along, he offered a huge dowry."

"So Father married you for your money?"

"Yes. Yes, he did." The admission to his daughter, that there hadn't been any more to it than that, hurt more than it should have. Jane had to swallow against the terrible lump in her throat.

Emily was surprised to see the tears of hurt spring to Jane's eyes. All this time, she'd imagined that Jane had tricked her father into marriage. He was so handsome, so dashing, accompanied by only the most beautiful, glamorous women. From the beginning, Jane had seemed so ordinary. He wouldn't have married her unless she'd worked some ulterior plan. Now, seeing the tears left her confused. "You didn't wish to marry him?"

"No. I didn't. I'm sorry if the truth hurts you, but I had very little say in the matter."

"And what does my father think about you?"

"I'd say he thinks very little about me, probably. I left London the day after the wedding, and I haven't heard a word from him since. I'd say he was glad to have my money, but even more glad to be rid of me." There were those tears again. Such awful admissions, but better that the girl learn the facts up front rather than letting her garner any false hopes about her parents' union.

"But ... but ... that's horrible." Emily couldn't believe the flood of compassion she felt for Jane's plight. The girl knew better than anyone what it was like to stand on the outside of her father's life looking in.

"Well, I wouldn't say horrible. It was an arranged marriage, and I could have ended up in a situation much worse."

"If he doesn't love you either, what's to become of us?"

As Emily's eyes flooded with tears of her own, Jane wondered how she'd ever be able to leave Rosewood when this beautiful, lonely girl needed her so desperately. "I was hoping you and I could build a life together. That we could be friends and companions."

"You would wish to be friends with me? After the way I've treated you?"

"You haven't done anything to me. You've simply been trying to come to terms with the shocking news caused by my arrival."

"I am sorry, though, for the way I've been acting."

"I know, dear." Jane smiled down at her and held out a hand. "Friends?"

"I've never had a lady friend before. I believe I'd like that ever so much." Emily clasped Jane's hand in her own.

"Now, why don't you tell me why you were hiding in here?"

Emily paused, wondering if she'd be able to explain it so Jane would understand. "I was hiding from Master Morris."

"Your visitor?"

'Yes. I don't have to go sit with him, do I?"

"If he's a friend of your father's, it would be impolite of us to snub him."

"But perhaps, just this once, you could go without me."

"Why is it that you don't wish to see him? Has he offended you in some way?"

"Well, you see ... it's just that"—Emily blushed bright red and looked down at her feet as the words gushed out—"it's just that he always makes me sit on his lap even though I don't like it, and he insists I kiss him good-bye. 'On the lips, now,' he says, because Father told him we're to be married! I don't have to marry him, do I?"

"Marry?" Jane's brow creased in concern. "You must have misunderstood."

"No, no. He said it. That Father was going to have us marry this year 'on my birthday,' and 'wouldn't that be grand?' I think it would be horrible. If I married him, I'd have to go away with him, wouldn't I? I don't want to. I want to stay here with you and Richard and Mrs. Smythe. And my horse. And I was thinking we might get a dog. A very big one."

The girl *had* to be mistaken. She was only eleven years old. Even Phillip, in his jaded state, wouldn't do such a thing. Would he? A trickle of dread pricked her spine, because she knew girls were wed at twelve years all the time. "Emily, you don't have to meet with him. Not ever again. And I'll speak to your father. I'm certain you just misunderstood what Master Morris told you. Don't worry on this overly much. Promise me that you won't."

"All right, but it has been keeping me quite vexed for some time now."

"I can imagine that it would. You run along."

"Thank you, Jane." Emily ran forward and hugged her tightly around the waist. Jane hugged her back for a long moment until Emily pulled away. "Is Meg truly to be my governess?"

"If you'd like her to be."

"I think I would."

"Good, we'll try it then and see how it works. Why don't you go find her? I was thinking we will all need some new dresses and perhaps a few gowns for the Harvest Fair coming in September. I'm sure there will be several events and parties to attend. You can talk with her about what would be appropriate and what colors we should select. She has a grand eye for fashion, and she'll know all about the latest styles in London. We'll need to call for the seamstress in the village."

"You'll get a new one also?"

"We'll both get several."

A few minutes later, Jane entered the drawing room to find Morris sitting by himself, quietly sipping a cup of tea. At first glance, viewed in profile, he seemed harmless enough, young and handsome, foppishly dressed in his blue coat and tan breeches, his black boots shined to perfection. When he heard Jane enter and looked her way, she was surprised to see he was much older than she'd imagined. The thought of him calling on Emily was distressing. No wonder the girl was begging for help. How long had the *visits* been going on, and what did the Earl really know about them?

Morris was obviously expecting to see Emily, and when he didn't, his blue eyes turned a frighteningly deep shade. Jane had the strangest flash of memory from her childhood, of sitting on her uncle's lap in a darkened corner and trying to pull away from his grasp. Funny it should surface now.

She couldn't have said precisely what it was about him that made her so uncomfortable, but it only took one look for her to know that Emily would never spend another moment in the man's company.

"Master Morris? I am Jane Wessington."

"Pleased to meet you, Lady Wessington. I must say, with the Earl still in London, I wasn't expecting to find you here."

Obviously, she thought. He stood and bowed over her hand. As his skin touched hers, she had to fight the urge to pull away. Once he let go, she waited until he'd glanced away, then wiped her palm against her skirt. "I'm told you're here to call on Lady Emily."

"Yes. I am an old friend of the Earl's. Since I am home more often than he, he likes me to stop by to check on the girl. She is quite dear to me. I care for her as though she were my own daughter."

His words rang hollow, and Jane couldn't help the feeling of revulsion that crept over her. She wanted the man gone, and no matter how terribly he reported her behavior to her husband, she wanted to make it clear that he wasn't welcome back. "I'm sorry, but Lady Emily is very busy just now. I've retained a new governess for her. She's receiving instruction at the moment."

Morris knew it was a bald-faced lie. He'd seen the child through the window, skipping in the garden, moments before Lady Wessington entered the room. His eyes darkened, his face flushed. He hated most women, but especially women like Jane with her air of authority and superiority. "Perhaps I could wait. I'm sure the Earl would like a report when I return to London."

"There is no need for you to trouble yourself. I'm afraid I've rearranged her days, and her schedule is now extremely full. Her time will be completely occupied until nightfall.''

"I see," Morris said, rising.

He did see; Jane could tell. The message had gotten through loudly and clearly, and although he was doing a good job of controlling his temper, inside he was seething. "Thank you for stopping," she said as sweetly as she could, but her lack of sincerity was obvious.

"What shall I tell the Earl when I see him?"

"You needn't tell him anything. I will tell him everything he needs to know. Good day, sir."

The butler, with impeccable timing, was waiting at the door with Morris's hat, and he stomped out and off without another word.

"Anything else, milady?" the butler asked.

"Yes, there is one thing, and I want you to spread the word among the staff. Master Morris should never again be allowed to call on Lady Emily. If he shows up requesting a visit, entrance should be denied. To avoid any unpleasantness, you may tell him you're simply following my orders and dare not go against my wishes."

"And what about the Earl's instructions?"

"Don't worry, I'll handle the Earl. No matter what, that man is not welcome around Emily."

She turned and walked away. Deep in thought, she didn't hear the butler remark, "Well done, Lady Jane. Well done."

Chapter Seventeen

Phillip rode through the village outside Rosewood and couldn't believe the attitudes of the people. For years, other than by an occasional wave when he passed, he'd barely been acknowledged. Now, people were smiling, stopping what they were doing to shout a hello. The greetings went on and on, and he couldn't remember the last time he'd seen the people looking so happy or so eager.

Charles Fitzsimmons's prognosis was extremely grim, and against everyone's advice, Gertrude had insisted on transporting him back to Portsmouth. At the group's departure, Phillip had set out on his own to deliver the news to Jane. With his conscience still stabbing at him like nasty insect bites, he'd decided to bring the message himself. Most of the time, he told himself he was only making the journey because he was her husband and it was only appropriate that he deliver the news.

In those rare moments when he was completely honest with himself, he admitted that he simply wanted to see her again, to make amends. He didn't know where the feelings were coming from, or why they were so strong, he only knew that he couldn't refuse to act on them.

With beautiful summer sunshine bathing the countryside, he'd decided to travel alone to Rosewood. It was a peaceful, glorious trek of solitude and scenery such as he had not enjoyed since his days as a boy when he'd regularly sneaked off with Richard Farrow to their secret hiding places. When he lowered his protective barriers enough to admit it, he realized he missed those times. The innocence. The carefree, playful days. He missed Richard, too, the only true friend he'd ever had.

He turned off the main road and rode through the gates to the estate. He'd loved this place as a boy, had always seen it through Richard's eyes as a grand and glorious playground. As an older youth, he'd begun to recognize it as his heritage, a place of great beauty and prosperity which would be placed in his trust.

But, as a man fully grown, he'd only seemed to cling to the worst of the memories, those of lonely months and years spent pining away for some attention from his father, of the strict and authoritarian tutors who beat and berated him on a regular basis, of the great, misplaced love for Anne which had shattered his heart and his life.

The place seemed truly alive on the bright summer day, and he slowed his horse so that he could have a lengthened enjoyment of the ride to the manor house. From nearby, female laughter sounded, then a man's roar, and others joined in. Curious as to what horseplay was in progress and who was involved, he reined his horse off the drive and into the woods.

He cleared the trees to a grassy meadow. At the other

side was one of the long streams which ran across the property. By the water's edge, a picnic was in progress. No one noticed his approach, and he watched for a few minutes, dumbfounded by the sight before his eyes.

Meg and Emily dangled their bare feet in the stream. Jane sat on a blanket, more lovely than ever in a simple blue dress that revealed her shoulders and the tops of her breasts. A large straw bonnet covered her face and shaded her arms and chest. Graves sat on one side of her and Richard Farrow on the other. He held his temper in check until Farrow laughed at something Jane had said and she responded with a pat on his knee.

Seeing red, he nearly started across the meadow, but stopped himself when Graves rose to his feet and pulled Meg to hers. Meg blushed prettily as Graves whispered something in her ear.

"Now that we're all here together," he announced with a huge smile on his face, "I wanted to tell you that Meg has finally agreed to become my wife."

Surprised silence, then shrieks from Jane and Emily who jumped up and started hugging the pair. Jane faced Graves, clasping both his hands in hers. "I told you to ask her again."

"I'm glad I followed your advice. She finally said yes."

"He's been wearing me down," Meg offered, laughing gaily.

"We thought we'd have the ceremony during the Harvest Fair," John said, "to add to the festivities."

"Splendid," Jane agreed.

Something about the homey scene, about the tight circle of happy friends, stoked Phillip's temper as nothing had in a long time. He felt terribly betrayed by all of them. But by Jane especially. She was supposed to be lonely, miserable, pining away as he was. Not content and happy and comfortable in the new place she'd made for herself.

Spurring his startled horse, he trampled through the baskets and across the blankets, tumbling everything off to the side. Everyone stopped in their tracks at his approach.

"Wessington!"

"Milord!"

"Father!"

Jane could not have been more surprised if the Good Lord himself had appeared in the meadow. In the times she'd imagined what her next encounter with her husband would be like, it had been much different from this. She'd envisioned herself sitting in the parlor, the house and grounds looking superb, she and Emily beautifully turned out, the staff trained and ready to make a magnificent occasion of his visit so he could see and appreciate all the good things they'd accomplished in his absence.

Instead, Wessington looked mad as a hornet. Determined to defuse the situation in any way she could, she smiled up at him. "Hello, milord husband. What a pleasant surprise to have you join us. Did you just arrive?"

"Yes," he responded tersely through clenched teeth.

"So you've not been to the house. I'm so glad. I wanted to be present when you returned so that I could give you the grand tour." Taking in his dusty countenance, she added, "You must be thirsty and tired. Please join us, won't you? I believe you know everyone here."

She gestured toward the assembled group, seeming to be oblivious to the tension in the air. Could she really be so thick? "Get on my horse, Jane. We're leaving."

"But we've only just arrived ourselves. Please rest for a moment, and then I'll escort you to the house."

"Now, Jane!"

His tone of command caused her smile to disappear. He was terribly upset about something. Probably Richard's presence, and perhaps Graves's, but that didn't mean he had to be so rude. "No, I'm not ready to leave."

"Wife, I will not argue the issue with you. Come here."

Jane placed her hands on her hips, her temper rising in direct accord to his own. "I absolutely will not."

"What did you say?"

"I said: I will not. I've neither seen nor heard from you for nearly four months, then you ride in here and begin insulting me and my friends, and I tell you I won't—" She never got the chance to finish before she found herself sitting across Phillip's lap, his arm wrapped tightly around her waist. Her hat flew off and fluttered silently to the ground.

He scanned the assembled players. "Graves and Meg, you're discharged."

"You are not," Jane called over her shoulder, kicking and struggling.

"Cease!" he shouted at Jane, so closely that her ears began ringing. His furious glare fell on Richard. "Get off my property. And if I ever see you within a hundred yards of my wife again, I'll shoot off your other leg."

With that, and no acknowledgment of Emily whatsoever, he whirled the horse around and took off at a jolting gallop. At the house, a stableboy came running, and Phillip tossed him the reins as he swung Jane, then himself, to the ground. "Inside. Now!"

"I'll not do anything when you're shouting like this. What is the matter with you?"

"What is the matter with me?" He shouted it again, much louder this time. "What is the matter with me?" He was not altogether certain why he was so angry, but something about seeing Jane sitting next to Farrow, laughing with John Graves made him snap. It was as though he were outside his body, watching a crazy man stand in the drive and shout at his wife.

"Yes!" her voice matched his in volume. "What is the matter with you?"

Without responding, he grabbed her around the waist and swung her over his shoulder. An astonished footman opened the door just as Phillip stormed through with Jane pounding on his back and shouting near-obscenities. The butler, on hearing the commotion, appeared down the hall. Wessington glared at the man, daring him to say anything. He wisely remained silent. "Make certain my wife and I are not disturbed."

Taking the stairs two at a time, he raced down the long halls, twisting and turning his way to the master suite at the end. Inside, he stomped to the large bed and deposited his load. Jane bounced several times but managed to keep from embarrassing herself by falling to the floor. As he hurried to the door and angrily turned the lock, she came to her knees.

"Have you gone completely mad?"

"What were you doing?"

"Sweet Jesu, I was having a picnic."

"What were you doing with those men?"

"They are my friends. They work for me."

"I'll not stand for it!"

"For what? Am I not to have any friends? What did you think? That I would retire to the country and lock myself in a closet? Was I never to come out?"

"That's not what I mean, and you know it."

"What do *you* mean? It's a beautiful summer day. We've all been working very hard—which you would have noticed if you'd arrived like a man possessed of his senses instead of like a crazed animal."

"You will not cavort—"

Jane laughed. "Cavort? Really, sir, listen to yourself."

"Don't you dare laugh at me."

"Or what? You'll strike me? Lock me in my room? Make me go without my supper?"

"Don't tempt me."

She started toward the door, carefully skirting him.

"Just where do you think you're going?"

"This is probably something you should know about me: I don't respond well to orders or threats, and I've never been much good at shouting matches. I'm leaving. We will speak later when you have calmed yourself."

"We will speak now."

"Speak of what? That I was having an innocent luncheon with my friends?"

"There is nothing innocent about Farrow. I won't have him near you."

Jane was thoroughly surprised by his tone. If she wasn't careful, she'd almost convince herself that he was jealous. "And what about Graves? Is he also unacceptable in your eyes?"

"I've spent the last month paying Bow Street runners to find him, and he's been playing house here all the while."

"He's not been 'playing house' as you call it. He's been working, and working hard for me."

"And I did not grant him leave to assist you."

"He understood that fact, sir. That is why he left your employ."

Phillip shouted at the idiocy of it all. "If he *left* my employ, pray tell me, what is he doing here?"

"He is working for me."

"No longer."

"Sir, I am perfectly capable of selecting my own staff. You will not discharge him. I will not allow it."

"Did I fall asleep and wake up in Bedlam?" Phillip shook his head in disbelief. "Did you not hear me, Jane? I have fired the man."

"I heard you, sir. And your action makes no sense, so I've no intention of listening to you."

"It's becoming clear to me that I should never have let you retire to the country alone. You definitely need a firmer hand."

Her husband's words terrified her. The last thing she wanted or needed was to have the Earl overseeing the day-to-day running of her life. She tried for calm. "Sir, he loves Meg, desperately and beyond reason. He wants to marry her."

"I heard the blabbering idiot."

"Then you realize that he couldn't let her come here alone."

"The man's a fool. To give up a position with me for the sake of a woman?"

"I think it's wonderful that he could love another so deeply."

Jane's clear gaze said it all: Phillip refused to believe that others loved, simply because he could not love himself. Sounding petulant and spoiled, he said, "I needed him."

Jane couldn't help the smile that began to play at her lips. "Why, milord, I do believe we've hurt your feelings."

"What?" He gasped at the ludicrous suggestion.

"We've hurt your feelings, so that must mean you have some." She clasped her hands together. "Now we're getting somewhere." Walking to the chair by the window, she sat casually, adjusting her skirts around her legs. "Calm yourself, and tell me what we've done that's so dreadful."

Phillip sputtered, trying to hold on to his anger, but

it was so difficult to maintain when she sat there smiling
so placidly. To avoid looking her in the eye, he began
pacing back and forth. "What is Farrow doing here?
I've left you alone here for a matter of months and that
snake in the grass raises his ugly head."

"Master Farrow has always been here."

"Jane, do not lie to me. I sent him away years ago.
What I want to know is: how did he manage to find his
way back?"

"I have many faults, milord, but fabricating the truth
is not one of them. I regret to be the one to inform
you, but he didn't leave. He has always been here."

"Doing what?"

"Seeing to the place. While you were in London gambling and womanizing, he was here. Year after year, he
kept a tight fist on a very slippery rein. If he hadn't
stayed on, I've no idea what might have become of your
family home."

"Who knew of this?"

"Everyone here. Master Thumberton. Most of the
merchants and suppliers. People in the village. Some
of the neighbors, I expect."

Phillip felt like a fool, with good reason. Everyone
had certainly played him for one. How they must all have
been laughing behind his back! The embarrassment of
it only refueled his anger. "He'll not remain."

"Of course, he will."

Phillip stiffened and turned to glare at her.

"He loves this place. He loves the people and the land.
And he is a remarkable agent. We need his guidance and
assistance."

"I'll not have him about the estate."

"If his presence offends you, I'll see to it that he
remains out of sight while you're here." Smiling wickedly, she said, "How long shall I tell him that will be,

milord? A day or two? Or perhaps you'd thought to grace us with a week of your time?''

Phillip bristled at her mocking tone. In actuality, he'd planned on remaining a day or two, not much more than that. The first of the house parties to which he'd been invited began in another week, but he'd never let her realize how close she was to being right. "With all that is occurring here, perhaps I'll not leave."

From talking to Richard, she knew that the number of days Wessington had spent at the estate in the past decade could nearly be counted on one hand. She muttered under her breath, "That will be the day."

"What did you say?" he roared.

"I said: 'twould be nice to have you stay. And will you stop that infernal pacing?" When he continued, she rose from her chair and stepped in front of him. He was so consumed by anger that he didn't see her. She bounced off his chest, lost her balance and fell to the floor, landing ungraciously on her rear.

Only when the unceremonious thump registered in his ears did he notice what had happened. "What the devil . . . ? Are you all right?"

"Yes, yes, I'm fine," she insisted, resisting the urge to rub her sore backside.

"Let me help you." He reached for her arm, but she yanked it away.

"Leave me be."

"Let me help you." She scooted across the floor, and in exasperation, he rested his hands on his hips. "Why the devil must everything be such a fight with you? I will assist you." Brooking no further argument, he reached for her hand and raised her to her feet. Once standing, she jerked her hand from his.

"Thank you," she managed, but she didn't sound grateful.

"I must admit, Jane, that I read several reports on your character before we were wed, and I failed to see any mention of this temper of yours."

"My temper?!" She whirled on him. "I'll have you know that I have a very pleasant nature. If you did not provoke me at every turn—"

"I? I provoke you? So it's my fault, is it, that you turn into an unreasonable, shouting shrew every time I'm in your presence?"

"Do you seriously expect me to silently cope with your rude, surly attitudes, and your high-handed manner?"

"Give me one example of how I have treated you badly in the time I've known you!" The moment the words left his mouth, he knew the argument was lost. Of course, he'd treated her badly. After a lifetime of acting however he pleased, he barely noticed when he offended someone. Jane simply refused to suffer in silence when she was wronged.

Seeing his consternation as a chance to escape, she walked purposefully to the door. "I grow weary of this discussion, and I have many chores to accomplish. If you'll excuse me—"

"I don't excuse you."

"Then I'm afraid I must beg your pardon, because I am frightfully busy and must get back to work. My luncheon picnic was only meant to be a short break from my duties."

"We are not finished speaking."

"Perhaps you're not, but I am. I cannot abide this bickering."

The thought of her leaving bothered him. He didn't want her to have things to do that were more important. He wanted to occupy her time, and she couldn't seem to wait to get shed of him. Of course, he had been a horse's ass since arriving, but he was a charming man who could certainly figure out how to change her mind. "Fine. Then we shall speak of other things." Leaning against a chair, trying to look casual, he asked, "How have you been?"

"You are unbelievable"—she shook her head, reaching for the door—"and I am dreadfully busy."

Used to crowds and social interaction, he was unwilling to acknowledge that they helped to keep his personal demons at bay. The prospect of spending the afternoon entertaining himself in this big house or around the estate, even though it was supposedly his home, was daunting. "What will I do all afternoon if you won't stay to chat?"

He smiled, trying to make light of the question, but she heard through it to the longing which lay underneath, and her look was one of pity. "I don't care. Drink or gamble or whatever it is you do when you're up and about in the daylight. I'll make sure your supper is arranged for nine."

With a sharp *click,* the door closed behind her. In the silence, he realized that he hadn't even mentioned the reason for his visit.

Chapter Eighteen

After an incredibly long, boring afternoon and evening, Phillip entered the drawing room at one minute of nine, expecting to see his wife and perhaps his daughter dressed and waiting for him to escort them to supper. The room was empty and silent. Wondering if they'd rudely gone ahead without him, he poked his head into the dining room. It, too, was empty except for a quartet of servants who stood perfectly poised, dressed and fastidiously ready to offer assistance for his every whim.

The long table, capable of comfortably seating thirty, glittered under the beautiful chandeliers. At the head, one pathetic-looking place setting waited. Feeling as though he were walking to an appointment with the guillotine, he forced one foot in front of the other until he reached the opposite end of the room. A servant held out his chair.

"Wine, sir?" the first man asked.

"That will be fine."

The man began to pour and the glug of the liquid as it chugged into the crystal goblet echoed around the empty room. The tip of the bottle nicked the rim of the glass, and the *ping* seemed so overly loud in the silent place that the Earl jumped.

Although he wasn't sure what he'd expected by showing up at the estate unannounced, this was hardly the homecoming he'd imagined. He managed to suffer through the first three courses, each scrape of silver across china causing him to wince, until he decided he could no longer bear the solitude. After only nibbling at the fish which had been so deliciously prepared, he pushed away the plate. "I believe that will be all. Thank you. You may be excused."

The servants looked at each other, their distress obvious, as they wondered if they'd offended somehow. "Is something amiss, sir?" one of them found the courage to ask.

"No, everything was excellent. I'm simply more tired than I thought after my long journey."

Another inquired, "Would you like us to send a tray up to your room, sir? Perhaps you'd feel like a bite later on."

He knew he wouldn't, but they all looked so hopeful. "Yes, perhaps. Thank you."

One man scooped away his plate, another his glassware, the third his eating utensils, and they shuffled off. As the three men left the room, the fourth servant, a young woman, followed, walking behind his chair. He turned slightly and caught her eye. "I've not seen my wife. I hope she hasn't taken ill. Has she eaten?"

"Milady ate some time ago, sir."

"I see." The devil made him ask. "Did she dine alone?"

"No, sir. Several people were present. *Working* sups,

she calls them. They were making plans for the morrow.''

"What sorts of plans?''

"Well, about the crops and the harvest and whatnot.''

"I'd like a word with her. Do you know where she is at the moment?''

"Already abed would be my guess. Exhausted usually by this time of the evening, sir. Gets up early, that one does. And works from dawn to dusk. Never saw the likes from a lady like herself.'' The girl blushed prettily. "If I may say so, sir, we're all quite taken with her.''

She hustled out after the men, leaving Phillip alone to brood. He poured himself a glass of port and contemplated the long night stretching ahead. With few prospects for enjoyment, he wandered down the hall, eventually ending up in the library. There were books and papers scattered everywhere, and he sat behind the desk, sifting through the piles. With nothing better to do, he picked up a notebook entitled, *Five-Year Plan*, and began to read.

Two hours later, shortly after midnight, Jane walked into the library and was completely shocked to see him. A single lamp illuminated the desktop as he carefully read one of her diaries. Off to the side, he had a piece of paper on which he appeared to be making a long list of notes. Her heart pounded. Was he criticizing her efforts? Changing? Canceling? Would all her hard work come to naught with a stoke of his pen?

So absorbed was he in what he was reading, he failed to notice her arrival, and she took the moment to study him. In the shadows, with his shirt undone, his hair tousled from running a hand through it, he was more handsome than ever. While always before he'd been carefully playing the part of the bored aristocrat, in the quiet darkness of his own library, unobserved and unaware, he seemed a different man. Gentle, studious, pensive. He looked younger and sadder and so terribly alone.

Jane's maternal instincts pushed her to say something—he seemed so approachable like this—but she didn't, because she stood in the doorway, dressed only in her nightgown and robe, the same nightclothes she'd been wearing on the evening he'd proposed at the apartment in London. Never again would she let him see her in such a state of undress, because it might encourage him toward exercising his marital rights.

During their heated argument earlier in the afternoon, there had hardly been time for him to discuss their situation regarding coupling. Certainly, his responsibility to provide an heir would require that they resume marital relations at some point in time, but she wasn't about to tempt fate. Taking a step back, she meant to slip out undetected and head to her room. As bad luck would have it, he looked up just as she made her move.

They stared at each other silently, until Phillip broke the tension by lifting his wineglass and taking a careful sip. "Hello, Jane."

"Hello, milord."

"Call me Phillip, please."

"I'd rather not be so informal, sir. We hardly know one another."

Phillip gave a derisive snort. "What are you doing wandering the halls?"

"I couldn't sleep. I was thinking to work a bit."

"From what I hear, you work all the time."

"There's much to do, sir." She shrugged. She was dying to ask what he was notating, but refused to give in to her fears that he was disapproving of her tasks. After the horrendous day she'd suffered due to his arrival, she couldn't bear to hear any of his criticisms. "I trust your supper was well served."

" 'Twas excellent, if a tad bit lonely. I had expected your company."

"My apologies then, sir. After the anger you showed me earlier, I hadn't imagined that you would wish to dine with me."

God's teeth, but he enjoyed her frankness. "You've done a good job with the house and the servants, Jane. I'm well pleased with what I've seen."

Jane couldn't believe she was blushing from the compliment. "Thank you, sir. I had so hoped you would appreciate what I've done on your behalf."

"I do. Very much."

The exchange became increasingly awkward. It seemed as though he wanted to say something more, perhaps apologize when he didn't quite know how, and she felt as though she were choking on the apprehension. She had to leave before he shattered their precious peace by saying the wrong thing.

"Well, then, I'm sorry I interrupted. I bid you good night."

Although he wasn't certain, she seemed to be wearing the same nightclothes she'd had on the evening they became engaged. The night he had been so thoroughly enchanted and aroused by her he'd barely been able to keep himself from stealing her maidenhood. Was she remembering just as he was? She turned to go, and he desperately didn't want her to leave.

Knowing exactly how to get her to stay, he said, "I've reviewed your numbers for years four and five, and I don't see how you figure the projected profit."

The comment caused her to stop in her tracks, and she whirled around, amazed that he'd gleaned so much from his review. She and Richard had haggled endlessly about the numbers he'd just mentioned. Very suspicious. "I thought you didn't understand anything about figures."

"I never said I didn't understand them. I simply don't care for the tedium of bookwork, while you obviously enjoy it very much."

The comment sounded like a criticism. "I'll not apologize for my interest."

"You shouldn't. From the moment I first learned about you, I suspected that our differing interests would make us a good team." He lifted his glass and toasted her. "After reviewing some of your work, I'd say I was right. You've done very well. I'm impressed. Your idea, to begin by fixing small pieces then working toward bigger ones, would never have occurred to me. I'm truly grateful, and extremely intrigued by the entire process."

She was blushing again. He was sincere, and the knowledge that he appreciated the extent of her hard work was the only welcome news she'd received in a good long time. "I must confess I acted out of necessity. My dower funds will not last forever. After I arrived here and reviewed the books, I knew we'd need to take action before too long. So I began on my own."

"A wise move."

"I've taken some liberties, but I didn't think you'd want to be apprised of what was happening here. From everything I've heard, you would not care."

"That's not true. This place is my heritage, and caring for it is my responsibility. I do have some questions, just so I may have a better understanding. Would you mind spending a few minutes?" He reached for a chair in the corner and pulled it behind the desk, next to his own.

In her current state of dishabille, Jane knew she should refuse. There would be plenty of time in the morning to discuss money and estate plans. However, in the short time she'd known her husband, he had rarely seemed so accessible as he was at the moment, and she longed for a smoother relationship with him, one in which they could converse without shouting.

"If you wish, I would be glad to." She moved to the desk and sat next to him. It took all her willpower not to reach out and stroke his cheek with her hand. Instead, she forced her gaze back down to the books stacked on top of the desk.

Phillip smiled at her obvious discomfort as he wondered how long, if ever, it would take them to get past the dreadful night of their wedding. They had to find a common ground on which they could live and work without all the emotion that seemed to flare every time they were together. "I've made a list of questions. Shall we go over them?"

"That would be a good start."

For the next few hours, Phillip asked questions and Jane answered them, opening books or notes, pointing out ledger statements, adding debit and credit columns. The tension that had marked his arrival gradually dwindled. The quiet room, the darkened surroundings, the shared interest in the task at hand, all lent themselves to providing an atmosphere of intimate conversation, which both seized hold of without realizing it.

Gradually, Phillip's interest moved beyond the intellectual. Jane's assured nature, her casual manner in answering his questions and her relaxed attitude in dealing with him, began to attract his attention in other ways.

With each passing minute, he found himself watching her rather than listening. Distractedly, she reached for his wineglass and helped herself to a sip. When she finished and set it back on the desk, he reached for it and sipped slowly from the very spot her lips had touched. Eventually, he moved closer until his arm rested across the back of her chair.

Jane couldn't believe how much she enjoyed the time she was passing with her husband. Contrary to all her preconceived notions, he was bright and inquisitive. Able to point out flaws in her logic without offending. Able to change the direction of her thinking with subtle suggestions which helped her to see things in a better light. He was funny and talkative. And actually, very sweet. For a moment, she felt herself longing for what might have existed between them if they hadn't gotten off to such a rocky start.

For some reason, the room suddenly seemed quieter. Wessington seemed closer. She glanced to the side, only to find him staring at her intently.

"What?" she asked. His beautiful dark eyes glowed intensely.

Without responding verbally, Wessington leaned across the few inches which separated them and rested his lips against hers. The contact lasted only a moment, long enough for Jane to feel their warmth and sweetness, before she jumped back as if she'd received a jolt. She rested her fingertips against her lips.

One corner of his mouth lifted in a smile, and a previously unnoticed dimple graced his cheek. With a lock of hair falling across his forehead and beard stubble shadowing his face, he looked positively wicked.

"Why did you do that?"

"I couldn't help myself." Without giving either of them a chance to think further, he leaned closer again, resting his hands on the arms of the chair, effectively trapping her. He pressed his lips to hers, tasting the wine she'd sipped. Licking her lips, he asked silently for them to open. At the slightest parting, he took immediate advantage, making tentative love to her mouth, tracing his tongue along her teeth, finding her tongue and offering sweet invitation. He rose, pressing her back into her chair.

Jane was not sure what had happened. One moment, she was discussing farming, and the next, Wessington had his lips locked with her own. At the first contact, she should have refused the invitation, but as usual when she was in his presence, her body welcomed what her mind would not tolerate. He was such a handsome, virile man, used to getting what he wanted from women, and she simply wasn't experienced enough to know how to refuse. Still, after their wedding night, it seemed odd that her body could so readily accept his advances.

His tongue stroked her own, causing that strange heat to swell and pull against her lower belly. Knowing now what would occur if they continued, she couldn't imagine why nature would cause her body to crave such a thing. Mating was a painful, disgusting experience which she had no intention of ever repeating.

As Wessington deepened the kiss, her panic started to mount. Did he intend to enforce his marital rights here in the library? What if she refused? Would he force his attentions? As her husband, he had every right to do so.

She pressed a palm against his chest and wrenched her lips away from his. "Please, Wessington," she gasped, out of breath, "please don't."

Phillip gazed into her luminous emerald eyes. Where a moment ago, they'd been confused but accepting, now he saw only resolve and something else. Fear. She was afraid of him.

At his moment of hesitation, she braced her feet against the floor and rocked her chair backward, effectively removing herself from the circle of his arms. She jumped to her feet. Clutching the lapels of her robe closed, she said frantically, "Please, sir, I don't want this from you."

Amazed to find that his own wife was frightened of him, he reached out a hand in supplication, as though gentling a skittish horse. "Don't be afraid of me, Jane. I would never hurt you."

"That's a lie. You've already hurt me. I'll not let you do it again." She whirled and fled from the library before he could make a move to stop her.

Her bare feet carried her down the hall until he could no longer hear the soft fall of her steps. Walking to the sideboard, he refilled his wineglass and gulped down the contents.

He had kissed her passionately, and he'd wanted to continue. To go on and on until he had taken her right there on the library desk. Why?

It would be easiest to convince himself that his sudden desire for her occurred because he was ready and she was available. But if simple lust were the reason, then anyone would do, and he could have bedded any number of tavern wenches on his journey to the estate. No, in all honesty, somewhere in the back of his mind, he knew that he'd been holding himself back until he arrived so he could bed Jane, the abstinence on the way only serving to make his joining with her more enjoyable.

Because of her wedding night, she was afraid of the sexual act, but that fear was of his own making. He was an experienced lover and had the skill to show her how it could be between them. Without giving further thought to the matter, knowing only that he had to have her and have her now, he followed her to the room she'd taken for herself, one of the smaller guest rooms far on the other side of the house from his own.

Silent as a mouse, he turned the knob and slipped inside. Jane was already abed, and the room was dark. He could still smell the lingering smoke from her extinguished candle. He tiptoed to the bedside, standing and waiting for his eyes to adjust to the darkness, then reached down and rested a hand on her shoulder, just able to feel her shape through the heavy bedcovers.

Jane had thought she'd heard someone open the door, but had dismissed it as her overactive imagination until she felt the hand on her. Wessington, with his unmistakable presence, stood next to the bed. What did he intend? Her heart pounded with fear.

"What are you doing here?" she whispered. Before he could answer, she leaned over and relit the candle, giving shape to his figure. She felt safer with the light burning.

"I find myself overcome with desire. I wish to make love to you," he whispered back.

"I'll never do such a thing again."

The covers had slipped to her waist. Through the thin fabric of her nightgown, he could see her nipples. Her pulse was throbbing at the base of her throat. Unable to resist, he reached for a breast and gently traced the contour. At the same time, he leaned down and rubbed his cheek against her own. "Don't be afraid."

"You can't do this." Her panic increased as he reached for the covers.

"I'm your husband, Jane," he responded, his exasperation clearly evident. "It's all right. I'll be ever so gentle with you. I swear it."

"You don't understand," she said, pushing him away. "Emily is here with me."

"What?" he pulled back and looked across the bed, seeing for the first time the other figure sleeping peacefully next to his wife. "She's nearly grown. What is she doing here?"

"She was very distressed today."

"By what?"

"By you!"

"Me? But I did nothing to the girl."

"Exactly my point. She was crushed. You've been here all day and didn't spare her a second."

Phillip refused to be moved by the girl's feelings. Somehow he sensed that if he succumbed once to thinking about her in a kind way, he would lose his dispassionate method of dealing with her. He couldn't afford to do that. "Wake her, and tell her to return to her own room."

"I will not."

"Then I will."

He made a move as if to step around the bed, but Jane jumped up and stopped him. "If you wake her, sir, you'll only frighten her. I don't believe even you would be so callous to a child sleeping so peacefully under your roof. Even if it is someone you despise so much as your own daughter."

"I do not despise her."

Jane stood her ground, watching her husband, wondering what he would do. Phillip, for his part, found his rampant desire quickly fading as he faced Jane's ire and pondered the prospect of waking Emily.

He'd simply wanted a tender tumble with his wife. Not another fight with her. It was too late, and he was too fatigued by the past days.

"Go, milord. To your own bed. You're not welcome here."

Phillip eyed her dispassionately. He could not remember when a woman had ever refused him. With his pride sorely wounded, he vowed that his wife would not persist. "We will speak more of this in the morning. I will accommodate you on this occasion, but not again. You'd best prepare yourself." With that, he turned and strode from the room.

Jane let out the deep breath she'd been holding and sank back onto the bed.

Chapter Nineteen

Emily skipped into Jane's room in a wild burst of energy, bringing with her smiles and excitement. "Jane, Jane," she stated breathlessly, "you'll not believe this."

"What, dear?" She'd been up for hours already, riding the grounds, inspecting the gardens, had barely slept after her nocturnal encounters with Wessington. Exhaustion was wearing her down, and she had to stifle a yawn.

"You'll not believe it."

"Calm yourself, Emily. With all your jumping about, you'll never quiet long enough to tell me the news."

"Father wishes to see me! At eleven. In the morning parlor."

She rose and hugged the girl, even as she breathed a sigh of relief at Wessington's decision. "See, I told you he was simply busy yesterday. Now, we must hurry if you're to be ready. We'll pick out the prettiest of your new dresses."

"How about the pink one?" Emily asked, as they rushed down the hall toward her room.

"I was thinking about the blue. It brings out the color of your eyes in such a lovely way." Two maids joined them, and along with Meg, they spent the next hour preparing her for her presentation to her father.

Promptly at eleven, Jane followed Emily into the parlor, crossing her fingers as the girl entered in the hope that Wessington would notice the changes. Her naturally curly hair was perfectly ringleted about her pretty face. Her new dress, with its crisp petticoats, swished delightfully as she moved. The girl had a bearing and charm which belied her young years.

Poised and confident, she walked straight to the Earl and made a perfect curtsy. "Hello, Father. Welcome home."

"Hello, Emily. Thank you for being prompt." He motioned for her to take a seat, then turned and indicated they had a guest. "Master Morris has come to call." Wessington, seeing Jane hanging in the back, motioned her to a seat also. He looked at Morris. "Have you met my wife, Lady Wessington?"

"Yes. I've had the pleasure."

Morris flashed Jane a look of triumph as though to tell her that he would have his way in the end. He rose and bowed over her hand, then Emily's. Jane watched carefully, giving him no opportunity to linger near the child.

The four of them sat in the sunny room, sipping tea and munching on the delicious scones Cook had prepared. The two men talked about various affairs they'd attended in London and various people with whom they were acquainted. Occasionally, Morris would ask Emily a question which she answered politely. The rest of the time, she stared at the floor, looking sullen and morose.

When the hour ended, the Earl excused them, and they left together. Throughout the entire ordeal, he had not made a single comment about Emily; he'd not asked any questions about how she'd been doing; he'd failed to notice her dress or deportment.

Jane was furious. "I'm sorry, Emily," she offered as they reached the stairs and were sufficiently out of earshot. "I know you expected something else."

Emily had managed to hold back the tears until that moment. They flowed freely now. "Father hates me," she cried softly. "He always has. What a fool I've been, thinking it wasn't so." She whirled and started up the stairs, two at a time. "It's no use. It's no use pretending anymore . . ." She disappeared around the corner.

Jane heaved a heavy sigh, wondering how many more upheavals were going to occur due to Wessington's presence. Once Morris departed, the Earl headed to the library, and she followed. He looked up from the desk as she closed the door.

From the determined look in her eye, he couldn't help but wonder what the matter could be. Perhaps she didn't like Morris any more than he did himself. The man was a dreadful bore, but also a wealthy, respected neighbor, and they could hardly send him packing when he came to call.

Resolved not to fight with her, he tried to start on a better foot. "I can't remember when I've seen Emily quite so prettily turned out. You've done a good job with her."

"She was hoping that you would notice . . ." She wearily shook her head, letting the thought trail off, unable to come to grips with her emotions over the entire issue of her husband. Would she ever understand this man?

Looking down, her eyes settled on the papers on the desk, and she was greatly disturbed by the few words she managed to read upside down. "What's that you have there?"

Her direct gaze irked him, for he felt himself ten years old again and being scolded by his tutor. How did she manage that so well? He reached to take the papers away, but she stopped him by grabbing them first.

"So it's true then? You plan to wed her to that man?" She quickly scanned the pages. "She told me you'd decided, but I was certain she had to be mistaken." With great effort, she sat back in the chair, the papers gripped in her hand.

"She told you about it?"

"Yes."

"I've never spoken to her or anyone about it—except Thumberton. How did she hear?"

"Morris told her some time ago. The news frightened her terribly."

Phillip scowled. "Well, I haven't decided any such thing. He made an offer, and I told him I'd think about it. That's all."

"Is that why he was here today? To see if you'd made up your mind?"

"One of the reasons. He also wanted to call on Emily. He said you won't let him."

"Of course, I won't. It's improper."

He pointed to the contract in her hand. "What would you have me do?"

"Simply tell him no. She's too young."

Phillip had never passed much time thinking about Emily's marriage prospects, so he didn't realize how silly he sounded when he asked, "What if she never receives another offer?"

Jane laughed, incredulous that he could be so blind.

"Have you never taken a look at her? She is exquisite. You will have dozens of offers from which to choose. In fact, I would lay bets that you'll be fighting off suitors with a stick, but it will happen in a few more years when the time is right." Without pausing to wonder if she dared raise the subject, she continued softly, "I know you harbor a great deal of animosity toward Emily because of what happened with her mother."

"What did you say?" Phillip rose slightly from his chair, his eyes flashing angrily. "Who has spoken to you of such private matters?"

"Calm yourself, please. What happened between you and Anne, between you and Richard, is well known. I could hardly *not* have heard the gossip."

"The relationship I had with Anne is none of your concern."

"But it is, milord. Her betrayals changed you." He opened his mouth to protest, and she silenced him with a raised hand. "Because of her, you trust no one; you care for no one. She continues to overshadow your relationship with me and with Emily."

Phillip shook his head in violent disagreement. No matter what others thought or said, Anne had no continuing effect on his life. "You're wrong."

"Am I?" Jane's piercing gaze looked far into his hardened heart. She stood and rounded the desk, taking his hand in hers as she dropped to her knees. "Please do not punish Emily simply because you hated Anne. If you feel she's too much of a burden, relieve yourself by giving her care completely into my hands. I couldn't love her more if she were my own child, so I ask—no, I beg—you not to do this to her. If you will grant me this one favor, I'll never ask another thing of you as long as I live. I swear it."

Phillip was terribly moved by her devotion to the girl

and couldn't help wondering what it would be like to have the full force of Jane's affection focused on himself. If he wasn't careful, he might almost find himself jealous over his wife's feelings for his daughter.

After hearing her plea, he sighed. How could he resist such a heartfelt request? "I'll tell him no."

"Please swear it."

"I swear it."

"Thank you."

He reached for her other hand and helped her to her feet. "Get up, now. I need to speak to you of another matter. The one which brought me here."

"What is it?" she asked, not at all certain she wanted to hear the answer.

"I have some news of your family."

"My family?" Jane's thoughts were instantly confused. Her family was the farthest topic she could imagine the Earl wanting to discuss. "What about them?"

"It's your father, Jane. It appears he's suffered an attack of apoplexy."

Her eyes widened, her mouth formed a silent O. She swallowed hard. "Is he still alive?"

"He was when last I saw him."

"Oh, dear." She looked down, suddenly very interested in the cameo pinned to her bodice.

"I meant to tell you yesterday, but I never seemed to find the proper moment. That's why I came out from London."

"And his condition?"

No sense lying. "Very grave. The doctors were not hopeful."

She walked to the window, staring off across the gardens and wringing her hands. The news was incomprehensible. Charles was such a vibrant person. In thinking back on her entire life, she couldn't remember a single day when he'd taken to his sickbed. The idea of him stricken down was impossible for her to process.

One of Wessington's comments came back to her. "You said you'd seen Father?"

"Yes. He was in London with Gregory and your sister, Gertrude."

"Whatever were they doing in the city?"

"They were discussing business matters. I ran into them at a society affair." Phillip hoped the explanation would suffice, for he didn't want to reveal the true reason for their London visit unless it was absolutely necessary. "I was with your father when he was laid low. We were speaking privately."

"Did he . . . did he ask about me?"

She looked so young and vulnerable that he didn't have the heart to shatter any illusions about her father. "Of course, he did." Phillip smiled. "He wanted to know all about you. How you were doing. How I was treating you."

His eyes had that mischievous twinkle she'd only witnessed a few times. "And what did you say to that?"

"I said I was being the very best of husbands."

"You're impossible." Wessington's slight attempt to lighten the moment was her undoing. Tears welled in her eyes, and she turned away. "I need to go home."

He moved to the window and sat on the sill facing her, resting a hand on her waist. Her eyes were glistening emeralds, and he longed to kiss away the lurking tears. "I don't think it's such a good idea for you to go home right now."

"Why? He's my father. I belong at his side."

"Have you communicated with them since we wed?"

"No. When I left home, my father asked me not to, until six months had passed. I obeyed his wishes in the matter."

"So you have no idea what they were doing in London?"

"You said they were there on business."

"Yes. They were there talking to bankers and making pronouncements about a new branch of the family business. An *import* business." Phillip waited for the facts to sink in.

Jane's eyes widened. "But I've never spoken to Father about my idea."

"Who else knew about it?"

"Gregory." Jane couldn't believe how guilty she felt at simply mentioning Gregory's name in her husband's presence.

"Would he have told your father about it?"

"Of course not. He knew I was still planning it." Phillip gave her a hard, assessing look, daring her to realistically assess what he was implying. She lowered her eyes, looking at his chest. "What are you saying? That Gregory stole my idea?"

"All I know, Jane, is that your father told me it was Gregory's idea."

Her brow furrowed, and her head suddenly started aching fiercely. She rubbed her temples. "You're wrong. You must have misunderstood."

Seeing her obvious torment, he had no desire to press the point, but he'd seen enough of her family to know that they bore her no goodwill. "Perhaps I did," he agreed. With a gentle tug, he brought her closer and she rested against his thigh. In her unsettled state, she didn't appear to notice or care that he held her in the circle of his arms, that a buttock rested against his leg. He cradled her face in his palm and edged her cheek to his chest. She accepted the silent offer of comfort.

After a time, she looked at up him. "Is he still in London?"

"No. Your sister insisted on taking him back to Portsmouth."

"But that's ludicrous."

"The doctors all advised against it, but she was adamant. I didn't feel I was in a position to stop her."

"So he's home?"

"If he's still alive, Jane. He's seriously afflicted, I fear."

"I need to go to Portsmouth. Please help me."

"Jane . . . I must advise against it."

"But you don't understand. He was always a good father to me." Wessington looked as though he intended to argue the point. "He was!" she insisted. "Then we parted on such bitter terms. I couldn't live with myself if he passed away while we were still at terrible odds."

Against his better judgment, he sighed and agreed. "All right. If it's what you truly want, I'll see to it."

"I don't wish to cause you any trouble. If you just tell me the best way to go about it, I can make the arrangements myself."

"I'll not have you running off across the country by yourself." There was more to it than that, he realized. He wanted to travel with her, just as he wanted to be with her in Portsmouth to protect her from whatever might happen at the hands of her family. Where the sudden protective instinct came from he couldn't say, but it was there—a vivid, tangible emotion he couldn't shake. He had to go with her.

"I'm sorry to say that time may be of the essence," he said.

"It's that serious, is it?"

"Yes, I think you should prepare yourself for the worst."

"Thank you for being so frank with me. I feel it simplifies matters."

"Yes, I'm finding the same thing." He smiled, extremely pleased to see her smile in return. "We could take the coach, but it would add many days to our trip. If we rode together, we could make good time. What do you think of such an extended journey on horseback?"

"I want to get there as quickly as possible."

"Then horseback it is." He stood her on her feet. "We'd best get busy. We'll leave first thing in the morning. There's much to do before we depart."

Chapter Twenty

Richard saw Jane leave the library in a distressed state. His heart pounded as he considered all the ghastly things Phillip might have said or done to her. The problems between Phillip and himself ran deep, the matters complicated and impossible to fix, but he'd not hide in the shadows while his old friend did injury to Jane.

With anger fueling his limping gait, he hastened to the library door and entered without knocking, allowing himself his first chance in over a decade to assess his friend. Phillip was turned in his chair, sipping a glass of wine and staring out the window onto the gardens. The worried wrinkle on his brow, the sad turn of the lines around his mouth, all gave testament to the way time had marked the passing of the years. With his pensive gaze, his depressed countenance, Phillip looked utterly alone.

"What did you do to Lady Jane?" Richard asked, more softly and gently than he'd intended.

Phillip was astounded at how familiar the voice sounded, even after all the years of never hearing it. He sat completely still, momentarily letting it tickle old memories of childhood. The only truly happy times of his life had been spent in Richard's company. Because of what had happened with Anne, Phillip had blocked out all thoughts of him, so that when he looked back on his days as a boy, he had no fond recollections.

"Ah, the ugly snake finally rears its head." Phillip turned in his chair. "What are you doing here, Farrow? I thought I'd ordered you gone."

"I never left."

"So I heard. Whatever gave you the audacity to think you could remain after I forbade it?"

Richard hated to shatter another of Phillip's illusions, but it was long past time he learned the truth. "Your father asked me to stay."

Phillip barely managed to swallow his mouthful of wine. Would his own father have betrayed him so completely? Had no one ever cared a whit for him? Not even his own father? "That's a bloody lie. He knew how much I hated you."

"Believe what you will." Richard shrugged. "My own father died shortly after you left. The Earl went through several agents in a handful of years. No one knew the properties as well as I, so he finally offered me the job. I accepted."

"Have you no shame? To stay here, to worm your way into the affections of my family? To show your face to me?"

Richard knew he should let Phillip vent his anger, but he had bigger fish to fry at the moment. "I saw Jane in the hall. She looked very distressed, and I want to know what you said."

With a deadly look in his eye, Phillip assessed him.

"Isn't it interesting, Farrow, how you always seem to take such a keen interest in my wives?"

"Don't forget your daughter, also. I care for Jane and Emily, and I won't have you hurting either one of them."

"I must say, you're quite bold for a man I'd just as soon kill as look at. Take some advice and hold your tongue."

"You'd kill me?"

"Without hesitation."

"If you couldn't kill me years ago, why should I fear you'd do it now?" The question hung in the air. Both recalled how Phillip had aimed the pistol at Richard's heart. Unable to fire, but unable to walk away without exacting some vengeance, he'd lowered the barrel and shot Richard in the leg. The surgeon's knife had saved Richard's life but not his limb. Ever since the day he'd awakened, crippled and maimed, he'd always felt half a man. Had never courted or married. Would never allow himself the joy of a family.

"I'd have preferred death to the life you left me," he said.

"And what of the life you left me?" The emotional question surprised them both. Although everyone knew how much Phillip had been irrevocably changed after the incident, he'd never given voice to the irreparable anguish his dear friend had caused.

"I never said I was sorry. So I'm saying it now."

"A pitiful utterance. Unwelcome and very, very much too late."

"Phillip, I was a boy. I had no sense that what I was doing with her was wrong."

"You—were—my—friend." Anger glistening in his eyes, Phillip rose from the chair. He gulped down the dark red liquid, then set the glass on the desk. The stem broke with a loud crack and the ruined goblet fell to its side.

So many questions were poised on the tip of his tongue, questions which had tortured him for years, but his pride kept him from finding the relief he sought by asking any of them. He waved Farrow away, dismissing him with a gesture of his hand. "You're truly a piece of work, Farrow. I don't believe I've ever encountered a more nervy, cheeky bastard. Be gone. I can no longer bear the sight of you."

Through all the years, Richard had hoped for a reconciliation with Phillip. In his mind, he'd played it out a thousand times, imagining what he would say and how it would go. Now that the time was here, he couldn't find the proper words of remorse to pierce Phillip's hardened heart. He shrugged, defeated. "Cry peace, Phillip. She was not worth it."

Although Phillip had believed the same for many years, he'd not admit it to the likes of Farrow. "Since she was my wife, I'd say I should be the judge of whether she was or not."

"Of course, you're right." Richard made one last attempt before stepping from the room. "I've missed you these long years. I've missed having you as my friend."

Phillip had missed Richard, also. Every season, every year. With a sudden surge of memory, a cascade of events tumbled through his head. The two of them running off to the river and diving in the creek on a hot summer day. Sitting in the hayloft, telling stories about the vicious pirates they would be when they grew up. The urge to round the desk and hug him was overwhelming and frightening.

Instead, to keep from acting like a fool, he simply

said, "My wife tells me you have done a good job with the estate."

Bowing slightly, Richard accepted the compliment. "It has been hard."

"I thank you for seeing to it."

Richard breathed a sigh of relief. They spoke like two strangers, but at least they were speaking. "It has been my pleasure."

"My wife's father has taken ill. We'll be leaving tomorrow for a visit to Portsmouth."

"How long will you be gone?"

"I cannot say. I'm not sure the gentleman is still alive." Acting calm and in control, he sat back in his seat, although his insides were in the greatest turmoil. "You will see to things while we're away." He made the statement, but nearly grimaced at how much it sounded like a request.

"Certainly. Lady Jane has begun many projects. I would not let any of them suffer in her absence."

"Good." Phillip picked up some papers, indicating the discussion was over. "Send Graves to see me."

Richard closed the door quietly, and Phillip sat very still, hearing the man's peg leg thump with each step as he made his way down the hall. His face felt flushed, hot, and he wished he had a cool cloth to lay on it before Graves made his appearance. Over the years, he had mastered well the looks and attitude necessary to his position. Who would ever have imagined that they would be so hard to summon to the fore when they were truly needed?

A short time later, Graves knocked and had the audacity to walk in with his head held high, showing no signs of remorse. Phillip eyed him silently, scrutinizing his demeanor and dress, hoping to push him into displaying a chink in his flawless deportment.

Unfortunately, the bastard refused to be cowed. He looked Phillip directly in the eye, his shoulders back, his figure stiff and straight. Once it became obvious that his assessment wasn't accomplishing anything, Phillip broke the silence. "Well, you bloody bastard, what do you have to say for yourself?"

"Will you be staying for the wedding?"

Phillip snorted. "I ought to turn you out without a character."

"But you won't, sir." Graves smiled and shrugged. "You're glad I'm here."

"If you'd just told me how badly you wanted to come, I'd have let you."

"I did tell you, sir. Six times. You wouldn't listen."

Phillip motioned him to a chair, and he sat.

"Love is a fleeting emotion, John. I hope you know what you're doing."

"It must be horrible to be so cynical." Graves noticed the broken glass on the desk. He moved it off to the sideboard, grabbed a new one and poured Phillip some more wine. "I hope you spend enough time around your wife to have a little of the lovebug bite you. With your surly attitude, it certainly couldn't hurt."

"I hardly need lessons on love and marriage from the likes of you." Phillip grabbed the glass Graves offered and took a swig of the sharp liquid.

"Really? Well, I just enjoyed a wonderful bit of afternoon delight with my betrothed." With a devilish wink, Graves asked, "So, how are you and Lady Jane getting along?"

"Bastard," Phillip muttered.

"What was that, sir?" Graves laughed. "I didn't quite catch it."

"By Christ, you're an irritating ass, but I'm glad you're

here in spite of it. Jane and I are leaving for Portsmouth."

"For how long?"

"I don't know. Her father's been stricken with apoplexy. We're going for a deathbed visit—if there's still a bed to visit."

"So, it's grave, is it?"

"Extremely."

"What can I do to help?"

"See to things for her while she's away."

"Certainly. Whatever you need, I'll do."

"I'm counting on you."

"Of course. Do you think you'll be back for the harvest?"

"Why do you ask?"

"I was just wondering if we should postpone the wedding. Meg had hoped that Jane would be her matron of honor." He flashed Wessington his crooked smile. "And I had hoped you'd stand up with me."

"Me?"

"Of course, unless you think it would be too far below your station?"

Phillip had never been asked to stand up for anyone. Had never been close enough for anyone to ask. He was flattered and embarrassed to find himself so. He had to clear his throat before he could respond. "I would be honored. You must postpone it until we return."

"I don't want you to go." Emily stood by the window of Jane's bedchamber, staring out across the grounds to the fields and hills beyond.

Behind her, Jane was buckling the hasp on the portmanteau she would tie onto her saddle. Wessington had sent other bags in a small, quick carriage, but they wouldn't meet up with the driver until Portsmouth, so Jane had packed a useful amount for the trip. "We've been through this, Emily. You know I must."

"But what if something happens to you?"

"Nothing will. I'll be with your father. He'll take good care of me."

"Couldn't I come with you?"

"You know you need to get back to your lessons, and I don't know how long I'll be away. It's for the best if you remain behind."

Emily turned from the window and stared at Jane. She loved her now, fiercely and passionately, and could hardly remember the times before Jane had arrived. To think of her leaving so soon was frightening and hurtful. She wanted to say: what about *me,* but as she was so unused to giving her own needs precedence, she couldn't find a way to voice the selfish thought. "What about all your work?"

"Richard will watch over the farm. John will watch over the house. And Meg will watch over you." Jane finished with the buckles and turned to the girl. She looked so lost that Jane's heart ached. Sitting on the bed, she patted the mattress. Emily hesitated, and Jane reached out a hand until she took a few slow steps across the room and eased down. "Are you afraid about my going?"

"Yes," she whispered as though the feeling was shameful.

"Why?"

"What if Master Morris comes around?"

"He'll not be allowed."

She nodded. "What if I get hurt or sick? Who'll take care of me?"

"Meg will, sweetheart. You know she'll do a good job."

Emily finally turned and looked her in the eye. "What if you don't come back?"

"You silly girl. Whatever would make you think such a thing?" Jane knew the answer of course. Emily's fears of being left alone were justified by the fact that she nearly always had been. She rested an arm across the girl's shoulders and pulled her into a tight hug. "I promise I'll come back for you."

"Swear it," Emily said against Jane's chest.

"I swear it. And if my stay becomes prolonged, I will send for you."

"I could come and stay with you in Portsmouth?"

"Yes. Would you like that?"

"Oh, I believe I would. Very much."

"It would be an adventure for you, I dare say. You could see the ocean and the city. We could ride on some of the ships my father is building. We could share my room like best of friends."

Emily had never been anywhere but to the nearby village. "That would be grand, Jane. Just grand."

"Are you feeling better now?"

"Just a bit."

"Let's get going, then. Your father is waiting for me downstairs."

Emily sighed with resignation as they rose together and headed down hand in hand. Richard, John and Meg, along with a few of the upper-level staff, waited in the front foyer and gave Jane quick hugs and words of reassurance.

Phillip, dressed casually in breeches and boots, had just finished tying a bag on the back of his saddle. He turned as Jane and Emily stepped through the door. For the first time, he was struck by what a pretty thing

Emily was. The bright pink of her dress brought out the rosy hue in her cheeks, the azure sky was reflected in her eyes; and her dark ringlets danced in the light as she bobbed down the stairs next to Jane.

Jane herself was prettier than usual. Her green velvet riding habit perfectly silhouetted her trim figure, and the color of the fabric increased the deep emerald of her eyes. The sun flashed off the golden highlights of her beautiful chestnut hair as she pulled a bonnet over her head and tied the green ribbon under her chin.

They made a lovely picture, and it occurred to Phillip that he was a very lucky man.

He watched as they came closer, just the two of them. Others had said their good-byes inside and had chosen to remain there while Emily saw to her parents. Only a lad from the stables stood by to offer assistance.

"Are you ready?" Phillip asked the rhetorical question as Jane stepped next to him. He reached for her bag and handed it to the boy who went to work at strapping it on Jane's horse.

"As ready as I can be."

"Let's be off then." He offered her a hand, but she didn't take it, turning instead to Emily.

"I'll miss you." She held out her arms, and Emily fell into them.

"Don't forget your promise," the girl whispered.

"I won't." Jane smiled and kissed her on the forehead. "And I'll try to write every day to let you know what's happening."

"So will I." They hugged again, and Emily started to cry.

Jane's own eyes were tearing at the thought of how much she'd miss the girl. "Now, don't start that. Your father will think we're a couple of watering pots."

"I'm sorry. I can't help it. I'll miss you so much."

"I love you, Emily."

"I love you, too, Jane."

They hugged each other hard again, and Phillip couldn't believe the lump in his throat. The emotion between them was so visible, so palpable. He wanted to reach out and touch it. To breathe it in. To keep some of it for himself. What would it be like, he wondered, to have the two of them include him in their magic circle? His heart ached at just thinking about it.

Jane pulled back first. "We need to get going. Say good-bye to your father."

Emily turned to him, her lovely cheeks damp with tears. "Good-bye, Father. Have a good trip."

She spoke as though to a casual acquaintance, showing him her most polite courtesies. Not for the first time lately, Phillip ached with the realization of all that had been lost over the years. Something glorious had slipped away, and he had no idea what to do about it or how to get it back. "Good-bye, Emily."

Surprising them both, she jumped forward and wrapped her arms around his waist. With her face against his chest, Phillip was assailed by the clean scent of her, the vibrant energy of the petite form pressed so tightly against his own. It was the first time in his memory that the girl had ever touched him. He placed his arms across her shoulders and hugged her back as tightly as he could.

Unable to resist the sudden urge, he placed a light kiss on the top of her head. "I'll miss you." The words sprang from somewhere deep inside, and after they were spoken, Phillip felt a terrible weight begin to dissipate.

"I'll miss you, too, Father." Emily stood on tiptoe and kissed his cheek. Without waiting for a response or a reaction, she turned and ran to the house.

Phillip rubbed his cheek, stunned, surprised and

shocked by how wonderful the quick embrace had made him feel. Jane also stood on tiptoe and kissed his other cheek.

"That was wonderful," she whispered.

Yes, Phillip thought, we're off to a good start. Unable to think of how to respond, and unable to talk around the lump of emotion choking him, he helped Jane mount, and they rode off together.

Chapter
Twenty-One

Phillip halted his horse in front an inn where he stayed occasionally. He dismounted and handed the reins to a stable boy as Jane's horse sauntered into the yard.

"I thought we'd never arrive." She heaved a sigh of relief.

Smiling, he held up a hand. "Tired?"

"More so than I imagined I could ever be and still be awake."

Phillip chuckled. "Let me help you down."

Jane's brain gave the order to move, but her legs didn't seem to receive the message. "Hmmm . . ." She shifted in the saddle, feeling pain in places she hadn't previously known existed. "I seem to be a bit more stiff than I thought."

"Not surprising." He reached up both hands and settled them on her waist. "Can you grab my shoulders?"

"I believe my arms still work. Let's see." They did, and she gripped her hands together behind his neck.

"Lean into me." Phillip tightened his grip about her waist and lifted her from the horse. "That's it. Just relax. Let me take all your weight." She was a tiny thing, and he pulled her close, taking his time in lowering her to the ground, enjoying the feel of her mound as it slid across his stomach and groin, her breasts as they passed down his chest, her thighs as they pressed against his own.

Jane felt her feet touching the ground. Phillip was holding her tightly, and she had to admit, it felt good to have him do so. The day they'd passed together had been pleasant; he had been so playful and funny that she could almost see herself falling for his charms.

Still, nothing had prepared her for how difficult the ride would be, and she was exhausted in the extreme. As she took a tiny step away from him, she swayed slightly. He immediately gripped her about the waist, loving the excuse to keep her pressed tightly against the length of his body. "Hold on. I've got you."

"My legs don't seem to want to follow instructions."

"It happens after a long ride. Just rest a moment. Let your legs become reacquainted with the ground." Gradually, he shifted more and more of her weight onto her until she managed to stand on her own. "Better?"

"Much."

"Something tells me you were fibbing the last two times you told me you wished to continue riding." He raised a questioning brow.

"Perhaps. I didn't want you to think me a complainer."

He tapped a finger against the tip of her nose. "I might think many things about you, Jane, but never that you complain. Next time you're tired, you must tell me."

They moved through the door together, Jane managing to walk under her own power, but Phillip kept a steadying hand on the small of her back, ever alert to grab her in case she lost her equilibrium and started to fall. The manager recognized Phillip when he entered, and with proficient haste, they were shown to their adjoining rooms. A maid was sent to tend to Jane; supper and baths were ordered.

Jane sat on the bed as Phillip gave instructions, fatigue quickly overwhelming her senses. Phillip kept watch on her out of the corner of his eye the entire time he talked to the servants he'd sent scurrying off to their tasks. He stepped to the bed, standing right in front of her, but his presence hardly registered, so he slipped a hand under her chin and raised her face. Her eyes weren't focusing too well. "I've ordered a hot bath to be sent up immediately. That should help with some of the stiffness in your muscles."

"It sounds perfectly lovely."

"I thought it would. I'll have my own next door; then I'll join you in here for supper in one hour. Will that give you enough time?"

"More than enough."

As Wessington turned to go, she managed to grab hold of one coherent thought. "Sir?"

He looked over his shoulder. "What is it, sleepy head?"

"Thank you for today."

"My pleasure." He smiled and walked out.

Jane sat immobile on the bed, letting the maid undress her and help her into the bath. The woman was pleasant and efficient, and Jane was grateful that she wasn't required to offer much assistance. Her arms and legs were completely beyond her control, her neck and back muscles a tangle of knots, her bottom black and blue from banging against the saddle all day.

When Phillip entered an hour later, refreshed by his own bath, but also extremely tired, he found Jane beautifully naked and sound asleep in the tub. Her head was tipped to the side, her cheek resting against the edge. Her sweet, full lips were slightly parted, the deep breaths of heavy sleep passing in and out. The maid had not washed her hair but had brushed it thoroughly, and it hung loose and radiant past the rim to the floor.

He stepped closer. The water level just reached the bottoms of her breasts; her nipples were visible above it. Below, in the soapy water, he could just make out her form, the slim waist, the hips, the chestnut hair protecting her womanly secrets. Her knees were drawn up and open in a most unladylike fashion. The sight of her, naked, wet and slippery excited him as nothing had in a long time. But the rest—the air of vulnerability, the quiet exhaustion, the simple beauty—stirred other things inside. He felt the strangest urges. To protect. To shelter. To cherish. To care.

He wanted nothing more than to bury himself inside her tight, sweet sheath, but he was surprised to also realize that he'd be perfectly content simply to hold her while she slept.

A knock sounded on the door. "Enter," he said softly.

The maid came in, carrying the supper tray. She set it on the table, then turned to Phillip with a knowing smile, whispering, "I tried to wake her a few minutes ago. 'Twas impossible."

"She had a hard day."

"Yes, but the water's getting cool. I can't think it's doing her tired muscles any service."

"I agree. Help me, please, and we'll put her straight to bed."

"Certainly, sir." The maid turned back the covers, then grabbed a towel.

Phillip rolled up his sleeves, baring his forearms, and reached into the water, slipping an arm under Jane's knees and the other behind her back. He lifted her and held her dripping form over the tub, while the maid gave her a quick drying. Jane didn't move, except to shift closer to Phillip, rubbing her cheek against his chest as though trying to burrow closer to his body's heat.

He tucked her under the covers, pulling them up and over her breasts. In sleep, she looked so young, so trusting. He leaned over and kissed her lips, then sat at the table to eat his meal. When the maid returned half an hour later, he was still sitting there, his plate empty, watching his wife.

"Shall I take the tray, sir?"

"Yes. But leave the cheese and bread. If she stirs in the night, I'm sure she'll be famished." The woman efficiently rearranged the food, tidied up and shuffled out. Phillip watched her go, then turned back to Jane. Funny, how things worked sometimes, that this glorious creature had fallen into his life.

Knowing he should go to his own room, but also knowing he couldn't have left her side if a pistol had been held to his head, he stood and slowly disrobed, his ardor increasing as each piece of clothing fell to the floor. Naked, he walked around the room, snuffing the candles and extinguishing the lamps. At the side of the bed, with only the glow of the moon shining through the window for illumination, he stood silently, watching the rise and fall of the bedcovers. A breast had escaped confinement, and the nipple taunted him with promises of deep, hidden pleasures.

Stifling a groan, he pulled back the covers and eased in next to her. The bed was warmed by her body heat, and he was assailed with the fresh smell of her skin, the perfume of her hair, the musk of her sex. Jane lay on her back; he stretched out next to her, letting his body touch the entire length of hers. The agony was exquisite, and he shifted her to her side, curling his legs behind hers and spooning her bottom against his crotch.

One arm slipped under her neck, the other lay across her waist. His hand cradled the weight of a breast. As if Jane welcomed his presence, she shifted her backside, some unconscious part of her wanting closer contact with his heat and energy. Closing his eyes, he bit back another groan, kissing her shoulder and pressing his loins against her. It was going to be a very long night.

Jane's first distracted thought was that she was in the middle of a glorious dream. She'd birthed a beautiful babe, with Wessington's face and Emily's glorious blue eyes. It suckled her greedily, easing the ache that seemed to plague her nipples of late. Arching her back slightly, she moaned with pleasure. Ah, yes, this was what she'd been seeking.

Her brow furled in confusion as she came closer to consciousness. The physical pleasure of the dream was so exquisite, she couldn't bear to feel it end. Just a while longer . . .

When Phillip had awakened a few minutes earlier, he'd found, much to his delight, that Jane had fully accepted him in her bed. She had turned to face him, an arm across his stomach, a leg twined with his. Soft breath tickled the crook of his neck. Her nipples played with the smattering of hairs across his chest. Her relaxed stomach rested against his, her mound pressed against his cock.

He was rock hard.

Judging from the hint of daylight poking through the shade, they had an hour or two before the maid would come with breakfast. Since he couldn't imagine the agony of going another day without venting some of his passion, it seemed the perfect opportunity to introduce his wife to the true pleasures of lovemaking, as he should have done on their wedding night.

Once again, he cursed himself for a fool. If he'd bedded her properly the first time, he'd have been enjoying her all these long months, and with her natural affinity for the emotional, she'd be an experienced temptress by now.

No time like the present to begin her lessons anew.

He rolled her onto her back. In the dim light, her nipple flirted. Gently licking and wetting, he nipped until it was tiny and pebble hard. Only then did he suck it into his mouth. He licked, then suckled, then licked again, teasing and playing. With his teeth, he nipped his way around, then kissed where his bites had fallen, then nipped again, ending the teasing by pulling her deep into his mouth and working his tongue against the sensitive skin.

Jane groaned softly and arched her chest, her body knowing what it liked and seeking more of it. Happy to give her what she craved, he moved to her other breast, kissing the valley between the two, before finding the rough ridge surrounding the other nipple. Much as he'd done with the first, he nipped and teased, licked and sucked, waiting forever before finally taking the nipple deep into his mouth.

While his lips worked their magic, his fingers found

their way down her stomach and into the thatch of chestnut curls. Her body was already wet with desire, her creamy essence pearling around the hairs and moistening his fingers. Suppressing a groan of frustration, he pulled his lips away from her nipple and rested them against the soft, silky skin between her breasts.

Easing a finger into the hot shaft, then another, he found the damp heat unbearably delightful. As if to torture him, Jane unconsciously flexed her interior muscles, tightening herself around his hand, holding him there, pulling him deeper inside. He moved his lips back to a breast, suckling her hard while he worked the fingers gently back and forth. It took every bit of restraint he'd ever mustered to keep from burying himself inside her.

When he did, he wanted her awake and participating. For some reason, her acceptance of his physical self had taken on grave proportions in his mind. He wanted— no *needed*—to have her.

The delicious pain invading Jane's body finally pulled her fully awake. In the back of her mind, she knew she should have been more surprised to see Wessington in her bed. But she wasn't. He was there, and her traitorous body was glad of his presence.

He instantly sensed she'd awakened and raised his mouth from her breast to smile into her eyes. His smile must have melted hundreds, if not thousands, of female hearts over the years, and Jane felt there was something perfectly lovely about having it focused on herself. He eyed her curiously, as though he expected her to scream or cry out, but surprisingly, to both of them, she regarded him silently.

"Good morning," he finally said. He kissed a path up the swell of her breast, across her neck, her jaw, to the corner of her mouth, where he playfully worked on her bottom lip.

"What are you doing in my bed?"

"I realize that, so far, I've been a very bad teacher, but don't you know?"

The mischievous smile he flashed her could have come from the Devil himself, he looked so wicked. Jane wondered how any woman had ever resisted him when he looked so. "I don't want this from you."

"Really? I could swear your body is telling me the opposite." The protest sounded feeble to his ears, and even if she meant it in some small part of her heart, he wasn't about to back off. With careful finesse, he worked his way back to her breast, his mouth hovering over her nipple so that each moist breath teased the aroused flesh.

Deliberately, he pulled his hand away from between her legs, watching as her hips moved at the sense of loss, trying to regain his touch. He took a finger, moist with her body's juices, and laved her nipple. With the hard nub soaking wet, he blew his hot breath across it, feeling her body squirm against the sensations he was causing.

"Tell me you don't want this, Jane." He blew again against the nipple, lowered his lip till it just grazed the tip, then pulled away, refusing to give her the relief she sought. He moved to the other breast, wet the nipple in the same manner and blew on it. "Tell me, Jane. Isn't this exactly what your body has been craving for so long? Haven't you dreamed about this at night? Haven't your breasts swelled and hurt at the thought of what it would feel like to have my lips around them? Tell me, Jane," he finished in a whisper.

How could he know how much she truly wanted this when she hadn't known herself? How could he know?

His lips hovered just on the edge of her extended nipple, torturing her with their closeness. Her breasts ached painfully. They were full and hard, and she longed for the sweet relief she'd felt during her dream. Somehow her body knew what she craved. Raising a hand to the back of his head, she pulled him closer.

With careful attention, he went to work again, sucking and licking. Each touch, each subtle shift of pressure, each tilt of his head brought a reaction from her. What a gem he'd uncovered.

Jane couldn't stand the painful pressure Wessington was creating. Each flick of his tongue, each tug of his lips, sent a surge through her body as though she'd been jolted by lightning. Her limbs seemed on fire, the blood in her veins roasting her from the inside out.

He left her breasts, and she nearly pouted as he withdrew the pleasure his mouth had provided, except there wasn't time to pout. Moving up her chest, he nuzzled her neck, teasing her earlobe until she squirmed in agony. Leaving a trail of moist kisses against her skin, he sought her mouth.

With tender urgency, he brushed his lips over hers, his excitement growing with each passing moment. Although she probably didn't realize it, her body was matching his, movement for movement. As his hands roamed across her shoulders and arms, hers moved up and down his back. When his knee slipped between her thighs, her hips arched to meet it. As he bit back a groan of pleasure, so did she. As had happened the other few times he'd touched her, he was so ready for her that he felt fourteen again and busy with his first lass. He was a man of great sexual experience. How was it that she aroused him so quickly and so completely?

Knowing he needed to slow himself down, both to

prolong his own pleasure and to increase hers, he worked on her lips, urging them open.

"Kiss me back, Jane, just as you did in London." His tongue begged invitation, begged again, until almost shyly her own met his in playful suggestion. "Yes, that's it."

Jane opened her mouth, receiving him, learning the pressure and shape of his lips, the feel of his teeth, the shape of his tongue as it worked against her own in a firm, insistent rhythm. Her hand moved along his neck, pulling him closer. Under her fingertips, she could feel the steady pounding of his heart, and a secret thrill passed through her as she realized he was as fevered as she.

The fur of hair on his chest brushed against her swollen nipples. The rough hair dusting his thigh abraded the soft skin of her own. He raised a knee, applying greater pressure against her woman's spot, and Jane discovered a new swirl of sensation, so exquisite that it was nearly unbearable. The only way she could ease the ache was to flex her hips against his roving thigh; each time she did, Wessington's ardor seemed to increase. He'd shifted until most of his body was covering hers, but for some reason, he didn't seem heavy. He only seemed welcome. The sensation of having a man lying on her, bearing her into the mattress was a new one and, she found to her satisfaction, a delightful one.

Phillip knew he couldn't stand the suspense of wanting her much longer. He let his fingers trace a swirling path down across her breasts, her waist, her navel until he once more reached her curly thatch. Without teasing or hesitating, he slipped into the wet heat, two fingers pushing inside. Moving them in a carnal rhythm timed to correspond with the thrust of his tongue, he let her body learn the rhythm to come, except that it already seemed to know.

Her hips flexed against his hand, but the motion no longer eased the excruciating agony growing between her legs. Something was happening. Something she didn't understand. Her body seemed to be spiraling toward a place where she had never gone before. The journey was unknown as was the destination, and, when Wessington shifted over her and moved between her legs, 'twas the first time she became frightened. His hardened member pressed against the moist spot at the center of her thighs, begging entrance, but that wasn't what scared her. It was something more. Something different. She didn't want to find out what it was, but she didn't want to let it escape either.

"What's happening to me?" she asked, a worried look in her eye.

"It's pleasure, love," he said in a voice so tightly controlled that she barely recognized it. "Don't fight it."

"But I don't know . . ." Her protest was cut off by the movement of his thumb across a hard nub hidden in the wet folds. The touch on a spot she'd never known existed on her body shot fire through her abdomen and beyond.

Phillip raised back on his elbow, wanting a better view of her as he eased her over the edge. She was ready, waiting, her body practically begging him to take her where she needed to go. He pushed just the tip of his shaft inside her wet sheath, fighting with every bit of his self-control to keep from burying himself to the hilt, then rubbed again across the center of her sex. 'Twas hard, enlarged. She jumped.

"Say my name." He stroked it again.

Jane looked into the beautiful face of her husband.

There were beads of sweat on his brow as though he was in great physical pain, his breathing heavy and labored. Some powerful emotion swept through her, too near to love to examine closely.

"I feel so strange," she whispered.

"Say my name," he demanded again, caressing that agonizing spot another time.

A spiral started through her, beginning at the hot point of sensation where his thumb kept striking and moving out across her belly, to her breasts, to her limbs. She arched her back, no longer able to fight that which seemed determined to sweep her away. Her brow furled in confusion. "Phillip . . . what . . . ?"

"Say it again," he smiled, driving her further to the cliff toward which her body seemed to be hurling itself.

"Phillip . . ."

With a final hard flick of his thumb, he pushed her over the edge, and she went flying into space, stars bursting behind her eyes, a darkened universe of fireworks and explosions making itself known to her. And then she was free-falling. Through space, her body arching with need, seeking more than she was given, begging for mercy that it would end soon, but never wanting it to stop.

Phillip caught the cry of pleasure the moment before it burst from her lips. As her body tensed with passion, he grabbed her buttocks, lifted her and rammed deep inside her, absorbing every shock which shuddered through her. The moment went on and on as Jane writhed and fought against the blissful agony engulfing her. It took all he had to keep from joining her, but he wanted her to experience every moment of her first pleasuring and he wanted to experience it with her.

Slowly, gradually, the spasms subsided. Jane's body relaxed, her mind became cognizant of her surroundings. Phillip lay fully on top of her, her thighs spread like a wanton's, his man-part completely buried inside her. She'd fallen from a very high cliff, but her husband had been there to catch her. "It didn't hurt," she whispered in surprise.

"No. It never will again." He smiled down at her joyfully, brushing a kiss against her eager lips.

"It doesn't seem finished."

"It's not." Tightening his buttocks, he moved deeply, touching her womb, delighted to see how her eyes opened wide with shocked pleasure. He pulled all the way out until his tip just hovered at the opening of her body, then pushed all the way in again. "Move with me. Like this."

He started pushing in, pulling out, and Jane immediately learned his rhythm as her own. As if her body knew some secret code, she raised her hips and wrapped her legs around him, loving the deep growl of pleasure she heard coming from him as she flexed and arched, allowing him fuller access to her body. The pleasure he'd given her had been exotic, incredible, but unsatisfying, because even though it had ended, she felt incomplete. This was what she needed, she saw now, this fullness, this hard press of his flesh against hers, this tug and pull as their bodies strained together toward fulfillment.

The tension in his loins had reached such an alarming state that he nearly spilled himself, but he held back, wanting her to join him when he reached his peak. He moved in a deliberate rhythm, helping her learn the way, pushing and working, their bodies sweating and sliding as one. The pressure built until his ears rang with it, his blood pounded. Nothing, no one existed except Jane, lying so beautifully open and welcoming beneath him.

Pleasure was building in Phillip; Jane could sense it. His arms and legs flexed, his stomach tightened. The muscles in his neck tensed in thick cords. A strange, exciting thrill of anticipation began as her own body responded to his. This time, she knew what was coming and what the end would entail. And, with heartfelt certainty, she knew he would join her. She would not make the journey alone.

Phillip could tell she was once again near the edge. So was he. Bracing himself with one arm, he used the other to lift her hips, wanting to be closer but not seeming to be able to join closely enough. Jane, sensing his need, reached around and grabbed his buttocks, shifting her hips, pulling him deeper, closer, tighter. It was his undoing.

"Now," he pleaded, out of breath. "Come with me."

"Yes. Now." Jane arched up off the bed as Phillip's entire body tensed, and he growled his pleasure low in his throat. Feeling his essence spilling deep inside, dampening her womb, set off her own explosion of pleasure. She pulled him close as shudders of ecstasy rocked both of them.

Thoroughly sated, they held each other, tenderly, quietly, Phillip feathering soft kisses across her brow. Their racing pulses slowed together until Jane could feel the beat of his heart deep inside, throbbing through his shaft in constant rhythm with her own. It was a stirring sensation unlike any she could have possibly imagined.

Her eyes damp with tears from the emotion of it all, she rested a hand against his cheek and whispered, "I love you."

Chapter
Twenty-Two

Not knowing where the words had come from, Jane covered her mouth with her hand, wishing she could take them back. Her husband probably thought her an inexperienced ninny, but the passion that sizzled between them had briefly overwhelmed all of her senses.

Phillip's heart turned over at the declaration, and he smiled down at her. On his wedding night, he'd let Margaret frighten him about the disaster that would loom upon hearing those very words spring from Jane's lips. Now he couldn't imagine why he'd let the thought worry him. Nothing had ever sounded sweeter.

"I'm sorry. I shouldn't have said that," she said with a slight shake of her head.

Panicked that she'd say she didn't mean it, he kissed her cheeks. "Don't be sorry. Not for anything that happens between us when we're together like this. Anything is allowed as long as it makes you happy."

She ran her hand along his cheek, letting the stubble prickle her skin. "Is it always like this?"

"Rarely. But I daresay it will be like this for us much of the time."

"Why is that, do you suppose?"

"I've often wondered the same. My only explanation is that some people seem to have a physical connection that's unexplainable. I do not know what causes it or why it exists. It simply does."

"Has it felt like this for you before?" Jane knew she was at risk by asking, for the ache in her heart would be great if he answered truthfully.

Phillip was glad he did not have to lie. "No, it's never been like this for me before."

A soft knock sounded on the door, and Phillip bid the maid to enter. She quickly puttered around the room, starting a fire, setting out hot water and towels. Jane, never having suffered such a moment in her life, lay naked beneath her husband, shielded by his body. With her red face buried against his chest, she hid her eyes as the woman completed her chores.

Phillip kissed the top of her head. "Don't be embarrassed. She'll be gone in another moment." He looked at the maid over his naked shoulder. "Bring us some breakfast, please, but take your time."

The maid gave him a knowing, experienced smile and left the room, and Jane heaved a huge sigh of relief when she heard the door close, causing Phillip to chuckle at her refreshing innocence. He'd had all manner of people stroll through his sexual encounters—from maids to butlers to old lovers to new lovers to strangers—and nothing bothered him anymore. "You are splendid, my dear." He smiled, kissing her ear.

"I've never been more embarrassed in my life. What-ever must the woman be thinking of me?"

"Oh, I'd say she's thinking that this very lucky hus-band is enjoying a bit of morning pleasure before a long and arduous day. She's probably extremely jealous."

Jane's heart did a little flip-flop as he smiled and kissed her hand. She raised up on an elbow, suddenly shy again, and pulled the blanket closer, shielding her naked breast from his view. "I thought we were in a hurry. How come you told her to take her time with our morning meal?"

Phillip reached out and slipped a hand under the blanket, revealing the hidden breast for his avid assess-ment. The nipple puckered immediately, and he flicked his finger across it. "I want to love you again before we rise."

"You can do it more than once?"

The surprise and shock in her eyes caused him to laugh aloud. "I can do it numerous times if the spirit moves me."

"But I didn't do anything. How is it that you're aroused again so quickly? And so easily?"

"Part of it is the newness of it. Of being close to you. Touching you and seeing you. But it's also because you're so beautiful." He traced a hand down the swell of her chest, pausing to circle the swollen mounds. "Your face. Your hair. Your lovely breasts. All conspire to ignite my passions. I find I can't help myself." He pulled at the covers that had wedged between their bodies and shifted her closer so she was once again stretched against him.

As her nipples brushed the hair on his chest, Jane was shocked by how quickly her body responded to his. She wanted him again already. "And if my physique someday fails to inspire you? What then?"

He chuckled as he reached under the covers. His hard, aching shaft was at full attention. Wrapping his hand around hers, he squeezed tightly and showed her how to stroke him back and forth, enjoying her look of wonder and satisfaction as she touched him for the first time. "There are many ways to work your wiles on me. I plan to enjoy teaching you every one of them."

The maid gave them a long, leisurely hour to completely sate themselves, and they took full advantage of the time. But, as Jane was quickly learning, the physical side of loving could quickly become addicting if practiced correctly. As she'd first assumed about her husband, he was an ardent and skilled lover who took great pleasure in learning the ways of her body, just as she hungered for more knowledge of his own. As they rose, and Phillip helped her wash and dress, she was shocked to find herself thinking about what type of loving would await them in the night to come.

The days to Portsmouth passed quickly, the nights even more so, as the lovers enjoyed an easy companionship during the daylight hours. Darkness brought them what they both craved, times of wild abandon or quiet tenderness. They slept little, but barely seemed to notice as the journey continued. Their senses were on overload as they loved and talked and learned of each other.

As the miles wore on, Jane's contemplative silences grew longer, and he could tell her thoughts were increasingly on her home and what they would find there. In the pleasantness of their days together, the heat of their nights, it was easy for him to forget why they were on the road. For Jane, the reason was always there just below the surface.

The last morning, as they rode into the city, she barely

talked at all. He allowed her to journey in silence, content to know he was close by if she needed him. They moved through the town and out the other side, passing numerous small country homes and estates until she stopped at the gate to a modest-sized two-story Queen Anne gracefully set on a small hill.

Below, off in the distance, was a protected harbor, and he could just make out the masts and sterns of numerous ships in various stages of construction. Odd, but for a workday, the place looked devoid of activity. He got a bad feeling but said nothing, not wanting to alarm his wife who was plenty nervous already.

"This is it?" he asked quietly, hating to disturb her reverie.

"Yes. My home."

Phillip winced at the phrase. He didn't want her to still be thinking of this small, plain place as her home. Although she'd told him what an unassuming man her father was, he found it hard to believe that a person possessed of such great wealth would live so frugally.

"Do you think they received our message?" Jane asked.

"I'm sure they did." There was a touch of uncertainty in her hesitation, and he leaned across and covered her hand with his own. "It will be all right, Jane."

"Yes, I know." She tried for a smile, but it didn't quite reach her eyes. Wanting to be the first through the gate, she turned her horse and started up the drive, not going more than a few yards before she reined the animal to a quick halt. "Oh, no."

Phillip looked up at the house, noticing for the first time the black wreath on the door, the black curtains draped over the windows.

Death.

They'd arrived too late.

* * *

Jane woke from her nap and judging from the shadows it was late afternoon. Her small bedchamber seemed so different now. Where once it had been her private haven from the secret turmoils of the household, now it just seemed little and plain and remarkably dreary. Why had they lived this way when they were, by all accounts, an incredibly wealthy family?

Father. Father was the answer. He'd been a hardworking, thrifty man. Almost miserly at times. No matter how well the business was doing, how much they thrived, he insisted on economy. Growing up, she had never enjoyed the servants or the gowns or the wonderful foods or all the other glorious things money could buy. He'd lived a simple life, so they had, too.

Had he enjoyed his life? Had he ever been happy? Jane didn't know, but she could never remember him ever spending any of his hard-earned wealth on an unnecessary purchase. No hair ribbons for his girls simply because they'd look pretty. No stick candies from the market as a surprise. No new gowns for a coming-out dance. Just work and saving and more work.

Now he was dead. Dead three days and buried the day before Jane arrived. He'd never regained consciousness after the seizure in London. If he could do it again, Jane wondered, would he change anything? Have a little more fun perhaps? Work a little less? Play a little more?

She shook off the morbid thoughts and rose to glance across the grounds sloping down toward the Shipworks. When Phillip had tucked her in for her nap, he'd said he was going down there. With so many interesting things to see, he was probably still there. She smiled, thinking how curious life was. Who would ever have imagined that she would be glad he had come with her?

Upon arriving hours earlier, he had been such a god-send, deftly handling their entrance into her childhood home where she didn't appear to be wanted or needed. He'd been the one to deal with Gert's rude and impertinent welcome by swiftly putting her in her place. He'd comforted Jane. He'd ordered her bath and put her to bed. And, most surprisingly, he'd acted like a devoted, loving husband, protecting her from any insult or abuse. If she didn't know better, she'd start believing he cared for her.

Jane smiled at the thought, but quickly chased it away. With Phillip down at the harbor, it was the perfect time to speak with Gregory. He hadn't been home when they'd arrived, but hopefully, with the supper hour approaching, he would be now. She wanted to seek him out and spend a few moments resolving things between them. It had been four months since they'd seen each other.

The thought of her brother-in-law left a bad taste in her mouth, for somewhere along the line, her memories of Gregory had changed dramatically. Or perhaps she had changed. Where once he had seemed charming, now he simply seemed overbearing. Not wise and thoughtful but bossy and selfish. Romantic had become manipulative. Misunderstood had become pitiful. His handsome features now seemed plain. And his trying to cheat on his wife, with her very own sister, left Jane angry and disgusted, both with herself and with him. Whatever had she been thinking?

She dressed quickly without summoning the maid Phillip had demanded Gert provide for her. It only took a few minutes to don the simple walking dress, to braid her hair. Down the stairs she tiptoed, knowing at this time of day she could find Gregory in the library if he was about at all.

As she entered the room, no one was present. She walked to the desk and surveyed the papers scattered there, shocked to see that the numbers looked familiar. Scooping them up, she scanned the columns. The pages contained her estimations of start-up costs for the import business. The factoring was her own, but the handwriting was Gregory's. Phillip had been right! Gregory was a liar as well as a thief.

Well-known footsteps sounded in the hall. She'd know Gregory's stride anywhere after spending years listening for it. Quickly masking the distress on her face, she moved to the window, making every effort to look calm when he entered.

Gregory paused in the doorway, a smile breaking across his face when he laid eyes on her.

"My dear, dear Jane. How good it is to see you at this horrible time. You must be devastated." He said it loudly, so any lingering servants might hear. "Let me express my most heartfelt condolences." Looking around covertly, he closed the door, then quickly stepped to her side, taking both her hands in his as he whispered, "Let me look at you. I swear you grow more lovely by the day."

Jane had to bite her lip to keep from laughing aloud. After all the years she'd pined away, cursing Fate that she couldn't have him for her own, she'd painted a picture of him in her mind as some sort of Adonis. Had he always been so short? Had his blond hair always been so thin on the top? Had that heavy paunch always circled his middle? Had his eyes always been so pale, his skin so marked? His breath so foul?

She took a step back. "Hello, Gregory."

"Hello, my love." Without warning, he pulled her into his arms. "I've been lost, absolutely lost without you. I can't believe you're here."

Jane's face was mashed against his chest. Her breasts pressed rudely and intimately against him. His erection was pressing against her stomach, and she again had to squelch laughter. Had he always been so poorly endowed?

She fisted her hands between them and broke the contact of their bodies. "I thought we should talk about—"

Gregory cut her off. "Yes, my darling, we must talk, but first . . ." He lowered his mouth to hers and kissed her.

As though in slow motion, Jane saw his face coming toward hers. She was mesmerized, not wanting the unwelcome contact, but not able to keep from wondering what his kiss would feel like now that she had been kissed by Phillip, a man who truly knew what passionate loving was all about.

After being taken to heaven and back by her husband, it was hard to call what Gregory did *kissing*. With eyes closed, he pressed his dry and chapped lips to hers. Holding his mouth against her own, not brushing, not rubbing, not teasing with his tongue, he just stood there. Yet, his body trembled as though in the throes of the most exciting passion.

With her eyes wide open, she watched him and felt not a flicker during the offensive embrace. His audacity, after they'd not seen each other for months, and after she was a married lady, was extremely insulting. She pushed him away and moved behind a chair, using it as a shield to protect her from any further advances.

"Really, Gregory, I hardly think that was appropriate. Please don't try such a thing again. I won't allow it."

Gregory looked shocked, then hurt, the emotions playing across his face as though he'd stood in front of the mirror and practiced them for her benefit. "I'm cut to the quick, Jane. I've waited so long to be with you again. Every minute of every day since your departure has been pure torture for me. And then to find that Charles married you to that . . . that . . ."

"That what, Gregory?" Not that she cared one whit for Gregory's opinion of Phillip, but she was terribly curious to hear what he would say.

"That . . . nobleman!" he sputtered as though it were the worst sort of epithet.

Jane laughed. "You hardly know him. What could you possibly find detestable?"

"The man's so rude. Ordering us to stay in his home while we were in London. Making us sleep in his beds and eat his food, then treating us as though we weren't good enough to share his table. He has the most atrocious manners. Telling us what to do at every turn."

"Yes, he can be quite overwhelming when he wants to be. It's one of the things I enjoy most about him."

"Jane dear, you can't tell me you're seriously taken with the fellow?"

"Actually, I find I am. The longer I'm married to him, the more I've come to realize that he is the very best thing that ever happened to me." With a great deal of surprise, she realized she meant every word.

Gregory was upset. Always before, he'd held the upper hand, had easily made her feel guilty or unworthy. Something had changed with her because his old tactics certainly weren't working. He wanted to hurt her and wished he knew how. "I can't see how you could hold any serious affection for a man with his reputation. Why, in London all we heard was—"

Jane cut him off. "Speaking of London, what were you and Father doing there?" He reddened and stepped behind the desk, shifting papers as though hiding things he didn't want her to see. Little did he know, it was too late. She'd already seen the evidence with her own eyes.

"We were there on business."

"What kind of business? Something to do with the Shipworks?"

"Well, yes . . . yes, it did have something to do with the Shipworks."

She loved watching him twitch under her condemning gaze and thought about prolonging the torture. Finally, after his numerous inane attempts to explain, she decided to have mercy on him. "My husband tells me you were there seeing bankers about my import business."

Caught red-handed, he paled. "It's not what you think."

"Really? You didn't steal my idea and present it to Father as your own?"

He rubbed a hand over his worried brow. "You don't understand, dear."

"Oh, I think I understand perfectly, and I am not your 'dear'. You are a liar and a cheat. A forger. A thief. You are a prevaricating opportunist who schemes, manipulates and cheats on his wife with her naïve, younger sister!" With each accusation, Jane's anger rose until she was certain she'd have hit him if he'd been standing closely enough. "Have I left anything out?"

"You bloody fool, I did it for us," he spit out at her.

"For us? How could any of your manipulations possibly have been for my benefit?"

Gregory didn't dare mention any of the secret discussions he'd had with Charles over the past year; while he was an ambitious man, he also knew his limitations. Charles had only been incapacitated a few weeks and dead a few days, yet already, the burdens seemed overwhelming. He needed Jane's help to keep things running smoothly and successfully. She had to be courted and wooed so she would remain in Portsmouth for a time.

In his most placating tone, he moved toward her, his hand out and reaching for hers. "Jane, dear, after all we've meant to each other over the years, I hate to see us fighting."

With the venom she felt clear in her eyes, she said, "We haven't even begun to fight."

Jane turned away, searching for self-control. As Gregory laid his hand on the center of her back, another unwelcome advance, the door flew open.

Gregory jumped back, but Jane stood her ground, glancing over her shoulder to see that Phillip had entered. The look on his face was calm, dispassionate, but she could see from the tense lines of his long frame that he was furious.

"Lord Wessington," Gregory squeaked. "How nice to see you again."

"I was looking for my wife. I see I've found her." He turned his burning gaze to Jane, and she met it without flinching.

Gregory cleared his throat. "This wasn't what it looked like, sir. I was . . . I was merely comforting my sister-in-law."

"Really? It looked to me as though you were kissing my wife."

"Phillip," Jane said, "I can explain . . ."

He locked his gaze on Gregory. "I shot the last man I caught kissing my wife."

Gregory trembled visibly, his Adam's apple bobbing as he swallowed. "Milord, I assure you, I was doing nothing of the kind. I was merely offering solace."

"Trust me, Gregory, if my wife needs comforting, I'm perfectly capable of it. Come here, Jane." He held out a hand to her. Jane took the few quick steps to his side, and he pulled her into an embrace. As he hugged her tightly, he ran his hands up and down her back in a proprietary gesture to let Gregory know that *he* had the right to touch her, while Gregory did not and never would.

She buried her face against his chest. "I'm sorry, Phillip. Please forgive me."

"It's all right," he whispered against her hair, and she raised her eyes to look into his. Surprisingly, he was smiling down at her.

"You're not angry?"

He shook his head. Returning from his walk, he'd seen them from outside as he approached the back of the house. His heart had nearly stopped beating in his chest as he saw Jane in the arms of another, but on stepping closer, it was immediately clear that she was not enjoying whatever Gregory was doing to her and was, in fact, trying to push him away. The dolt didn't seem to realize that she was not participating in the embrace.

He'd watched in silence and seen right away when Gregory had gotten himself into deep trouble. Thinking he'd better rescue the idiot before Jane killed him, he had hurried to the library before she could inflict any permanent damage.

"We will speak more of this later. When we're alone." His tone suggested they would do other things when they were alone, things Gregory could only begin to imagine. He turned his attentions back to his red-faced brother-in-law. "I'm going to take a wild guess and say that Jane's found out what you were doing in London with her father."

"Really, Wessington"—Gregory cleared his throat—"I don't think this is the proper time to talk business. Charles is hardly put in the ground."

Behind them, a footman stepped to the door. "Master Fitzsimmons," the man said to Gregory, "the solicitor's here. Should I show him in?"

Gregory looked panic-stricken. Behind him, the solicitor's footsteps could be heard as the portly gentleman lumbered down the hall without waiting for an invitation. On stepping into the library, he eyed Jane and her husband, looking as nervous as Gregory, who made quick introductions.

"Hello, Jane," he said. He'd been her father's solicitor for decades and had known her since she was a girl. "Gregory told me he wasn't expecting you for several more days." He raised a questioning brow at Gregory. "Perhaps we should postpone this until another time?"

"Yes. That's an excellent idea." Gregory came toward the door and started ushering the man from the room.

Phillip's imperious glare stopped them both in their tracks. He didn't like this one bit. "What brings you out from town so late at night, sir? What couldn't wait until morning?"

The solicitor flashed Gregory a furious look, then shrugged. Jane would find out soon enough. He just hadn't wanted to be there when she did. "We were going to read Charles's will."

"And Gregory wanted it done before we arrived?"

"Well . . ." The man hemmed and hawed, looking to Gregory for assistance.

"We just wanted to get the painful task over with," Gregory offered. "No use upsetting Jane unnecessarily."

Phillip stared down the solicitor. "Is my wife mentioned?"

He cleared his throat. "Well . . . ah . . . yes. She is mentioned."

"Then by all means, don't let us interrupt. Do come in."

Chapter
Twenty-Three

" 'I, Charles Francis Xavier Fitzsimmons, the Third, being of sound mind and body, do hereby declare this to be my last will and testament ...' " The solicitor adjusted his spectacles, glanced surreptitiously at Gregory, then began reading the introductory paragraphs, which mentioned several longtime employees by name as heirs to small cash gifts.

Jane, who was still in shock over her father's death, hadn't had time to ponder his estate. When the solicitor raised his eyes and looked straight at her, she felt such a frisson of fear that her entire body tensed. Phillip noticed and reached across, slipping his hand around hers, offering his silent comfort and strength.

" 'To my daughter, Jane Fitzsimmons Wessington, I bequeath the box containing her mother's jewels, as well as the portrait of her mother hanging in the upstairs hall' "—Jane smiled at this, and Phillip squeezed her hand—" 'the remainder of her bequest to be considered the dowry paid to her husband, Phillip Wessington.' "

Phillip raised a brow. Jane didn't seem to fully grasp the consequences of what the solicitor had just announced. But for a box of jewels and a painting, she'd been disinherited. Not unusual for a female child, but considering the Shipworks was Jane's whole life, and Gregory not Charles's blood son, it seemed unduly harsh.

The man continued reading. " 'To my son-in-law, Gregory Fitzsimmons, in recognition of his hard work and dedication to the family businesses, I leave the bulk of my estate . . .' " Listing Jane's childhood home, the Shipworks, various properties and investments, the solicitor read on for several minutes until he came to the end, a short paragraph ordering Gregory to take care of Gert and to manage the Shipworks so that their sons could proudly carry on the family name.

There was a long silence after the solicitor finished his recitation. Looking confused, Jane finally sat forward in her chair. "That's it?"

"Yes. That's all of it." The man's eyes held a great deal of sympathy.

"But he's just given my home, my business, my . . . my life . . . to Gregory!"

Quietly, he offered, "Charles felt you had your own life, now that you'd married."

She stood, agitated. "But he said if I left, if I married, he'd let me come back. I did everything he asked. This is my home, my place." She pointed toward the harbor. "Those ships are mine! I spent my life helping him build them."

The solicitor shrugged, hating the moment. Having never liked or trusted Gregory, he'd argued with Charles about making all the changes, but the man couldn't be swayed. Lamely, he offered, "He felt Gregory's contributions had been substantial."

"You!" Jane whirled on Gregory, as years of memories came flooding back. Years of completing Gregory's work, of fixing and changing. Going along when Gregory came up with reasons to tell Charles that the work had been his own. She saw it all clearly now. He'd played her for a fool. "You can't even add a column of figures correctly without my help."

Gregory played the moment as a man insulted. "Your father didn't think so."

"I can't believe this." She shook her head in dismay. "To think of all the years I covered for you—lied for you and took the blame for you. All the years, I let you . . ." She couldn't speak of their flirtation. Not in front of her husband. Not in front of anyone. "I trusted you."

"I've not misplaced your trust, Jane. You'll be welcome to continue at the Shipworks in any fashion your husband will allow." He flashed Wessington a placating smile. The Earl seemed to have an affection for her, and Gregory hoped he'd allow Jane to dabble at the business—just enough to keep Gregory himself on the right track.

"My father went to his grave thinking the import idea was yours, didn't he?"

"Well, of course it was mine, but I mentioned your assistance to him numerous times."

"I'll just bet you did, you wretched scoundrel. I hope you drown in the flood of debt that's going to come washing over you."

Her assumption that he'd fail angered him greatly. He'd show the little witch. He stood in a huff. "I refuse to be insulted in such a fashion in my own home."

"My, aren't you quick to claim it as your own?" Jane wanted to scream and tear out her hair. "I have to get out of here. I can't stay here another moment." Looking to her husband, she said, "Phillip, may we leave? Please?"

"Certainly. As quickly as possible." He rose, shaking hands with the solicitor, whom one could hardly blame for the mess. Deliberately, he walked past Gregory, intentionally snubbing him. The Good Lord could only guess what kinds of machinations he'd worked on Charles over the past few months or maybe even years. Lucky for Gregory, there was little likelihood they'd ever meet up with one another again.

With a steadying hand on her back and another on her waist, he escorted Jane out of the room. Refusing to give her a chance to run into her sister or Gregory again, he walked her to the door where he informed a surprised maid that they were leaving immediately. Giving the name of an inn with which he was familiar in the town, he asked that their things be packed and sent there. Then, walking around to the stable behind the house, he saddled their horses without waiting for assistance from one of the limited number of servants in the small household.

An hour later, ensconced in their room in town, Phillip sat her on the bed and poured her a glass of wine. "Drink this down. It should help calm you."

She did as he bid, then said, "I can't remember being this angry in my life, except, well . . ."

"Except with me?"

"Yes." She blushed. They'd not spoken of their wedding night since he'd returned, both seeming willing to try starting over and seeing no need to rehash their horrible beginning. "It's water under the bridge, Phillip. Let's not dredge it up again."

Since he'd acted like the most incredible cad, and been shot at for his efforts, his wedding night was the last thing he wanted to discuss. He changed the subject, asking the question he'd been dying to pose ever since he'd looked through the library window and seen Fitzsimmons mauling her. "Were you in love with Gregory?"

Jane snorted in disgust and rose to stare out the window. "I've always considered myself an intelligent person. I can't believe what a fool I was."

Having made the mistake of falling in love with Anne, Phillip could only sympathize. "Love does strange things to a person. How long did it last?"

"I pined after him for years."

Phillip laughed. "Jane, you're only twenty."

"He married Gert and moved into our house when I was thirteen."

"He must have started in on you when you were quite young."

"Oh, yes," she responded, thinking back to how much she'd enjoyed the attention, the flattery, the secrets and sharing. "From almost the first day. Do you suppose he's planned this all these years?"

"Probably."

"And my father?" Jane couldn't finish voicing the question. It would take a very long time to come to terms with his string of betrayals.

"He's the reason I felt so certain you shouldn't come here. In London, he was so taken with Gregory, and so glad that you weren't there, almost as if he was relieved that he wouldn't have to face you. Was Gregory the reason he sent you away?"

"Gregory was simply the excuse he used. He caught us kissing." She turned her head to look over her shoulder, wanting to look him in the eye when she said, "That's all I ever did with him, Phillip. I just kissed him. I was a virgin when we married. And greatly inexperienced."

"I know, and I feel considerably blessed by my good fortune." He moved to stand behind her and laid his hands around her tiny waist, his warm breath tickling the hairs on the back of her neck. "I never had the chance to thank Gregory or your father for sending you to me."

She'd never thanked them, either, simply because it was only beginning to occur to her that Phillip was a wonderful, wonderful husband. He had been marvelous, so supportive, throughout the trip to Portsmouth and the short stay at home, through the ordeal with Gregory. She wanted to show him how much she cared for him. She *needed* to show him.

"Kiss me, Phillip," she whispered.

From the look in her eye, and the sultry tone in her voice, he knew what she wanted and couldn't believe that his first thought was to refuse her. He didn't want to refuse her anything as long as he lived. "I don't think that's a good idea. You're tired and upset. Let's get you in your bath and put you to bed."

"Kiss me. Now." Without waiting for his cooperation, she stepped into him, leaning forward slightly so that her entire body was stretched out against his. Her nipples hardened against his broad chest, her thighs flexed against his own. Rising slightly on her toes, she reached around and grabbed his buttocks, then shifted her hips to better ease her mound against him.

Phillip hardened instantly. The cause was lost. A bath certainly would have relaxed her, but he was more than happy to use other methods. She started kissing his neck, working her way up to nibble at the corner of his mouth, bringing a smile to his lips. "I've created a monster."

"I can't help myself. What you do is so wonderful, I simply lose myself in you. That's what I need right now."

She kissed her way across his lips, pausing to speak. "Not to think. Not to worry. Not to plan."

A knock sounded on the door. He'd ordered a bath when they'd arrived, and a maid was outside with the tub. Two burly men brought it in and set it in front of the fire, then followed with jugs of water. The maid bustled around the room, setting up a screen, laying out towels. As she departed, Phillip gave an order that they were not to be disturbed until morning.

"Are you going to wash your hair?" he asked in the too-silent room, his voice sounding husky and full of promise.

"No. I'll just brush out the snarls."

"I want to do it for you."

Jane wasn't about to argue the request. Everything he'd shown her so far had been full of wonder and promise. He led her to a stool in front of the mirror. Before letting her sit down, he deftly worked the buttons and hooks on her dress so it fell to the floor around her feet. The silk and lace of her chemise barely hid anything from his critical gaze. The cool air on her shoulders and chest, as well as Phillip's touch at her back, evoked prickly goose bumps up and down her arms. The anticipation was incredible.

Phillip untied the ribbon and pulled the pins from her hair, letting the heavy rope swing down her back. He threaded his fingers through it several times, loosening and straightening the long mass. Leaning down, he whispered in her ear, "I love your hair."

His breath, tickling her neck, created new sensations. Her breasts tingled, the woman's spot between her legs began to ache. The feel of him, working through her hair was so exquisite. Never would she have imagined that such a simple act could seem so intimate, so loving.

He told himself that he finished quickly because he

didn't want her bath water to cool overly much. In truth, the simple act of brushing her hair was so dear that he was frightened. The feelings trying to work their way to the surface of his heart were startling. He'd never felt this way about anyone, and he wasn't entirely sure he wanted to start now. Wishing for a return to the safer ground of simple lust, he laid the brush down and started unbuttoning his shirt.

Jane turned on the stool, only to see he was disrobing. From viewing her husband, she'd learned that the male body was a beautiful thing, and she never had her fill of looking. "What are you doing?"

"I thought we would bathe together."

Jane's eyes widened. The things he came up with! "What a wicked idea."

"I find the idea to be greatly arousing." He reached for her hand and placed it on his hard phallus. Through the fabric of his breeches, she could feel his erection, and she moved her hand across it in the manner he'd taught her.

"How can we both fit in the tub at the same time?" she asked, staring at her hand and what was waiting underneath.

"We'll make ourselves fit."

"I want to wash you." A few days earlier, she'd probably have died before being able to voice such a notion, but Phillip was methodically dashing so many of her inhibitions that she wasn't afraid to make the request.

"I'd like that very much."

Finished undressing, he stood before her in all his naked glory. She wrapped her fingers around his rigid shaft and worked him with her hands, each slow stroke rubbing the sensitive tip against the silk of her chemise. Somehow she'd known it would feel good to him, and his groan of pleasure made her smile.

He stopped her hand and broke the contact between their bodies, amazed anew at how such simple actions on her part were able to completely unman him. "You'd best stop, or we'll never make it to the water."

She chuckled and reached for the hem of her chemise. "Should I take this off?"

"No. Leave it. I enjoy seeing your breasts play against the fabric." He ran a hand across the swell, toying with the firm bud in the center, then led her to the bath where he eased down into the hot water.

Jane, kneeling beside the tub, wasn't certain how or where to begin, so she reached for the cloth and wet it under the water, then began rubbing it across his chest. It didn't provide her with close enough access to his warm skin so she quickly dropped it in favor of using her hands. She worked up a good lather, then let her fingers glide across his skin, washing across the swirl of dark hair on his chest, down his flat stomach, his hard thighs, behind his knees.

With his legs resting open and relaxed against the edges of the tub, she ran her finger along the inside of the right one. The oddest birthmark was there. A figure eight. She ran her fingers around and around the shape. "What's this?"

"It's a mark on the firstborn sons in my family. Passed on from generation to generation."

"It's the sign for infinity."

"It means I'll lust after you for all eternity."

Even though she loved the physical things he did to her, she was still unused to his casual sexual banter. Before meeting him, she'd had no idea men and women spoke to one another in such a fashion. She smiled, "You are terrible."

"No. Just insatiable." He pulled her into his arms, kissing her long and deeply, using the moment to scoop the hot water against her bosom so her chemise hung snugly to the peaked tips. As he sucked on one through the wet cloth—a new sensation for Jane, one which quickly had her squirming—he said, "Who'd ever have imagined that you would be hiding such precious gems under all that clothing?"

When he said such things, she had no idea how to respond verbally, but she was growing much better at responding physically. Using the bath as her excuse, she explored him in every place she loved to touch in the dark hours of the night. From Phillip's teaching, she knew what he liked, but so far, she was still shy. Working her hands up his legs, she paid extra attention to the tender skin on the insides of his thighs, moving in circles, higher and higher, until with each stroke, she just brushed the soft sacs hanging between his legs.

'Twas the first time she'd been so bold, and he was dying. If she brushed him one more time like that, he'd . . . He closed his eyes against the pleasure, groaning low in his throat. "You're killing me."

"You like that, do you?"

"Very much."

"I hope you realize what a wanton I've become. 'Tis all your doing."

"It has been my pleasure to show you the way."

Jane chuckled and leaned into the water, searching for the soap she'd dropped. The splash of water soaked her bodice again, the fabric now tight against her breasts, accentuating every peak and curve. "Up on your knees."

Phillip complied, resting his fists on the edge of the tub, the water slapping against him midthigh. His manpart, hard and pulsing, stood out proudly. Jane took the slippery soap and ran it the length of it, then back, then lower to lather between his legs and up the cleft of his buttocks. She dropped the soap, using her hands to work the lather around, fondling the sacs as she stroked the skin of his shaft back and forth in the steady rhythm he loved. The feeling of having him in her hands, of holding such control over him, was as arousing to her as it was to her husband.

"Enough!" Phillip hissed, as her fingers slid over the throbbing tip. "Enough. Come here." He pulled her into the tub, chemise and all. On her knees, with her back to him, she felt him working the fabric slowly, up her thighs, her hips, her stomach. Tugging it past her breasts and over her head, he threw it on the floor.

She shivered slightly as the chemise departed, so he dipped his hands in the hot water, finding the soap and running it deliberately up her body, much as she had just done. Up her thighs, between her legs, her stomach, breasts, across her shoulders, down her back. He worked the soap and water until she was as hot and slippery as he.

"Grab the edge," he commanded in a harsh tone, his arousal now painful, his need to spill his seed uncontrollable.

She leaned forward and held on, feeling Phillip behind her. He nudged her knees apart as much as he could in the small tub, then slipped his hard member between her legs, where it demanded entry. This was how he'd taken her on their wedding night, and he'd not tried it again. Until now. Although nothing about the experience was the same, she still tensed, her body instinctively remembering the pain, her mind the humiliation. "Phillip, please . . ."

Completely attuned to her body's needs, he could sense her agitation over what he wanted to do. "You trust me, don't you?"

Did she? She closed her eyes as the truth struck her.

Their bond had changed, evolved and forged, until now, she realized, she'd trust him with her life if necessary. "Yes," she nodded in confirmation.

"Welcome me." He placed a hand on the center of her back, tipping her forward slightly, then grabbed for her hips. With one thrust, he plunged in all the way to the hilt.

Jane gasped at the sensation of having him fill her so completely. With one hand, he reached for her nipple and began to twirl it in a maddening circle, while the other moved between her legs to stroke the bud of her sex.

With her beautiful buttocks slapping against him, his shaft moving in and out, the need for release quickly grew out of control. He'd resolved never again to take his own pleasure without helping her to find her own first, but his arousal was so great that he couldn't wait. Holding her close, he pushed in all the way. Again. And a final time, the growl of pleasure escaping his throat sounding like that of a wild animal.

Jane felt the tip of his sex against her womb, the welcome surge of his seed. His body leaned over hers, his arm wrapped around her stomach, holding her buttocks tightly against his groin. His body spasmed, then relaxed, although his breathing, hot and heavy, pulsed across her back. His own passion spent, she knew he was finished. But what about her own? She'd not had this happen before and wasn't sure of what to do. Her body was thrumming with desire, her pulse was racing, her breasts were swollen painfully, her woman's core was crying out for release.

Before she could think of how to move from the dreadful pinnacle on which Phillip had left her dangling, he pulled away and twirled her around so she was facing him. Not knowing what was coming, she watched in fascination as he worked an arm under her hips and raised her, his mouth kissing a trail down her stomach. When he touched her there with his mouth for the first time, she gasped.

"Phillip!" Although she wasn't sure why, she struggled against the pleasure he was inflicting with short flicks of his tongue.

"Everything's allowed between us, love, remember?" His tongue slipped lower, entering where only his fingers and shaft had gone before. "Close your eyes. Let me have you this way."

She did as he asked, closing her eyes and gripping the rim of the tub. He moved his tongue back to her hard center, licking and tickling as tendrils of fire shot out from her stomach to her limbs, the pressure building higher and higher. As she reached the edge of her cliff, Phillip wrapped his lips around the firm bud and sucked, pushing her over into free fall.

As always, he held her tightly in his arms as she spiraled through space and time, catching her when she returned. This time, gently kissing her lips and allowing her to taste her own sex.

"I love you," she whispered for the second time ever, now against the salty tang on his mouth.

Phillip remained silent, but his heart swelled and ached.

Much later, he woke in the night with a start. Jane wasn't by his side. He'd grown so used to her presence that the darkness seemed overwhelming without her. In a shaft of moonlight, he found her, wrapped in his shirt, sitting in a chair and staring into the remnants of the fire.

He sat up, swinging his legs over the side of the bed. The movement caused her to turn and look at him.

"I'm sorry. I didn't mean to wake you," she said softly.

She looked so lonely. So forlorn. "Are you all right?"

"I was just thinking."

"About what, love?"

"About what I'll do now. I've no home, no family, no employment. I feel so lost." She looked back to the fire. "It's a horrible thing to find yourself twenty years old and to suddenly learn that you don't have a place, that there's no one in the world who cares about you."

The despair in her voice brought back that unwelcome ache in the center of his chest. He rose and moved to her side, stroking his hand across her hair. "I care about you."

She looked up into his eyes which were so hard to read in the darkness. "Do you?"

"Very much. And Emily cares about you. Besides, you've other good friends. Richard, John, Meg." He slipped into the chair, moving underneath her and turning her so she sat astride his lap, her cheek resting on his shoulder. "You're already building a new life to replace what you've lost here."

Feeling confused and hopeless, she shrugged. "I don't belong anywhere."

"You belong by my side, Jane. Your home is with me." Phillip couldn't believe the next thought which sprang into his head unannounced, but he gave voice to it before he had time to contemplate the consequences of what he was asking. "Could you think of Emily and me as your family?"

Jane pulled back and stared at him with love in her eyes. She knew many things about Phillip, things he probably didn't even realize himself. It was hard for him to trust others. Hard to care. Hard to love, simply because no one had ever taught him how. What he was asking, although it sounded like a modest request, was a monumental step on his part. A step toward a better life. Toward friendship. Toward hope and believing mutual dependence was a good and valuable thing. If he was willing to offer so much, so would she.

She hugged him as tightly as she could and whispered in his ear. "I would love to consider you and Emily as my family. If you'll have me."

Phillip shrugged as though her decision didn't matter much to him one way or the other although, in fact, it meant everything. Over the years, he'd convinced himself that he didn't need to love or be loved, but lately, he found himself thinking back on his position more and more. Since meeting Jane, he'd realized there was an emptiness somewhere inside him, a barren spot left vacant by those who should have, but had never, cared about him. What would it feel like to have that barren spot filled in? Was he brave enough to find out?

He brushed his lips lightly across her temple. "Be my family, Jane. I'd like that more than anything." In response, she hugged him again, as though she'd never let go, and the ache around his heart eased for the first time.

Chapter
Twenty-Four

Jane sat in the meadow grass with Emily, the same place where three months earlier, Phillip had screamed and shouted because he'd found her picnicking with her friends. The October day was as bright and hot as any she could remember, and if someone had told her the calendar was wrong, that somehow time had moved backward and 'twas still mid-July, she'd have believed it in a heartbeat.

What a difference three months could make. Phillip seemed a different man. Although he still had moments when he managed to be incredibly difficult, he seemed to have found some of what had been lost to him so many years earlier. Much to Jane's surprise and delight, he'd decided to forgo the autumn invitations he received daily to attend house parties and hunting excursions. Instead, he spent time relearning the ways of the estate and reacquainting himself with the servants, villagers and tenants who had faithfully served his family for generations.

With much grace, he'd stood up with John at his wedding to Meg. With enthusiasm and humor, he'd helped as the crops were brought in, then presided over the festivities during and after the harvest. With awkward, but successful, attempts at parenting, he'd established a bond with Emily. Even his relationship with Richard was on the mend. Just the previous afternoon, Jane had peeked out the library window and seen the two of them talking near the stables. Of all things, Phillip was smiling.

With herself, he was more than anything she could have imagined finding in a husband. By day, he was courteous, affectionate, concerned. By night, he was as passionate as ever, his lust for her only seeming to increase. If she hadn't known him as well as she did, it would almost seem as though he were in love with her. Considering his past, she wasn't certain the emotion could ever overtake him, but that was all right. She had enough love for both of them.

Yes, what a difference three months could make.

Emily's voice brought her out of her reverie. "What did you say, dear?"

"I said, 'tis so dreadfully hot, let's go swimming."

"What if someone sees us?"

"No one's about, Jane. Please, let's do."

Jane hadn't gone swimming since she was a young girl. Glancing around, she saw that Emily was correct. They were alone, and even if someone happened by, they'd never be seen through the copse of trees shielding them from the lane. "Why not?" She smiled at the girl.

"Yes." Emily clapped her hands in excitement.

They helped each other with hooks and ties, stripping

down to their chemises and drawers. One of Emily's petticoats snagged on the heel of her boot, and Jane knelt down to help her untangle it. While she was pulling free the last of the offending fabric, the girl's knees were visible. On the inside of her right one was the same birthmark—the mark of infinity—that was on Phillip's leg.

Tentatively, Jane touched the spot as though afraid it might disappear. Thrilled and shocked to find it there, she shook her head in consternation. Had no one ever looked closely at the girl? Or had everyone just assumed, as Phillip had, that the mark only appeared on firstborn males? To think of all the years both father and daughter had suffered because he'd been convinced his unfaithful wife had left him to care for another man's child.

The enormity of her discovery was disconcerting. Still on her knees, she glanced up at Emily. "Did you ever show your father this birthmark?"

"Really, Jane, the things you say are so funny sometimes. As if I'd show Father my legs!" Emily laughed at the thought of doing something so outrageous. "You can be so silly."

"Yes, I can, can't I?" As far as Jane knew, Emily had no idea about what type of woman her mother had been, what had happened between her parents or why the birthmark was so significant. Jane was not about to broach such subjects. She stood, pulling on Emily's hand. "Last one in's a rotten egg."

Together, they ran into the water, laughing and splashing, shrieking with delight as the cold water soaked their undergarments.

Phillip rode slowly along the country road, enjoying the unseasonably hot weather. Coming back from a visit to the village, his eyes surveyed the fields and cottages he passed on the way to the estate. Winter would last long enough, and he couldn't get over how much he relished the unexpected extension of summer.

Somewhere he'd lost his way the past few years, convincing himself that he hated the estate. Approaching the turn up the long lane to the house, he inhaled deeply, loving the smell of the fresh grass yellowing in the autumn sun. Overhead, a shower of colorful leaves danced off the trees, covering his shoulders with orange and red. He picked one up off the saddle, twirling it by the stem.

Happiness was a tangible thing, he'd learned lately. Something missing most of his life, but given to him now like a precious gift to be protected and cherished. He'd found a true and good friend in John Graves. Slowly, he'd been building a new relationship with Emily. His connection with Richard was improving daily—something he had never imagined happening in his lifetime. Using the excuse of estate business, he'd found himself drawn to the man's company more and more. The bond which had always existed between them was still there, bruised but unbroken by the sins of the past.

All because of Jane. Standing square in the middle of his life, she was the center of this new universe filled with laughter, friendship and love. Gradually, he was learning that devotion and trust were not frightening things, but emotions to welcome. Rubbing a hand across his chest, he sometimes wondered if the ache he felt there was actually the thawing of his cold, miserable heart.

Ahead, he could see a rider approaching. Before he could turn up the lane, the man waved and hailed him with a hearty hello.

"Wessington," Morris greeted Phillip, riding up alongside.

"Morris," he nodded back. "We haven't seen much of you lately." *Thank God*, Phillip added to himself.

"I've been in Sussex. At Roberta's party. Thought I'd see you there."

"I had matters to attend to here. I couldn't get away."

"I must say you missed quite a do. Never seen the likes."

Phillip shook his head at how much a man's life could change in a matter of months. Roberta's parties had always been his favorites in the past. Somehow this year, nothing she'd offered as entertainment enticed him in the least.

Laughter and the sound of splashing water trickled up through the trees as they passed the spot where Phillip had interrupted Jane's picnic in the middle of the summer. What a jealous, insecure, pompous ass he'd been that day! If Jane had never spoken to him again, he'd have deserved the punishment.

Morris reined his horse to a halt when he heard the female laughter and chatter. He recognized Emily's voice right away and had to see what she was about. All summer he had stayed away from his properties, hoping distance would temper his desire for the girl, but it hadn't worked.

With hardly a glance at Wessington, Morris walked his horse through the trees. Phillip followed, realizing belatedly that the voices they heard belonged to Jane and Emily. Across the meadow, mother and daughter frolicked and splashed in the cool water, oblivious to being watched from afar. Their undergarments were soaked and clinging to their skins.

Still on their horses, the two men were far enough away so that neither could view anything unseemly. The pair they watched looked like forest sprites caught in an afternoon of play. Phillip gazed at Jane, knowing every curve and valley, and thinking her breasts looked slightly bigger, her stomach paunched the tiniest bit. His pulse fluttered as he wondered if she might be increasing and neither of them had realized it yet. Who would ever have imagined he'd find himself excited about such a possibility?

Without giving a thought to Morris sitting next to him, he whispered, "My Lord, she's beautiful."

Morris surveyed the same scene, but saw a very different actress in the lead role—Emily, with her flat chest and body that looked like a young boy's. He was hard as a poker. Hardly meaning to speak aloud, he agreed with Wessington. "Yes, she is. I can't wait."

The passion in Morris's statement brought Phillip's head swinging around. Thinking at first that he was talking about Jane, Phillip nearly made a nasty comment until he realized that Morris's gaze was fixed on Emily, and if Phillip was seeing what he thought he was seeing, the man was completely aroused. The way he was eyeing her enraged Phillip as nothing had in years.

Reining his horse toward the lane, he said, "Come back up to the road."

"What?" Morris asked, completely distracted by the girl in the water.

"I said, 'Come back up to the road.' " When the thick idiot continued to look, Phillip said angrily, "Morris, you're staring at my naked wife and child."

Morris wanted to keep looking at Emily. Seeing her like this only fueled the sick desire that raged through his veins day and night. The craving was growing out of control again, and it had been over a month since he'd managed to assuage some of it at his favorite brothel in London. There were always plenty of children in the city ready to do anything for food and shelter; he took advantage of that as often as he could. But the young whores couldn't satisfy him completely. Even though he always selected the brunette ones and pretended they were Emily, Emily was the child he wanted, and he intended to have her.

He wanted to go down to the water and join her. To play next to her, finding an excuse to touch her in her secret places, using the water as a shield. The thought of it was a delicious agony, but something in the Earl's tone brought him back to reality, and he forced his attentions away from the stream. "My apologies. I didn't mean to appear rude."

"Of course not," Phillip muttered sarcastically. Once they were back on the road, the two females safely shielded by the trees, he looked Morris in the eye. "I've meant to tell you for some time now that I'm not ready for Emily to marry. She's much too young."

Morris couldn't believe what he was hearing. After all the years he'd waited! He hated the whine in his voice when he said, "But she's almost twelve."

"Yes. Almost. And much too young to wed."

"When, then?" Morris asked, trying to control his temper but hardly succeeding. He felt cheated, tricked. Played for a fool.

"Oh, I suppose when she's eighteen or nineteen. After she's had a Season or two in London."

"But I can't wait that long!"

"I wouldn't expect you to wait." Letting a moment of silence play out, Phillip added, "Even if you were still interested in a few year's time, I'd never agree."

Two angry red splotches appeared on Morris's cheeks. "You've raised my hopes. I've been patient so long, and now you've ruined everything."

"I'm certain you'll find someone else interested in your money."

"I'll raise my offer."

Phillip shook his head in disgust. More and more, he'd been thinking that he'd spent the past few years viewing the world through some kind of fog which was only recently beginning to clear. "Just go, Morris. And don't come back. I don't want to see you showing your face 'round here again."

From behind the line of trees, Morris clearly heard Jane's voice. She was the cause of all this. Before she'd come along, everything had been going smoothly. Margaret had had the contract in Wessington's hand. Possession of Emily had been only a signature away. Jane Wessington had ruined everything, and he'd get even if it was the last thing he ever did. "You'll be sorry," he muttered, bringing his horse around with a furious jerk and starting back toward the main road. "You'll be bloody sorry."

Jane had not noticed Phillip or Morris until Phillip turned his horse and practically dragged Morris through the trees. Her heart had nearly stopped beating when she'd seen the dreaded neighbor sitting so comfortably beside her husband. She thought she knew Phillip's thinking these days, but did she really?

Unfortunately, Emily had heard the same commotion and had looked around in time to see the two men.

"My birthday is in three weeks," she finally mentioned, so softly that Jane barely heard her.

Of late, Phillip seemed so taken with the girl that Jane couldn't believe he'd consider doing anything to hurt her. "He won't do this, Emily."

"You don't know that," she insisted with a wisdom

far beyond her years. "He's been different for the past few weeks, so you think he's changed. It doesn't mean he has."

"He *has* changed, Emily. He loves us in his way."

"Maybe . . . or maybe not. Maybe, he's just passing his time until he finds something better to do."

"Who told you that?" Jane tried to sound outraged, but she couldn't quite manage it. With a very guilty conscience, she'd often wondered the same thing in the small hours of the night as he lay sleeping next to her.

"I hear things." She shrugged. "Everyone's saying it. They just don't talk about it in front of you, because it would hurt your feelings."

Jane grabbed both Emily's hands and squeezed. "He will not do this to you. Or to me. I swear it."

Without responding, Emily pulled her hands away and walked out into the water. Jane followed, and they were both standing thigh deep when they heard a horse's hooves coming across the meadow. Phillip trotted up to their blankets and dismounted. Their clothing, discarded quickly, lay around in piles. They were both silent as he approached the water's edge.

"Is this a private swim party, or may anyone join you?" Without waiting for an answer, he tugged off his boots and waded in. They were both eyeing him suspiciously, and he might have laughed if they hadn't both been trembling; Jane with fury, Emily with fear. What agony he must have put the girl through all these long months.

Jane finally spoke. "What did Morris want?"

"He wanted to find out if I was going to allow him to marry Emily." Both females shrank back from him. In the past, he'd always held himself aloof from emotional outpourings, thinking them unseemly and beneath his exalted state. Now, at seeing both in such obvious dis-

tress, their reactions hurt him. He never wanted to see
either of them looking at him like that again. He smiled,
and said, "But I sent him packing. I told him I thought
his feelings for Emily were inappropriate and I didn't
want him ever showing his morbid face 'round our
property again. Ever."

Jane finally took a breath. "Really?"

"Of course, really, you silly goose."

"Oh, Phillip, oh . . . Thank you. This is the nicest
thing anyone's ever done for me." Trying to run, but
unable to in the deeper water, she took a few sluggish
steps.

Phillip met her halfway and drew her into his arms.
Over her head, he could see Emily still trembled a few
feet beyond. He held out his hand, but she didn't move
to take it.

"You really sent him away?" she asked quietly.

"Yes. Forever. He'll never bother you again."

With that extra measure of reassurance, she fairly
leaped out of the water in one astonishing movement,
landing with her arms wrapped around his shoulders
and her legs around his waist. She started planting endless kisses across his cheeks and neck, her tears splashing
down his chest. "Thank you, Father. Oh, thank you,
thank you . . ."

The weight of her and of Jane, the two embracing
and pulling on him, caused him to lose his balance,
and he tumbled down into the cool stream, gritting his
teeth against the frigid dunking. As they hit the water,
it absorbed Emily's weight, and he bounced her on his
thighs. The action raised the leg of her drawers, baring
a good portion of her leg. Jane reached down, stroking
the girl's skin, grabbing his attention with her eyes.

He looked down to where her fingers traced a delicate
line on the inside of Emily's knee. The sign of infinity.

A perfect copy of the one on his own leg. His eyes widened in shock, and his mind whirled with the implications of the silent message she was sending.

"How long have you known?" he mouthed, nodding toward the mark.

"I just saw it a few minutes ago myself."

Emily was his child! What a fool he'd been for listening to Anne's hateful words telling him the babe had been sired by another. All of Emily's life, he'd held her at arm's length because of it. To think of all that had been lost because of Anne's treachery.

He pulled Emily so tightly against his chest that it was likely she couldn't draw breath, but he didn't care. "I'm sorry, my beautiful girl, I'm so sorry."

Emily sensed that some monumental event had just occurred, but she had no idea what it was. She hugged him back. "It's all right, Father. Really it is."

"I've been such a fool. The biggest fool in the whole world. Can you ever forgive me?"

"Of course, I forgive you, Father." She looked over at Jane, her confusion evident.

Jane knelt in the water, silently watching the pair. Her husband, her daughter. Her family. Her life. For the remainder of her years, she wanted to remember everything about this moment. How the stream trickled over the rocks. How the birds chirped in the trees. How the horse munched on the sweet grass along the bank. How the sun warmed her skin.

Two identical faces stared at her, identical looks of bewilderment raising their identical brows. Together, they reached for her; she opened her arms and leaned into them, whispering, "What a wonderful, wonderful day!"

Chapter
Twenty-Five

Jane looked out at the rainy November afternoon. The sun-filled days of late October were only a memory now, and winter had set upon the land with full force. She supposed she should be downstairs with the other guests, socializing, but there were only so many minutes in the day that she could stand to chat with unknown women who were determined to carry their discussions no further than the topics of needlework and fashion.

While others were playing, she had several estates to run. Even though they were away from home, on their first official visit as husband and wife, she couldn't let too many hours pass without working. Phillip teased her, but he understood. She thrived on making herself useful, and keeping busy made her happy. Already, with her steady attentions to his vast properties and investments, his personal fortune was growing, but, along with increased prosperity, came increased responsibilities. The tasks were endless, but she didn't mind.

They were staying at a duke's estate just outside London. Their host's daughter's engagement ball was to be a magnificent social event, one attended by several hundred of the upper crust of Society, so of course, Phillip had been invited. The Duke and his father had been lifelong friends.

Jane hadn't been surprised when he'd showed her the invitation and said he'd like to attend. After all, before they'd met, his life had revolved around the London social scene, and he'd sheltered himself at Rosewood for months, passing up invitations to dozens of gatherings. She could understand his desire to get about again. What had surprised her was the fact that he wanted her and Emily to join him.

Jane had agreed reluctantly, hating to leave Rosewood, and dreading the fact that she'd be back among the wealthy, bored members of the peerage whom she'd so disliked when marrying in the city the previous spring. She relented because she knew Emily needed to broaden her horizons and because Phillip seemed so excited by the prospect of the trip that she couldn't say no.

Their first two days at the Duke's home had passed quickly. Emily had been befriended by several girls and was having the time of her life. Phillip was seeing old friends, and she found herself fascinated by this side of him she'd not seen before. For her part, her fears about attending had proved to be unfounded. As the wife of a well-known and well-liked nobleman, she was treated with deference and respect. If anything, she felt herself a great curiosity, the woman who had lured the notoriously single Wessington into matrimony.

With minimal effort, she forced her attention back to the letters in front of her. She'd brought the stack from home, not having time to go through it before they'd left. The third letter brought her sitting up straight, and the movement exacerbated the recurring pain in her lower back. She rubbed a hand over the spot as her eyes scanned the contents of the letter, and she could barely stifle a gurgle of laughter. Behind her, the door to their suite opened, and Jane knew, without looking, that her husband had entered.

Phillip watched Jane, sitting at the desk in front of the window, her papers scattered about. The day's light was just fading, and she was silhouetted by the lamplight. Her hair glowed with red highlights, her graceful form cast distinct shadows on the wall. As always, while catching her so silently absorbed in some project or other, he couldn't help thinking how perfectly lovely she was. The fact that she was rubbing her back again instantly caught his attention.

He stepped behind her and placed a tender kiss on her exposed shoulder. "What has you sitting here, chuckling to yourself?"

Holding up a folded sheet, she opened it for his inspection. "Look who's written."

"Gregory?" He raised a questioning brow. "What the devil does he want?"

"Well, he rambles on and on, but as near as I can decipher, he can't seem to get the import business going, and the Shipworks is late on a contract. And would I like to come home for a spell to help out?"

"Cheeky bastard, isn't he?" He scanned the contents, then tossed the letter on the table. Scooping Jane off the chair, he seated himself and lowered her onto his lap. "I hope you're going to tell me that you're prepared to watch him cook in his own soup."

"Well, I had thought we might let him stew for a time. Then, perhaps we might offer to buy the import business."

Phillip shrugged, considering. "We could move it to London. Purchase some older warehouses and fix them up."

"My thinking exactly." More and more, their minds walked the same path.

"Sounds like we could get it at a good price." Jane chuckled at that. "Perhaps we should offer for the Ship-works as well."

"Now, that's a grand idea. I'll start working on some figures."

She reached for her pen, as though intending to start that very minute, which caused Phillip to laugh and still her hand with his own. "Not this moment, my dear countess. We've a party to attend." Phillip stroked a hand across the small of her back. "I saw you rubbing this when I came in. Is it hurting you again?"

"Just slightly."

With one hand on her back, he moved the other to caress the front of her chest, his fingers cupping the bottom of one breast and then the other. In turn, he lifted each slightly, testing weight and size, then slid up to likewise measure the nipples. As always, they sprang to immediate attention.

Loving the feel of his hands on her breasts, she tipped her head back and, for her effort, received a gentle kiss on the mouth. "What's your verdict, kind sir?"

"They're definitely bigger. Fuller." He massaged her breasts again. "And your nipples . . ." To prove his point, he tugged at the bodice until one of the rosy tips sprang free, allowing him to trace it with the end of his finger. "Absolutely wider, longer. A deeper shade of red."

She twisted at his merciless ministrations. "I think they're more sensitive, also."

"Are they? I'd better check." He lowered his head,

sucking the elongated tip, taking it deep inside, wetting and tickling it with his tongue. As Jane arched her back, offering more of herself, he chuckled. "Yes, I'd say they're much more sensitive."

"Do you truly think I'm increasing?" They'd been having the discussion for days.

"I told you, I've thought so for several weeks."

"But I don't feel much different." This wasn't entirely accurate. She became exhausted easily, seemed tired all the time, had a nagging backache and headache, grew more and more nauseous around food and odors, and couldn't shake the uncontrollable feeling that something miraculous had recently occurred.

"When we get to London, I'm sending for a midwife. We'll find out the truth."

"Are you sure you want to know?" The words were out before she could pull them back.

"Of course I do. Why wouldn't I?"

She shook her head and looked out the window. "No reason. I misspoke."

"Look at me." With a finger to her chin, he turned her back to face him. "You think I wouldn't want our child?"

One corner of her mouth lifted in a smile, and she leaned closer, resting her breasts against his chest, her lips nearly touching his own. "I'm just a little frightened by the whole idea. I'm being silly, I know."

"Listen to me now, Jane. I can't imagine anything more wonderful than you carrying my child."

He looked so sincere that her heart eased a little. "What if we have a girl?"

"I hope we have a dozen girls. With your green eyes and Emily's spunk."

More and more, he always seemed to say just the right thing. She kissed him along the cheek till she found his mouth, overcome with the need to show him how much she cared about him. With nimble fingers, she worked at the front of his breeches. He was instantly hard and pulsing.

"You shameless hussy, what do you think you're doing?"

"Pay attention, sir. I'm certain you'll figure it out soon enough."

"Dear heart"—he laughed, cupping her face in his palm—"I've died and gone to heaven."

I love you.

The emotion swelled up from some dark corner.

Say it, you fool. Tell her!

He longed to, but the words, so long repressed, had a way of sticking deep down inside and refusing to come forward when ordered.

Just then, chatter and laughter in the hall brought them both sitting up straight, adjusting fabric and closing openings. Emily burst into the room from her adjoining bedchamber.

She couldn't help noticing her parents' red faces. They were blushing as though she'd caught them doing something they oughtn't. "Have you two been kissing again?"

"I'm afraid so," Phillip readily admitted. "Jane is so pretty, I can't seem to help myself."

Emily thought they were incredibly romantic. Her new friends all thought so, too, with the way her father was always holding Jane's hand, smiling as though they shared a special secret and whispering into her ear. They were all talking about it. And, of course, all the girls agreed with Emily that her father was too handsome by half. "Is it all right to do it in the middle of the afternoon?"

Phillip's eyes were round as saucers, and it took a huge

swallow from Jane's glass of wine to stifle the laughter wanting to bubble out. Jane couldn't believe he was actually blushing. Her own cheeks felt a little warm. "Yes, dear, it's all right. As long as you're with your husband." A lame response, but one she hoped would suffice. Wanting nothing more than to change the subject, she asked, "Did you have a pleasant afternoon?"

"Absolutely splendid. And the most wonderful thing has happened."

"What's that?"

"Penelope Heathrow is having eight of her closest friends to a private supper right in her own room, and I've been invited."

"My goodness"—Phillip smiled at his daughter—"what an exciting prospect."

"Yes, so I must get dressed." Turning to Jane, she looked terribly worried. "Whatever should I wear?"

Winking at her husband, Jane extended her hand to Emily. "Let's go take a look, shall we?"

For the next two hours, the women primped and preened until it was time to head for their various meals. The trio walked down the halls of the vast mansion, Phillip and Jane wanting to escort Emily to her party before heading downstairs to their own. Just as they rounded a corner near the stairs, a door opened and Margaret stepped into the hallway.

A moment of awkward silence ensued. Margaret, lovely as ever in a flowing gown of soft, blue velvet, eyed them. There was a hint of malice in her eyes as she said, "Lord Wessington. *Lady* Wessington," emphasizing Jane's title, making it clear she didn't think Jane deserved it. Almost sounding rude, but not quite, she added, "Lady Emily, how *interesting* to see you out and about."

Emily stepped behind Jane as though fearing Margaret might hurt her. Jane seethed with anger at the woman's venomous tone, and the manner in which she was regarding Emily raised Jane's protective hackles. Only Phillip's reassuring hand tightly gripping her own kept her from making a scene.

"Lady Downs." Jane returned the greeting with a brief nod of her head.

"Hello, Margaret," Phillip said coolly. He hadn't seen the woman in months, had often reflected on how peaceful it was to be parted from her, only to have her show up at his first outing with Jane. He took a step, indicating the encounter was over. "If you'll excuse us? We're a bit late."

"But, of course. Don't let me keep you." She eyed the proprietary way he held Jane's hand, the way his other rested on the small of Emily's back. What she'd heard through the grapevine appeared to be true. They retreated down the hall, and she fumed, furious that she could hear their words.

"I'm sorry, love," Phillip said in a tone Margaret had never heard before. "I'd no idea she'd be here."

"It's no matter, Phillip."

"But it is. It's embarrassing to you. I can't know what the Duchess was thinking when she sent out invitations. I'll speak with her."

"No, no. Don't do that. The damage is done. Let's not make more of it. She's here and we're here, and I simply refuse to allow her to ruin our time together." Their voices trailed off, and Margaret could hear no more.

She went back into her room, pressing a cool cloth to her face and slowing her breathing. After his wedding night, Wessington had dumped her like so much extra baggage, and she'd not seen him again. Still, she ached to have him back in her life. He was the only man who truly understood her. Besides that, it was galling to have anyone, especially the likes of Phillip Wessington, thinking he'd rid himself of her, all because of that plain chit he called wife. She'd get even for all the troubles Jane Wessington had caused and enjoy herself greatly in the process.

Several hours later, the ball in full progress, colorfully clad dancers swirled in beautiful circles. Feeling suddenly dizzy, Jane tugged on Phillip's arm, and he leaned down to better hear her.

"Are you all right?" he asked, but immediately saw that she wasn't.

"Just feeling a trifle strange at the moment."

"An attack of vertigo, is it?" he asked, barely able to hide his knowing smile. Inconspicuously, they stepped out of the line of dancers, and Phillip eased her into a chair. Try as she might, Jane couldn't prevent the yawn which made its way to the surface. Phillip instantly noticed the fatigue she hadn't wanted to acknowledge but could no longer hide. She was nearly asleep on her feet.

"I think I'm just overly tired."

"Shall we retire?"

Jane glanced around the room, at the spinning dancers and the laughing, chattering crowd. Besides the dance itself, there was wagering, also card games and cigar rooms in which the men could congregate. Phillip was in his element, and much as she'd like him to go to bed with her, she hated to deprive him of his fun. The attack of dizziness passing, she stood carefully. "I don't want you to miss any of the party. I'll see myself upstairs."

"I wouldn't dream of letting you go up alone."

"Don't be silly. Stay and enjoy yourself."

Phillip looked around. It had been ages since he'd attended a gathering like this one. There were people with whom he wanted to talk, gossip he wanted to hear, stories he wanted to tell, liquor he wanted to drink. A roll of the dice wouldn't be so bad either. He smiled down at Jane. "Are you certain?"

"I want you to stay on one condition."

"What's that?"

She stood on tiptoe and whispered, "That you promise to wake me when you come to bed."

"That I will promise you, Lady Jane. That I will." Suggestively kissing the back of her hand in good-bye, he smiled as she turned and made her way from the ballroom. At the door, she gave him a smile and a wave of her fingers. And a wicked wink to seal the bargain. He grinned from ear to ear, wondering if anyone had seen her send her subtle love message and not caring a whit if anyone had. Watching until she disappeared from sight, he then headed for the gaming tables.

Not a minute later, Margaret appeared at his side.

"Hello, darling," she whispered seductively, favoring him with her most delectable pout. "I could swear you've been avoiding me."

Phillip knew the look she was flashing; she had nothing but trouble in mind. "What do you want, Margaret?"

"What do you think I want?" She rested a hand on the center of his chest and rubbed in small circles. "I'm so glad you've finally returned. It's been positively unbearable without you."

Attempting to appear casual, he reached for her hand and removed it from his person. She managed to keep hold of his fingers. Only by yanking them away would he be able to separate himself from her grasp. No one appeared to be watching, but one never knew for sure. He refused to make any kind of scene. "I think we need to talk. Privately."

"Excellent. How about my rooms, in thirty minutes? You know where they are?"

"I'll be there."

Exactly on time, he stepped into her sitting room. Almost as though she'd planned things carefully in advance, the room was prepared for his visit. A cozy fire sparked in the grate. Scented candles burned. Wine was poured and waiting. The door to the boudoir was open, and he could hear Margaret in the other room, humming softly as she changed her clothing.

Phillip relaxed onto the small sofa in front of the fire. The location provided an erotic view. Through the partially open door, he caught glimpses of Margaret in various stages of undress. As always, she took plenty of time preparing herself, and he had a long opportunity to think about the coming encounter. He knew he should speak his piece and go, but he refused to talk through the door or enter her bedchamber, so he waited for her to appear.

Momentarily she entered, dressed in a sheer negligee which hid nothing. Her breasts, her nipples, her mound, all were completely visible through the thin fabric. She was, and had always been, a glorious sight. Coupled with her lack of sexual inhibitions, she was every man's fantasy. Except for Phillip, who was simply glad to be shed of her.

Margaret misread the assessment in his gaze and told herself she'd moved wisely, that with a few flicks of her tongue, she'd have him back in her bed. Once she had him completely snagged, she had every intention of making sure his wife heard all the appropriate gossip and rumors.

Phillip stood as she crossed the room. "We need to talk."

"Later, darling. I have more pleasant things in mind right now."

Before Phillip realized what she intended, she stretched her body full against his, raising her mouth to his at the same moment she grabbed his hands and laid them on her breasts. He jumped back as though burned, but didn't move far enough, for she was too determined to let him escape so easily.

"Show me how much you missed me," she demanded, reaching for his ass and rubbing herself against his crotch.

It wasn't until that moment that she began to understand what was happening. Or what *wasn't* happening. His body showed no sign of rising desire. She hesitated, her confidence temporarily shaken.

Looking down at the beauty who had previously stirred his blood so easily, and often, he felt absolutely no lust for her. Not wanting to sound overly cruel, but needing to make his point clear, he answered her demand for attention with, "I'm sorry, but I can't show you anything, for I haven't missed you. Not a bit."

"I can't believe this." She flexed her hips in frustration.

"Give it up, Margaret." He reached behind and removed her hands from his buttocks. "I'm going back downstairs."

"What? Whatever are you saying? Jane's gone to bed. We can spend hours together."

"But I don't want to spend hours with you." He took her hand and moved it across his crotch, letting her feel his flaccid state. "I'm no longer interested in continuing our relationship, and I won't have you hounding me over it."

Margaret continued to stroke his uncooperative organ, unable to believe what he was saying and what she was feeling between his legs. Impossible! No man had ever resisted her. "You must be joking."

"No, I'm not. I'm going down to game for a time; then I'm going to bed. With my wife." Phillip stepped back, and she moved closer, refusing to let him break the contact. He picked her up and physically set her away. "I simply came up here to say that whatever we had is over. I'm not interested in starting it up again, and I don't want you approaching me. I won't have Jane upset by your antics or your tantrums."

Red-faced, she was angry and embarrassed. To be put down—by Wessington of all people. In her view, emotional attachments were the silliest, and he had always believed the same. In her most scathing tone, she said, "Why, if I didn't know better, I'd swear you had developed tender feelings for her."

"More than you know. I love her." Phillip grinned stupidly. All these months, he'd been unable to speak the words to Jane, but he felt good saying them now. At having Margaret, of all people, know how deeply his emotions ran. As soon as he could exit this dreadful scene, he would head to his rooms and say those words to his wife. "I love her very much."

"But you can't mean it. Look at me!" Refusing to believe or accept that she'd been bested for Phillip's attentions, she wrenched at the front of her gown, exposing her full, exquisite breasts for his purview.

Phillip stared, unmoved, then raised his hands to the straps, trying to tug them up her shoulders. "Could we please have some dignity about this?"

A movement in the mirror caught Margaret's eye.

The door to her room was opening. Phillip couldn't see the door or who was on the other side, but Margaret could. She stepped forward and pulled him into a deep embrace.

Chapter
Twenty-Six

Morris watched Wessington and his wife. Across the crowded ballroom, they stood in the long line of dancers, their steps following an intricate pattern. The tune was a popular one and would continue for many minutes. Knowing the Earl as he did, there would be plenty more after that. They were obviously enjoying themselves and were thoroughly involved—in each other and in the party.

There would never be a better time.

He'd carefully moved through the crowd during the evening so that everyone was aware of his presence. No one would be able to say when, or if, he'd left the ballroom. He'd pop out and be back without being missed.

One minute he was standing near the rear door of the grand ballroom, the next, he was silently gliding up a back stairway he'd found during the previous day's preparations. Peeking out the door at the top, he saw the expanse of hall was dimly lit and quiet. Just as he'd suspected, no one was about.

Silent as a snake, he walked to the door he sought and tried the knob, breathing a sigh of relief that it was unlocked and he would not have to waste time opening it. Ducking inside, sweat popped out on his brow.

For several moments, he rested his back against the door, steadying his breathing and adjusting to the darkness. Gradually, he could make out the bed a few feet away. The person in it slept soundly, the covers rising and falling in a steady rhythm. The very sight made him hard as a rock. He loosened the front of his breeches, then, in one swift move, tugged back on the covers and lay down.

Emily Wessington, dazed from being awakened from her deep sleep, opened her eyes wide, trying to breathe against the hand covering her mouth.

"If you make one sound, I'll kill you. Do you understand?" She just lay there, frightened and confused about what was happening. "Do you understand?" he hissed.

She nodded as much as she could.

"Good. Just do everything I say, and I'll try not to hurt you," which was a lie. He intended to hurt her as much as possible. He reached a hand beneath her nightgown. "This will be over before you know it."

Jane entered their silent room. The maid had been by to turn down the bedding; a small fire crackled in the grate, and a single candle burned on the table. Standing in front of the mirror, she reached to take the pins out of her hair, but she was much more tired than she'd imagined. She dropped her hands and moved to the bed. Resting on the edge, she worked her fingers

through the curls and tangles. The pillow beckoned
invitingly. Knowing she should check on Emily, she
meant to shut her eyes for just a moment, but as soon
as her head hit the feathers, she slept.

A noise awakened her. Not sure where she was, she
had to look around the room to gather her bearings.
Had she lain there for minutes or hours? Tense and
alert, but hearing only the sound of her pounding heart,
she relaxed.

Just as she closed her eyes again, she heard her name.
"Jane . . ." Like a whisper from a ghost. The sound sent
goosebumps rising along the backs of her arms. She sat
up, dangling her legs off the side of the bed. "Who's
there?"

No response.

Feeling a trifle silly, she shivered in the cool room
and thought to undress and snuggle under the covers,
but decided to check on Emily first. Grabbing a wrap
draped on a nearby chair, she moved to the door adjoining their bedchambers. Holding her single candle out
in front, she silently pushed open the door and froze
at the sight.

At first, Emily had not known what was happening.
Her sleep had been so deep that it had taken her many
moments to come fully awake and realize that Morris
was in the room with her. While her existence had been
a sheltered one, some part of her knew what he was
trying to do.

Fighting with every bit of her strength proved useless.
He was too big and too strong. In one quick movement,
he ripped her favorite nightgown, the one Jane had
given her for her birthday the previous week, and it lay

in tatters on the bedcovers. She whimpered against his hand.

He slapped her hard, wanting to silence her but hurt her as well. "Shut up! Do you hear me?" His hand went back to her mouth. "If anyone hears you, I'll kill Jane. Now lie still!"

The slap hurt unmercifully, and tears flooded her eyes. Next thing she knew, he was working between her legs, with a knee, with a hand, and then she felt him down there, ramming and hurting as though he wished to split her in half. With the last of her strength, she bit his hand and he jerked it away.

"Jane . . ." she managed to get out, before he hit her again. She knew calling out was pointless since her parents were still downstairs at the ball, but she couldn't help calling for her mother, her friend.

Jane stood like a statue for several moments, her mind not able to process what she was seeing. For more than a few seconds, she wondered if she was really awake, if perhaps she wasn't sequestered in some horrifying dream from which she couldn't awaken. But no. The bed was moving. The people on it struggling. She stepped closer, then, outraged, set aside her candle as she leaped for them.

"Get away from her." At first, the man didn't appear to notice her presence. She reached for the collar of his coat and pulled to no effect. "Let her go!" Reaching for the water pitcher next to Emily's bed, she swung it as hard as she could. He saw it coming at the last second and shifted, deflecting the blow with his forearm. As he turned, she saw his face captured in the dim glow of the fire coming from the other room. "Morris!"

"You bitch," he whispered, his voice full of murderous venom. "You keep ruining everything."

He lunged for her, and she tried to jump away but

couldn't manage fast enough. Tackling her to the floor, he hit her hard in the face. Wincing at the blow, Jane thought she might lose consciousness and knew she couldn't until Emily was safe. "Emily, run!" she shouted, wondering if the girl still had her wits about her. "Run! And scream!"

Jane opened her mouth to do just that, but Morris stopped her by wrapping his fingers around her throat and squeezing as tightly as he could. Prying at his fingers, Jane couldn't make any headway at loosening them. Just then, Emily leaped off the bed, pounding him about the head and shoulders with a heavy object.

"Let her go," she cried, pummeling him until he lost his balance. Jane pushed him away and rose to her knees, screaming bloody murder.

Morris, quickly assessing the danger of his situation, jumped to his feet. Frightened and enraged, wanting nothing more than to get as far away as possible, he fled down the hall.

Jane and Emily knelt in the room, listening as his hasty footsteps retreated. Several seconds later, another set came from a different direction. Jane stood on wobbly legs and hurried to the door. Peeking out into the candlelit hall, she saw a footman hurrying toward their open doorway. Glancing over her shoulder, she noted that Emily was curled into a ball in the corner. Knowing the scandal the situation would cause and wanting to contain it as much as possible, Jane ran a hand over her dress, straightening it as much as she could before stepping closer to the light spilling in from the hall.

"Milady, are you all right?"

Although she doubted he could make out anything in the room, Jane pulled the door to her so the man could not see inside. Smoothing out the lines of fear and rage etched on her face, she said as calmly as possible,

"Could you please have someone go downstairs and find my husband for me?"

"Certainly, ma'am."

Jane hesitated. She didn't want this man roaming through the party looking for Phillip. There'd be gossip enough as it was. "I've changed my mind, sir. I need two of my servants. Meg and John Graves." She gave him directions to their room in the servants' wing. "Please tell them that they cannot arrive too soon."

The footman wondered at her disheveled state. She seemed injured and frightened, and he hesitated to leave, but perhaps the matter was better left to her own servants. "I'll be back with them as quickly as I'm able, milady. Until I return, perhaps you would like to lock the door."

"Yes, I believe that might be wise. Thank you."

He quickly walked away, and she followed his suggestion. Knowing the door in the main bedchamber to also be unlocked, she reached for Emily's hand. The girl seemed dazed and confused, and Jane reached down and put a hand on her shoulder. "Emily dear, can you hear me?"

Emily finally looked up into her eyes. "What?"

"Let's go into my room. Can you stand?"

"Ah . . . yes. I believe so." Before Jane could help her to her feet, she looked up imploringly. "I think I'm going to be sick," Emily said and she leaned to the side and retched over and over onto the floor until there was nothing left in her stomach.

Jane stroked her back, cooing words of comfort until the moment passed. With a steadying hand, she then helped her to her feet. Emily was completely naked, but Jane found her wrap and draped it over her shoulders. In the other room, she eased her down on the mattress, covered her with a heavy blanket and started for the door.

"Don't leave me," Emily begged in a voice filled with fear.

"I'm not. I'm just locking the door." She quickly completed the action, then went about the room, lighting each and every lamp and candle. They were both shivering, so she stepped to the fireplace and threw another log on the dying embers. "Are you all right?"

"No. No, I'm not," Emily whispered.

Jane reached for the pitcher and poured water into the basin, then soothed Emily's brow with a cool cloth, letting her sip some water from a cup to wipe the taste of sickness from her mouth. Pulling her close, she rocked her against her breast. "It will be all right," she crooned, although she didn't know if it would ever be all right again.

"I want a bath."

"Yes, of course."

"I want to leave. I don't want to stay here. It's not safe."

"All right. Let's wait for John and Meg. They'll be along in a minute. John can find your father, and we'll all go together." It was difficult to speak, and she put a hand to her throat, feeling the bruising there. On her cheek, another bruise swelled where she'd been punched. With a trembling hand, she rubbed her brow. If Emily hadn't jumped on him, perhaps the man would have strangled her. "Thank you for coming to my aid," she whispered, kissing the girl on top of her head.

They stayed like that, holding one another in silence, each tick of the clock marking the passage of time. It seemed an eternity before they heard steps in the carpeted hall, before Meg's tap came on the door. Emily had been still for so long that Jane wondered if she was asleep, but the rapping instantly brought her alert. "It's Meg, dear. Sit right there; I'm just going to open the door."

She had to pry the girl's arms from her waist. Hurriedly, she drew the pair inside.

Meg saw Jane first, then Emily huddled on the bed. "Whatever . . . ?" She looked over at John with fear in her eyes.

Jane leaned forward and whispered, "Morris attacked her in her bed."

John gasped and reached out to steady Meg, who swayed at the news. "The bloody bastard! Wessington will kill him."

"I hope so," Jane agreed vehemently.

"Where is Morris now?"

"I don't know. He ran off when I entered her room."

Meg put a hand on Jane's face. "But it looks as though you had a sort of altercation with him. Did he strike you?"

"Yes, but I'm all right. Just banged up a bit."

"What can we do?" John asked.

"I want to get her out of here as quickly and quietly as possible. I thought we'd head to the city. The town house should be ready for our arrival. If it's not, I don't care. We can't stay here."

"Yes, yes, I'll go find Wessington."

"And have our carriage brought 'round. I want to dress and leave. I'll have you send our things. After we go, check the other room and make sure there are no signs of what happened."

"Did he . . . ?" Meg didn't finish the sentence, but they all looked over at the girl, huddled quietly on the bed.

"No, but I won't have malicious gossip of this following her."

"Quite right, Jane," John agreed, then left to find her husband.

Meg tended to the two women, helping them dress and prepare for travel. There was plenty of time, because it seemed forever before John returned alone.

"I couldn't find him," he apologized.

"I don't want to stay here," Emily reminded all of them.

"No, dear, I don't want to either." She glanced at John as she tied the bow on Emily's bonnet. "Did you look in the gaming rooms?"

"Yes, Jane."

If she'd glanced away just then, she'd have missed the look he flashed Meg. As it was, she saw some sort of message being exchanged by the pair. "What?" she demanded.

" 'Tis nothing."

"Tell me."

"Jane . . ." He rubbed a worried hand over his eyes and sighed. "Just leave it be. We'll sort it out on the morrow."

"We'll sort it out now."

Hands on hips, her angry stance indicating she was ready for a fight, Jane wouldn't leave without knowing what he knew. John realized it. He shrugged.

"He was last seen talking to Lady Margaret."

"And?"

"They left."

Jane thought her heart would stop beating in her chest. "Together?"

"Apparently."

"How long ago."

He stared at the clock on the mantel as though it held the answer. "It's been quite some time now."

Jane worked her bottom lip, wondering what the

information meant. Could Phillip have gone off with Margaret as soon as Jane had left the ballroom? Refusing to believe that he would hurt her in such a fashion, she had to move on. She couldn't dwell on his actions; Emily's needs had to come first. "We'll leave without him. Is the carriage ready?"

"It's waiting out in the front drive. I won't have you traveling alone. I'm going with you."

"Let's be off then." With Jane's arm across Emily's shoulders, they headed out the door. "Meg, would you stay here and see to things?"

"Certainly. I'm sure the Earl will return shortly, and I can inform him right away of what's happened."

Meg's doubt that Wessington would show up soon was clearly apparent in her voice, but the three adults pretended she meant what she said. Meg hugged Emily, promising to see her in London the next day.

"Lock the door," John told her by way of good-bye.

As they walked down the long, silent hallways, Jane was grateful for the dim lighting, for the lavish affair downstairs which was keeping everyone occupied. She simply wanted to get the girl outside, into the carriage and off to London before they ran into anyone who might wonder what they were about, leaving in the middle of the night.

Around the next corner was the turn for the stairs. As they approached, Jane couldn't help but notice the door to Margaret's rooms. It seemed to grow as they neared it, becoming larger than life. Could Phillip possibly be inside at this very moment?

Try as she might to force her eyes to the center of the hallway, they refused to stay there, insisting instead on drifting back to the door. Wanting to hurry past, but not able to, she noticed that the latch had not caught when the last person had entered. When they were abreast of the door, female laughter came through it. The murmur of a male voice followed.

Emily stopped. Her eyes devoid of any expression, she stared up at Jane. "That's Father."

Jane's face went white. Her heart stopped beating. "You don't know that."

"It is," she insisted quietly.

John looked puzzled and concerned. "What is it?"

"That's Margaret's room," Emily answered because Jane couldn't. "Father is in there with her."

The three of them turned and faced the door, looking at it as though the very force of their combined gazes could magically penetrate the wood and allow them to see inside.

The silence became unbearable, and Jane knew she had to make a decision. Open the door and learn the truth or move on down the stairs. If she opened it and found Phillip inside, she would die. Perhaps not at that very moment, but slowly over the next few weeks and months until her broken heart simply quit beating. With what she and Emily had already endured during the night, this was one truth she could not face.

Before she could get them moving again, Emily stepped forward before either adult could stop her and laid a hand to the wood, shoving the door open. "See," she said dully, "it's not latched."

The door swung back and there, in all her glory, was Lady Margaret Downs, the bodice of her see-through negligee pulled low to reveal her admirable naked breasts. Holding her tightly in what looked to be a passionate embrace, was Phillip Wessington, Earl of Rosewood.

Jane gasped.

Emily smiled vacantly.

"Wessington," John roared, while Margaret leaned closer to Phillip, looking coy and greatly humored.

Phillip stared in confusion. Emily and Jane dressed to leave. John with them, a bag in hand, a pistol in his belt. Panic immediately seized his heart. He thrust Margaret away and took a step forward. The trio took a step back, as though he carried leprosy or plague. "Jane, what is it? What's happened?"

"See, Jane," Emily said dispassionately, "I told you he hadn't really changed."

One tiny part of Jane's frantic mind tried to tell her that she should get all the facts before making a decision. The other part, the larger part, told her that she was seeing exactly what lay before her eyes. After leaving Phillip alone for a matter of minutes, his first act had been to make his way into the arms of his mistress. In her naïveté, Jane had assumed his affair with Margaret had ended long ago. How stupid to think that what had passed between herself and Phillip in the past few months had had any bearing on his life at all.

Tears burning her eyes, she shook her head. Her voice raspy with pain from Morris's throttling, she said, "You never really cared about us, did you?"

Phillip reached out a hand, ready to say something, but John pushed them out the door before he could open his mouth.

"What the bloody hell is the matter with you?" John asked in disgust. Quietly, he closed the door and ushered Jane and Emily down the stairs and out into the waiting carriage.

Chapter
Twenty-Seven

Morris woke with a start, the hand around his throat choking him to frightful consciousness. 'Twas too dark to see the figure looming over the bed.

A male voice, low and cold, whispered, "I've let you alone all these months. I wanted to make certain you rested peacefully in your bed, that you went to sleep dreaming easily, thinking you'd gotten away with it."

Morris grabbed at the man's wrist, trying, to no avail, to ease the pressure. He rasped, "What? Who are you? What do you want?"

"I'll not call you out. You don't deserve an honorable death."

The grip on his neck eased slightly as the man moved away. Flint sparked, and the single candle on the nightstand made the shadows in the room larger than life. Before he could even think of escape, the hand returned, pressing him back against the pillows until he gagged with the strain of it. The man leaned over the bed again, giving Morris his first and last view of who threatened. His eyes widened like saucers. "No. Oh, no."

"Yes, you bloody coward. 'Tis I. Look closely and speak the name of the man who will kill you this night. Let it be the last sound you utter in your filthy life."

"Wessington . . ." he hissed, begging with his eyes, struggling with his legs, but 'twas all for naught.

Phillip pressed the barrel of the pistol against the center of Morris's chest and blew a hole through his evil heart.

Not caring if anyone saw him or not, he slowly descended the stairs. A lone servant, having heard the shot, hovered in the shadows, but one glare from Phillip sent him scurrying. Phillip then stepped out into the drizzle and slipped away in the night. Spoiling for a fight, he walked London's streets, wishing someone would jump out from the shadows to rob or taunt him. No one did, and he walked in sullen misery until dawn finally gave him an excuse to return to his lonely, quiet house.

Inside, he bathed and dressed, heading first to see John and Meg. They worked just down the street, having been hired by an acquaintance. In her final act before she and Emily ran away, Jane wrote them both a glowing letter of recommendation. He knocked at the door and presented his card. A new face answered, a man he'd not seen before on his routine visits.

"The master of the house is hardly awake at this hour, Lord Wessington," the butler offered.

"I'm not here to see Lord Heathrow. I've come to speak with John and Meg Graves. They're up and about by now. Would you fetch them for me, please?" He stepped inside, not giving the man a chance to refuse. "I'll wait in the first parlor."

"Of course, sir," the servant responded, not at all certain he was doing the right thing.

Many minutes later, the pair entered, looking like his old friends but like strangers just the same. The hostility emanating from them was a tangible thing.

"What is it you wish this time, Lord Wessington?" Graves asked, barely able to contain his dislike.

"What do you think I want? Have you heard from them?"

"No, and I'd not tell you if I had." He turned toward the door, taking Meg's arm as he went. "You must quit calling on us. We're happy here, and I won't jeopardize our employment by having you repeatedly bothering us."

They walked away, leaving Phillip with only his bitter thoughts as companions. For several minutes, he watched the fire, contemplating his world and his future without Jane and Emily. How could life be so unfair that he would lose the both of them before he'd hardly found them?

As always these past months, the questions flew through his mind with lightning speed. Where could they be? Were they all right? Would he ever find them? And, most importantly, if he did find them, would they ever forgive him?

Were they still alive? No, no, no, he'd not go down that road again. That question always crept in with the others, and he refused to pay it heed. Somewhere, Jane was out there; he felt her presence as surely as he felt his own heart beating.

Groaning in frustration, he left the parlor and walked to the door. On the front walk, he stood for a moment, wondering where to go next. With the step of a forlorn, old man, he trudged toward his carriage, not hearing the door open behind him.

"Lord Wessington, wait, please."

He turned at the sound of Meg's voice. Hope flared. During all the times he'd visited, asking if they'd heard from Jane, she'd not spoken a word. "What is it, Meg?"

"I just wanted to say ... to say I'm sorry for your troubles." She came down the steps. "I can't bear seeing you like this. Is there anything I can do?"

"You can tell me where she is."

"I don't know, sir, truly I don't."

Meg was simply too honest to tell such a lie, so he believed her. "You spent the most time with her, Meg. Where would she go? She must have said something to you."

"I'm sorry. I've thought on it so often, but I just don't know. John and I would go after her ourselves if we could figure out where she is. I wish I could help."

"Just promise me you'll tell me if you hear from her."

Meg knew John would strangle her if she ever told Wessington anything, but she couldn't stand another moment of his anguish. "You have my word, sir, if I hear from her, you'll be the first to know."

"Thank you." He walked on, oblivious, to his waiting carriage. The driver flicked the reins and lumbered along next to him. Finally deciding on a destination, Phillip climbed inside, and they headed to Thumberton's offices.

He was announced and shown in right away. Thumberton leaned across the desk and shook his hand. "Any news?" the solicitor asked.

"Not a word. And yourself?"

Thumberton shook his head.

"How about the trust account?"

"I'm sorry, Phillip," Thumberton shook his head again. Phillip had placed a large amount of money in an account for Jane. In case she contacted Thumberton for assistance, the solicitor was authorized to give her anything she needed, even if she refused to disclose her whereabouts. "Any word from Bow Street?"

"No," Phillip sighed. "I sent a man to Portsmouth again, although I can't believe she'd go back there."

"Keep trying, Phillip. She's bound to turn up." Phillip looked so despairing that Thumberton wanted to round the desk and hug the poor lad. Only the watchful eyes of his clerks kept him from doing so.

Feeling each of his thirty-one years, Phillip stood slowly. "Good-bye, sir. Contact me immediately if you hear anything."

"I promise I will."

Phillip stumbled out into the morning, seeming surprised that the sun could be shining and the day progressing as though everything was normal. Nothing had been normal since that fateful November night. Jane and Emily had vanished before he reached London the next day, taking with them only a few items of clothing and a handful of coins, and leaving behind only a short note.

Reaching into his pocket he pulled it out and reread the words. Long ago, he'd committed them to memory, but he loved looking at the scroll of her hand.

Dearest Phillip,

It is with the greatest regret that we leave you now, but Emily and I have talked over the situation and feel we cannot stay. Not in London and not at Rosewood. We've never belonged anywhere, the two of us. No one has ever cared for or about us, so perhaps it's for the best that we take care of each other at this dreadful time.

How I wish things could have been different between us. I think I loved you from the very first time I ever saw

*you, but my love was never enough. How broken is my
heart! I feel as though it may simply quit beating.*

*I hope you find whatever it is you are so desperately
seeking—whatever it is that Emily and I could not give
you.*

*Love always,
Jane*

"Oh, Jane, where are you?" he whispered, running
his fingers over and over the ink as though by doing so
he might glean some idea of her whereabouts.

At the house, he was greeted by the cold, accusing
stares of his staff. No one knew why Jane and Emily
had gone into hiding, but given Phillip's reputation,
everyone was open to the conclusion that he'd committed some horrible deed against them. Phillip had never
corrected the misconception. He'd make no excuses to
anyone, because Jane's forgiveness was all that mattered.

In his study, he leafed through the pile of mail. The
first piece was a cryptic note from Richard on conditions
at Rosewood. He was one of the few who knew what
had occurred, probably informed by Graves, and it was
clear from the tone of each of his scant missives that
whatever chance they'd had to reestablish their bonds
of friendship was now completely destroyed.

He tossed the letter aside, then briefly glanced at the
others. On the bottom of the stack was one in a feminine
hand. Curious, he broke the seal and looked at the neat
script. It was signed Elizabeth Carew. The name meant
nothing to him, but he began to read.

*Lord Wessington,
    I doubt if you'll remember me, but I met you when I
accompanied Jane to London last spring when the two
of you first became engaged. Recently, your messenger*

*was 'round asking questions about Jane, and I couldn't
help thinking that I might know where she's gone. Jane
owns a small cottage she inherited from her mother many
years ago . . .*

Phillip's heart pounded with excitement. He couldn't
help feeling optimistic. This was the first real lead they'd
had in months.

Jane stirred the soup and tasted a bit on the tip of
the spoon. "That will do nicely," she murmured to
herself. As if in agreement, the babe which had swollen
her belly gave a swift kick. "You think so, too, do you?"
With a half-smile, she absentmindedly rubbed her hand
across the spot where the tiny feet were pushing so hard,
trying to find a way out of her womb.

If she did say so herself, she had developed a knack
for cooking and was becoming quite proficient at it.
There was something greatly soothing about preparing
food with your own hands, and she wondered why she'd
never tried it before. Mrs. Higgins had taken time to
show her the basics before hurrying off to stay with her
dying sister, leaving Emily and Jane alone to fend for
themselves. Her departure turned out to be the best
thing that could have happened.

Their days were now filled with the ordinary tasks
of living. Cooking, cleaning, washing, scrubbing. The
mindless chores kept them busy and tired, and they had
no time for fretting over whether they'd done the right
thing.

They were happy—or as happy as either of them
could expect to be under the circumstances. They had
each other, a family of two. If Emily wasn't recovering
as quickly as she might, that was no matter. The days

stretched ahead of them like an endless river. There was plenty of time for her mind and soul to heal. As for the babe, when she came in a few weeks, she would be delivered into a loving home. She might not grow up with mansions and ponies and gowns, but she would know, each and every day of her life, that she was dearly loved by her mother and sister.

As usual, Jane experienced a terrible twinge of guilt as she thought about the fact that Phillip would have another child and not know. Quickly, she pushed the thought away. What possible difference would it make if he knew? He wouldn't care. He didn't care. He'd had his chance to love and raise a daughter and had shirked his responsibility toward her. His feelings toward this child would be no different.

Her mind in torment, pictures whirled through her head before she could stop them. The London Season was in full swing, and she imagined balls, parties, women. So many women. Was Margaret still his mistress? Did he have others? The images were so wrenching, so heartbreaking, she closed her eyes against them, trying to force them back down deep inside where they belonged.

How could he care so little? How could she have been such a blind, naïve fool? And how could she continue to care about him so much after all this time? "Water under the bridge," she scolded. "Stop torturing yourself."

The babe kicked hard, and Jane took a deep breath, held it, then sank into the chair by the small table. With her head resting in her hands, she heard the brisk knock on the front door. It was rare when anyone visited, especially so late in the day. They had few neighbors, and the distance to the village was lengthy. The knock sounded again, and she didn't have the heart or the energy to answer. "Emily, could you get the door, please?"

She heard Emily's footsteps, heard the door open, heard her words of greeting, then gasped with shock and surprise.

"Hello, Father." Emily eyed him dispassionately. Standing there in his casual clothes, he looked the same but different. Thinner. Older.

"Hello, Emily." Phillip had to swallow past the lump in his throat. She looked so changed that at first he hadn't recognized her. Her aged, wise blue eyes were too big in the thin face. Her beautiful hair was cut short and slicked back, and wearing black shirt and pants, she looked like a boy. He reached a hand out to rest it on her shoulder, but she flinched away before he could.

Jane appeared behind her, explaining, "She doesn't like anyone touching her."

"My apologies, Emily," he murmured. This was none of what he'd expected. Gad, it had been months since the attack. Would the girl ever recover? His mind in turmoil, he searched for a way to start the encounter again by turning his attention to Jane.

She looked beautiful. Sad and tired, but her face was filled out, her skin lustrous and smooth. He wanted to reach for her as he'd done with Emily, but it would be too painful if she flinched away in the same fashion. Standing silently, he tried to locate some of the words he'd carefully rehearsed, but found they'd completely disappeared.

No longer able to abide the tension, Jane finally broke the silence. "What are you doing here?"

"What do you think?"

"I've no idea."

"I've come to take you home."

Emily huffed. "I'll never go back." With beseeching eyes, she turned to Jane. "He can't make us go, can he?"

Jane didn't know how to answer. "Go inside, dear. Let us talk for a moment."

Emily hesitated, then slipped away, leaving Jane standing alone. Phillip was finally able to see what Emily's body had hidden. Jane was pregnant. Severely so, her stomach rounded, her breasts huge and full. His first urge was to shout at her for keeping such a secret, but he knew he was on shaky ground. He'd be lucky if she let him inside. Taking a calming breath, he held it, then let it out slowly.

"Were you ever going to tell me?"

"I can't imagine why you'd want to know."

"You think I wouldn't want my child?"

Jane merely shrugged. "I don't know, Phillip. Where you're concerned, I truly, truly don't know."

"But it's my child. Perhaps my son . . ."

"I feel it will be a girl."

He couldn't keep the edge out of his voice. "And you think the fact that it might be a girl makes this all right?"

"You already had one girl you didn't want. I couldn't see any reason to saddle you with another."

"I *did* want her. I . . ." Unable to believe the emotion warring inside, he looked away, staring down the road until the unbidden tears passed and he could once again face his wife in an unruffled, neutral manner. "I need to speak with you. May I come in?"

He looked so desperately lonely standing there. Her maternal instincts warred with her good sense; she wanted to embrace him and offer comfort until the look of loss and hurt was gone from his eyes. She knew better. "I don't think that's a good idea."

Just then, the skies decided to cooperate with Phillip. The gray clouds which had threatened rain all day let loose with a deluge of huge, cold drops. "Would you send me on my way in this downpour?"

"I suppose not." Resigned, she stepped back and he entered.

Phillip eyed the small front room. It was plain but clean. The interesting aromas coming from the kitchen gave it a homey feeling. No fire burned in the fireplace, though, and the room was cold. Emily sat in the corner on a stool. "Emily, why don't you get one of the servants to light the fire."

"We don't have any servants."

"But who's taking care of you?" He whirled around to face Jane.

"I usually have a woman here, but she had family obligations to attend." Phillip looked so shocked that Jane wanted to laugh. "It's not a big deal, Phillip. No one ever died from doing a little cooking and cleaning."

Phillip ran a frustrated hand through his hair, wondering how much they must hate him if they'd rather live like this than suffer his presence at home. "Fine, I'll start the fire." There was a tiny bit of kindling next to the fireplace, but no logs for burning once the fire was going. "Where are your logs?"

Emily shrugged. "We're out."

Phillip raised a brow. "What do you mean?"

"We don't have any right now. We bring wood up from the beach, but it's hard now that Jane's gotten so big. I'm not very good at chopping the stuff into pieces, and Jane can't do it at all anymore. We're going to wait until after the babe, then restock our pile."

"You are, are you?" He reached out and grabbed

Jane's hand, running his thumb over her fingers. Besides the fact that her hands were freezing, they were rough with calluses. "You've been chopping wood. And cooking and cleaning and Lord knows what else in your condition. Don't you have any sense?"

She jerked her hand away, hating the fact that she loved the feel of his warm skin on hers. What a fool she was. Would she never learn? "There's nothing wrong with me. I'm perfectly capable of doing my fair share of the work."

"Aren't you listening to me?" His voice rose in direct proportion to his temper.

"Yes, I am. You want a fire, and a fire you'll have." She stomped to the door, ready to fling it open just as he grabbed her hand and turned her around.

"I've had enough of this. You're both coming home with me. Right now. Emily, go upstairs and pack your things."

"I won't."

Jane braced her hands on what she could still find of her waist and readied for a fight. "You can't coerce your way in here and then start ordering us around."

"Can't I? Just watch me." He turned his attention back to Emily. "This is the last time I'm telling you. Go and pack your things. If you refuse, we'll leave without them."

The panicked look in Emily's eyes was Jane's undoing. She softened her angry stance. "I'll never force Emily back to London. Besides, even if I wanted to go with you, I can't travel in my condition."

Phillip looked back and forth at the two females who meant everything in the world to him. This encounter wasn't going at all as he'd planned. He'd anticipated calm and reasonable discussion, followed by apologies and forgiveness. He didn't want to fight. He loved them both so much his heart was nearly bursting, and he couldn't bear to have them staring at him as though he'd just sprouted a second head.

"Fine. If you can't travel, we'll remain here until after the babe arrives." They both gasped. "I smell something wonderful in the kitchen. What's for supper?"

Chapter
Twenty-Eight

"You can't stay here," Jane insisted.

"Of course I can." Realizing that he hadn't had any sound nourishment since early morning, he turned toward the kitchen. "I'm starving. Let's eat."

Without waiting to see if they would follow, he went into the other room. It was warm and cozy with an aroma that promised delicious food. There was a pot of something on the counter, and two bowls were sitting beside it. Since it was one of the few times in his life that he'd ever been in a kitchen, Phillip had no idea how to dish up the food. Thinking to pick up the pot and pour, he began to reach for it just as footsteps sounded.

"Don't touch that! It's hot." Jane's voice was filled with irritation. "I'll do it. Sit down before you hurt yourself."

He sat on one of the chairs and watched silently as Emily set the table and Jane finished the supper preparations. Her long, nimble fingers stirred and sliced as she easily worked her way around the small room. The sight was fascinating and soothing. The food was simple, just a stew, fresh bread and summer garden greens, but it looked wonderful and smelled even better. His first bite proved it was tasty as well.

"Did you prepare this?" he asked Jane.

"Yes," she answered stiffly, as though waiting for a criticism to follow.

"It's very good."

She hesitated as though she'd heard him wrong. "Thank you."

No other words were spoken until Phillip finished his bowl and asked for a second helping, which Jane provided. He finished that one as well and asked for a third. With hearty aplomb, he ate as though he hadn't a care in the world. Jane and Emily, on the other hand, barely swallowed any food.

Jane could feel his eyes on her. She tried to keep her attention focused on her bowl, but Phillip's presence was so overwhelming that it did no good. The urge to look at him was uncontrollable, and every time she risked a quick glance, he was staring at her as though he wanted her to speak. What did the man expect her to say? The tension mounted, and the pieces of meat in the stew seemed to grow until each bite nearly choked her.

When he spoke again, although it was softly, both women jumped. He looked at Emily. "I thought you might be interested in a bit of news I heard just before I left London." He waited and waited, and waited some more. They sat, stirring their stew.

Finally, Jane could no longer stand the suspense. Looking at her bowl, she said, "What is the news?"

"Frederick Morris is dead." Jane's head snapped up,

her eyes locked on his. Emily's remained fixed on her
bowl. For the first time during the meal, she'd stopped
her incessant stirring. Her body was completely rigid.

"What happened to him?" Jane asked.

"He was murdered. Shot through the heart in his
own bed in the middle of the night."

"I'm so glad," Emily whispered softly.

"Do they know who did it?"

"No, but 'tis rumored that he finally crossed the
wrong man, the wrong family." Phillip's gaze bore into
Jane's, daring her to make the connection, to realize
what he had done, to understand the depth of his rage
over what had happened. "He'll hurt no one ever
again."

Jane watched him intensely. From the unruffled certainty in his eyes, she was sure he'd killed Morris himself.
In another time of her life, she might have been
shocked. Not now. Many was the night she'd lain awake
in the lonely darkness regretting the fact that she'd not
taken gun in hand herself. Whatever had happened to
the despicable creature was exactly what he deserved,
and if his death had been at Phillip's hand, so much
the better.

"That is the very best news I've heard in a long,
long time." Certain Emily wasn't looking, she mouthed,
"Thank you."

Phillip nodded an acceptance.

Emily shifted, cleared her throat. Still looking down
at her food, she said, "Jane, I'm frightfully tired all of
a sudden. Would you mind if I skipped the dishes this
evening?"

"No, dear, why don't you run along to bed?"

"Will you be coming shortly?"

"Yes. As soon as I've straightened up a bit." The girl
nodded, then stood. Although she tried to appear calm,

she was shaking. "Say good night to your father," Jane urged.

"Good night," Emily murmured without looking at him.

Jane and Phillip sat in silence, listening as she crossed the front room and headed up the stairs. The sounds she made were magnified in the small house, and they waited while she walked around overhead, readying herself for bed.

Phillip looked at Jane. "She's terribly changed."

Jane shrugged. "She's much better than she was." She started removing dishes from the table, taking them to the counter where washing water she'd already heated awaited.

"May I help you?"

"No, thank you. This will only take a moment." She could feel Phillip's eyes on her back, watching her every move, every twitch of muscle, every shift of position. Just as during the meal, the tension grew and grew until she wanted to shriek at him. Finally, she finished with the last piece of washing and set it aside.

When she turned to face him, her features were a mask of composure while her insides were churning with nerves. "If you'd like to wash, there's some extra hot water in that basin. I'll bank the fire and put out the lamps." She set a candle on the table. "This should see you upstairs."

"Where is *our* room?"

Jane nearly sputtered at his audacity. *The idea!* "Your room is on the left at the top of the stairs."

"Where will you be?"

"Across the hall with Emily."

"No, not tonight. Tonight, you'll sleep with me."

The facade she'd tried so desperately to maintain shattered with a resounding crash. If this man thought he could walk back into her life and begin marital relations as though nothing had happened, he had to be crazy. "I will sleep with Emily as I always do," she spit out at him. "She is afraid of the dark and afraid to be alone."

"I'm sorry, Jane, but I'm afraid you won't be able to change my mind."

"Why you wretched cad!" She waved an angry fist. "How dare you come in here and think you can . . . you can . . ." Just then, the babe took the opportunity to kick hard. She'd grown so big of late that the force of her blows was occasionally wicked to endure. This jab landed hard against a rib, and Jane groaned and bent over.

Phillip was instantly by her side. "What is it? The babe?"

She pressed a hand against her stomach. "No . . . y-yes," she stuttered. "She just kicked me."

He took her hand and helped her to the chair. "Calm yourself for a moment. Take a deep breath." He watched her relax. "That's better," he assured her and himself when she managed to take a breath again. Gently, he rested his palm against her abdomen and was rewarded with a hearty kick of his own. His eyes widened like saucers. "Is that the babe?"

"Yes." Because his touch felt welcome and familiar, Jane didn't want him so close, but he looked so awestruck that she couldn't refuse to let him feel his child moving about. She reached for his wrist and shifted his hand further to the side. "And here, too."

"Why, it feels like a foot. The pad of a little, tiny foot."

"I think she's tired of being cramped up inside. She's ready to come out."

As if in agreement, the babe gave another strong kick,

and Phillip chuckled. "She's going to be a feisty one, isn't she?"

For long minutes, they sat in a suspended silence as Phillip marveled at the movements going on inside Jane's belly. Eventually, the babe quieted, and he raised his eyes to his wife's, wishing he could see through them to the thoughts racing inside her head.

"I've missed you," he whispered, then gave in to temptation and leaned forward over the few inches that separated them.

Jane was mesmerized by his gaze, by his closeness, by his presence. By the heat of his hand and the smell of his skin. Even after all that had happened, after all he had done, he still remained so familiar, so loved, so cherished. At the last moment, just a split second before his lips brushed hers, she turned her head. "No. I can't."

"Yes, you can," he insisted, as he settled for nuzzling against her cheek and brow. "I've missed you. I know you've missed me, too."

"No, no . . ." She pushed back the chair. "No, you're wrong. I haven't missed you for a second." She stood and walked to the kitchen door, vastly relieved that he didn't try to stop her. Afraid of the look she'd see in his eyes, she didn't turn around. "I'm going to bed. With Emily," she added, in case he was still intending anything else.

"Get her settled in sleep, and then come to me. I'll be waiting."

"I won't come." She fled the room and lumbered for the safety of the stairs.

Emily appeared asleep when Jane crawled in beside her. She looked so young but, at the same time, so old. Jane longed to lean over and kiss her forehead, but didn't. The touch wouldn't be welcomed. Instead, she shifted around, trying to find a comfortable position which was nearly impossible in her swollen condition.

In a sleepy voice, Emily murmured, "I'm so glad Morris is dead."

"So am I."

"Things will be much better now; I just know it."

"I believe you."

"I don't need to be so afraid anymore."

"I'm glad."

Emily yawned and was silent for the longest time. Just as Jane thought she'd drifted off, she asked, "Do you think Father killed him?"

"I don't know."

"I hope so."

So do I, Jane thought to herself, but she didn't think it would be appropriate to say such a thing to Emily.

"Can Father make us go home?"

"Don't worry about it now. Try to get some rest."

Jane stared at the ceiling, listening to Emily as her breathing slowed and steadied. She had no idea what might happen. Phillip was her husband and Emily's father, which gave him the right to do anything he wished to either one of them. They had no right to refuse any of his commands, and if he ordered them home and Jane refused to go, he could take the babe and Emily and leave without her. He could divorce her, leave her alone in a world where she'd never see her children again. A horrid universe swirled unchecked through her head, and due to her emotional state, tears sprang to her eyes as she imagined every possible, terrible thing Phillip could do to them.

She could hear every sound he made as he washed, as he headed up the stairs, disrobed, laid down. He was probably lying there much as she was, only he'd be smug and confident that he'd have his way in the end. The longer she thought about him and his high-handed manner, the angrier she grew, until her sadness of a few minutes earlier was completely washed away by clean, burning fury.

How dare he disrupt their lives this way!

She threw back the covers and tiptoed across the hall, no small feat in her condition. The arrogant rogue was sitting up with the pillows propped behind, naked to the waist, casually leafing through the pages of a book she'd left on the night table. On hearing her enter, he tossed the book aside. With one hand, he reached out to her. With the other, he held back the covers.

Knowing he always slept in the nude, Jane panicked. The last thing she needed was to see him in the altogether. "Let's get one thing straight right now: I am not sleeping with you."

Phillip was making every effort to appear composed and relaxed while on the inside his nerves were humming. Waiting to see if she'd come had been torture. "Yes, you are. Tonight and every night of our lives from now on. I don't intend to sleep apart ever again." He gestured to the spot next to him on the bed. "I'm getting chilled holding the covers like this. Come."

He expected her to instantly comply! She had to swallow twice before she could clear enough of the outrage from her throat to be able to speak. "You despicable wretch. Of all the rude, insensitive, foul, demeaning—"

As though he hadn't a care in the world, he leaned back against the headboard and laced his fingers behind his head. "I see you're upset. Why don't you tell me all about it, so we can move on to more enjoyable things?"

"Tell you all about it?" she sputtered. His casual attitude only served to further inflame her. She felt like stamping her foot and screaming, but she refused to give him the pleasure of seeing her so out of control. "Oh, I'll tell you about it, all right. You stroll in here, complaining about the life we've built for ourselves, ordering us to feed you and house you, ordering us back to London, ordering me to your bed. Well, I won't stand for it, I tell you. I won't!"

"What would you have me do, Jane? Leave the three of you here to fend for yourselves? I've been frantic with worry, imagining the worst. I can't believe you'd do such a foolish thing as run away, and now that I've found you again, I've no intention of ever letting you out of my sight. You're coming home with me. You're coming back to my bed. You might as well prepare yourself for the inevitable. Your attitude will go a long way toward helping Emily make the adjustment."

Since Jane had never thought Phillip would search for them or, if he *did*, that he'd never actually look hard enough to find them, she'd never let her mind wander to this point in time. Of course, he'd insist they come back. What other option did he have but demanding their compliance?

Defeated, she let her shoulders sag and blindly groped for the chair, sank into it. The months of worry—worry about Emily, their financial state, the babe, Phillip—finally took their toll. She started to cry silent tears and buried her head in her hands. "What do you want from me, Phillip?"

"I want to sleep with you by my side."

He moved off the bed and knelt in front of her. Taking her wrists, he pulled her hands away from her face. His tough, tenacious, beautiful fighter was finally reduced to tears. "Look at me, Jane."

"No." She tried to hide her face, embarrassed to have him see her in such a state.

He cupped her cheek in his palm so she couldn't

look away. She looked so lovely, so miserable. "Are your memories of our loving so horrible that you can no longer bear the thought of sharing my bed?"

"No, I always thought it was special, wonderful. Magnificent. But it didn't mean anything to you. Are you such an animal that you must rut with every woman you see?" She gestured around the room as though it were filled with women. "Fine, then. Go find another. I'm sure there are girls at the tavern in the village. Any one of them would be happy to service the great Earl of Rosewood."

"I don't want a tavern girl. I don't want anyone. I want you and no other."

"Stop it, Phillip, please. This is killing me."

"Jane, there's been no other woman in my bed since I walked through the doors at Rosewood last summer. There's been only you."

She groaned, rubbing her hand over her heart as though it were breaking all over again. "Don't lie to me. It only makes things so much worse between us."

"I'm not lying to you, Jane."

"Are you saying that all these months you've been in London, you've been . . . been . . ." Jane couldn't find the word she was seeking.

"Celibate? Yes, I have been."

Her mouth dropped in shock. "What about Margaret?"

"Margaret means nothing to me. I hadn't seen her for months before the Duke's party, and I've not seen her since."

"How can I believe you?"

Phillip shifted his hands so he was holding both of hers in his own. "Jane, listen to me. I swear to you that I went to Margaret's rooms that night with an innocent heart." He waved a dismissive hand. "It started harmlessly enough—on my part, anyway. She approached me in the ballroom, and I didn't want others to see us talking, so I followed her to have a private talk, to tell her it was over between us. Over for good."

"You have a funny way of showing a woman it's over."

"When I got there, she was undressed and intent on resuming our affair. I never even considered it. Not for a moment."

"But I saw you kissing her. I saw the two of you—"

"I know what you saw, but it wasn't real. I told her we couldn't go on, because I didn't want to hurt you. She refused to believe I'd set her aside, and she threw herself into my arms. More than once. It was a dreadful scene. You saw part of that when you walked in. I thought on it later and decided perhaps she saw you entering. I wouldn't put anything past her." He reached for her shoulders, squeezed tightly. "But it wasn't what you thought you saw. I swear it."

He seemed so sincere, so upset. "I don't know, Phillip. I'm so confused."

"Then let me tell you what I told Margaret about you that night that put her in such a state: I love you, Jane. I love you so much. I was going to leave her room and come straight to ours to tell you. You're my life! I can't go on if you don't forgive me. Please say that you do." He reached around her waist and rested his head against her swollen bosom. "Please, I can't go on like this. Tell me you forgive me."

At the string of heart-wrenching declarations, Jane was unable to keep from wrapping her arms around his shoulders. She pulled him close, letting him snuggle while she comforted him by running her fingers through his hair and down his back. Many things were still unresolved, many things still uncertain, but one fact remained true and overriding: Phillip loved her. There was no way he'd have spoken the words if he hadn't meant them. While he might not be the perfect husband, and while he certainly had human faults, he loved her.

Knowing that, there was only one thing to do. She gave a resigned sigh. "You must promise me one thing."

"Anything."

"Promise me that you'll never see Margaret again."

"Never. Never again."

"And that you'll never take another to your bed. I've found I can't bear the heartbreak of even thinking about such an event. Swear it to me."

"That's easy." He pulled back so he could look her in the eye. Taking both her hands in his once again, he vowed, "On bended knee before you, I swear that I shall always be your true and faithful husband. You have my word on it.'

"Then I forgive you."

"Truly?"

"Yes. I love you, Phillip. I'm not always sure why, but I can't seem to help myself where you're concerned."

"Then I am the luckiest man in the entire world. Now, will you come to my bed?"

From the gleam in his eye, she knew he wasn't thinking about sleeping once they arrived. "How can you find me desirable in such a state?"

"You're beautiful, Jane. More beautiful than I've ever seen you." He rose to his feet, gloriously naked before her and reached out his hand. "Come."

"What of Emily? What if she stirs?"

"I'll hear her and wake you. You can go to her."

"All right, but you'll have to help me with everything. Sometimes I can't even climb into the bed without assistance."

"It will be my pleasure."

*   *   *

Later, much later, Jane lay on her side, watching her husband. Moonlight bathed his face, and he looked so young, so handsome and vulnerable. She ran a hand across his hair, his shoulder, his chest. She loved him beyond all thought, all reason, but if, at that very moment, someone had asked her why, she'd have been hard pressed to answer. Who can ever truly know the way of the heart?

There were still problems to work out, difficult topics to discuss, arrangements to be made, but she wouldn't worry about that now.

Now, she would lie beside him and relish how wonderful it felt to be back by his side where she belonged. Tomorrow, they could begin working on figuring it all out.

Her hand rested over his heart, and she felt its steady beat. Thinking Phillip slept soundly, she was surprised when he reached out and covered her hand with his own.

In a sleepy voice, he whispered, "Don't ever leave me again. Promise."

"No, I never will. I will always stay right here."

He patted her hand, then drifted back to sleep. Jane smiled and joined him.

Chapter
Twenty-Nine

Emily lay in her bed in the small cottage and stared up at the ceiling. Across the hall, her new baby sister, Mary, gurgled and cooed. It was still dark outside, but through her window, she could see the first hint of dawn in the eastern sky, meaning Mary was now five hours old.

Jane's contractions had begun the morning after Father arrived. She'd labored hard through both days, all of one night and a good share of another. Because of the full moon, several women had gone into labor at the same time, so the midwife hadn't been able to come until the very end.

Father had panicked, but not Emily—for Emily had known what to do. The midwife had previously coached her and given her supplies just in case the babe came quickly before help could arrive. While Father went running around frantically wringing his hands, Emily patiently set up the room, helped Jane change clothes, prepared the herbal brews.

After a few hours of worrying and pacing, Father had calmed enough to help. By the time the midwife showed up, they'd been at it for so long they barely noticed her arrival or assistance as the slippery girl spilled from Jane's body.

Jane had cried. Emily had cried. Father, too, had cried; Emily still couldn't get over it. Right there in front of everyone, he'd cried like a baby. And he'd said he loved them all. Over and over. He'd said it right out loud, just like that so everyone could hear. Emily was still amazed at how he'd hugged and kissed her. She'd let him do it, too, and it felt good. In between tears and embraces, he'd told her that she'd have to show Mary the way of things because she was the older one, and that he was glad Mary would have such a grand big sister to teach her and care for her.

A bright star gleamed on the horizon in the fading night. It seemed to be shining directly on her. She closed her eyes and made a wish that everything would always remain just as wonderful as it was at that very moment.

Mary stirred again. Jane had just fed her awhile ago, so she couldn't be hungry. Emily had heard Father get up and bring her to their bed, had heard her parents whispering while Mary suckled, so she didn't know why Father didn't get up again. Perhaps he and Jane were simply too exhausted to hear her.

The midwife had said Jane's experience had been a particularly harsh one, and she shouldn't get out of bed for several days. The days and nights of labor had also been so hard on Father—he'd not rested during any of it and had seemed overcome with emotion afterward—that it was almost as if he'd done the birthing himself. Emily smiled. Who would ever have imagined that her stern, serious father would put on such a passionate display?

Sighing with happiness, she silently rose from her bed and tiptoed to the room across the hall. In the small cradle, Mary's eyes twinkled, much like the stars out in the night sky. The two sisters gazed silently at each other, and it seemed to Emily as though she could read the babe's mind.

Please pick me up. I don't like being alone.

"Neither do I," Emily whispered.

I'm scared of the dark.

"So am I."

Their parents didn't stir as Emily reached into the small bed and lifted the bundle, returning with her to the other bedroom. Emily lay on her side, and Mary snuggled next to her. Propping the babe's head in her hand, Emily smiled down at her little sister. "Father says I must show you the way of things," she whispered again. "There's so much to learn, we'd better get started."

Yes, I want to know everything.

The words rang as clearly in Emily's mind as if Mary had spoken them aloud. Emily held out a finger, and Mary wrapped her tiny fist around it and squeezed hard.

Emily swallowed back a flood of tears. "Let me begin by telling you all about Father. And about Jane. Let me tell you about our family . . ."

BOOK YOUR PLACE ON OUR WEBSITE AND MAKE THE READING CONNECTION!

We've created a customized website just for our very special readers, where you can get the inside scoop on everything that's going on with Zebra, Pinnacle and Kensington books.

When you come online, you'll have the exciting opportunity to:

- View covers of upcoming books

- Read sample chapters

- Learn about our future publishing schedule (listed by publication month *and author*)

- Find out when your favorite authors will be visiting a city near you

- Search for and order backlist books from our online catalog

- Check out author bios and background information

- Send e-mail to your favorite authors

- Meet the Kensington staff online

- Join us in weekly chats with authors, readers and other guests

- Get writing guidelines

- AND MUCH MORE!

Visit our website at
http://www.kensingtonbooks.com

More Regency Romance
From Zebra

More Historical Romance From
Jo Ann Ferguson

Available Wherever Books Are Sold!

Visit our website at **www.kensingtonbooks.com**.

Embrace the Romance of
Shannon Drake

When We Touch
0-8217-7547-2 $6.99US/$9.99CAN

The Lion in Glory
0-8217-7287-2 $6.99US/$9.99CAN

Knight Triumphant
0-8217-6928-6 $6.99US/$9.99CAN

Seize the Dawn
0-8217-6773-9 $6.99US/$8.99CAN

Come the Morning
0-8217-6471-3 $6.99US/$8.99CAN

Conquer the Night
0-8217-6639-2 $6.99US/$8.99CAN

The King's Pleasure
0-8217-5857-8 $6.50US/$8.00CAN

Available Wherever Books Are Sold!

Visit our website at **www.kensingtonbooks.com**.

Discover the Romances of
Hannah Howell